PERILOUS

RISE OF THE CHARIOTEER
BOOK THREE

SUSAN LASPE

First Printing, 2024

ISBN 978-1-7377188-4-0

Cover Art & Layout by: Susan Laspe

Year of the Frog Publishing, LLC

6209 Mid Rivers Mall Dr. Ste 202

St. Charles, MO 63304

http://susanlaspe.com

ALSO BY SUSAN LASPE

Rise of the Charioteer Series

Sorcerous

Treacherous

For healthcare workers and all you do for us.

CAST OF CHARACTERS

AERON DREFAN: knight of Chaddesden

AESCULAPIUS: greatest healer in the world (at one time)

ASTERION: The Minotaur

BRYNWEN MASSON: healer and midwife-in-training, twin of Talfryn

CECIL: older son of Franco

CIRCE: Roman goddess, sorceress, relative of Padric

FRANCO: guide, tracker

GARRICK DE CLIFTON: Captain of knight corps in Derby, father of Padric

GREGORIO FIORI / TELEGONUS: tutor in Chaddesden, Derby / immortal son of Circe and Ulysses

HELIUS: Roman god of the sun, father of Circe

IASO: healer, daughter of Aesculapius

LENORE: wife of Franco

MANDALIN RICHAL: Princess of Rellea, daughter of Morfrey

MORFREY RICHAL II: the Roman god *Dis Pater*, king of the underground city of Rellea

OMBAG: cobalus (goblin) thief

PADRIC DE CLIFTON: knight of Chaddesden

PASIPHAE: sister of Circe, a witch/sorceress

PAYLA: daughter of Pasiphae, priestess of Mithras, immortal
RANULF RAWLINS: knight of Chaddesden
SHADOW DRUID: an ancient creature dressed as a Druid, underling of Janus
SIMON: younger son of Franco
TALFRYN MASSON: farmer, twin of Brynwen
ULYSSES: peryton (half-stag, half-bird), relative of Padric

PART I
GOAT & ORACLE

"No man or woman born, coward or brave, can shun his destiny."
— Homer, *The Iliad*

CHAPTER 1

End of July, AD 1356

At last, a night when rain clouds and the night sky weren't competing with one another! After a fortnight of straight rain, this night was clear, and the stars glistered bright. Gazing up at the heavens, Brynwen could not have dreamed of a more perfect evening.

Her fingers entwined with Padric's as they lay on blankets covering the soft, dewey grass and gazing at the stars.

"That constellation"—he pointed at a cluster of stars with his free hand —"is Cassiopeia. You can see the shape of the letter M or W, depending on how you look at it." He was all smiles.

It made her heart dance when his enthusiasm burst in this manner. He'd have been a brilliant teacher if he hadn't become a knight.

"Oh, I think I see it. It looks like an M." Brynwen returned Padric's smile. "What about...that one?" She pointed to what looked like a bunch of stars southwest of Cassiopeia, but Padric seemed to know each one by heart.

The knight regarded the constellation in silence for a few heartbeats.

Then, in a gentle voice explained, "It is Pegasus."

Ah, that's why he is so quiet suddenly. It had only been one month since they had left Cataractonium where they had nearly died saving the world from Janus, the villainous two-faced god of time. Helius and his pegasi, or winged horses, had unwittingly been involved in bringing about the world's near destruction, but in the end, Padric and Talfryn had stopped Janus—though only just.

"You can see Pegasus's neck, legs, and tail." He traced the lines with his finger.

"He is the father of all winged horses, isn't he? Didn't Circe call them 'pegasos' or something like that? It's the Latin form?"

Padric turned his surprised gaze on Brynwen. "You paid attention!"

"Of course, you can't expect me to sleep through all your lectures."

Padric chuckled. "Of which I am extremely felicitous." He leaned over and planted a quick peck on her temple.

Warmth spread through her when his lips touched her skin. "So, what is next, oh professor?"

Once more, Padric leaned back and studied the sky. "Hmmm, since you are so knowledgeable...I will find a challenging one." His eyes gleamed. He pointed upward. "That one. What think you it could be?"

Brynwen studied the cluster of stars to the far-east of Pegasus, nearly hidden by the trees. She traced the constellation with four points and a stem, trying to picture in her mind what it might be. A hill, a bare tree, a Roman god. "A boat?"

"Ah, could be...I was thinking it looks more like Grandfather's rickety old cart."

Brynwen rolled her eyes. Her brother lay on his own blanket not five feet from them. "Talfryn, you promised to keep quiet."

"I said no such thing. I said I wouldn't tell Grandfather about all your kissing and merrymaking." He snickered under his breath.

"It is Ursa Minor, if anyone cares," Padric said. "Also known as the Lesser Bear. Its most famous star is Polaris, the North Star. With it, you can always locate the north."

"But what if it's cloudy?"

Brynwen huffed. "Talfryn—"

"Well, that is enough for one lesson." Padric leapt up and helped Brynwen to her feet. Talfryn moved to rise, but Padric held up his hand. "Ho, I would like a private word with your sister for a few moments, if I may."

Talfryn, returned to his sitting position, smiling at them knowingly. "Very well then." He laid back down and closed his eyes, head resting on his crossed arms. "I see nothing. Nothing going on here. At. All." With that, he began to whistle the new catchy ditty he'd picked up from the bard in Chaddesden.

Brynwen and Padric grinned at each other. Her giggle made him smile like a fool, the grin she cherished the most and wished he would give more often. But being a knight, he rarely had time for such joviality.

Out of earshot of Talfryn, Padric gathered Brynwen in his arms. They were warm and comfortable around her, and she leaned into him as he locked his fingers behind her back. A pang of guilt struck her for betraying her grandfather's wishes, but it wasn't enough to make her pull away.

"Do not be cross with your brother. He is only being a good chaperone...well, a decent one."

"I know." Brynwen sighed. "If Grandfather were chaperoning us, we would have to be arms-length apart."

"Although, it is past his bedtime. Likely, he would be snoring by now."

They laughed, imagining Eduard curled up in the grass and snoring loud enough to wake all the wildlife in the vicinity.

He leaned in and kissed her soundly. As always, her toes curled, and it left her breathless. She didn't want this night to end. Tomorrow would bring her back to her life of endless patients and making ointments. *And*, she scrunched her nose, *her betrothal.*

Last Sunday, her betrothed, Jasper, and his parents had invited Brynwen and her family over for the evening meal. It was most awkward, especially whenever Jasper tried to catch her eye. She barely spoke a word all visit and later received a long reprimand from her grandfather about 'ungrateful children these days.' In that instant, she'd opened her mouth to tell him of her feelings for Padric, but something had held her tongue.

"Bryn"—Padric breathed heavily—"have you told your grandfather about us yet? I wish to court you properly instead of all this sneaking around."

Unable to look him in the eye, she bit her lower lip and studied the folds of his tunic with feigned fascination.

It wasn't as though Padric had not tried convincing Eduard of his intentions of courtship. She had been standing outside the cottage door and heard her grandfather's gentle but firm refusal. Nothing Padric said could sway the stubborn older man. To him, Brynwen's future with Jasper was settled. Secure. Nothing could dash all her hopes and dreams more than that moment.

If Padric, the commander of his own unit, couldn't persuade Eduard Masson, how could she possibly hope to do so?

Padric's lips crushed together into a half-frown. "I will take your silence as a negatory." Gently, he set his hands on her shoulders and slid them down to her elbows. "I trust you will tell him soon. But I must warn you, delaying it will only discourage his disposition toward me all the more."

The swish of wings sounded behind her.

Padric's gaze rose over her shoulder, and his breath caught.

"What is it?" Brynwen looked around in the darkness but saw nothing. When she brought her attention back to him, he stood as still as a stone, transfixed by something she couldn't see.

"Padric?" She shook, afraid Janus or the cloaked man stood behind her. She wished she'd thought to bring the lantern.

The hoot of an owl descended from a nearby tree. With lightning speed, it snatched a rodent off the ground and swooped into the black foliage of a neighboring tree.

She sighed in relief and released a nervous laugh. "It's only an owl."

Yet, this revelation failed to relieve Padric's fear. Instead, his eyes lost focus, his hand took on a tremor, and his breathing shallowed.

What was wrong with him? He never froze at a challenge, but his tremors revived a memory from months ago when he had been trapped under the tree before transforming from a centaur into a faun. Could it be related to that? "Padric?" When he didn't respond, she grabbed his arms and shook them. "Padric, what's wrong?" Nothing. Out of ideas, she brought her arm back and slapped his cheek.

It worked, for he blinked away his daze.

"I am so sorry." Her stinging fingers hovered over his cheek. "Did I hurt you?"

His speech returned slowly. "What…Bryn? Where did…?"

Talfryn arrived at their side, lantern in hand. "What happened?" His eyes darted around the dark expanse. He had his hatchet in the other hand, ready to fight. "I heard your shouts."

"I don't know." Brynwen shook her head. "There was an owl over there, and Padric's whole body shook." She grabbed Padric's hand. "Padric, why did it affect you so?"

"I… I know not." Padric's voice was weary. "It was as if the owl called to me. Does that make sense?" He combed trembling fingers through his dark-blond curls, which appeared silver in the moonlight and were thankfully without little horns sticking out of them any longer.

Talfryn shook his head. "Not at all, mate."

"Talfryn, lift the light," said Brynwen, worrying her lip.

Brynwen cupped Padric's cheek, half-lit and half-shadowed, to study his complexion in the dim light. The dark circles beneath his eyes troubled her. How had she not noticed them before? "Are you sleeping well?"

He shrugged. "The last few nights have been rough." He placed a hand over his stomach and grimaced.

Perhaps that was all—he was merely weary from his duties and not eating well. "Padric, you do too much. Your knightly duties, training in shapeshifting, making rounds to the Returned—"

"Courting my sister…"

Brynwen nudged Talfryn's arm. "When do you find time to rest? Are you eating well?" She felt like a nagging mother, but she couldn't help worrying about him.

Padric's eyes shifted. "When I can. I am fine," he snapped, as he tore his face away from her hands and the light. Then he puffed an impatient breath and snatched up Brynwen's hand, entwining her fingers with his. "Forgive me, Bryn. Mayhap you are right. But I am confident everything will return to normal soon enough. We are all under intense scrutiny concerning what transpired over the last several months, as you are all too well aware."

Oh yes. They had returned to Chaddesden nearly a month ago, and the villagers who had remained at home were joyful to have their family members and friends returned to them, but they had many questions. Questions no one who had returned from Cataractonium could answer without causing great distress and anxiety. How did one disclose Roman gods and goddess had kidnapped and enslaved them and that magic was involved?

"Has your father questioned you?" she asked.

"Thoroughly. I despise lying to him, yet I cannot tell him much of the truth."

"Slavers would be accurate enough." Talfryn gave a nod of his head.

"The Returned seek you, me, or any of the knights who were there. They seek comfort and believe their loneliness will be lessened by speaking with those of us who share their secret." He sighed, then yawned. Again, his stomach growled. "Mayhap 'tis best to return you both home for the evening. Then find a snack in the barracks kitchen."

Heart saddened, Brynwen could only nod. Since coming back to Derbyshire, she rarely had the chance to see Padric, and now they had to cut short their evening together.

They approached the farm in silence, Padric holding her hand all the while. She didn't know what to say to him. Perhaps tomorrow she could ask him about the matter when he was more refreshed.

At the cottage, she wouldn't allow him to depart until she had secured a sleeping tincture in his hand. She gave him a quick peck on the cheek, fully aware of Talfryn's presence. "A few drops should be enough." The chamomile flowers, lemon balm, and valerian should be enough to calm his nerves and help him sleep better.

"Till the morrow." Padric returned the peck. A pang filled her, inwardly wishing he would give her a toe-curling kiss like earlier.

"Till then," she replied with stars in her eyes.

CHAPTER 2

Blinking away sleep, Brynwen was halfway down the ladder from the loft when Talfryn's feet padded onto the floor. The pounding on the cottage door persisted. Samuel popped his groggy head over the edge of the loft. Eduard, who had been sleeping on the cot on the main level of their cottage, hobbled to the door, swinging it inward in irritation.

"What's so important, young man, that you wake us with all this clamor at such an hour?"

Brynwen reached the floor and peered around her twin brother's left shoulder. Though still dark—perhaps another hour or two until sunup —she could make out the strong shoulders and sour countenance of Padric's friend Rawlins. The young knight begged entrance. "It's urgent, Master Masson. Please," he added as an afterthought.

Eduard grumbled and stepped aside to let Rawlins pass. The dark, brooding knight barged into the cottage and paused just across the threshold. He had dressed in haste, his nightshirt partially tucked into his trousers, boots unpolished, and black hair tussled. In one hand, he clasped a brown sack slung over his back. The most extraordinary item to note about the knight's appearance was the gray goat at his side, held close by a rope around its middle.

"Miss Brynwen," he addressed her as he stepped forward. "Talfryn."

"Sir Rawlins." Brynwen dipped her head slightly toward the knight. "What is so urgent? Are you well?"

"I know it's the middle of the night,"—Rawlins said in a rush—"but I had nowhere else to turn. You're the only ones I know who might be able to help him. *Somehow.*"

Brynwen raised an eyebrow and glanced down at the gray animal. "What are you doing with a goat?"

"Is he a new recruit?" Talfryn asked. "I thought they require better grooming before being brought on board."

"Hilarious," Rawlins drawled. "Does he look at all familiar to any of you?"

Brynwen, Talfryn, and Eduard scrutinized the gray goat, who had become bored and sniffed the ground near the herb table. Its eyes glazed over at the sight of the potential munchies. Inching closer to dissuade it from its current course, she recalled why she disliked animals in her home. "Familiar how?"

"Did you bring a friend for Hay and Stack?" Talfryn knelt on the ground in front of the animal. "For they are most stingy with their meals and don't care to share. Where'd you get this fine fellow?"

"In Padric's cot," replied Rawlins. "Tied with this rope. Chewing up the cot's stuffings."

Brynwen looked up at that. She was too tired for games. "And Padric is...where?"

"I thought it odd a few hours ago when Padric wanted to tie himself up to the bed. He even asked me to ensure the knot was taut. Before that, the last few days his cot was empty come morning, and he came in late, directly from the stable, appearing for all the world as though he'd been rolling around in the hay. Serill'd overheard the stable hands talking about finding a knight asleep in the straw several days straight, and we've all noticed Padric's strange behavior lately. He's been tired and on edge. At first, I thought you two'd had a spat." His cheeks reddened like ripe cherries, and he glanced quickly at Brynwen, then away again. He cleared his throat. "Anyway, this morning I woke to find this goat tied to his cot. *Eating the straw* of his mattress."

The twins and Eduard stared at Rawlins.

Brynwen rubbed her face, trying to awaken. Had he just implied that Padric had switched himself with a goat?

After a few moments, Talfryn's eyes widened. "Are you saying—"

"Wait, wait, wait." Brynwen held up a finger. Her brain raced, trying to discern Rawlins's crazy insinuation. "You are *not* saying *this* is Padric." She squinted again at the gray goat as it tugged against the rope.

"That's exactly what I'm saying. Look, he *is* the same shade of gray as Padric as a faun, isn't he?"

Falling to her knees, she grabbed hold of the goat's horns. It tugged to free itself, but she kept her grip. *Oh no!* The horns were the same shape as those worn by Padric in his faun form. And its eyes...the same green as the moss in the forest. *His* eyes. "Padric?" she stroked the goat's furry face. "Are you in there?"

The goat gazed at her with apt attentiveness. Three heartbeats later, it lost interest and searched for something to chew. Her heart dropped. But then the goat nudged her hand.

"Are you trying to tell me something, Padric?"

It nudged her again.

"He's saying he's hungry." Talfryn rummaged through the cupboard and found a carrot, which the goat gobbled up. "How do we turn him back?"

Again, Rawlins shrugged. "I thought *you* might know."

"Us?"

"Beg your pardon, Miss Brynwen, but your curatives are legendary."

She blushed. "They are hardly legendary. I know nothing about turning a goat into a man. Or vice versa. Were Circe here, she might help. But only Signore Gregorio can contact her." How could this have happened? She'd thought he had everything under control. Well, mostly under control. "He did act odd when he spotted the owl last night."

"He did," Talfryn agreed.

"What exactly happened?" Rawlins asked.

Brynwen explained how Padric had frozen, and they hadn't been able to get his attention for a little while. She'd tried not to let it show, but being helpless to do anything for him had terrified her. She felt the same now. Was there anything she could have done to prevent it? Could *On Healing and Other Remedies* be of assistance?

Rawlins dragged his hands through his disheveled hair. "I don't know what else to do with him, and I've got to return to the barracks. The captain's coming first thing, and I'll have to think of an excuse for his absence. Something to do with the mayor. In the meantime, can he stay here?"

"Absolutely not." Eduard dusted off his hands. "I won't allow it."

Surprised, Brynwen gaped at her grandfather. "Why ever not, Grandfather?"

"Remember, you are betrothed. Sir Padric shouldn't be here."

A headache pulsed behind her temples. Not even dawn yet, and she'd already encountered two problems. "What? This has nothing to do with any betrothal." *One I don't want.* "He needs help, regardless of who he is or what you think he might do. He has nowhere else to turn." She spun to face Rawlins. "Of course, Padric can stay. Perhaps he will come around on his own. Preferably before I have midwife rounds to attend this afternoon." Again, she regarded the goat and imagined it nodded in agreement.

Eduard harrumphed and folded his arms.

The knight slung the sack from his back and handed it to Brynwen. "Perfect. Here's his uniform and boots. I'm leaving Firminus in your barn." Stoic *and* prepared.

"If you see Signore Gregorio, can you send him our way? He might know something," she requested.

The knight gave a curt nod.

"You said he's always himself in the morning?" Talfryn took the lead rope from Rawlins, who nodded. "Then we only need to wait a bit, right? Meantime, Padric-goat, you can bed with Hay and Stack in the barn. Doesn't that sound like fun?"

"Sooo much fun," Talfryn muttered hours later.

To Talfryn's utter dismay, during the rest of the night, Padric-goat neither returned to his human state, nor stayed in the barn. The gray-furred creature escaped at every opportunity, and Talfryn constantly chased after him. Most of the time Padric-goat ran to the cottage. Talfryn wondered if it was because of the carrot or the remaining times the white goat siblings Hay and Stack escaped right along with him, though they darted directly toward the cabbages in the fields.

After enduring a last rough go, Talfryn ended up spending the rest of the night in the barn with the animals. The moment he returned to the cottage at dawn, completely disheveled and bleary-eyed, his furry, gray friend followed him. Upon seeing Brynwen, Padric-goat made a beeline toward her.

"You look as gray as the goat, Tal."

He looked past her—and her remark—and trudged to the ladder. Their grandfather was finishing tying his belt around his work tunic. "Oh, good, Talfryn, there you are. Do Hay and Stack approve of their new friend?"

"Well enough." Padric had seemed to advance in his shapeshifting abilities, with barely an issue transforming into a faun and centaur since Gregorio started working with him. *What if Padric advanced to the next stage, and he's now stuck as a goat forever?* He just hoped his friend would be back to his old self by the end of the day. He couldn't do this every morning for the rest of his life.

"And where do you think you're going?" Ladle in hand, Brynwen placed her hands on her hips, the utensil dripping porridge onto the rush-covered floor. Padric-goat muttered in delight and devoured the entire puddle in one long lick, then raised his head to nibble on her apron. Bags under her eyes, she appeared to have gotten just as much sleep as him.

"Up to get a na…" A large yawn took over before he could finish the word *nap*.

"Oh, no. Gerda will be here any minute. And Rosa, and any number of people wanting my attention today."

"After the nap," Talfryn muttered.

Samuel clambered down the ladder, whistling one of the bard's newest melodies. "An Ode to the Fair Herbalist" was based on a true story and told of a maiden who saved her beloved, brave knight from a tragic death by venom most foul. Talfryn caught the rolling of Brynwen's eyes at the tune. Their brother whirled around and, seeing Talfryn, clapped him on the back and spun him around toward the door. "Oh, good. I was afraid you'd left without me."

"Wha...what?" Talfryn asked. *Was I supposed to do something?* He racked his brain, but nothing came to mind except longing for his cot.

"The ol' stump, remember?"

"Ummm...stump? Oh, yeah. The oak stump. In the yard. The one you're going to carve for Edina."

Samuel chuckled. "That's the one, little brother." He tussled Talfryn's hair like he was a lad of five. "Let's get to it."

"But..." He looked at Brynwen for help, but she only glared. Obviously not happy about the goat potentially eating everything in the cottage. He sighed. "Right, I'll get my hatchet."

"It's on your belt," Grandfather pointed out.

Seriously loving *today, and it's only just started.* There were no more excuses. "Yep, let's go then. Padric-goat, have fun with your *friend*, and save some of the food for the rest of us, all right?" As he closed the cottage door behind him, Brynwen didn't seem to know whether to scowl at him or the goat.

CHAPTER 3

"Not another one," Brynwen muttered to herself. From the window of her family's cottage, she spied the wife of Chance Regers and the younger five of their seven children walking down the path, not five minutes since her last patient left. Trailing them strolled three people Brynwen didn't recognize: a middle-aged man with a long, brown beard, an elderly matron wearing a black veil, and a beautiful young maiden with raven tresses. With deep regret, Brynwen refrained from escaping out the side window and dashing toward the forest to hide until they'd left. Padric chewed on his third carrot of the morning.

"Fret not." Rosa, the midwife, came to stand beside her. "Soon, the hype will settle down, and everything will return to normal."

Brynwen frowned at her mentor and second-mother. "How soon is *soon?*"

The moment they'd left Cataractonium to return to Chaddesden nearly six weeks ago, word of Brynwen saving the lives of Sir Padric and Signore Gregorio Fiori from the deadly poison—manticore venom—with a miracle cure spread like wildfire. What they didn't know was that the source of the poison was actually Padric's tutor, Gregorio, who had been transformed into a manticore by someone under Janus's influence. She still couldn't wrap her head around the fact that the enthusiastic Italian tutor was really an immortal, let alone Padric's ancient ancestor.

That single act had made Brynwen as much of a hero as Talfryn, Padric, and his knights. Like Padric, she was constantly pulled in all directions. The Returned, as those taken by Circe were now referenced, came to see her for treatments at all hours. The townsfolk started calling on her at dawn and throughout the day until the last rays of the sun slipped behind the hills. They referred their families and friends to her. Sometimes patients followed her on her way to attend to expectant mothers; and when she returned from those visits, there was always a long line outside the cottage door. Grandfather quickly became irked at his quiet farm being overrun by everyone under the sun. Some days, she would go to bed in tears from exhaustion.

Brynwen's gaze turned to her favorite thing about the farm: her garden. A hired maiden by the name of Gerda attended the plants required for her medicinals. Gerda went to the market for the supplies she couldn't cultivate in her own growing garden, such as vials, jars, and surplus plants.

Not to seem stingy, and although she dearly loved helping others in need, being always bombarded with ills—most real but some feigned—took its toll after a while.

On the same note, her twin brother didn't make it out unscathed, either. Villagers descended on him with queries and worries. Would the gods kidnap them again? What could they tell their loved ones? Some youngsters thought he was a knight. Every week, a new friend dragged him to a "secret meeting" in someone's barn to go over and over these same queries. Sometimes, he'd drag Brynwen to the meetings if she wasn't too exhausted. It was all becoming tiresome.

Gerda stood up from the garden and brushed off her apron and skirts. "Good morrow, Goody Regers. I'm afraid Miss Brynwen's with another patient." Gerda, bless her, did her best to assuage the townsfolk coming down the lane for Brynwen's medicinals on the most harried days. "Would it be much trouble to return later?"

Mrs. Regers was unconvinced. "My children and I walked all the way here to see Miss Brynwen."

"And what might their ailments be?"

On cue, all the children proceeded to cough. The eldest daughter, Annabeth, coughed the loudest.

The midwife, Rosa, glimpsed out the little window at the sight. "Good thing you've prepared your coughing syrup in advance."

"It's the sixth cough this week," Brynwen said. "The second by this brood. And look at how Annabeth is staring at Talfryn, chopping up the stump on the other side of the farm." Doe eyes from a twelve-year-old. Brynwen rolled her eyes.

"Here they come. I suppose Gerda couldn't dissuade her this time."

"Apparently not."

As the family continued on toward the cottage, Gerda shrugged her shoulders in apology to Brynwen.

Brynwen eyed the midwife. "Shouldn't you be sitting down, Rosa? Your foot will swell again." She reached for the front door latch.

"The foot will be fine. Don't glare at me like that. I will not have my own pupil giving me the eye. That's *my* job." She chuckled and obliged Brynwen by sitting down on the cot, regardless.

Taking firm hold of Padric-goat's lead rope, Brynwen opened the front door. "Goody Regers! What a pleasant surprise to see you again so soon. All is well with you and your children, I hope? Hello, and welcome." Brynwen nodded to the three strangers who entered last. Before she could ask who they were, Goody Regers spoke up.

"'Tis all my children ya see before ya. The eldest two, Bernie and Barnie, are well and workin' hard like your good brothers outside." She gave a proud smile.

"Goat." The two-year-old maid with a wisp of blond hair pointed at the gray creature tied in the corner.

"That is Pad—Patty. He's staying here for a bit."

"Can we pet the goat?" the four-year-old lad asked Brynwen.

Brynwen considered refusing but thought better of it. It might at least distract Padric-goat and the younger children for a few minutes. "Yes, but be careful. He might nibble at your fingers."

"Yes'm," he said. Glee on their faces, he, the toddler, and one more brother skipped across the small cottage to pet the goat. The goat allowed it as long as he could eat his carrot in somewhat peace.

"Here, goaty-goat," said one small child with straight golden hair. "Eat car-rot."

They talked to him as though he were a child, and two of them tried to sit on him at once, though he'd have nothing to do with that.

First, Brynwen studied Annabeth, a plain girl of twelve with strawberry blond locks, who gazed out the window with longing. She made quick assessments of the other children's flushed, healthy faces from their walk. Nary a cough to be heard. "Another coughing syrup is what you're after?"

"Goodness, yes, we gobbled your last batch right up." With seven children, it was no surprise...

"I will be right with you, sir, mum, miss. Please make yourselves comfortable while I prepare Goody Regers's cough syrup." She motioned to the matron by the door and pulled out a chair for her by Rosa. When no one else was looking, Brynwen gave Rosa an exasperated look. Rosa's eyes crinkled in mirth.

Goody Regers had barely sat down on a wooden chair by the table, the baby on her lap, when she began the small talk. "Saving that nice young knight and all from that poison. 'T'were so clever of you, it were."

The ears of Padric-goat perked up, but he continued to chew his fourth carrot.

Brynwen's cheeks heated. Last week, Goody Regers had gone on and on with that story. It seemed she couldn't let it alone. Daring a quick glance at the three strangers, they didn't seem a bit surprised at the gossip. "Honestly, I did nothing more than—"

"My Chance, praise the Lord, returned to me unscathed. His cousin saw the young lieutenant on his deathbed. Then the next day he was parading around, all whole and hearty. How wondrous and clever you are." Her smile lit her full face. The children nodded in vigorous agreement. Three of their brown heads were perfect, childlike replicas of their mother's. Not everyone shared Goody Regers's good opinion, though. In town, Brynwen had heard the term "witch" and "black magic" more than once, along with icy stares.

Cheeks thoroughly aflame, Brynwen handed the mother a jar full of the coughing syrup flavored with sweet honey from Talfryn's beloved bees. A recipe from *On Healing and Other Remedies*—which the sorceress, Circe, had lent her—included an improvement upon her own mixture. "Here you are, Goody Regers. This should relieve Annabeth and any of the other children who get a cough."

"We are much beholden to you for seeing us." She handed Brynwen a small sack of grain. "Children?"

"Thank you," they said, nowhere in unison. It made Brynwen brim with contentment and bid them farewell. *For at least another couple of days.*

She spun to chide Rosa for ignoring her, but then spotted the other three people patiently making small talk with the midwife and held her tongue.

"Forgive me for the wait. How may I help you today?"

"Please, call me Merta," the elder matron said. "And this is my nephew Arthur and granddaughter Isabel." She had an accent similar to those up north in Yorkshire, yet different somehow. "It's my hands. The arthritis is getting worse by the day, and I don't know what to do. Working with my hands is essential for my livelihood."

Brynwen held in a grimace of pity for the matron. "May I see?" Hands were an important part of most tasks in the labor force.

Merta nodded. Brynwen took one of her fragile appendages and studied it, flipping it over to see the lines and veins on her palms. Letting go, Brynwen went to her workbench and opened *On Healing and Other Remedies* to the first page. Like every other time she'd opened the book, she spied the capital letters "HA" written under the title. She wondered if the odd choice of a word represented the initials of the author. In her mind, she pictured the remedy she wanted—arthritis relief—then opened to a random page. There, at the top, she found the recipe she needed: *Remedy for Arthritic Pain.* The principal ingredients were ginger, aloe vera, and willow bark. But she'd also add feverfew since it helped other arthritic patients.

Even after all the weeks since Circe allowed her to borrow it, she still found it uncanny how every time she opened *On Healing and Other Remedies*, it turned to within a page or two, if not exactly, on the recipe she searched for, whether it be for medicinal use or the odd cooking recipe. Just to be certain, she would go through the next couple pages, ending up returning to the original page the book "chose." Without a doubt, this was a most remarkable magical book. How could Circe have ever wished to part with it? At first, its remarkable magic sent shivers up her spine. But now, it excited her every time she used it. Talfryn disapproved, of course, but if it enhanced her skills threefold, all the better. Why waste such a helpful and lifesaving gift?

Her brother did not appreciate how near Padric and Gregorio had come to dying had it not been for this book. Since then, new mothers and their babies would have suffered without it, and patients with strange ailments could have died. No, she could no longer do without it. Not ever. She could only pray Circe would forget she had it.

"You have a lovely garden," Isabel said. "The lavender is especially colorful and lush."

Brynwen smiled. "Thank you. The Lord blessed us with an abundant lavender crop this year, thanks to Gerda's expert green thumb."

They nodded in agreement.

After mixing the ingredients with the beeswax in a bowl with her wooden spoon, Brynwen lathered a good helping onto the older woman's hands. They glistened from the wax and oils. "How does that feel?"

The woman's face perked. "I say, they feel better already."

"Great. I will put the rest in a jar for you."

Arthur cleared his throat. "Pray, what herbs did you put in the ointment?"

A blush crept up Brynwen's throat. Hoping they didn't notice, she quickly recited the ingredients from the book. "Ginger, willow bark extract, and feverfew are the principal ingredients. I've added a touch of beeswax to make it creamy." Beeswax wasn't in the book, but it helped to make salves and creams.

From her pocket, Isabel produced a bag of coins and placed it in

Brynwen's hand. Brynwen was so shocked, she didn't quite register the woman's heartfelt thanks. "I...I beg your pardon, but this is too generous. I can't possibly accept this much." The ingredients cost a halfpenny at most. She turned to Rosa for support, but the midwife's expression was just as surprised.

Isabel shook her head. "This is not just to pay for my...grandmother's hands. We have need of your help."

"Oh?" Brynwen asked, the money forgotten.

"Yes," Arthur said. "A terrible sickness has taken hold of many people in our city to the north. Many have died, others remain ill, and we can find no cure. Would you come and help us?"

Brynwen stared at him, stunned. "A sickness? Do you know what kind? How far north?"

"It is in the Yorkshire Dales. We have a theory but would like you to see them for yourself."

"Here is the list of symptoms." From his pocket, Arthur pulled out a twice-folded piece of parchment. The material was thick, made of a fine quality one might see at the Wilmots' mansion in Chaddesden. Neat handwriting listed the symptoms:

> *Abdominal pain*
> *Chest pains*
> *Nausea*
> *Vomiting*
> *Bedridden by morning*
> *Severe cases end in death*

"It almost sounds like food poisoning. But that can go away within a few days. Could it be poisoning?" *But why would someone want to poison all these people?*

"That is what we wish you to discover," Isabel said.

"We must go back home quickly to attend to our patients," Arthur stated with regret. "Unfortunately, our city is difficult to locate. In three days, make your way to the inn at the address provided at the bottom of the page. From that point, a guide will take you to Rellea."

"To Rellea, in three days? But, why come all this way to ask *me*? Surely there are many physicians or healers much more qualified than me. Rosa, for instance."

Isabel wrung her hands in her dress. "Your name came at the highest recommendation, Brynwen. We need you."

This was all so sudden. She turned to Rosa for support.

The midwife smiled sadly, her hands folded in her lap. "Of course, child, you should go. I imagine I can handle our patients until you return."

"You won't go with me?"

"Traveling these days is out of the question for me. Besides, you know so much already, and I think you will do just fine on your own."

"But what about Grandfather and Samuel? I just returned. They won't be happy with me leaving again so soon."

Rosa patted Brynwen's hand. "We will deal with your grandfather."

That seemed enough for the travelers. Arthur gave a graceful bow. "See you in three days, Brynwen."

Isabel and Merta curtsied, then all three left.

Still perplexed at her late visitors' request, she muddled over how she'd get herself and all her herbs to the Yorkshire Dales in three days' time.

Rosa chuckled. "It seems you have your work cut out for you, my sweet. I don't understand what happened while you were away, but it seems to have come to good in the end. Oh, look, another patient comes for you." Sure enough, a couple more villagers traveled down the path leading to the cottage. Rosa had never asked what really transpired while Brynwen had been traipsing up north. She had heard the rumors but had ignored them until Brynwen might share the tale herself. *But how can I tell her? Rosa is patient, and I could never lie to her. She's not just my employer, she's like my mother.* There was naught to do but to keep her mouth closed on the subject.

❦

AFTER ROSA LEFT to tend to her own affairs, and a lull finally came to the cottage, Brynwen's grandfather and brothers came in for a break. Goody Regers's comment about saving Padric still bothered her, and Talfryn pulled her to the side.

"What's wrong?"

Absentmindedly, Brynwen twisted her finger around her braid. "A healer from up north summoned me to help with a terrible sickness, and they wouldn't take no for an answer. How did this all get out of hand, Tal? I only followed a recipe from a book, and now I'm deemed a hero. Circe was there, though—she helped them, too."

"But it was with your book."

"Which she *let* me borrow. It isn't mine."

"Well, you're one of the only ones who can read it."

"What do you mean?"

He shook his head. "It's in Latin or the like. I can't read a word of it."

"Nay, it's in the King's English. Isn't it?" That set Brynwen wondering. And worrying. Either she was raving, or Talfryn was, for she couldn't read Latin. If ever she saw Circe again, she would ask about it.

Talfryn cast a wary eye on the tome. "Speaking of which, aren't you using it a lot? You never used to use any written recipes before."

"That's because I didn't have *On Healing and Other Remedies* before. Rosa has a couple of books she uses all the time. Besides, this makes my medicines so much better. You've heard everyone say so."

"Aye," Talfryn said, resigned. "I have." *But I don't like it*, his eyes said.

CHAPTER 4

"Are you sure I haven't seen this goat before? He looks awfully familiar."

"Nay," Brynwen answered quickly, avoiding her cousin's gaze.

"You look pale. Have you eaten enough today?"

Brynwen looked up from her infant goddaughter, Amalia, cuddled in her arms, to her cousin Alice. "Not much. I was too busy with patients all morning." She absently patted the baby's back. Though only six weeks old, Amalia's head grew blonde hair like her mother; one lone curl swirled around her forehead. There was no doubt as to her father's blue eyes and mother's button nose.

Try as she might, Brynwen couldn't stifle a yawn. After Padric's unconventional arrival at her doorstep that morning, she'd felt as if she was taking care of her own infant. Even though it wasn't his fault, the stress tied her stomach in knots with all she needed to do, plus trying every spare moment to find a cure for him in *On Healing and Other Remedies*, but it came to naught. To top all of this, her duties for the day weren't close to complete. She needed to mix more soothing balms for the two patients expecting her that afternoon. However, a peek down at the baby cured her of that notion. Perhaps a few more minutes' break wouldn't hurt…

"How has she been this week?" Brynwen shifted to get a better grip on the tiny maid.

"Oh, much less trouble now that she has a routine," Alice replied. "Except for the sleeping part. Jack and I don't know if we'll ever sleep again."

Brynwen chuckled.

Alice grinned slyly. "Yes, well…how is your handsome beau? He is quite popular lately."

"What do you mean?" Brynwen asked, her voice a high squeak. "I have no beau."

"Oh, come now, cousin. You know exactly who I mean. Tall, blond hair, wears a black and crimson uniform…"

"Nope." Brynwen was unable to avoid the scarlet coating her cheeks and neck. "I don't know who you're talking about." *Good thing Grandfather is outside and can't hear this.*

Alice rolled her eyes. "All right, fine. How is your *non*-beau?"

A hysterical laugh almost erupted from Brynwen. How dearly she wanted to spill all to her cousin—but there seemed to be no need, as she already knew. *Who else also knows?*

"My non-beau is fine." It came out in a rush. She was displeased to note Alice's grin growing wider. *The nerve!*

A lump grew in Brynwen's chest. Guilt flooded over her. Instead of caring for him, she kept berating Padric-goat for getting underfoot and chewing everything in sight. She ended up leaving the goat tied to a tree under the supervision of her brothers and grandfather. *Please come back to yourself soon, Padric. I miss you.* She still couldn't understand how he had become stuck as a goat. *How didn't I know he was dealing with this all week, if not longer?* More guilt twisted her gut.

Alice tickled Amalia's cheek. "Can she be teething already, do you think?"

Brynwen released a glad breath for the change of subject. "It's possible. I'll have to refer to my book." Turning to the workbench, she opened *The Book of Healing*. Above the workbench, the wind picked up through the open window. The lavender she'd tied up with twine and hung on a hook earlier in the week to dry for her Miracle Mix bopped her in the head. The violet stalks got tangled in her hair. With a scowl, she snagged the stalks out of her auburn locks, a few of the buds falling onto the workbench. She sighed. Glancing out the window, she started.

Two people on a horse approached the cottage. The last two people Brynwen expected to see: Roana and her husband, Hamon.

"Oh, no." She continued to brush the lavender out of her hair.

With dark, curly tresses spilling from her cream-colored bonnet and her eyes glistening, the Sibylline Oracle looked radiant as she rode atop a dappled gray horse. Even from this distance, Brynwen could feel Roana's deep-purple eyes gaze into her soul. Hamon sat before her, cheeks bright red and hair bedraggled from the ride. He halted the horse between the barn and the garden.

Brynwen handed her goddaughter to her cousin and excused herself. Luckily, Gerda had gone to the market for more supplies and wouldn't return for a bit. Donning a smile as she opened the cottage door, she called out, "Roana, Hamon, so good to see you!"

Roana waved. "Brynwen! You as well. But you don't have to pretend with me. I know I'm the last person you wanted to see today." Already on the ground, Hamon lifted her from the horse as though she were a fragile flower. "Forgive us for coming unannounced," she continued, "but I had no choice." She gave Brynwen a hug.

"Regardless, it is good to see you both again. Did you have a pleasant trip from Nottingham?"

Hamon dusted himself off before replying. "Thank you. There was little foot traffic on the road today, so we made good time."

"That is good news, indeed. Pray, if you came to see Padric—Sir Padric, that is—I am afraid he is...ah...indisposed."

"Yes, yes." A smirk pried at Roana's face. "I am well aware of his unfortunate condition."

"You..." *Oh.* "Of course. Then can you tell me—"

"Presently. He shall be himself again presently. But this time I did not come for him. Nay, I came for *you.*"

Brynwen let out a breathy laugh. She stopped when neither Roana nor Hamon laughed with her. "Me?" Her heart rate picked up. First, the people from Rellea, now, Roana. What was going on today?

"Come." Roana beckoned her to follow.

Brynwen peeked over her shoulder at Talfryn in the distance, taking turns plying away at the stump with Samuel and Grandfather; Padric-goat tugging on his tether nearby. Deep in their task, they hadn't noticed the new arrivals. "Are you sure they shouldn't come too?"

"Nonsense. They'll find out soon enough." Roana ushered Brynwen around to the back of the cottage.

"There must be some mistake."

"It is no mistake." Hamon waved his hands to dismiss her argument. "Roana knows what she is about."

Mollified, Brynwen followed them to the grove of trees a short distance behind the cottage and paused in the birches' shade. Welcoming the coolness, Brynwen took a moment to study the Sibylline Oracle. Something seemed different about her this time. Despite her urgency to speak with Brynwen, Roana's face glowed.

Roana faced Brynwen with grave eyes, the opposite of how they had looked a few minutes before. "A vision came to me, one most urgent. Brace yourself—the effects shall be...fierce."

Before Brynwen could protest, Roana's body stiffened. Her eyes shifted from purple to deepest pitch. The dappled sunlight through the tree cover clouded over as the Oracle's lips moved to chant:

> *O tu filia medici divini*
> *Denuo dono tuo utere.*
> *Sub profundo, periculum regni,*
> *Semitae currunt sine ulla luce.*
> *Per eum socium tuam viam inveni*
> *Ut perfringas lucem diei.*
> *Ut exsecrationem vincas saxum reperi*
> *Aut tuos dies versu ultimo fini.*

> O thou daughter of the healer divine
> Cast your gift another time.
> Beneath the depths, a kingdom's plight
> Paths run with nary a light.
> Through an ally find thy way
> To break through the light of day.
> Find the adamant to end the curse
> Or end your days with this last verse.

To say Brynwen was unprepared would be an understatement. The onslaught of head-splitting agony threatened with no gentle urging to tear her head in twain. Bright, blinding letters connecting into words blazoned before her vision as a red-hot poker set to her eyes. Grabbing her head in both hands, she tried to keep the pressure from building.

"What did you do to me?" Her voice sounded pitiful to her own ears. "Please stop it."

"I can't," came the reply.

Brynwen blinked. Darkness. Then the Oracle's words formed in her mind, red-gold letters swimming, consuming everything before her. *No,* she thought. *This isn't right.* The words came alive, twisting, pushing their way in, even as she pushed them away. It was important. *Urgent. What am I to do?*

Black spots danced around the text. Her chest constricted with anxiety over the jumbled words. Loud bleating barraged her ears. The last of her resolve oozed out of her and onto the hard ground, and she pitched backward into nothingness.

EVEN AS A GOAT, Padric appreciated the Massons for putting up with his antics.

It was all Padric-goat could do to keep from getting under-foot as he waited for the family to bring him something to eat. He knew his actions this day were deplorable against Brynwen and Talfryn, his dear friends. His stomach led the goat-part of his brain, the one that constantly took over. With great difficulty, he tried to keep the rest of his senses intact. And yet, he could not find the concentration to become human again. There always seemed to be something to distract him from the task he had set himself. Too distracted to be ashamed of his own horrible behavior for over five seconds.

Eating, somehow, made him hungrier and caused him to allay this hunger with great alacrity, thus getting himself into deeper and deeper trouble. More trouble than he had ever been in his life.

Talfryn had tied him to a sapling close to the stump. "If you're lucky, I'll get you something to nibble on," he promised. Then he strode off and took turns with his brother in the odd ceremony of chopping at a tree stump, which didn't look at all edible. In the meantime, Padric-goat thought his stomach would fall out from hunger. He wondered if the small humans would return to feed him some more. But they never did. Dejection and hunger—mostly hunger—set in.

A few minutes went by, and discomfort squeezed at his stomach. *See how they starve me here? I am nothing but skin and bones!* Dreams of vegetables and piles of hay danced through his brain until the intensity grew. He fidgeted and danced around, suddenly feeling repulsed by the food in his dream. All the while, no one noticed him dying of hunger.

No, he realized. *Not hunger.* It nagged at him with great urgency.

"Talfryn! Something is wrong. Do you not feel it?" Padric-goat said.

"We'll finish up soon, Padric-goat. Then you'll feast. Promise."

"You do not understand! Something is happening*!"*

Then he spotted her—Brynwen was speaking with a dark-haired young matron and a man. He knew them. Again, he pushed to concentrate through his anxiety. *They are...yes!* The memory of his first encounter with them flashed through his eyes. *But what are they doing with Brynwen?*

Brynwen looked back over her shoulder, and the couple ushered her behind the house toward the forest. None of the three humans destroying the tree stump noticed a thing.

"Nayyyy!" Padric-goat cried. The foreboding he felt was uncontrol-

lable. *"Untie me! Untie me at once, insufferable humans! Fine, if you won't help me, I'll do it myself."* He gnawed at the rope around his neck.

"All right, all right, I have returned, Sir Goat." Talfryn arrived, one hand holding his hatchet, the other tugging out a small bit of cloth tied with a string. Once untied, he offered it to Padric. Padric-goat shook his head, refusing the delicious-smelling sweetmeat within the cloth.

"Free me."

"He's not hungry?" Samuel asked.

"I see that." Talfryn frowned. At last, he appeared to see that something was wrong with Padric-goat. "Hold still. I'll untie you from this tree."

The moment the rope fell loose, Padric-goat darted forward, his horn knocking the snack out of Talfryn's hand. The surprised farmer was nearly dragged off his feet.

Padric-goat did not wait for Talfryn to follow. He skillfully maneuvered around the shouting humans as they tried to grab him.

Talfryn's shouts were getting closer as he rounded the corner of the cottage. Seeing Brynwen clutching her head and crying in pain made his heart stop.

Beyond her, the dark-haired Oracle stood with eyes dark and empty, chanting a prophecy.

"Stop it! Roana, you are hurting her!" Padric-goat cried as he charged toward them. Toward *Brynwen.* What everyone else heard was: *"Naahhhh!"*

As he hastened, Padric tried to transform. *Please!* Yet his body refused to cooperate.

CHAPTER 5

$\mathcal{B}$rynwen gasped.

"*Now!*" Padric screamed.

Reaching deep inside, he searched for his humanity. *She needs me.* Deeper. *There!*

Acute pain shot through his stomach and limbs as he reached out for her. He watched in horror as his front hoofs uncurled and formed fingers and knuckles.

Brynwen's knees buckled.

Padric caught her just before her head hit the ground. The internal pain subsided to discomfort as he cradled her head. "Bryn," he called softly around shaking breaths. He swept stray auburn hair from her face and caressed her cheek with his fingers. *Why, oh why did I wait all day to change back? I could have helped her. I could have—*

"Bryn!" Talfryn dropped to his knees by his sister's head, his chest heaving. "What happened?" His eyes grew wide as he spotted Padric holding his unconscious sister. "You." He scowled and pointed a shaking finger. "You could've changed back all this time?"

Padric noticed food splattered on Talfryn's sweaty tunic from pieces of the sweetmeats meant for him—or rather, the goat. If Padric was still a goat, he might have attacked his friend for the scraps. Deep crimson flew up his neck. This day was not getting any better. "Talfryn, I—"

Brynwen groaned, eyelashes fluttering.

Padric's chest constricted, praying for the timely lessening of his beloved's harsh ordeal. He caressed a loose hair off her forehead and softened his voice. "Bryn, you are safe." Relief flooded his veins when her hazel eyes popped open and gazed into his.

She blinked, eyebrows scrunching, then pressed the heels of her hands into her closed eyes. "Oh, my head. My eyes, they burn."

Padric's face blanched. *No, this cannot be.* "Bryn?"

"What's happened?" Talfryn's eyes were wide.

"We shouldn't have come," came a deep, whispered voice. "I knew this would happen."

Padric's head shot up. In all the excitement and fear for Brynwen, he had failed to remember Roana and Hamon. They were on the ground not two yards away. The Oracle's cream-colored skirts spread about her, bonnet strings tangled in her dark hair, cheeks the color of bleached flour. Hamon cradled her to his chest and whispered to her, his eyebrows knitted with worry. Although her eyes were closed, she mumbled a short phrase over and over. Padric caught parts of it: "Beware...false sun."

What does that mean?

"Hamon? What are you and Roana doing here?" he asked, although he could guess the answer. His mind still reeled from transforming and catching Brynwen. Somehow, Roana's magic had brought him back to his senses. "Did Roana give Brynwen a prophecy?"

"Well, we're not here to sell ale, that's for certain." Hamon growled. "Why else would we be here?"

"What'd you do to my sister?" The harshness of his question seemed to surprise even Talfryn.

Padric's eyes furrowed. "Why would she give a prophecy to Brynwen?"

Hamon raised a glare at Padric. "Because she is the only one who can accomplish the task."

It was like a slap to the face. Padric's cheeks heated, but he tamped down a retort. "Fair enough. How does Roana fare?"

"She'll be fine once I get her home."

"Of course. One more question, if I may? What did Roana mean about—"

Eyes opening wide, Brynwen grabbed Padric's arm. "Padric, you are you again?"

He smiled and pecked a kiss on her forehead, his worries momentarily forgotten. "You noticed. Can you sit up?"

"I think so." A wince pinched her face when she moved.

Slowly, Padric helped her to a sitting position, but kept her close. He had no wish to be overbearing, but a protective instinct sometimes took over. She blinked repeatedly. Padric knew what that meant all too well. "From experience, the fiery text of the prophecy may last several hours. But eventually it will be a mere inconvenience, despite its dire warnings."

The inquisitor in him pushed to query about the prophecy, but the other half wished not to rush her. She needed time to regain her wits.

Looking at the ground, she nodded, her forehead screwed up in discomfort. "I must help Roana." Brynwen pulled away from his protective arms and knelt in front of the Oracle. Hamon pulled his wife up to a sitting position, leaning against his chest. The effects of the prophecy had not taken away Brynwen's drive to help, but as she examined the Oracle, she blinked and shook her head many times as though struggling to see through a fog.

Roana answered Brynwen's questions as the latter performed her examination. At the end, Brynwen asked, "How far along are you, Roana?"

"Ten weeks, give or take."

Padric shook his head in wonderment at Brynwen's uncanny ability to know these things. Although it was her occupation, he learned something new about her every day, increasing his attraction to her.

"You must come to rest in the cottage for a bit," Brynwen encouraged. "You must eat and drink something."

Hamon shook his head. "We should get going. Besides, we can't intrude on your hospitality after all this."

"Please, a bit of food and rest would be a great restorative before your journey home."

Roana brushed a strand of dark hair out of her eyes. "Only for a bit, Hamon? I could use the rest."

Her husband narrowed his eyes to protest, but seeing her pale complexion, agreed. "My nephew is tending the tavern, and he's not always...reliable," he explained. "Thus, my haste."

"I see." Brynwen nodded in understanding. "We won't keep you long, then."

Making to get up, Padric felt a breeze along his chest. Upon realizing how little clothing he was wearing, his body stiffened, and he hoped nobody would notice. He'd gone to bed in nothing but his underpants as the night had been warm. Nor did he have a pair of boots or stockings. So engrossed was he in the situation, he had failed to notice this slightly important detail previously. He tried to make himself look as small as possible. *How do I keep getting into these situations? Perhaps no one will notice.*

Although the women were loath to bring his plight to light, Talfryn was none so worried. He slapped Padric on his bare shoulder.

"It's all right, mate. I'll get your clothes."

"You have them?"

"Yep, one sec."

"Wait, do not leave me here," he hissed; but Talfryn had already dashed around the corner of the cottage on his mission. With no one noticing, Padric got up to follow. When he was about to round the house, he stopped short. A man walking beside a cart and a brown horse with a weary head passed on the road at a pace fit for a turtle. "Perfect," he muttered, "I should have stayed as a goat. Mayhap I can find a bush..."

"Why do you need a bush?"

Spinning, Padric stood nearly chest-to-chin with Brynwen. She blinked a few times as though something were in her eye. All the heat flared through his body, and he froze. "N-no reason." *Please keep your attention on my face...*

"Good." She gazed up at his face and patted his bare chest, a smile forming, and his stomach flipped. "Because you owe me for this morning."

Padric nearly choked, recollecting eating half her family's food stores. He gave a nervous laugh. "You have me there, I am afraid." He cleared his throat and raised a hand to rub the back of his rather sweaty neck. Half a dozen steps behind Brynwen, Hamon raised an eyebrow. When Padric's gaze again rested on Brynwen, her smile faded. "Mayhap you should rest for a bit, Bryn. The prophecy can be a bit unsettling."

"I don't have the time. I have patients..." she said, breathless. She swayed and raised a hand to her head. "I see two of you between the blaring prophecy."

He caught her before she collapsed. "Only two of me?"

When she smiled, he knew she would be all right.

Her hands gripped his arms for support. "Will you help me inside?"

Alarm bells went off in Padric's mind. *Where is Talfryn with my clothes?* "I would, but..." He glanced around the corner and spied the man and cart still in sight. His nostrils flared in frustration.

Unaware of his distress, she peered up at him expectantly. He caught Roana and Hamon trying to hide their mirth at his plight. "Gladly, milady." He glowered at the couple as he took her arm in his.

Getting his hint, the Sibylline Oracle and her husband moved to the lead so he and Brynwen could follow. But not before snickering as they passed them.

Biting his tongue from barking a retort, he steered Brynwen. "This way." As they walked, he promised her that the intensity and strangeness would soon fade. However, curiosity and worry almost got the better of him, as he wished to press Brynwen and Roana about the prophecy. *What is it about? Can she understand it? It is in Latin, after all.*

Leaning against Hamon for support, Roana glimpsed behind her. "Yes, Sir Padric, it's the same for everyone who receives a Sibylline prophecy. They can comprehend it in their own language regardless of the original Latin. It is a great wonder."

Can she read minds, too? "I see." This was something to mull over. The feeling of helplessness crept up his spine. He could have neither prevented Brynwen from receiving the prophecy, nor from its effects. She stared straight ahead to something beyond the Oracle. Padric knew the feeling all too well. "I would spare you this burden and take it upon myself if I could."

Brynwen nearly jumped. Gaining her bearings, she shook her head. "It's mine to bear. For whatever reason, Roana gave it to me."

"And you would see it through?"

Her lips set in a firm line. "Yes."

THEY ENTERED the cottage with no trouble. The moment the door closed behind them, Talfryn tossed a sack at Padric. He released Brynwen's arm to catch it, surprised at its unexpected bulk. Opening the sack, he discovered his uniform and boots. Relief flooded through him. *Thank you, Rawlins.*

When he looked up again, he met the glower of Eduard Masson, who, along with Samuel and Alice, had finished being introduced to the couple from Nottingham. Padric gulped. *It appears Brynwen does not need to tell Eduard where her heart lies—he already knows.* "Good afternoon, Master Eduard, Samuel, Alice. Please, forgive my antics from earlier. My memory is a tad fuzzy." His stomach rumbled loud enough for all to hear. "Alas, I recall eating some of your food, and I promise to repay your generous hospitality."

Eduard's grin did not meet his eyes, but he waved Padric off. "No need, lad. You've had your share of adventure with my family today." *See that it doesn't happen again,* his expression said. Mortification struck Padric's chest. *I will bring a week's worth of food to compensate for the day. What else can I do to earn Eduard's trust?*

Padric clutched the sack like his life depended on it. "I will be off to the barracks now. I thank you again, Master Eduard, for your family's hospitality. Samuel, Hamon, Roana, Alice." Padric made a polite bow, sparing a glance at the twins, then fled the cottage like a storm chasing a colt, not caring one bit if a neighbor came strolling down the lane at that moment.

So much for learning about the prophecy.

"I'll help with the horse," Talfryn announced, following behind him.

Once in the barn, Firminus puffed a greeting and bumped Padric in the chest with his enormous nose. "Looks like I owe you an apology, too, Firm." He dumped the sack of clothes out on some fresh straw and dressed while Talfryn saddled the horse.

A huge grin spread across Talfryn's face. "So, what d'you remember from this morning?"

Padric had to think for a time. "I remember eating. A lot. And that is about it. Did Rawlins bring me here?"

"Ah. Yep, I suppose your stomach overtook your brain, so you mightn't remember. Happens all the time to Hay and Stack." He nodded knowledgeably. "Rawlins brought you, Firminus, and the clothes. He was pretty grumpy about losing sleep, you know. He also mentioned Captain Garrick needed to see you as soon as possible."

"The mayor." Padric ran his hands through his curls. Following a vigil for the fallen in Cataractonium, the mayor had celebrated the return of the townsfolk with fanfare. A wolf-like monster called an *aeternae* had killed one knight in Padric's unit, Leowyn Masson. They had proclaimed the young man a hero. Padric and his returning knights had received ornate wooden plaques heralding their bravery and many thanks. Since then, Padric had met with the mayor again to review the security measures of Derby and Chaddesden. He had made the appointment for today with the captain, but never specified the reason. Surprises from the mayor were never good. The very thought made his stomach rumble again.

"Promise me you will make Bryn take a break for a while."

Talfryn chortled. "Good one. That's like asking Stack to stop eating my socks every morning."

<h1 style="text-align:center">CHAPTER 6</h1>

"Enter."

Padric opened the door to the office of Captain Garrick de Clifton. As usual, Padric found the room orderly with the familiar polished mahogany desk, chairs, and bench. A bookshelf filled with military tomes stood to the left of the door. To its immediate right hung a large map of Derbyshire and the surrounding towns, and beside it, an illustrated map of England. Garrick sat at his desk, the window behind him casting a long shadow across his face.

"Captain." Padric hid his unease as best he could.

"Padric." Garrick got to his feet and rounded the desk. Padric groaned internally when his father used his "captain tone" on him. "Where the devil have you been? Your sergeant said you were on an urgent matter. What was the pressing issue that caused your delay?"

"I beg your pardon, but I was detained, sir."

"'Detained,' eh? Was it that little healer you have been seeing?"

"What?" This was not at all where he had dreamed the conversation would turn. "Well…in all honesty, 'tis the truth, but not the reason. There was an issue—"

"You have duties. To your men. Your city. Your country. Court the maid on your own time, lad."

"Sir, I did not come here to make excuses. I came at your summons before sunset. What is so dire that you must upend all of Derbyshire searching for me?"

Garrick folded his arms across his chest. "When it is difficult to get the attention of one's own son, one must improvise."

"Well, I am here, sir. What has happened?"

"Whispers have spread that up north, a man transformed into a goat and saved thousands of people from slavers. Others say he transformed into a horse, and that ancient gods and fiery, flying chariots were involved.

"Each day, the story builds to a greater and more absurd crescendo. I have been disregarding these rumors for several weeks. And yet still they come." He gestured to a stack of papers. "The latest word I received claimed that this mystical savior was a knight of Derbyshire, a certain Sir Padric de Clifton, and was this man-turned-goat or -horse. These rumors have even hit upon the ears of the mayor himself. He has asked me to put an end to this talk before it gets out of hand. Now, would you care to explain these rantings?"

Padric stood dumbstruck, heat creeping up his neck. He had planned everything so carefully and his hopes to thoroughly quash the gossip out of the populace had seemed sound. He had spoken with each person who had returned from Cataractonium and urged secrecy—not for his own safety, but theirs. The clandestine meetings were meant to keep the harrowing adventure a secret until the townsfolk forgot it. Yet, someone had slipped up.

Dare I tell him all, and undermine all we have worked toward?

It was a preposterous idea. Yet, if he got stuck again as a goat, how could he explain?

Recovering somewhat, Padric feigned a smile and waved his hand in amusement. "You would listen to the hearsay and stories of some town drunkards?" Although he highly doubted they were the only ones with loose lips. "Wet their tongues enough, people will spill anything they fancy."

"The bard is making songs of this hero's deeds."

That is no surprise. First Brynwen, now him. Durand the bard could make a song out of any subject, regardless of its veracity. It could be of some benefit, however, because everything he sang about seemed incredible, even to those who had witnessed everything in Cataractonium.

"Another interesting rumor I heard involves the young maiden you are courting." He glanced at his notes. "Brynwen Masson is her name, I believe. She healed you from a deadly venom. Am I correct?"

"I owe her my life, but that is no secret."

"However, some people might not be impressed with her accomplishments, despite her supposed powers of healing."

Padric's chest constricted as he wondered where this line of talk was going. "What? Nay. I have heard those rumors of her using witchcraft, but I know this to be untrue. They do not know her as I. As a midwife, Brynwen may have more healing knowledge than the average person might, but that is no reason to call her a witch."

"You haven't known her long."

"I have not, but I know her well. I know her character. You must not disregard the fact that she attends Mass every Sunday."

"Not everyone attends Saint Mary's, though," Garrick reminded him. "Regardless, you might warn her to be more careful in the foreseeable future." His eyes fell and voice lightened. "For your sake, son, I do not wish to see you get hurt."

This was indeed troubling. Garrick had met both Brynwen and Talfryn upon their return from Cataractonium and had thought the twins an agreeable pair. Of course, Padric could not tell him of their complete involvement with Circe, Helius, and Janus, but he had told him the story agreed upon by all the Returned about the slavers. Garrick was astute, and every day Padric wondered when his father would piece the true story together. It sounded more and more like he had fallen on the answers, as insensible as they were, although he did not understand the truth.

Padric's shoulders straightened. "I shall share the warning next I see her, sir."

"Excellent," Garrick grumbled. "Is there anything you wish to tell me? You look as though you have something to say. You know you can always talk to me."

That was the rub. Never had Padric kept secrets from his family. It broke his heart more than anything. But if he told his father now, he would break the oath he and everyone else who had returned from Cataractonium had made. *Best to keep to the story.* "Not at all, sir. I merely wish to return to the barracks to attend to my men. We have training."

Garrick gave him a hard look. Without a hitch, Padric's heart started racing. *He knows.*

"Padric, what are you hiding?"

Inwardly, Padric grimaced. "Sir—"

A sharp set of knocks rapped on the door. Three quick taps.

The captain muttered under his breath. "Enter." He sat back, face transferring to indifference.

Padric turned to view Rawlins poking his head through the open door.

"Beg pardon, Captain, but the Lieutenant's needed at the training field."

Garrick's expression hardened. "Very well. The Lieutenant will be right with you."

"Yes, Sir."

The door clicked behind Rawlins, and Garrick stood. With haste, Padric ascended to his feet and reached for the door handle. "I will take my leave, Captain." Perhaps he could exit quickly without an altercation.

"One last thing," said Garrick. Padric hid his dismay behind a stoic facade. "Your mother and sister miss you and wish you would visit with them more often. Would the evening meal this tonight be bearable?"

Padric's shoulders nearly sagged in relief. Tonight. "I miss them awfully. Tonight would be delightful."

"Excellent. She is making your favorite dish—you know how your mother likes to dote over you." He cracked the slightest smile. "We look forward to seeing you at the usual time." Garrick was back to his usual self. All Padric had to do was make sure his father did not corner him with more questions during his visit, and all would be well. In all honesty, though, he did not know how long he could keep up this pretense.

"Until then, give them my love." Padric exited the office and only breathed after the door closed behind him.

CHAPTER 7

"Thought you'd need a rescue." Arms folded across his chest, Rawlins shoved off the wall across from Garrick's office. "Byron saw you trudge your way to the captain's office. Also, I found your tutor. He's waiting for us by the training field."

"Ah, good old Byron. And at last." Padric breathed. "Where has Gregorio been all day? Any moment now, I may have a relapse of this morning. To top it off, the captain suspects me." *I cannot go on like this indefinitely.*

"He's got a right to be suspicious, but he may be lenient on his son if he finds out. Mine'd lock me up without batting an eye—were he still around." He scanned the area in a tactical manner. "Now we're alone, you can tell me why I woke up to you eating yer mattress in a gray, furry coat at an ungodly hour this morning."

A sudden twinge took residence in Padric's neck. He rubbed it with his first two fingers to get the kink out, to no avail. "It is a complicated story, and I would prefer to tell it only once. I hope Gregorio has some answers, because I tire of this."

"As long as you don't turn into a manticore or that horned wolf thing." Rawlins shivered and his eyes glazed over. In a flash, his customary stoic attitude returned.

"Sir Padric, Sir Rawlins," came a voice from a little way behind them.

They spun on their heels, and Padric's stomach flipped. Led by fellow knight Aeron Drefan, the Masson twins made their way to Padric—Brynwen with furrowed brows and a determined gait, her hand on her satchel. Talfryn took a long stride by her side.

Aeron, with his customary impeccable uniform and ebony hair, stopped before them and waved at the twins. "They insisted on following me, sir."

Rawlins regarded them warily, as was his wont. "Well, what are you two doing way out here?"

"We normally walk well out of our way past the training grounds to get to the farm. Good for the old legs, so they say." With a cheeky grin, Talfryn patted his legs. "Never understood that saying, actually."

Padric caught Brynwen by the arms, disregarding propriety. He smiled down at her. Their encounter with Roana earlier had worried him. "Are you well? Please tell me your vision has not worsened in the hour since I left you." Her eyes appeared clearer and more focused, at least.

"It's manageable enough, but that's not the only reason we're here. I couldn't help thinking about you and your…uh…indigestion. So, in between the last couple of clients, I concocted this tonic for you. We knew you'd have training this afternoon and wanted to bring it to you right away in case you needed it." Out from her satchel, she procured a stoppered vial of clear liquid.

"It's not poisonous." Talfryn raised his eyebrows. "I know, because I tried it. It's kinda sweet, actually."

Before Padric could ask about the tonic, Talfryn waved over Padric's shoulder. "Look, it's Teleg—er, Gregorio."

The skin of Padric's forearms tingled. He turned to see the familiar, bright flash of a silver and blue amulet bouncing in the sunlight. Its owner's dark curls were streaked with gray. The immortal son of the Roman goddess Circe and hero Ulysses moved with brusque purpose toward them, carrying a corded blue bag. His usual worn red cloak was absent in the July heat. In the guise of the elder Italian tutor, Gregorio Fiori, the studious lines marking his face reminded Padric that Circe's son was, in fact, thousands of years older than he appeared. Despite this, Padric did not think he could ever call his friend by his real name of "Telegonus." His friend who was, in fact, Padric's many-great-grandfather.

Padric's eyes fell on the magic amulet hanging around Gregorio's neck on a thin gold chain. It had taken a while for Padric to sense magic, especially small traces. But after leaving Circe's magical barrier and staff, it had become easier to detect a glimmer of power radiating from items such as Gregorio's amulet. Too distracted to notice it earlier, Padric's skin had tingled when Roana had radiated her Sibylline power and transferred the prophecy to Brynwen. At least, that was his guess. It was all still new to him.

Gregorio smiled and held his arms wide. "Ah, it is so good to see you all in one place. My thanks, Sir Rawlins, for bringing my former pupil to me."

Rawlins nodded respectfully. He would deny it unto death, but Padric knew Rawlins's regard for Gregorio had risen tenfold by the immortal's ability to keep his true identity hidden for years, even from *him*, the knight who suspected everyone of hiding something.

A couple of passing squires greeted the knights. The group became silent until they were out of earshot.

"Padric, Sir Rawlins tells me you had an emergency with a certain—" Gregorio surveyed the vicinity for observers "—*goat problem*. Forgive me for not helping earlier. I was teaching my two pupils some Roman history out in the fields, and we only returned a short while ago."

Padric nodded.

"When I returned to my room afterward to change, I discovered a message from my mother. She desires an audience with you."

Padric cocked his head, knowing he should not be surprised. "Does she know of our eventful day?"

"That is the question, but she would say nothing more until you were present. You are all welcome to come." His gaze landed expectantly on Brynwen. "Especially you, my dear. Follow me."

"But training?" Aeron asked, pointing toward the field where his fellow knights, squires, and pages gathered.

Gregorio kept moving. "This shan't take long, I promise."

&a.

THE TUTOR LED the group to a grove of trees away from the road and held up the corded blue bag. Up close, Brynwen noticed the fine gold stitches around the trimming, little suns in the same shape as on Helius's sun chariot, which Padric had destroyed to stop the two-faced god Janus's fatal project. Opening the soft bag, Gregorio retrieved an orb large enough to fill his hand. Inside the glass, Brynwen marveled at what appeared to be stationary clouds and blue sky. It could have reflected the sky above, except for the few clouds amassing there.

Talfryn gasped, enamored with the orb. Either entranced or curious, he reached out a hand to touch it.

"Talfryn," Brynwen hissed.

"Oh, sorry." Talfryn retracted his hand and stuck it behind his back.

Everyone circled the orb. With the object in his left hand, Gregorio slowly waved his right over it and chanted an incantation in Latin.

A soft glow emanated from the orb, and the clouds passed under and over one another, swirling faster and faster until it made Brynwen's eyes cross. The swirls came to an abrupt stop. The clouds thickened until it looked completely white and misty. As they dissipated, a young maiden's face emerged with golden hair piled atop her head: Circe, Roman goddess and sorceress. Next, her father, the Titan Helius, the former Roman god of the sky, who still didn't look a day over eighteen and could have been Circe's brother.

Their appearance in the glass orb brought back conflicting memories. Beginning in December, Circe had slowly kidnapped hundreds of Englishmen and maidens to build a grand temple for Helius. His friend Janus, the two-faced god of time, had encouraged him to destroy Apollo with a powerful sun crystal as vengeance against Jupiter. However, the whole affair ended tragically when Janus betrayed Helius and tried to destroy much of the known world in the process.

Following them appeared another maiden with long, straight, dark hair, running halfway down her back. Yet, there was something about her eyes that mirrored those of both Helius and Circe.

Gregorio bowed. *"Mater."* Then, as the others came into view, he said, *"Avus, Matertera." Mother* and *Grandfather*, Brynwen remembered from her time in Cataractonium. But what was *Matertera?* She glanced at Padric, but his attention remained on the people inside the orb. She wondered about her friend Ulysses, who had remained with them, but didn't see him.

Padric greeted his family, but he didn't seem to recognize the dark-haired maiden either.

Circe nodded and smiled at the group, though there was a tightness in her lips. "We are glad you responded with haste. I would like to introduce you to my sister, Pasiphae."

Padric nodded as though he recognized the name. Brynwen was sure he had mentioned who Circe's siblings were at one time, but she couldn't remember. "Pasiphae" was a name one didn't hear often—or at all.

Aunt—*Matertera* meant "aunt." A wave of achievement swept over Brynwen at figuring it out.

Pasiphae bowed. "Charmed. Sir Padric, Circe has told me much about you." Brynwen couldn't help but notice her regarding Padric with a careful eye. *What does that look mean?*

"Gonus." Circe's eyebrows furrowed as she beheld her son. "What have you done to your hair and face?"

Gonus?

Gregorio bristled, shaking the orb for a brief second. "It is my disguise, *Mater.* I have used it for years."

The goddess scoffed. "It makes you look like a clown. No son of mine will have such horrid fashion sense."

Brynwen placed her hands on her hips. "Well, I, for one, think it makes him look very distinguished."

Nodding, Padric's lips rose into a grin. "Yes, m'lady, his disguise has fooled everyone in Derbyshire."

"No one's figured it out." Talfryn grinned. "Not even Rawlins here."

The knight glared daggers at the farmer. Brynwen feared her brother would perish where he stood.

"Enough about me. *Avus, Mater, Matertera Pasiphae,*" Gregorio said quickly, "what is so urgent? I have heard nothing from you for over a fortnight, and now your urgent message arrives. Did you find what you were looking for?"

A frown marred Circe's perfect mouth, clearly not yet ready to let the subject go. "Yes, well, a recent development has arisen." She paused. "Earlier this week, we received intelligence that Janus is planning something devastating for the gods on Olympus."

"Why am I not surprised?" Gregorio said dryly. "What is his plan this time?"

"He requires something of value, but it is unclear what. Only in the moors of the Yorkshire Dales can one find it."

"The moors?" Gregorio asked. "Whatever for?"

A blaze of red and gold letters stabbed at Brynwen's eyes. Her lips parted of their own accord, spilling the prophecy to one and all.

> *O thou daughter of the healer divine*
> *Cast your gift another time.*
> *Beneath the depths, a kingdom's plight*
> *Paths run with nary a light.*
> *Through an ally find thy way*
> *To break through the light of day.*
> *Find the adamant to end the curse*
> *Or end your days with this last verse.*

When she finished, spent, her knees gave out. Padric and Talfryn caught her arms.

The right eyebrows of both sisters in the globe rose.

Helius gasped. "Two prophecies so close together? How can this be?"

Circe regarded Brynwen with mirth. "It appears the Oracle has paid another visit to Chaddesden."

"She isn't the only one," Brynwen said breathlessly. Only Padric and Talfryn seemed to have heard her.

Padric's grip on her tensed. "Who else was here?"

"Roana was here?" Gregorio frowned, put out by the news.

"Is that the prophecy woman?" Aeron asked. "I thought she was done with us."

Rawlins gritted his teeth. "Apparently not."

Clasping Brynwen's hands, Gregorio rambled off a list of questions. "Brynwen, are you well? Are you experiencing headaches and vision quirks? Roana's prophecies are not...gentle." Shaking his head, he released her hands and rubbed the blue amulet about his neck between nervous fingers. "Forgive me, my dear, but Roana's prophecies both fascinate and frighten me."

Brynwen's cheeks turned scarlet. "I...I..."

A gentle hand rested on her arm, and Padric smiled. "It is all right, Bryn. He can help you interpret it."

"Yes, it's just...I'm still adjusting to it."

"Of course."

"To get back to it," Pasiphae said, "what of this adamant in the prophecy? If the healer is to find it, which is it?"

Gregorio scratched his chin. "'Adamant to end the curse.' It may refer to the time when the Titan Chronos turned the young man Adamas into an *adamastos,* which means 'unbreakable'. It is known to you as a diamond. This particular *adamastos,* or adamant, became known as the *lapis adamantis,* or stone of adamant and is believed to possess great healing properties."

"Is adamant not also called 'tears of the gods'?" Padric asked.

A snort came from Pasiphae. "No gods shed any tears for Adamas."

Circe shook her head in distaste. "A pity, Adamas was quite handsome."

Pasiphae rolled her eyes. "He is hardly the only one, sister."

"A sight more handsome than that Cretan Bull."

"Look, sister, you know very well that I was under a spell. And what about your littler peryton here, the way you give him doe eyes, eh?"

"That is completely different."

"Sure it is. Why, I think—"

"The stone of adamant, then," Padric interrupted. He eyed his many-great grandmother and aunt like he would quarreling pages, then stared at the ground in thought. "But what of 'beneath the depths, a kingdom's plight, paths run with nary a light'? What are these paths it references?"

"Paths?" Back on track, Circe's eyebrows knit together in thought. "Like the paths in a forest? But what forest could it mean?"

"The forests in the Mediterranean are lovely this time of year," Helius offered.

Circe raised an eyebrow at her father.

Helius bristled in return. "What? It was merely a suggestion."

"Paths of light," Pasiphae offered.

"What about the paths one takes to get to an answer?" Aeron asked. "Like a riddle."

"A riddle within a riddle. Lovely," Talfryn said.

Gregorio's fingers twitched in excitement. "It specifically says 'paths' in the plural. What else makes paths without light?"

"A maze of some sort?" Padric asked. "Mayhap made of bushes or trees to make it dark."

Thoughtfully, Gregorio nodded, the gears in his head seeming to turn in his favor. "Yes, a maze would make sense. Let's go with that for now. I am also curious about the meaning of 'beneath the depths.' It could mean the underworld. But I hope not. I have no wish to meet Hades again anytime soon." His mouth formed a thin line.

Again? Brynwen became curious as to what that story with Hades entailed.

Aeron furrowed his brows. "Doesn't that mean in the sea or death or something?"

"Yes and no," Gregorio replied, still puzzling over the matter.

Padric looked up suddenly. "The Labyrinth."

"Ah, now, why didn't I think of that? Indeed, the Labyrinth is deep underground, or 'beneath the depths,' if you will. Well done, my former pupil. Now, if the Labyrinth is near the underground city of Rellea, we have our answer."

The group both present and in the orb spent the next couple of minutes discussing the prophecy. Who was the ally? They brought up the Labyrinth or some equally important maze. But what could the curse mean? And so on.

Talk of the prophecy only made Brynwen's head spin and stomach twist. She felt more nauseated with each passing second. She didn't take part, couldn't think of it right now. As a balm, she shoved her hand into her satchel and felt the smooth tome resting within. *On Healing and Other Remedies* calmed her racing heart, where even a steaming cup of chamomile tea could not. Time to change the subject. "The prophecy isn't the only problem we have." All eyes looked at her, and she cringed. *Maybe speaking was a mistake.*

Twisting her finger around her braid, Brynwen cleared her throat. "I had more visitors this morning. Three people from a city in the Yorkshire Dales. A place called Rellea, I think. They want me to help them with a mysterious illness affecting their citizens."

The four immortals' mouths fell open. Circe recovered first. "Visitors from Rellea? That is a place I have not heard about in ages."

Intrigued, Helius tapped his fingers together. "Pray, what were the names of these visitors?"

"They were called Merta, Arthur, and Isabel."

All the excitement from the three immortals in the globe deflated. They did not recognize the names.

Frustration threatened to burst Brynwen's mind. "The question is: how am I to find the adamant *and* help these people at the same time? I won't forego helping them, but I can't let Janus succeed, either."

A smile lit the two orbed women's faces, but it was Circe who answered. "You must accomplish both tasks."

"Can we split the tasks between us?" Rawlins asked.

Sing-song laughter filled the air as Circe chortled at the question.

Talfryn's nostrils flared. "I'll take that as a no."

"The last known ruler of Rellea was a god called *Dis Pater*," Pasiphae explained. "For unknown reasons, he took his kingdom city underground in the Yorkshire Dales hundreds of years ago. Rumor has it that the Labyrinth is nearby.

"It was also rumored that he guarded the Labyrinth from curious, ignorant mortals who wandered too close to the entrance and never found the exit."

"*Dis Pater.*" Gregorio paced around the clearing, then paused. "Originally, *Dis Pater* was the god of land-based riches: fertile land, gems, and precious minerals. Because anything in the ground deemed precious is considered the treasure of the underworld, some people associated him with Pluto, the god of said underworld. He has mainly kept to himself and his domain for hundreds of years; until one day, over two hundred years ago, he and his subjects vanished."

Circe's grin grew wicked. "It would seem, Brynwen, your two missions coincide with one another. Is that not convenient?"

Sometimes, the goddess got on Brynwen's nerves. This was one of those times.

"Indeed, it is too convenient to be a coincidence," Padric replied.

"What if we go to your estimated location, and it's not there?" Rawlins looked perturbed as ever. "Aren't the Dales huge?"

A spark lit Circe's eyes. "What makes you think you are going, Sir Rawlins?"

It impressed Brynwen that the goddess knew his name. Then again, she *would* remember the name of the knight who had almost killed her in her weakest moment. After facing off with the terrible bone-covered wolf creature called the *aeternae,* Rawlins had nearly died on the ruins of Helius's temple. In a fitful waking dream, he would have strangled Circe to death had it not been for Gregorio and Brynwen calming him down.

Folding his arms over his chest, Aeron looked as impassive as Rawlins. "I'm going as well."

"If she will have me, I go where Brynwen goes—as do they," Padric replied, hands on his hips. "Which is where in the Dales, exactly?"

"Don't forget me." Talfryn straightened next to Brynwen.

The lingering bit of doubt she hadn't acknowledged in her taut stomach flitted away at all the statements of intention. *I won't have to go alone.*

Circe's lips parted to answer, but Pasiphae cut her off. "We are sending another member to join your party."

"Nalini?" Gregorio asked. "Eliva?"

"Payla."

The tutor gaped. "But...are you sure she should be involved? If the Labyrinth is there..." he trailed off. Despite his confusion, he seemed joyous about seeing this Payla person.

Brynwen caught Padric's eye, but he looked as clueless as she felt.

"She shall not forsake her training, regardless of where you go." Pasiphae shrugged. "Besides, it will be good for her to see some of the world again."

"Indeed, it will be good to see her, *Matertera Pasiphae.*"

"When she arrives on the morrow, you must make haste to leave immediately."

"Tomorrow?" Talfryn asked.

"If you wish to save both *Dis Pater's* people and thwart Janus, yes. However, I must warn you that if you enter the Labyrinth, there's a high likelihood of encountering Asterion. Be on your guard."

Asterion.

"The Minotaur?" Padric asked. "But did he not die thousands of years ago?"

Pasiphae smirked. "That, my dear nephew, is a myth."

CLAD IN BLACK, the knight stepped into the darkened evening, where the creature of shadow awaited him. Shade from the trees and hood partially hid the knight's face.

"Well?" The knight folded his arms across his chest. "Is it done?"

The Shadow rubbed together thin, perpetually chilly hands. *"Yes, the plan is in motion. Soon, the next phase will begin."*

"I can come with you. I'll be of more help to you there than here."

"Nay, you must stay with de Clifton and the healer. Otherwise, there will be unwanted questions. Tell me about the Oracle's visit and the healer's quest."

Surprise registered in the knight's expression, but then he shrugged. "The Oracle gave de Clifton's vixen a prophecy about finding adamant to end a curse." He informed the Shadow of everything which had occurred between Brynwen and the group earlier in the day. Each time he mentioned Brynwen, he subconsciously scratched at his forearm, where she had cut him over a month ago.

"*This guide, did they provide a name?*"

"None that I heard."

A plan formed in the Shadow's mind. "*You will stay by their side until I instruct you otherwise. Do I make myself clear?*"

The knight's eyes rolled in their sockets. "Perfectly. I've persuaded de Clifton to take me with him and his love on their quest." He said the word "love" as though it caused him great pain to do so.

"*Good, good! You are learning, young one.*" The knight grimaced at the diminutive term, which made the Shadow grin beneath the hood of the gray cloak. The Shadow was about to dismiss the knight, but the young man remained rooted to the spot. "*What else have you for me?*"

"De Clifton's shapeshifting abilities are advancing rapidly. However, he can't control them, which makes him vulnerable."

"*Yet. That is to be expected, based on his ancestry. He will master them soon enough, with or without aid. You must be careful.*"

"I can take him out the next time it happens, with no one the wiser. On the way, de Clifton could have a tragic accident down a ravine and break his neck. Mayhap, Telegonus could join him. I'll only need Brynwen to complete the task, then she and her brother can meet the same fate as their friends." He snickered, which made his features appear maniacal. Not for the first time, the Shadow wondered how sane this pupil was. Never had the Shadow asked the knight the reason for his animosity toward Padric de Clifton and would not ask now.

"*Patience. Wait until after you have retrieved the adamant to do the deed to de Clifton, Telegonus, and whomever you so desire. If de Clifton dies early, the healer may be too distracted by grief to be of use. We cannot afford to fail this time.*"

The knight stilled and clenched his fists at his sides as though wishing to throttle the creature before him.

"*Do not get aggravated. Savor the hunt, but do not allow vengeance of your heart to divert your path. He and all his friends will meet their demise eventually, whether by your hand or by Master Janus's. Is that not something to look forward to?*"

Unclenching his fists, the knight gave an ungrateful huff. "Fine. But when the time comes, de Clifton and his lady will meet their sorry fates at the end of my sword. Mark me, the day he is dead is the day I will be free. *Free.*"

Somehow, although having felt nothing corporal for centuries, a chill ran up the proverbial spine of the Shadow. The Shadow wondered about the troubling young man as the knight walked away. Keeping him in check was a priority, if only to halt him from ruining everything.

He will need some persistent watching. A plan of action formed in the creature's head. But for now, everything was going according to plan.

CHAPTER 8

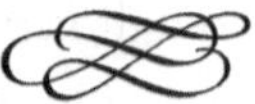

On the morning of their departure, Talfryn and Brynwen got to the Chaddesden market early. The stalls were just opening, and Brynwen wanted to do some last-minute shopping before the long journey to only the-mysterious-Payla-knew-where. The knights and Gregorio would meet them on the western side of the market, and Payla would find them there.

They'd bidden farewell to their grandfather, Samuel, and Rosa. Yesterday, Gregorio had begged Captain Garrick to allow Padric, Rawlins, and Aeron leave for a couple of weeks to help him with another family emergency up north. Due to his family's closeness with the tutor, Garrick grudgingly accepted.

Hopefully, this morning he hadn't changed his mind about letting them go.

Brynwen stepped up to the seed and herb merchant with a wide smile. While she bartered for his products, something metallic caught Talfryn's eye at the blacksmith's forge. The tallest maiden he had ever seen, covered from head to toe in a midnight blue cloak and white dress, spoke animatedly to the young, dark-skinned apprentice about a gleaming dagger with a fresh, leather-wrapped hilt. The few strands of dark hair falling from her hood bounced as she spoke. His eyes danced as he looked up at her towering frame, responding to her questions.

"Not a penny over four," Brynwen insisted.

Talfryn turned his attention back to his sister's bartering, which was winding down. Brynwen got her way maybe half the time, and, judging by her expression, this was one of those times. When he glanced again at the forge, the apprentice stood alone, tending his work at the bellows to stoke the fire.

Curiosity piqued, Talfryn peered around him, but couldn't find any trace of the maiden.

Brynwen finished paying the merchant and whirled around in triumph. "I've been waiting for this comfrey to be available for weeks. Insects have decimated the batch in my garden, despite Gerda's efforts to drive them away. Now, I just need one more thing." Her attention moved to another stall.

Talfryn followed his sister's gaze until it landed on the cloaked maiden two stalls down. She spoke with the owner of the stall over stacked crates containing white-feathered chickens, motioning with her empty hands in every direction like she was trying to describe something.

"Oh, there's Padric, Aeron, and Rawlins." Brynwen waved. They wore traveling clothes instead of their crimson and black uniforms and carried sacks over their shoulders.

Padric spotted the twins first, and his face lit up. He raised his arm in greeting.

A commotion buzzed behind Talfryn and Brynwen. Spinning around, Talfryn gawked at the sight. At least a dozen chickens squawked as they strutted or darted around, feathers sprouting from their wings as they attempted to take flight. The unfortunate owners of the chickens squawked in their own way as they chased the escaped fowl. Some bystanders bent down in a futile attempt to catch the escaped poultry.

"How did they get loose?" Brynwen asked.

"I've a guess." Talfryn smirked when he caught the startled eye of the cloaked maiden. She stood near the chicken owners' stall, trying to both close the busted gate of the top cage with one hand and clutching at a nearby chicken with the other. Meanwhile, more chickens continued to escape.

In a tick, Talfryn stashed his belongings in his sister's arms and sprinted toward the closest chicken zipping in their direction. He feinted right then left, an action he practiced nearly every other day on the farm thanks to his wily goats. "Got you. Gisela, right?" He scooped it up with one hand under the breast and the other between its shoulder blades. Once in his arms, he clutched its neck for security without strangling the jerking creature. It did its best to peck painful holes in his arms and chest. "It's okay, lass, calm down." By the time he reached the overwhelmed owner, the chicken had relaxed considerably and made no further protestations. "Good lass." He handed the creature over to its owner.

Picking the contents from his pockets, he dropped some extra seed on the ground. In seconds, a couple of chickens flocked to his feet. Without hesitation, he plucked them up by the scruff of their necks and crossed to the maiden.

Brynwen and Aeron came over as Talfryn stuffed the chickens in the crate the maiden held and grabbed the edge of the busted gate. "I've got it. Here's some seed for the chickens." He reached into his pocket and dumped the remaining helping into her hand.

"I didn't mean for this to happen." Flustered, she released the cage and tossed the seeds into the air.

As he fiddled with the bent latch, he called to Aeron and Brynwen. "Grab that bucket of seed and sprinkle some of it on the ground." They obeyed without question.

A handful of chickens discovered the seed with delight. Soon, the others followed. In another minute, humans had surrounded the chickens, and Talfryn and the owners hauled the pecking birds into their crate.

Satisfied they were secure, Talfryn wiped his brow. "Whew, that was fun."

Padric and Rawlins came forward, verifying that they'd caught all the poultry.

"What happened? Who let the chickens out?" the lieutenant asked. He gazed intently at the cloaked maiden who clasped her hands in front of her, head bowed in embarrassment.

"She did." The owner was a youngish farmer whom Talfryn had seen many times throughout the years but couldn't ever remember his name. He pointed at the culprit.

The owner's wife flashed angrily. "She ripped the whole cage apart. On purpose."

"Why would you do that?" Padric asked.

The accused's eyes and hands shot up in astonishment. "I didn't mean to, sir, honest. We don't have many chickens like this where I am from. In my excitement, well, my elbow hit the cage. Please forgive me," she entreated the couple.

"Where are you from that you have no chickens?"

"Ah, there you are!" Gregorio came running up and halted in front of the gathered group. "Sir Padric, I beg of you, please have mercy on my cousin. She is from a tiny, far-off place."

"Your cousin?" Talfryn asked. *Payla?*

"This is your cousin?" Padric asked at the same time. Indecision crossed his face.

"She nearly destroyed all our chickens!" The young owner reminded Padric. Then he shot a black look at Gregorio as if the whole thing were his fault.

Padric pulled out his coin bag. "What do we owe you for the damage?"

"I can pay." Payla reached deep within her cloak and pulled out a coin purse made of blue material with Helius's blazing sun on it. She placed a silver coin into the owner's hand. His eyes grew as round as the coin.

Like the owner, Talfryn gaped at the generous offer. He didn't think he'd ever seen a silver coin more than one other time in his whole life. It was enough to pay for a lifetime supply of cabbages for an entire village. Twice over.

"Isn't it enough?" Payla asked, bewildered at the silence.

Gregorio nodded and hooked an arm through hers. "It is more than enough, cousin. Let us go before they change their minds." He steered her to the eastern side of the market. Taking their cue, Talfryn and the others gathered their gear and followed.

❦

While the knights picked up horses from the stables, Brynwen and Talfryn trailed behind Gregorio and his cousin Payla on their way out of the village. Brynwen found the cloaked maiden quite curious. Her height easily matched Rawlins, who topped Padric and Talfryn by a couple of inches. The cloak she wore reminded Brynwen of a starry night filled with a bright moon and constellations.

When they'd left behind the chicken owners, Payla was quiet. But as the distance from the trouble grew, she became more animated. She clutched Gregorio into a fierce hug from which he nearly passed out. Then she showed him a new dagger she had bought, speaking at a quick pace, as though she couldn't get her thoughts out fast enough. The discourse could give Miriel Wilmot a run for her lung capacity.

Gregorio led them to a copse just north of the road. An array of antlers poked out from behind a tree trunk, followed by the familiar furry snout.

Talfryn's face lit up. "Staggy—er, Ulysses!" He dashed to the peryton and gave him a heartfelt hug. "I missed you. Gregorio said you'd come."

Following, Brynwen giggled at her brother's excitement and greeted her half-stag-half-eagle friend with a curtsy and scratch behind his ears. His eyes closed and white wings twitched in contentment while she scratched, reminding her of the goats at home. It was still hard to believe that this creature was once human, the great hero Ulysses whose exploits were memorialized in Homer's *The Odyssey.*

All the dark lines and gray hairs on Gregorio's face and hair melted away in seconds. Brynwen hadn't witnessed the change in person before and watched the transformation in wonder. He turned toward his cousin.

"Finally." Payla grinned as she stepped into the shade. She dropped her bag on the ground and slipped her wide hood off her head. Long, black hair like Gregorio's flowed out of the hood and down her back as she shook it free. But that wasn't what surprised Brynwen the most.

"What the…" Talfryn's mouth dropped as he gaped at Payla.

Brynwen reached for her knife. For a second, she thought Lilith, the deadly succubus from the ruined Mamucium fortress, had returned in a new form.

Horses nickered close by, then Padric's group led their horses into the clearing. All eyes turned to Payla in astonishment. Rawlins and Aeron reached for their swords. Padric put his arm out to stop them, although his eyes were hard.

"What's wrong? Haven't you seen horns before? Telegonus, didn't you warn them about…umm…" She pointed to her head, where a long, sharp horn grew straight for a few inches before hooking upward on each side of her head, like one would see on a bull.

Crimson blotched Gregorio's cheeks. "Well, I was about to when you ripped your hood off without warning. But now everyone knows, so it is fine."

"Yeah, fine," Talfryn murmured. To Brynwen, he whispered, "Ya know, her horns outrank Padric's horns by a lot."

"I heard that." Padric eyed Talfryn, who made a nervous laugh.

Gregorio waved as though quieting rowdy pupils. "Now that we are all here, we can make formal introductions. Allow me to introduce my cousin Payla, the daughter of Pasiphae and twin sister to Asterion, the Minotaur. Priestess in the Temple of Mithras." Next, he introduced everyone to her.

So many questions threatened to pour out of Brynwen's mouth, but she didn't know where to start. By the others' wide-eyed expressions, they felt the same.

"Sister of Asterion? Forgive me, but I have not seen your name listed in any of the texts I have studied. How could you leave out such an important detail, *o tutor*?" Padric glared pointedly at the scholar.

A sigh escaped Gregorio's lips. "Sí, Padric. I was under a strict oath of secrecy at that moment." He eyed his cousin, who nodded. "Let us begin our journey, and we will share the story along the way."

They mounted their horses, and once they were about a mile out, Gregorio began the story of Payla as promised.

"Cursed by Neptune into falling in love with the Cretan bull, its rendezvous with Pasiphae produced a set of twins: Asterion and Payla. While Asterion was born with the body of a male child and head and tail of a bull, Payla looked like a normal human babe, but with tiny nubs of horns on her head. Pasiphae's handmaid was able to spirit Payla away before her stepfather, King Minos, could ever discover she lived, so she would never suffer the same fate as her brother.

"Asterion was not as lucky. He was discovered by King Minos and forced to live in the center of the Labyrinth where he devoured the sacrificial young men and maidens of their enemy, Athens. Asterion became known as the Minotaur. Then, a young prince from Athens named Theseus thought to free his people by killing the Minotaur. That was when Ariadne fell in love with Theseus and vowed to help him."

"Ariadne was our half-sister." Payla frowned. "She betrayed my stepfather and brother to help *him*." A sneer of disgust showed on her face.

Gregorio nodded sadly. "She procured an enchanted string that would help guide him out of the Labyrinth afterward. Thanks to her, Theseus succeeded in killing Asterion, and in his gratitude for Ariadne's help, abandoned her on an island and never returned for her."

Payla's voice was thick. "I was unable to save my brother in time, but then a miracle happened."

"What miracle?" Brynwen's heart went out to the horned maiden. If something ever happened to her brother, she couldn't bear it.

"The gods gave him a second chance at life." Payla's eyes glittered for a moment before dropping. "But I have not seen him since that day."

A mixture of feelings swirled around Brynwen. Happiness that Payla's brother lived, yet also uncertainty over restoring the life of a monster. "That is wonderful. But tell me, where have you lived all this time?"

"Priestesses in the Temple of Mithras raised me up near Hadrian's Wall at the border of Scotland."

Talfryn's eyes were saucers. "How was it being the sister of the Minotaur?"

Payla gave a sad smile. "It was never easy, mind you. When we were children, whenever my stepfather left his home for a few days, my mother would retrieve Asterion from the Labyrinth and bring him to my temple where we would play. Back then, he was so excited to be freed for days at a time. But as we grew, he became angered by his predicament and jealous of the freedom I enjoyed, even though I was as much a captive to the Temple as he was to the Labyrinth. Our last time together, when we were about fourteen, was…difficult." She paused, frowning as though remembering that fateful day.

Brynwen wished to ask more about it, but Payla's expression became guarded and closed on the subject. "Pray, how does one become a priestess of Mithras?"

Talfryn scratched his chin. "And who *is* Mithras? The god of myth?"

Padric and Gregorio tried to hold in a chuckle, but Payla outright laughed, a high sound not unlike Circe's, but with much less restraint. She wiped a tear from her eye. "Forgive me, I have been on my own for so long and haven't laughed in ages. It is a long process, but at a very young age you go into the Temple of the god you will swear fealty to and undergo tests and training. If you pass, you can become a priestess and devote your life to the god or goddess."

"I liken it to a cloistered nun," Gregorio explained.

It didn't surprise Brynwen he knew this, as he had attended St. Mary's most Sundays. It occurred to her now that whether he attended because of Church law or because he wanted to be there, hadn't come up before.

"Precisely. Mithras is the god of oaths and justice, similar to my grandfather Helius, but on a much wider scale. He is also attributed with having influence over the sun, water, and cattle. His temple, where I live, is at the remains of the Carrawburgh Roman Fort in Northumberland."

"Near Hadrian's wall?" Padric asked. "I have always desired to go there."

Payla smiled brightly. "Correct. Mayhap someday, you can visit."

"Then why did your mother send you all the way down here if it is nearly halfway?"

"She thought it best we come up with a plan along the way." She grinned. Plus, Ulysses begged to come."

Brynwen was sure she saw the peryton blush.

CHAPTER 9

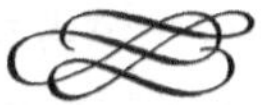

Unwinding the chain from his saddlebags, Padric wrapped the links around the sturdiest tree in the clearing. He wished to secure it before the sunlight faded, then perhaps invite Brynwen for a short stroll before turning in. With double the travelers and the need for vigilance, finding time to talk was challenging compared to their previous trip with just Brynwen, Talfryn, and him.

"So, that's what the chain's for." Talfryn cocked his head to the side. "That thing's been clinking in your saddlebags since we left home."

"Last night, I chewed through my rope and gnawed on Rawlins's bedding." It was extremely embarrassing asking the mending woman to mend yet another mattress. She had looked at him like he had three heads.

"It's still coming out of your pay," Rawlins called from the other side of the clearing.

"Believe me, I know." Padric sighed. "Having abilities is becoming more tedious than helpful." His stomach was still upset from many a night's partaking of hay, straw, and other non-human food. But at least this morning he had returned to human form with little of a hitch. *Now the question is, can I do it again?*

Talfryn nodded. "I don't doubt it. Let me know if you need help with the chain. I've learned a couple tricks from having to tie up Hay and Stack all the time." He yawned and headed for his belongings.

"Padric." Brynwen stood up from tending the fire and brushed her hands on her apron. "I can make you another tonic tonight."

"That is most thoughtful. Afterward, mayhap we can—"

"Nay, nay, nay." Gregorio barged in on them, the tutor's hands flying around his head. Payla and Ulysses marched in behind him. "A tincture is ill advised. Payla, Ulysses, and I have conferred, and we think the tincture you made for him two nights ago caused his predicament with transforming."

"What?" Brynwen asked, wide eyed.

"How so?" Padric asked.

Payla folded her hands together as though in prayer. "One ingredient may have interfered with your dreams and desires, Sir Padric. Brynwen, what ingredients did you use?"

Brynwen regarded the youthful-looking tutor with awe. "How could that be? I used basic ingredients." From her satchel, she withdrew the black leather-bound *Book of Healing and Other Remedies*.

The title was in a Latin dialect so ancient Padric could not quite understand; yet Brynwen could read it without incident, although she'd had no training in the language. It seemed to have been a constant companion of hers since Cataractonium.

"Here it is." Brynwen pointed at the ingredient list.

Gregorio frowned at the tome. "This book...*De Sanatione atque Aliorum Remediorum*...from where did you get it?"

Antlers hovered in close as the peryton tried to get a better look at the book in question.

"Your mother lent it to me. What's wrong? Can you read it?"

"*Mater*," he said it like a curse. The immortal swallowed. "Not I. Tell me, is there a name on the first page?"

"Yes. Well, of sorts." She flipped to the first page. "'H.A.' Do you know what it means?"

"It is the author, a brilliant man by the name of Aesculapius. 'H' is for Hepius, his birth name. But this book…" All the color drained from his face. "Jupiter destroyed both him and this book thousands of years ago. At least, they were supposed to have been. This is a dangerous book, Brynwen."

"Oh, no, not Jupiter again. Well, he obviously didn't destroy it. Maybe he just wanted everyone to think so."

"Jupiter," Padric said, recalling his mythology lessons about the king of gods residing on Mount Olympus. "I remember something about Aesculapius. He was a great healer who learned everything he knew from his father Apollo, was he not? Jupiter killed him because he healed too many people."

"I am afraid so."

"That's awful." Brynwen closed the book and held it before her but frowned in uncertainty. "I can't believe this book could cause so much grief. It has saved so many lives—it saved yours, Signore, and Padric's, from the manticore venom."

The immortal pursed his lips. "Be that as it may, it is a dangerous book. Be rid of it as soon as possible, Brynwen, I beg you." He strode off to a fair distance, scratching his head.

Payla nodded in agreement. "My cousin is right. It would be best for all if the book goes. I don't know why my aunt had it in her possession, yet I am sure she wouldn't give it to you without reason. It is something to think about, yes?"

Ulysses gave first Brynwen, then Padric, an imploring look, as though asking them to listen to the immortals' suggestions. Then he and Payla bedded down for the night in companionable silence.

Padric took a step closer to Brynwen. "Mayhap they are right, Bryn. If the book is as dangerous as they say, we should destroy it. Or return it to Circe and let her deal with it."

Indecision darkened Brynwen's expression. Her silence made him second-guess his speaking up, but how could he ignore the warnings of three immortals who had lived a thousand life experiences each? Of Payla, he knew little, but he regarded the word of Gregorio, his mentor, friend, and many-great-grandfather, above almost all others.

At last, Brynwen shook her head and clutched the book to her chest tightly. "You heard her, Padric. Circe must have given it to me for a reason. We'll just have to ask her next time we meet." Without another word, she ducked into her bedroll with her back to him and pulled her blanket over her shoulder.

Aeron appeared beside him. "That went well."

A sudden tiredness came over Padric, but he feared what came with sleep. "I will take first watch. After that, I cannot guarantee what form I will take come morning."

&

A LOUD "NAAAAHHH," followed by a sharp cry and curse from Sir Aeron, startled Brynwen awake. Snatching up the dagger she'd borrowed from among Rawlins's small armory, she launched to her feet. Heart in her throat, she squinted through the darkness for an enemy. She pictured the man in the green cloak stalking her, the long gash on the arm she had cut still bleeding even after more than a month.

The dark forms of Rawlins and Talfryn were already up, weapons drawn.

The clink of chains drew her attention to the tree where Padric had tied himself up with sturdy chains. The goat, nearly charcoal gray in the dark, pouted at those around the fire, bleating and quaking against his chains.

Near him sat Aeron, clutching his arm, glaring at the chained animal. "You mangy goat. I should—"

"What is happening?" Gregorio staggered to his feet, blinking away sleep.

Before he could finish the question, Rawlins and Talfryn were already rushing toward the irritated goat. Rawlins grabbed his horns while Talfryn yanked on the chain. This only infuriated Padric-goat more, and soon a three-way tug-of-war began. Shouts, curses, and hoofs flew everywhere. Padric-goat nipped at too-close fingers. Quick hoofs knocked Talfryn and Rawlins to the ground more than once.

"This is getting old," Rawlins muttered. "Hold that chain close."

"Trying," Talfryn huffed.

"Padric, you must stop at once, or someone will get hurt," Gregorio shouted.

Payla grabbed the chain while Ulysses paced back and forth, his intelligent eyes watching, yet unable to give aid.

"You're hurting him," Brynwen yelled over the din. She hastened toward the melee. "Padric, please."

Padric-goat glanced at her. Paused.

The pause was enough for the knights and Talfryn to shove Padric-goat's gray face into the moss at the base of the tree. Then they pinned the rest of his body to the ground. The fight was over.

Padric-goat glared at each of them, his eyes red with anger at being beaten.

"Good thing Padric thought to bring this chain," Aeron grumbled and rubbed at his hand.

"The good it did us," Rawlins growled. "We still aren't getting much sleep."

Talfryn wiped his brow. "Oh, I dunno. I'll sleep like a baby after this."

"Why does this keep happening to him? What if he gets stuck like this forever?" The fear of this happening to her brave, charming, handsome knight made Brynwen's heart threaten to burst.

Gregorio stepped behind her. "His shapeshifting abilities are growing at a rapid pace. Unfortunately, sometimes it is a slow process to master. It is unfortunate this occurs now, during our mission. I have done what I can for him, which honestly isn't much."

"How are we to complete our mission if he's like this?" Aeron asked.

Rawlins looked hard at Aeron, then down at the goat.

Brynwen exhaled and regarded her beau. Hesitantly, she knelt and caressed his furry cheek. He looked up at her, transfixed. "Can we do anything for him? What if I make him another tonic?" Her satchel was by her bedroll. She made to get up when Gregorio placed a hand on her shoulder and gently coaxed her back down, shaking his head.

"Nay, that will not help him. It is something *he* must deal with. But I have an idea. Try speaking with him. See if you can persuade him to change back to his human form."

"But it didn't work the other day. He only changed back under duress, not because he felt like it."

"That was then. Since then, he has become more attuned to you, has he not?"

"I suppose so." She curled her finger around her braid, unsure it would work.

"Then proceed. Remind him of who he is. At times, we all need a little reminder of this." He lifted his gaze. "Lads, let go of him gently."

Rawlins started. "But—"

"No buts. Please. If we are to gain the trust of his animal instincts, we must first show him some respect." The immortal nodded encouragement.

Finally, three dark heads nodded and slowly released Padric. When he didn't move, they backed off to a safe distance. Payla continued holding the chain, but out of Padric's immediate periphery. Gregorio ushered everyone else further away until they reached the other side of the clearing.

Brynwen took a breath and settled herself closer to Padric, tucking her feet under her skirt to get comfortable. *Where to begin?* She caressed his cheek again. Like Ulysses with Circe, Padric moved into her touch. "This would be more adorable if you were *you*." She sighed and bit her lip. "Padric, it's me. I know your stomach is overtaking your senses right now, but I need you to listen. I need you—we all need you—to be yourself again. Signore Gregorio says your abilities are growing, but I can't keep losing you to these fits of goatiness. As much as Hay and Stack appreciate your friendship"—she couldn't help but smile at this—"it's only making things harder for you to master yourself. Remember, you are a man, a knight. *My* knight." She imagined her grandfather glaring down at her.

"Naahhh," Padric-goat bleated skeptically.

She chuckled. "It is true. You are someone who loves his people and whom Talfryn and I can count on. You have so many good friends, and you have me." A tear escaped down her cheek and fell on Padric-goat's hoof. He watched it land on his appendage. "You are your own master, sir knight." As much as she liked the animals at home, she never felt inclined to kiss their faces like Talfryn did. Imagining trying to kiss the crazy, dirty heads of Hay and Stack, she scrunched her nose. But for the creature before her, she would. "Please come back to me, Padric." She leaned over and kissed the fur above his nose. "I will love you even if you stay a goat forever."

When nothing happened after a few moments, Brynwen's heart sank. "It was worth a try." She stroked his head between the horns. Padric-goat's body stiffened, then shook, similar to the stormy night when he'd been trapped under the great tree outside her home—the night they officially met.

Brynwen shot to her feet, but stared in horror as first the goat's legs, then his head, morphed. Gregorio and the others stepped in line beside her, their faces grim. Talfryn stopped at her right.

Her chest constricted. "This is what you went through every day in Cataractonium?"

"Aye." Talfryn shivered despite the warm evening.

How did you stand it? she wanted to ask.

Finally, Padric's tremors stilled. She rushed forward, releasing a great sigh as she sunk to her knees beside his fully human form. He lay still as if asleep. The others surrounded them.

She wondered if she should bother Padric or let him rest. Tentatively, she placed a hand on his chest and said in a soft voice like she would to soothe an expectant mother. "Padric?"

His eyelashes fluttered, then his eyes opened. Ebony in the shadows. "Bryn?" A deep groan escaped his lips as he sat up, the chains twisting around him, and patted his arms and ribs. "Every muscle aches." Then he placed his head in his hands. "Please tell me I dreamt about walloping you three."

"You didn't," they all said in unison.

Gregorio placed his hands on his hips. "I am afraid your extended training, what little I can give, will begin in the morning."

"Will this not interfere with our traveling?" Padric asked.

"We will work around it."

Padric nodded wearily and looked to the sky. "I will keep watch until dawn. The rest of you, get back to bed, as there is still a little time left before the sun rises."

Slinking into his bedroll, Rawlins grumbled. "No thanks to you."

Brynwen lingered while the rest of the camp settled down. "Padric, you already did the first watch."

"Yes, but this way I will not be a nuisance a second time. I had better get a hold of this soon, or I do not know what I'll do. There is no way I can continue to do my duty if I eat everyone's bedding and knock them senseless every night. My father is closer to the truth than he knows."

Like father, like son in their cleverness. She seized his hand and squeezed. "It will sort itself out. I know it will."

"But when?"

"Look at me. You will not do this alone, I promise."

Padric gazed at her intently, all his love, pain, and confusion present in that one moment, threatening to pull her off her feet. *How does he always have this effect on me? Even after I was terrible to him earlier?*

His hand hovered next to her cheek and caressed it, causing the butterflies in Brynwen's stomach to flutter. Moving his head toward hers, he said softly, "I love you, too."

CHAPTER 10

The next day

After studying Gregorio's maps depicting the area west of York while Payla argued with Rawlins and Aeron over the best location to begin their search for the stone of adamant, Padric caught the tutor's eye.

"Fear not, Padric, I have not forgotten about you. *Mater* has agreed to help with your training." Gregorio held up his orb. The white clouds swirled around.

Padric grimaced. "More breathing exercises?" Despite the tedium of breathing exercises, his hopes rose. The sorceress had a knack for seeing through his issues. Also, being the one who turned others into animals, she would know a thing or two about transformation. Perhaps she could put some perspective on things. It could not be worse than tying himself up to his bed or a tree night after night. "I would most appreciate any aid at all."

"You can say that again," Rawlins interjected, appearing at Padric's elbow. "He's going through mattresses and blankets like the bard goes through his cups."

"That is not fair," Padric replied. "My chewing on your mattress two nights in a row still only counts as one."

"You could also get some pointers from him." Gregorio nodded toward Rawlins. "His is a most natural talent, so complete is his obliviousness in possessing it."

Rawlins's nostrils flared. "Me? What're you on about?"

"See? Denial." Gregorio clucked his tongue and shook his head.

It took a few seconds for Padric to understand what the tutor meant. "Do you really think he has an ability like me? It would explain so much."

"Explain what? What are we talking about?" Padric had only ever seen Rawlins flustered a handful of times, and this was no exception as the knight's cheeks turned bright red.

A grin raised Padric's lips. "Your ability to disappear and reappear like a ghost. It is most extraordinary."

Narrowing his eyes, Rawlins reflected. "I'm quiet like a fox, mind, but nothing special there. Years of training."

"Your father noticed it, too." Growing up, Padric had heard the older man, now deceased, comment on it more than once. It had unnerved him something fierce.

"Who is your mother?" Gregorio asked.

"My mother?" Rawlins scratched his temple and shrugged. "Died when I was born. My gran was foreign born, though." He shrugged. "That's all I know."

"'Tis a sad thing, knowing not one's ancestry."

Rawlins's cheeks turned to cherry. "Listen here—"

Padric clamped a hand on his friend's shoulder. "I am sure Gregorio meant nothing by it." He gave the immortal a meaningful look. "Only that you should consider what he is asking. Mayhap you will stop sneaking up on me so often."

"It's 'cause you're not paying attention."

"Regardless, it may benefit you to join in Padric's training. Your ability to blend in may come in handy someday."

"Think about it."

"I might," Rawlins conceded. Nevertheless, he looked like he would rather think about skewering the closest tree.

CHAPTER 11

The village of Malham had a small town center, including a tiny two-story inn, a handful of shops, and a stable. Spread out from there, they spotted cottages on acres of land.

Talfryn jumped off his horse to stretch his sore legs. Padric hastened past him to help Brynwen escape her own horse, his hands around her waist, each gazing into each other's eyes…

Ugh, yep, there's no doubt—they're still smitten. At least they're done hiding their feelings from each other, so I can tease them properly.

He spotted the peryton, white wings hidden by magical cloaking, looking at the couple, and thumped his shoulder. "Ulysses, stop gaping, mate, and help me get these love birds inside before they make a scene in front of the entire village."

Romantic mood over, Padric turned to smirk at them. "Ha, ha. Now get inside. Forgive me, Ulysses, but I think it best you wait out here."

The peryton nodded in what Talfryn might consider mild disappointment.

It's not fair. He's one of us—even if his antlers won't fit through the door.

Once everyone except Ulysses was inside the inn, Talfryn took in his surroundings. A handful of paintings decorated the walls. A long bar with a tidy-but-bored-looking barkeep behind it stood to the left. On the floor sat eight square wooden tables with chairs. Three of the tables had occupants leaning over pints of ale and bowls of something thick, who stopped to stare at the strangers when they came in.

The barkeep, who doubled as the innkeeper, perked up when they walked in. He smoothed down his blue tunic and gave a welcoming smile. "How may I help you?" His shrewd eyes scanned the group, likely calculating in his head how much he could charge the strangers for food, drink, and rooms. Luckily, they had three intimidating knights, one more terrifying than the others, to keep the price down. The man's eyes stopped for a couple of heartbeats on Gregorio before moving on.

Curious, Talfryn thought.

They ordered drinks and pushed two tables together. By then, the other customers had resumed their meals and conversations.

"Where's this envoy?" Rawlins asked softly, his back to the wall, facing the door. Talfryn knew he'd already made note of both exits and who, if anyone, had concealed weapons on their person.

"That's what I would like to know as well," Aeron replied.

The door to the inn opened, drawing everyone's attention. Magic hood covering her horns, Payla shot to her feet. A bright smile lit her face, and although completely unnecessary, she waved at the man who entered. "Franco!" At least two dozen years older than Talfryn, the man sported dark hair with a hint of gray under a dark green cap and a week's worth of stubble from travel. His pinched face showed wariness as he surveyed the room before halting mid-stride. The next step he took made him limp and wince. Talfryn had been around animals long enough to know when they'd gotten into a scrape or were born lame, and Franco met the former condition. The other thing that gave it away was his dirty and torn clothing.

Payla gasped and pushed back her chair with a loud scrape on the floorboards in her attempt to get to him. "Franco? What happened?" She placed a steadying hand on his arm. Padric followed her.

"They...took them." He shuddered and would have collapsed if Payla hadn't caught him. She and Padric led him to the table and set him in the knight's vacated chair. "Payla? What are you doing here? You shouldn't be here."

"Lenore and your sons?" Payla asked, ignoring his question.

"Barkeep, we need ale," Padric called. "Who took them, Franco?"

The man sat in a daze for a moment, face haunted. Payla put a hand on his back and he jumped. The act woke him from his stupor. "This… Druid and his strange goblin-like servants. They attacked us as we were crossing the moors a few miles from here."

Padric started. "Goblins?"

Payla covered her face in her hands. "Please don't tell me—are they…?" A quick shake of his head made her shoulders sag in relief. "Thank the gods for that. Franco, you can trust my friends and cousin." In quick sentences, she told the group how she had found Franco as a wounded soldier after a battle against bandits—the lone survivor. She'd brought him back to health and returned him to his family. They discovered her horns and immortality but weren't frightened. In fact, after his recovery, she visited them frequently.

"Why did he take them?" Padric asked once the story was finished.

"Somehow, the Druid knew I had been hired to bring a healer to Rellea. He wants an exchange. The healer for my family. Tomorrow, or they die."

CHAPTER 12

Talfryn's mouth dropped. "Bryn? He wants my sister? No." He shook his head vehemently. Standing up abruptly, he folded his arms over his chest and nearly knocked the table over in his haste. "He can't have her. Not in a thousand years, I won't allow it." *I'm not losing her again.*

"Tal." Padric put a hand on Talfryn's shoulder. "We will not allow that to happen."

Franco's voice took on an edge. "But my family's at stake."

"So's mine," Talfryn said through clenched teeth.

"Hold it, hold it." Payla threw her hands between the two. "Mayhap we can find a way to save Franco's family *and* keep Brynwen safe. Did he say why he wanted her?"

"Nay, but he was very iron-willed about it. I offered my life for theirs, but he'd take nothing less."

Fingers stroking his chin, Padric sat in contemplation. Talfryn thought he saw tiny horns sticking out of his hair for a second, but when he blinked they disappeared.

Brynwen threw her arms out in exasperation. "You're all speaking about me as though I'm not here. I'm not worth the lives of a family."

Padric shook his head and took hold of Brynwen. "There are no other negotiations, Bryn. He must be an agent of Janus and knows what we are after. You are the key to this, and he wants only you."

Gregorio had been sitting in thoughtful silence until now. "Padric is right. If he gets you, Brynwen, Janus will triumph."

"Well, we need to rescue Franco's family." She stared at Padric.

"I agree, but we need a plan." He turned to the envoy. "Franco, where are you to meet the Druid?"

"Near one of the gigantic caverns in the Dales. But I'm to take her alone, no one else. I didn't know there'd be so many of you."

Padric's mouth dipped into a scowl.

Talfryn was about to protest.

"That doesn't mean we won't be nearby." Rawlins tapped his sheathed sword and dagger.

"Right," Talfryn agreed, a blush creeping up his neck. His hand grazed his hatchet, remembering the last time he'd had to use it. Nightmares had sprouted from that encounter.

Gregorio slipped his hand inside his leather satchel. "Everything is in the Dales, apparently," he muttered.

We hope, Talfryn thought.

The tutor looked about the room then splayed his long, heavy tome on the table and carefully turned the pages. Its worn edges and pages, discolored with age, took up most of the table space. *How old is this book, and how did it fit in his bitty bag?* Talfryn figured it might have to do with a certain resourceful blonde sorceress.

Franco studied the map. "We're here, and we'll enter the Dales here." He traced a line with his finger to a large area of the map with no markings of roads or towns. "The cave is somewhere in here. He said I'd know it when I see it, whatever that means."

"The king was last seen in this same area hundreds of years ago." Payla tapped the map near what looked like inked-in mounds.

The group studied the map until a tall shadow leaned over it.

"Oh, no, you don't want to go into that part of the Dales." The innkeeper shook his head. From a large round tray, he placed bowls of stew in front of each guest. "The area around the caves isn't safe."

All sounds from the other tables ceased. Some patrons craned their necks toward the party's tables.

The moment the food landed in front of him, Talfryn began eating in earnest. He hadn't realized how hungry he was until the savory stew met his mouth.

"Nevertheless," Padric replied, "we must go there."

He shook his head sadly. "Mind yer things, then."

"The place is haunted," an elderly man with a crooked nose and long white beard said from a nearby table.

Talfryn spit out his soup all over his portion of the table. "Haunted?"

"My aunt's husband disappeared from there years ago."

"Someone stole my brother's belongings—from right under his nose," another person with a short gray beard remarked.

Nearly everyone in the room claimed to know someone or something—mostly *something*—that was lost near the caves.

"Mark me, those caves are dangerous," the innkeeper repeated. His gaze rested on Gregorio. "Best be on your way—after a good night's rest in our charming village, of course."

"Of course, we will keep your warnings under advisement," Padric replied carefully. "Pray, what can you tell us of these ghosts?"

The innkeeper took a quick glance behind him, then leaned forward, his voice a loud whisper so everyone in the tavern could still hear. "Well, legend has it a king lived in these parts centuries ago. Aye, we've had many kings, but this one had magic, as did many of his subjects. Ruthless and rich in precious minerals from the caves, he had hundreds if not thousands of slaves to unearth all his riches. *Dis Pater*, or the Rich King, they called him. Or Dark King, so named for his long, black beard." His hand raised to his chin, then lowered to his knees. "Which he doted over, and his subjects paid homage to both him and his glorious beard."

Talfryn chortled, picturing a stooped over old king with a priceless bejeweled crown and a long, thick, black beard that reached past his knobby hose-clad knees.

Rawlins narrowed his eyes at the innkeeper.

"A Rich King, eh?" Aeron scratched his chin. "Then what happened?"

"No one knows. Some say he went to ground, hiding in one of those caves. Took his followers and slaves with him."

The man with the white beard raised his arms. "And his ghost haunts the land still, stealing things off people for his underground kingdom."

A chill traveled down Talfryn's spine. "Well, that's a cheery tale to hear right before bed."

"There are still hours left before bedtime," Brynwen pointed out.

"And plenty of time left to ruminate on ghosts following me around everywhere."

"Good point," she grumbled. "But we still have to go there."

"Aye," Padric replied. "Regardless of this rumor or legend or what have you, we must go."

"All right, but don't say we didn't warn you." The innkeeper gave a strained smile, wiped up a spot of stew which had escaped a bowl, flipped the dirty towel over his shoulder, and spun around, raising his shoulders at his regular patrons. They returned the shrug and resumed their conversations once more.

Padric studied the map with uncertainty and lowered his voice. "Franco, Gregorio, Payla, what do you make of his tale?"

"D'you really think it took hundreds of years for him to grow his beard that long? I mean, it takes me a week to grow a bit of stubble like this." Talfryn pointed to his unshaven chin.

"Tal." Padric folded his arms across his chest.

"It's an honest question."

Ignoring him, Payla turned to Franco. "How long have you been working for *Dis Pater*? What happened to your farm?"

"Extra income. Farming isn't as lucrative as I'd hoped. Sometimes people from the moors need a guide, and I provide service. This is the first time the king asked me directly."

"Is this *Dis Pater* known to be dangerous?" Rawlins asked Franco.

"Word is he's generous when he wants to be and ruthless against his enemies."

Padric leaned forward, hands on the table. "Do you think he might help us against the Druid? If we outnumber him, he would have no chance against us."

A hiccup of excitement traveled through Talfryn's stomach. "Aye! Ulysses could go. He can fly fast and ask the king for his army."

Franco shook his head wearily. "Won't work. It'd take too long to amass troops and travel in that short a time. I was a soldier for fifteen long years, so I'd know."

A sense of foreboding filled Talfryn's chest, chilling him to the bone. The remaining confidence he'd had from the morning before fled like a mouse from a hungry barn cat. He reached for his sister's hand and squeezed. "Then we really are on our own."

CHAPTER 13

"This is it." Padric needed no map, or even Franco, to know they had found the Yorkshire Moors. The place was massive and extended as far as the eye could see in each direction, with moors and hills covered in purple heather. They had followed the cliff's footpath north from Malham and stopped at the bottom. Payla had already dismounted and dashed into the heather. Butterflies and small animals scampered out of her way as her hood fell from her head. Padric spied Brynwen, astride her horse, gazing in wonder at the sight, and chuckled.

"You can go pick some, if you would like."

"Oh, I don't know. It is too pretty to pick. Well..." She looked slyly around her. "Mayhap just a couple. For research, mind you."

"Of course." Padric hurried off his horse to hide his amusement, then gripped her waist to help her down. "If you have not returned in five minutes, I shall dispatch all the knights in the kingdom after you."

"Will there be a certain lieutenant among the dispatched knights? I hear he is pleasant to look at."

Padric closed the gap between them, his voice growing husky. "If he is available, I will ensure he leads the search."

Brynwen stood on her tiptoes, her lips a hairsbreadth from his. He caught a whiff of lavender and honeysuckle.

She smirked, placing her hands on her hips. "Challenge accepted." Then she dashed off into the purple vegetation and picked the purple stalks which came up to her knees.

Ulysses bounded in after her to run around in circles, then unfurling his wings, he took off into the air. Brynwen's giggles were infectious. She sent a glance back at Padric with a huge smile, and butterflies danced around in his stomach.

Watching her, Padric realized he had never seen her so happy. So carefree. What was it about this place that infected her so? Another fluttering in his stomach made him wish to give chase and kiss her here and now, and he cared not if the entire world witnessed it.

"Too bad she isn't enjoying herself at all." With a tsk, Talfryn stopped beside him and folded his arms over his chest.

Padric grinned. "I know, 'tis a pity. Say, has it been five minutes yet?"

"Beg pardon?"

"Mayhap I should go make sure she is well—"

"Sir, come look at this," Aeron called from behind.

Grimacing, Padric spun around to find Aeron leading his horse down a hill toward them from the east. He pointed up at Gregorio and Rawlins at the top of the grassy hill. Franco stood nearby.

"Rawlins saw something in the ravine."

With regret, Padric left the twins, priestess, and peryton to their merrymaking and followed Aeron up the hill. Padric's breath caught when he crested the rise. They stood on not a hill, but a cliff dropping nearly three hundred feet toward rocks and boulders of the Gordale Scar Ravine. Knees nearly buckling at the long drop, Padric found himself back in Helius's flying sun chariot, the god by his side, speeding over the countryside with the wind whipping through their hair. Just before Janus attempted to kill them and Apollo...

A clap on his shoulder brought him back to the present.

"Careful, mate, it's a long drop," Aeron said.

"Aye," Padric replied with a raspy voice. *We might have flown over this very ravine. How strange, it was a few weeks ago, but seems like only yesterday.* Once he regained his bearings, he studied the expanse of limestone. A waterfall flowed down the other side of the ravine. The way down was too steep and there was no footpath nearby, so he could not get a closer look. "This truly is spectacular. Thank you for showing me." He could not wait to see Brynwen's expression when she came up the hill.

"This is one of my favorite views." Gregorio's heartfelt expression seemed more relaxed than it had in the last week. "It has been so long since I was last here, I nearly forgot its beauty. Another waterfall is just a short distance that way." He pointed north.

Padric could not help but smile at his tutor's wistful expression. "Mayhap, when we have finished our task, we can explore it some more."

"I would like that very much." Gregorio beamed at Padric.

"You have been here before. Is that why the innkeeper kept looking at you?"

"Alas, I am afraid so. I prayed he would not remember me, as he was just a boy then. I stayed with his family for a few days during an unrelenting spring storm."

"And you looked the same as you do now."

The youthful immortal nodded, his dark curls bouncing around his head. The other men did not seem to recognize me, which was a relief."

A quiet presence stepped up behind Padric. He grinned and said, "Rawlins, I see you've taken Gregorio's revelation to heart—good. Now, what's this about your seeing something of interest?"

Rawlins grumbled. "Someone, more like. Down there. The fellow ducked behind one of those boulders the moment I spotted him. Short fellow, too. I've felt eyes on us since we reached the Dales."

Padric did another quick scan of the area below, seeing no one at all, but he did not doubt Rawlins's word. "Could be one of the Druid's 'goblin' minions or someone from Malham Village. Unfortunately, there is much he can hide behind to deter our spotting him. Keep an eye on it?"

The sergeant nodded. "Aye, my thoughts exactly."

Gentle footsteps approached, the scent of honey and lavender wafted toward Padric, and he knew he need not draw his sword. A bouquet of violet heather greeted him as he turned, catching him off guard. Their bushy, aromatic scent overpowered every other sense. He sneezed.

"Sorry, Padric! I didn't think you'd turn around so fast. But don't these smell divine?"

Pushing the plants down, he saw her smile from ear to ear, infectious as ever. "Yes, love," he agreed without giving the plants another glance. "Whatever you say. Looks like you did not need rescuing after all."

She raised an eyebrow. "Is that a pout I see?"

"There is no pout."

"It is right there." She poked the corner of his mouth, causing his lip to quiver into a smile. "Ah, that's better."

Padric's breath hitched for the second time in as many minutes. *What power does this maiden hold over me? Is she a witch? If so, I do not care in the least.* On impulse, he leaned in and kissed her. At first, she gasped in surprise, but moved in to return the gesture. Her lips were warm and tasted of honey, and he lost himself in them. Loud whistles emanated from those around them.

With the greatest regret, he unlocked their lips. "Can a man not kiss his maiden without fanfare?" He tried to hide his blush. A pang of guilt filled his chest at the chastising look Brynwen's grandfather would give him had he seen the display.

"Nay," came the unified response.

"I think he's gone," Rawlins muttered. "No thanks to you two." He rolled his eyes and stalked further along the cliff's edge.

Who? Padric nearly asked, squeezing Brynwen's hand, his mind in a flutter. *Oh.* Combing a hand through his hair, he took a final peek down into the Gordale Scar Ravine, but saw no sign of anyone. *Hopefully it will stay that way until we finish our missions.* Yet, he knew better.

CHAPTER 14

*S*omething awoke Brynwen from her slumber. *What was that? A dream about heather? Running in it, dancing in it, sleeping in it, eating it, kissing Padric in it...*

How bizarre. She rolled over to fall asleep again, but her mind raced about purple heather. *Fine, I am getting up!* Over the last month, thoughts and dreams of plants and herbs kept her up or woke her for absolutely no reason. And each night, the dreams made her more and more curious about *On Healing and Other Remedies.*

She studied the tome. "What is it about you, book, that so draws me? I find I can't be without you." Sitting by the crackling fire, shadows dancing on sleeping Padric-goat, Talfryn, and the others, she opened to a random page and, without looking at the title, read a list of ingredients, including heather and many herbs from her Miracle Mix. *This looks like a recipe for insomnia, but with heather and lavender—something I need, apparently!* She'd played this game with herself ever since leaving Chaddesden: Peeking at the ingredients and then guessing the title of the recipe. Most times, she was correct.

Is the book trying to tell me I need to make this? Chamomile usually does wonders, but this... She frowned and stared into the fire. "Could be I just need a drink of water."

87

Grabbing her wooden cup and getting to her feet, she sidled over to the pitcher of stream water and filled her cup. Her eye fell on Padric's sleeping form, his breaths rising evenly in his chest. Warmth filled her own chest, watching him, relaxed and out of danger for the time being. Not wailing for food like last night. "Wait," she said under her breath. She regarded him again, at his human face, arms, and clothes. "Weren't you just a goat? Ugh, mayhap I am more tired than I thought." Next, her gaze slid to Talfryn, his usually lax body lying taught and mouth stuck in a frown. *Is he having a nightmare?* She thought to sit by him when the bright flash of firelight broke through her thoughts. The fire reflected on an exposed dagger on the ground.

"No, don't do that," Rawlins mumbled.

At least, that's what it sounded like he'd said.

The stoic knight was lying in his bedroll, clutching his favorite dagger in one hand, sword in the other, his tunic askew. Untied at the wrist, his sleeves scrunched up to his elbows from the warm night. For a moment, she feared he'd wake in a panic as he had done on the roof of Helius's temple. After being severely wounded by the beastly *aeternae*, he'd somehow found enough strength to nearly strangle the goddess Circe to death. According to Talfryn and Byron, he had fought the beast bravely and nearly died from blood loss. Having been mostly concerned with Padric, Gregorio, and Talfryn's health at the infirmary, she had left his care in the hands of other capable healers, such as Isemay and Miriel. A wave of guilt passed over her. She had not visited many other patients, as all her energy had gone to keeping Padric and Gregorio alive. A voice in the back of her head told her to not worry, that she'd had a lot on her mind. But her heart knew it wasn't right. *I must do better.*

Now, something obviously disturbed Rawlins in his sleep. It was only the second time she had ever seen him without a stoic or grumpy countenance.

Still gripping the dagger, his left hand shifted and caught the firelight, a dark shadow falling on his wrist. Curiosity getting the better of her, Brynwen leaned forward for a better view of the shadow.

She gasped, dropping the cup of water. "No…it can't be…no, no, no…"

The scar.

Her heel accidentally hit Talfryn's arm as she stumbled backward.

No, no, no. Somehow, she picked her way out of the circle of firelight and escaped into the deep dark of partial moonlight, running through the heather, running, until she fell to her knees in exhaustion. All her breaths stuck to her throat, choking her. *The scar. Long and jagged…*

Her hands tied together, she picked up the knife and retreated away from him. The remains of the sun glinted off gold on a silver chain as the cloaked man lunged for the decoy amulet. She raised the dagger, the glint of steel arcing and slicing his arm. He retracted his arm in shock. She retreated a step but tripped over Nessie's cage, sending them both pitching over the edge of the cliff.

Brynwen gasped, her chest constricting as she relived the cloaked man's treachery over and over in her mind. Twisted within the memory were Roana's prophecy and words of warning.

"He's here, among us," she sobbed. "Rawlins, of all people." Padric's oldest friend. *How could he betray us, least of all Padric?* It made her sick at heart. Could Rawlins have somehow communicated with the Druid that she was going to Rellea? That he had known about Franco's family's kidnapping? Angry tears flowed for what seemed forever until she could no longer lift her head. "It's my fault. I must warn Padric. But how? Rawlins is there. He's always *there.* And I am so tired."

Her thoughts were in such disarray, she took a brief break to rest her eyes. After getting some rest she would create a strategy to expose Rawlins for what he truly was. The word echoed in her mind.

Traitor.

Traitor.

Traitor.

⚘

"Brynwen."

A shake to the shoulder roused her from sleep. Cracking her eyes open, she recognized the stoic gaze and black hair of Rawlins. Startled, she cringed from his touch as though bit by a viper. *Get away from me!* she wanted to shout, but the words stuck in her throat. She could only

89

gape at him in horror. He had the advantage on her, lying in a bed of heather, his dozens of deadly weapons ready to murder her where she lay, though his hands were now empty. Her gaze fell to his left sleeve, rolled down and secured with the ties, all traces of the scar conveniently hidden from view.

Her action caught him by surprise, and he withdrew his hand from her shoulder.

Aeron approached in a hurry, clothes and hair in perfect order, relief spreading across his face when he saw her. "She's here," he cried over his shoulder. "We found her."

Excited shouts erupted behind them.

"Are you well?" Aeron asked.

–Rawlins remained silent, expression unreadable, mouth clamped, hands at his sides.

Bewildered, Brynwen sat up and nodded, finally finding her voice. "Yes, I'm fine." She refused to look at Rawlins, especially not at his forearm. *He knows I know! I must warn everyone. I must—*

Payla halted beside her, waving her hands in excitement. "Brynwen! I am so glad you're safe. I prayed to Mithras to watch over you, and he answered my prayer."

"Here, let's get you up off the ground." Aeron, Rawlins, and Payla each offered her a hand. She cringed inwardly. *Act natural.* She accepted Aeron's and Payla's and tried not to quake in fear as they pulled her up.

"Bryn!" Padric dashed in and grabbed her up into a hug, nearly squeezing the air out of her lungs. "I was so worried about you. How did you end up out here?" He released her and looked her up and down, cupping her dirty cheek in his firm hands to ensure she was uninjured. His mossy green eyes melted some of her unease like butter. If only he could hold her for the rest of the day, she knew he would keep her safe.

"It's funny you're checking *me* for hurts." She smiled, deflecting her own panic. Pushing the rest into the crevices of her mind.

Talfryn reached them and hugged her, this time squeezing all the air from her lungs. "You promised to never do that to me ever again." The anxiety in his voice was enough to assuage her fear for the time being.

I did? "I am sorry, Tal."

Antlers filled her vision, and Gregorio clapped her on the shoulder. "It is good we found you, Brynwen. If it pleases you, I will take the initiative in preparing our morning meal so you may rest and prepare for the day." He bowed to her.

"I'm fine, really."

Talfryn rolled his eyes. "You always say that."

She batted him with a glower.

"I insist." Gregorio spun to leave before she could argue.

"I suppose, I accept," she said to his retreating form. *Now I just need a moment alone with Padric or Talfryn.*

Despite her plan, there was never an opportunity to speak with either of them alone before they set out for the cave marked on Gregorio's map.

AN HOUR LATER, Padric and the others followed Aeron and Franco out of the colorful moors. The horses' hoofs clopped onto rocky ground littered with tall grass where the land jutted up toward the sky.

"The cave is just over here," Franco said. "No one's watching it."

"That we know." Aeron folded his arms over his chest.

Padric stayed by Brynwen's side. Keeping her head down, Brynwen's forefinger and thumb twisted the bottom of her braid. Since finding her on the moors, the few things he had said to cheer her up had fallen on deaf ears. He still did not know what had happened. Sleepwalking was not something she had done on their previous journey. *So what happened?*

"I nearly missed it on our first pass," Franco explained, "but then I looked at the right spot at the right time." He appeared somewhere between excited and anxious, leaning toward anxiousness.

Padric felt just as nervous, having two problems to deal with at once, and praying the Druid did not somehow make a third.

The cave had a large entrance, wide enough for Ulysses's antlers to fit through, but no one knew how long that might last. As they drew near, Padric heard a hum. Dismounting, a strange sensation tingled from his chest to his fingertips. "There is magic in this cave." *Magic belonging to what—or whom, though?*

Ulysses approached the cave and peeked inside. When finished, he swiveled his head to look at Padric as though confirming his suspicion.

Once more, they went over the plan of rescue. They were going in blind.

Franco's nostrils flared. "I still think it's risky. The Druid seems pretty clever—what if he figures out our plan? He may kill my family."

"It is a risk we must take," Padric said. "Would you prefer to be unprotected should something else go wrong? What if he has lied about something?"

The wheels of logic seemed to churn in the guide's mind. "Not too close."

"On my honor." Padric put a hand to his chest to emphasize the point.

As the knights prepared the torches, Padric drew Brynwen aside. He gazed into her hazel eyes, inhaling her honey and lavender scent, and caressed her cheek with his thumb. "We will not allow the Druid to take you, Bryn."

Brynwen bit her lip, gazing intently at the quiver of arrows at his shoulder rather than his face.

"Will you tell me what troubles you? Whatever happened this morning has me concerned for you."

Brynwen regarded him and pressed her lips together. With her fingers, she twisted her braid again. He cupped his hands around hers to stop her fidgeting. "Please, Bryn, you can tell me anything. You know that, right?"

A huff escaped her lips. "I know it, I do. But I have something to tell you, and I am afraid."

"Of me?"

"Nay—it is about..." Breaking off, her eyes searched the area as though to make sure they were alone. She whispered the knight's name. "Rawlins."

Padric's eyebrows furrowed as her words sunk in. "What do you mean it is about Rawlins?" *Something to do with the prophecy?*

"We're ready," Talfryn announced. He had rope curled around his shoulder, torch in hand, prepped and ready to set aflame. Franco stood beside him, eager to be off.

Padric grimaced and took Brynwen's hands in his. He gave them a loving squeeze. "We best not keep them waiting. But rest assured, my love, we will finish this discussion later. I wish to know everything you have to say."

Disappointment dulled her eyes, but she nodded. "Just watch your back, please." Her eyes shifted toward the others, then returned to Padric.

"I will." Now he wished more than ever to know what had upset her. He kissed her hand for a long heartbeat and gave his most reassuring smile. Her eyes brightened at the touch, which was what he hoped for. Ready, he raised the crook of his arm to her and smiled. "Would you care to walk with me in the cave for a few leagues, m'lady?"

With the hint of a smile, she curled her hand around his proffered arm and said, "I would be delighted, Sir Knight."

Brynwen was not the only one feeling trepidation. Whatever magic dwelt in the cave was likely much more powerful than the tingling in his chest suggested. He wondered if it had to do with the mysterious Druid or something else. He adjusted the bow and quiver at his shoulders and the sheathed sword at his side.

Taking a torch in his free hand, Padric gave one last look at the two who would remain. He hated leaving anyone behind. Yet, someone must stay, in case they never returned.

Payla and Gregorio clasped each other's arms just below the elbow, then she patted Ulysses's shoulder.

"Safe travels, my friends," Gregorio said. "We will pray for your safe return. And," he added, "if you find the king of the underworld, give him my regards." Suddenly, he looked very young as he waved them off. Ulysses nodded his sending forth.

"Stay safe," Padric replied to them both.

On the first step into the cave, a tremor traveled up Padric's foot. Neither Brynwen nor the others seemed to have felt anything, so he continued into the pitch darkness, keeping his senses alert. Before entering, Franco had warned any who had never been inside a cave before of the smells and dampness. Odors of mustiness and earth enveloped his nose. The humidity of high summer assailed his skin and clothes, and he could feel his hair curling ever more. He did not yet smell mold, but Franco said it could be a factor deeper within.

They walked in a nearly straight line for almost a mile, which Franco thought was strange, unnatural. After another half mile, the cave split into two junctions, both equally inviting in the dark.

"Which way?" Brynwen asked. After the first half mile, she had withdrawn her hand and stayed close to Padric, but now her hand returned, fingers tightening on his arm.

Franco studied the two passageways, then pointed with his head. "To the left."

"Then, left we go," Payla said.

From the back of the group, with a torch in hand, Rawlins approached and scanned the tunnels, keeping his sword at the ready. He scrunched his nose. "There's something else down there, and it stinks."

"How far in d'you think they are?" Talfryn asked in a raised whisper.

"Could be miles and miles," Payla said. "Some of these caves go deep and become labyrinths in themselves."

Brynwen's eyes grew wide. "Labyrinth? Like the maze in the prophecy? Do you think the Druid knows where the adamant is?"

Padric thrust his torch into every crevice. "We will not know until we scour every inch of these caves. Pasiphae will be displeased if we come back empty-handed. Let us make fast work of this task and be off."

"We don't have to go back to her," Aeron suggested.

"I'd rather not have an immortal witch on my bad side," Rawlins muttered. "Bad enough that there's two of them now."

"True," Aeron agreed.

Payla harrumphed. "One of those witches is my mother." Her horn scraped the side of the cave, causing dust and debris to drop behind her.

"Sorry." Rawlins spit out the apology without the least bit of remorse.

"It's the dryads I'm worried about," Talfryn confided. "They may look beautiful, but mark me, they're as deadly as a pack of hungry lions."

"That is a fact." Padric had trained against both dryads and lions in Cataractonium. It had been an interesting experience. And painful.

Noises sounded ahead in the tunnel. Franco scouted ahead and came back a few minutes later to report. "Found an opening to a cavern a little way off. Follow me."

Despite the four lit torches, the dreary darkness in this part of the cave made their light appear dull and useless for more than a foot in diameter. For whatever reason, only Franco's light seemed bright, and they followed it like lemmings in the dark. Their fingers brushed against the rough wall as guidance. Still, they tripped over bits of uneven ground as they went.

Curving left, the tunnel opened into a large cavern. Its sudden appearance caused Franco to halt mid-stride. Padric nearly collided with him.

But Talfryn barreled into Padric. "Ow," Talfryn grumbled. Then, "Ow!"

"So sorry, Talfryn!" Payla said.

"So much for the element of surprise," Rawlins drawled.

"This is it," Franco whispered. "I think, though, I reckoned they'd be here already. It's time."

They gathered inside the cavern, their torchlight never reaching the ceiling. Padric spun, spying the tall stalagmites pointing heavenward. "Is this the place?" He started as loud voices came from all directions of the cavern.

Padric dropped his torch and drew his bow and arrow while everyone else drew their weapons, each darting wary glances at all corners of the darkened room. Brynwen pulled out her borrowed dagger, her face the essence of determination.

"We are surrounded." Aeron panicked.

The voices rose again in crescendo, but after a few agonizing seconds, they died down to nothing.

No one attacked them.

Franco cleared his throat. "It is an echo."

"An echo-echo-oo..." bounced off the ceiling and walls in his voice.

The cavern was a new experience for Padric and the others from

Chaddesden. The Minster church in York was massive and echoes bounced throughout the building, but not to this eerie extent.

"Well, that wasn't embarrassing at all." Talfryn hooked his hatchet back onto his belt.

No, not one bit. Padric lowered his bow a fraction.

"What is this? I noticed it when we came in." Brynwen brushed her hand against a ledge filled with liquid. She dipped her finger into it, then removed her fingers and rubbed them together before sniffing them. "Oil."

"Oil?" Talfryn asked, confused.

Joining them, Padric and Payla studied the trench of oil. It traveled along the wall as far as they could see—which was not very far.

Aeron approached and looked up. "What is that?"

Payla whipped her head around. Her horn crashed into the back of Talfryn's head. "Ow!" he shouted again, knocking into the wall. The torch slipped from his hand, the flames landing in the trench.

The oil sparked, and a flood of fire soared down the trough. The blaze travelled along the wall at breakneck speed toward the far end of the cavern, nearly a hundred yards away. Heart pounding, Padric followed its trajectory until it halted at a jut in the wall. The cavern illuminated at once, causing more than one of them to give echoing gasps. Only one corner remained in semi-darkness.

Clasping her arms, Payla peered down at her feet. "Forgive me."

Talfryn was reaching for the fallen torch as Rawlins yanked it out of reach with a scowl at both him and Payla. "I'll take that. No more fire for you. Or you." He stalked away with it.

Brynwen gasped as she gazed all around them, spinning in a slow circle.

Following her gaze, Padric gaped at the sight illuminated by the wall of light. The cavern was much grander than he initially thought. Stalactites longer than a man reached down like a wolf's teeth from the high ceiling. The entire population of Chaddesden could fit in this cavern with room to spare.

Loud growling came from Talfryn's stomach, resounding off the walls. "I hope they come soon. I'm starving." Brynwen rolled her eyes and brought out a small, gray, cloth bag filled with oatcakes for her hungry brother.

In moments, Talfryn—his mouth filled with Brynwen's spiced oatcakes—sneezed, spraying bits of oats everywhere.

When the deafening echo died, everyone said "bless you" in unison, even Rawlins.

Talfryn sniffed and rubbed his nose on his sleeve. "Ugh. Thanks."

A voice beside Padric spoke. *"Welcome. It is about time you arrived."*

CHAPTER 15

$\mathcal{E}$veryone jumped.

Heart racing, Padric raised his bow, aiming the projectile while pivoting toward the voice. Everyone mimicked his action, but they saw no one. *Where did the voice come from?*

A piece of fabric crinkled in the distance. Padric had to squint to see in the dark corner but could make out nothing until a figure emerged into the light. Clad in a gray robe with long sleeves, the hood pulled down so low it hid the stranger's face in complete shadow.

"*Druidae,*" Payla whispered in awe.

Yes, Padric agreed. The cloak reminded him of a drawing depicting a Druid from of old. "I thought they were all gone."

"So did I."

"*At last, we meet face to face, Padric de Clifton,*" the robed figure said in a raspy voice.

Padric shuddered. The ancient voice had not come from beside him, but *from within his own mind.* Padric kept his arrow aimed at the Druidic figure. "It appears you have the advantage of knowing my name, yet I do not recall our having met previously."

"*That is not your concern.*"

"Ah, you see, it is very much my concern. Answer me, before your blood desecrates this cavern."

"It will not be my blood that spills this day. Give me the healer, and none shall spill at all."

This about confirms who the Druid is working for. At least, Janus has not found the adamant yet. Padric shook his head.

The Druid snapped his fingers, creating echoes in the cavern. *"I shall rephrase. Hand over Brynwen Masson, and you shall all go free."*

Every fiber of Padric's being screamed to deny the Druid's request. It took every ounce of willpower not to pick Brynwen up and carry her out of the cave to safety like a sack of grain. But then he remembered the innocent family caught in between.

Taking her arm, Franco marched Brynwen forward a couple of steps. "We've brought the maiden as demanded, Druid. Now give me back my family."

"Yes, tracker, well done. I was afraid something might happen to your lovely wife and handsome sons as a consequence of your failure."

"If you've hurt a hair on any of their heads..."

"Rest assured; they are intact. I must admit, tracker. I had my doubts as to your ability to bring Brynwen Masson to me, and that her family and friends would so willingly hand her over."

"It was my decision," Brynwen stated.

There was no doubt about that, but Padric suspected Franco might have become desperate enough to force her to cooperate had she refused.

Padric took a tentative step forward. "First, we must see the prisoners." He would not readily give Brynwen over for nothing.

"Cobali." The Druid snapped his fingers. From behind him emerged a short, human-like creature who poked its round head out from the darkness behind the Druid. Then another, with enormous eyes and a balding head. The creatures looked like they had escaped from the stories the old spinsters told small, naughty children. He struggled to recall the name of the child-eating goblins.

A handful more followed, escorting a woman and two lads, about ages ten and eight—Lenore, Cecil, and Simon.

"Papa!" the younger child shouted. He turned to his mother and brother. "He came for us. See, I told you he would!"

"It's all right, son. It will be over soon." Franco dragged Brynwen closer to the center of the cavern.

"This is an awful plan." Talfryn's hands fidgeted dangerously close to his hatchet.

"I know." Padric clenched his teeth, this close to hauling the tracker and healer back to safety, although it was already much too late for that.

"Bring the maiden to me, Franco, and your fair family will be released."

"Meet in the middle or the exchange is off," Padric said. If the Druid really wanted her, he must comply.

After a moment's hesitation, the Druid nodded. *"Very well."* He approached while the cobali dragged Lenore and her sons forward. Franco and Brynwen took a couple of steps toward them. "I'm sorry about this." Franco sent a quick glance over his shoulder, his voice barely carrying over to Padric.

As they approached the center, more goblins entered the cavern. Most were armed similarly to the first few, wielding clubs or short swords. Others were empty-handed. Their clothes were little more than rags, worn boots, and hats. Near the end, a very large goblin creature came out with a spiked club. Heart sinking, Padric counted close to thirty of the creatures, with the possibility of more hidden elsewhere. Rawlins drew the same conclusion as he cursed under his breath and brandished his weapons.

Any hope Padric had of getting Brynwen back seemed impossible. But he had to trust in Brynwen's choice, even if he did not like it.

After an excruciating amount of time, both parties reached the center of the cavern. Still unable to discern the Druid's face beneath the low, gray hood, Padric watched him like a hawk.

He heard the sound a second before a handful of small, dark shapes descended on them with fierce cries and gleaming eyes and weapons.

A GOBLIN HURLED onto Talfryn's back, nearly knocking him to his knees. It battered his shoulder with a club, squeezing his hips with his short legs and cutting off his air supply with his long fingers and sharp nails. "Get off!" he yelled. He reached for it, but the goblin or whatever the Druid called it was too quick and wriggly for him to grab hold of. It squeezed its legs tighter.

Payla was busy with her own goblin troubles. She spun, knives gleaming, striking at the creature on her back with expert precision, and it flew off with a shriek.

The others were likewise fighting multiple creatures that spilled out into the cavern, including from the way they'd come.

"Let go!" Brynwen cried out.

Talfryn turned in time to see two goblins grabbing her arms, trying to drag her away toward the Druid. Franco had abandoned her to help his family.

All the blood in Talfryn's body boiled.

"Bryn!" Talfryn struggled to reach her, but the goblin thing on his back didn't care and continued the onslaught. Talfryn bashed it against the wall of the tunnel, hoping the trench fire would scorch its ugly bottom.

The second time, it released its grip with a yelp. Talfryn crinkled his nose. "How cold they smell even worse cooked? I sure lost my appetite now."

Meanwhile, the goblins continued to tug Brynwen in the Druid's direction, pulling her farther and farther away. She tugged and fought every inch of the way, kicking their shins and punching their backs. Making them work for every step toward their goal.

Not again. A fierce fury built up inside Talfryn. *She's not leaving me again, and those things better not get in my way.* Some kind of instinct took over as he gripped his hatchet and struck down the goblin. Two more came to fill its place. Talfryn dispatched them with hardly a thought. They fell at his feet with a thud.

Nearby, Payla struck down another goblin with her knives where a pile of bodies grew high.

"Come on, Talfryn," she called after dispatching another goblin.

"Follow me." Payla continued in her dance of knives to make a pathway through the goblins, her motions reminding him of her Aunt Circe. She made much better progress than him. For one so clumsy, she was surprisingly graceful on the battlefield.

Unfortunately, Padric's team split up. Rawlins disappeared and then Aeron broke off toward the matron and lads. Franco went after them, too. Only Padric and Payla stayed to help Brynwen.

"What about Bryn?" Talfryn asked the other two knights, his cry landing on deaf ears. He knew it was selfish and petty but didn't care. When he and Payla were less than ten feet from Brynwen, Padric's face fell. Talfryn could see the indecision, then the determined look of resignation.

"Lenore and the children need help. It is up to you now." Without waiting for a reply, Padric took off toward the Druid with the others. He bowled over the three cobali blocking his path to the captives. One glance and Talfryn could see why—the creatures surrounded Lenore and her sons. A trail of blood streamed down the mother's arm.

"Talfryn." Payla caught his eye. "Make a path to them." She revealed her tactic with the next stroke.

"Got it." He mirrored her in a clumsy yet effective way. "Hey, that's not so bad!"

Once the tide had turned, Franco began fighting off the creatures, but he was badly outnumbered.

However, as they drew closer, the creatures' numbers only seemed to increase. Talfryn fought and fought the never-ending stream of goblins as he and Payla forged a narrow path to Brynwen. For his pains, he received his share of cuts and bruises and got knocked to the ground loads of times. Franco had said there were thirty goblins, but it seemed like over a hundred.

Seven feet.

Five feet.

Three feet.

Talfryn could reach out and touch her. If only the creatures would stop for a snack break. Then Payla struck the final goblin in the way.

Now only one goblin held onto Brynwen, looking rather intimidated by Payla's tall stature, pointy weapon, and shiny horns.

"He's mine." Talfryn set his jaw.

Attention only on its task, the goblin didn't see Talfryn's fist until it struck. It stumbled but stayed upright, releasing Brynwen to catch Talfryn's incoming hatchet.

"I had it under control," Brynwen grumbled.

Talfryn grinned. "I can see that."

A loud buzzing met his ears, the pressure in the huge cavern pressing down on his body as though a handful of lions sat on his chest. Then a white light appeared and blazed from a point not two feet from Brynwen. The light seared as though he stared at the sun, forcing him and Payla to stagger backward in pain.

CHAPTER 16

*P*adric saw the circle of light appear next to Brynwen. He watched in horror as it widened into an oval, unable to avert his gaze as it seared into his eyes. It grew to nearly Brynwen's height. From the center, a hand reached out and grasped her arm. Likewise blinded, Brynwen jerked, but it yanked her into the oval. The last thing Padric saw—or thought he saw—was a midnight blue cloak entering the light after them. Then—

The oval vanished. Brynwen with it.

Padric stared at the vacant place, dark spots dotting his vision.

She's gone.

Again.

His stomach plummeted, his knees ready to buckle. It was over in seconds. There was nothing he could do. Nothing.

"Bryn! No, Bryn! Bring her back! Bring her back, you vile..." Talfryn's voice grated harshly against the walls and ceiling of the cavern. Half a dozen cobali jumped him. He fought his captors with every fiber of his being and glared murder at the Druid. "Let me go. Bry—"

Talfryn disappeared among the cobali horde. Shouts erupted from his handlers as they beat him with fists, clubs, and thick boots. Padric and Payla could not get near their friend. They flinched as he cried out in agony.

In another few seconds, Padric, Aeron, and Rawlins made headway on extracting Lenore and her sons. Lenore and Cecil stood behind Aeron as Rawlins, now visible, was within reach of Simon.

The Druid shouted a curse in Latin, hands balled into fists of rage. Something had gone horribly wrong.

"We must stop them," Payla shouted.

Padric thought of a plan when the grating voice assaulted his ears again.

"*Stulti, omnia me facere debeo?*" It translated to "Fools. Must I do everything myself?"

The Druid's shout was harsh. Guttural. He threw a vial of a sickly yellow substance onto the floor. Shattering, smoke sprang from it in all directions.

Like a summons, the walls of the cavern trembled. Dirt, dust, and stalactites loosened from the ceiling and crashed to earth. The creatures fled back from whence they came.

"Simon!" Cecil tore out of Aeron's grasp and dashed toward his little brother, determined to help him. Lenore called after him, her voice lost to everything else. Franco took three steps before two cobali tackled him to the ground.

Padric and Rawlins made to help, but the ground split in front of them. Six cobali scooped the lads up, kicking and screaming, and raced them past the Druid into the shadows.

No!

The earth, walls, and ceiling continued to quake without mercy. It was hopeless. "Fall back," Padric directed.

The cobali directed Franco away at spearpoint. All the determination he had displayed fled as he realized how wrong everything had gone. He gave one final forlorn look at his wife before they shoved him forward.

A stalactite crashed to the ground next to Padric, nearly missing his leg as he dove out of the way. Pushing himself up, he raced to help Aeron tug on Talfryn, who hung limply in his arms. Taking one of the farmer's arms over his shoulder, Padric and Aeron followed Rawlins and Lenore at a half-run, avoiding pieces of collapsing ceiling on their way to the exit tunnel and their escape.

A feeling of unease told Padric something was awry. Payla was missing.

Rawlins glanced up, then spun around in alarm and dashed toward them, dodging more falling rocks. "Look out!"

Too late, Padric saw the stalactite as it crashed down toward him. A flash of excruciating pain erupted in his head and all went dark.

PART II
UNDERGROUND

"Let me not then die ingloriously and without a struggle, but let me first do some great thing that shall be told among men hereafter."
    — Homer, *The Iliad*

CHAPTER 17

Brynwen fell through the blinding light. Her stomach twisted and mouth opened in a silent scream as lights and sound rushed past, whipping her hair in all directions. The pull of the hand's iron grip dragged her out of the bright light. Knees shaking, she emerged into an unfamiliar place. Next thing she knew, she'd collapsed to her hands and knees. She groaned as her stomach reeled in agony.

"The discomfort will pass in a moment," said an unfamiliar male voice. A hand gently gripped her wrist.

Where...who...?

It was difficult for Brynwen to get her bearings. Her eyes felt crossed and tired. After another minute, though, her stomach calmed. She sat up and blinked into the startling brown eyes of a man. They stared into her own, checking for illness or something worse, she thought.

"Good, the worst is over now."

He straightened, and Brynwen got a better look at him. Straight hair, somewhere between brown and black in the dim light, swept across his brow. He was handsome, perhaps twenty years her senior, wearing rich clothing. A blue outer tunic with gold buttons and sensibly laced cuffs beneath a velvety red cape that flowed from shoulder to knee. Polished black boots traveled up to his knees, overlaying black trousers.

But what most startled her was the gilt crown upon his head.

A king?

"Who are you? Where are we?" A flush fell on her cheeks as she realized her rudeness. She blamed it on the bright lights and momentary illness. While trying not to stare, she took a quick survey of the room: gray stone with beautiful tapestries and rich red wall-to-wall carpet. Luxury she could never afford in any sense.

Instead of berating her, though, the well-dressed stranger's mouth twitched. "To outsiders I am known as *Dis Pater*, but to my subjects I am Morfrey Richal II, King of Rellea."

"You are *Dis Pater*? We have been looking for…" It was then she realized who wasn't in the room. "Where is my brother? My friends? Padric?" Panic constricted her chest until she couldn't breathe. He had left them there. "Please, you must save them too!"

King Morfrey drew his lips together. "I was not expecting others. This complicates things."

Neither Arthur nor Isabel had specified she come alone. "Please, sire. We were under attack, with children in danger."

"Children…" Resigned, he nodded and glanced behind Brynwen. "Yes, of course. Ulrich, open the door again."

"But your Majesty—"

"Do it, Ulrich."

"Yes, sire."

Turning her head, Brynwen saw an older man in gray robes and a matching beard who she hadn't noticed before. He blended in with the stones rather well. The man dipped his head before making circular motions with one arm. It produced the same buzzing sound she'd heard before. The white light appeared and grew round and blinding. This time, Brynwen shielded her eyes before it became too harsh.

After a couple seconds it became barely tolerable, and Brynwen looked at the oval as it cleared in the center. The king stood next to it, ready to reach in.

Beyond the "door," the sky appeared to blend with the earth. Heavy rocks and debris and stalactites collided with the ground. Rocks the size of her fist jumped through the round door. One would have hit the king in the leg had he not dodged it.

"Close it," King Morfrey demanded.

"Nay!" Brynwen cried.

The door shrunk and disappeared with a pop.

"Padric! Talfryn!" Stumbling to her feet, Brynwen rushed to where the door had been moments before.

It was gone.

Tears filled her eyes. "I'm too late." *They can't all be dead, can they?*

"It is too late, my dear."

"You don't know that."

"They could be dead."

All Brynwen wanted to do in that second was die with the others. *What will I do without them? It's my fault for allowing them to come with me in the first place.*

Ulrich bowed. "They may yet live, Your Majesty. Might we send some troops up top to find them?"

"Yes, Ulrich, do that."

Brynwen curtsied, trying to hold in her tears. "Thank you, thank you, Your Majesty. I owe you so much."

"Indeed, you do. Come, Brynwen Masson, I shall take to you the herbarium to begin your work." The king strode toward a door at the other end of the room.

Herbarium? Brynwen's hopes rose some. She had so many questions for Arthur and Isabel.

Ulrich gave her a heartfelt smile and nodded toward the retreating king.

Brynwen returned the smile. At least she had one friend in the palace. "Thank you, Ulrich. I owe you my life, too. Would they be able to look for my two other friends who didn't enter the cave with us?" She was grateful Gregorio and Ulysses were safe up top, at least, and hoped they could help find Talfryn, Padric, and the others. *Please, Lord,* she prayed, *please be with them.*

"We shall look for them, too. Thank you for coming to our aid." He bowed to her. "You had better hurry—he walks at a brisk pace."

Granting the magician a last smile, Brynwen made a hesitant curtsy and dashed after King Morfrey II of Rellea. With every step, she implored the Lord to help Talfryn, Padric, and the others escape the Druid and the rock-filled cavern.

✤

Hurrying down the corridor, Brynwen fretted about those she had left behind. They passed statues that looked oddly like some of the Roman gods in Cataractonium. Despite her limited knowledge of monarchs, she questioned the need for his personal presence instead of sending the magician alone. Also, he had plucked her from that cavern like a flower. Why wait until that crucial moment to rescue her?

Eventually, King Morfrey stopped in front of a beautifully painted blue wooden door and opened it. Brynwen's breath caught as the scene before her emerged into life.

They stood atop a small outcropping of rock with a stone staircase leading downward, affixed with a railing for safety. Below her, a city of many colors and levels splayed before her, bustling with activity.

Her eyes swept over the city, and she wondered how they had reached the surface so rapidly.

"Nay." The king didn't need to look at her to read her mind. "We have not emerged onto the surface. Welcome to Rellea." His arm extended over the city before them.

We're still underground. Despite their location, there was a sky with realistic clouds. It appeared to be daylight but with no sun. *What magic source can do this?* The buildings lining the street resembled those in Chaddesden, but taller and with brighter colors. People of various sizes and shapes moved around. She gasped when she saw a goblin creature like those who had attacked them. But the little maiden only stared at her with curiosity instead of animosity. Moving forward, they encountered various creatures of the underground, mostly goblins and human-like beings, some with pink or green hair. Centaurs, some fauns, a large, three-headed dog, nymphs, including naiads and dryads, and gray kind she hadn't seen before. The animals were the only things that remained normal: goats, sheep, horses, pigs, dogs, and cats. One cat scampered in front of her feet, nearly upending her. The oddest thing about it was its two tails.

It was not long before they entered the enormous stone palace with its tall spires and turrets and hundreds of windows. The place made Miriel Wilmot's manor in Chaddesden seem like a small cottage in comparison. Opening a side door made of wood and carved with designs in an expert hand, King Morfrey gave her an amused glance. "Follow closely, or you shall get lost."

Through corridor upon corridor, Brynwen marched, pumping her legs to keep up with the much taller King Morfrey. His fine cloak rustled elegantly behind him. Portraits and long ornate tapestries adorned the walls of the stone hallways and tall atrium. They passed by statues of gods or heroes or whoever they were. Unfortunately, they walked so fast, she barely caught more than a glimpse of one here and there. With a pang, she realized Gregorio would know who all these statues depicted. *Will he and Ulysses ever discover what happened to any of them?*

Servants in bright blue livery made her practical cream blouse and brown skirts appear worn and dull. *Perhaps I should have changed beforehand, not that I have anything remotely fancy to wear. I didn't know I'd be visiting a palace today.* She was beginning to realize that Alice and Arthur hadn't given her much information, which might have come in handy. The farther in they walked, and with each floor they ascended, Brynwen noticed King Morfrey's back becoming more rigid. His silence brought foreboding. "Your Majesty, what exactly am I to do in the palace?"

"You will know presently."

Lost and disoriented, Brynwen finally came to a halt in front of a wooden door. The straight faced faun servant knocked twice and entered unannounced. The king marched in right after him. Shocked, Brynwen hesitated until the servant raised his eyebrow at her. Remembering herself, she hastened in after the king.

Brynwen felt overwhelmed by the day's surprises. That changed when she stepped through the door. The sight before her took her breath away. Brynwen could only dream of the healing tools that filled the large room. In Circe's room, there had been many herbs, books, and jars of samples. In contrast, this room had beakers filled with colorful liquids, and books covered the five workbenches. Thirty or more types of herbs hung on hooks near the three windows. Floor to ceiling shelves filled with leather-bound tomes and jars of specimens, ointments, and tinctures filled every inch of wall space.

It was then that she noticed an older man standing in the room, his back to the door.

"Aesculapius," Morfrey said.

Brynwen spun at the name. *What did he say?*

"Aesculapius."

Didn't Gregorio say the initials H.A. on the front page of On Healing and Other Remedies *stood for the great healer Aesculapius?* The name wasn't easy to remember, but she was confident it was at least close.

The man ignored the king. Brynwen ogled the ruler, waiting for the hot temper she imagined royals to display when disregarded in such a manner by a subordinate. At least, that was how her golden-haired friend Miriel Wilmot would act.

However, King Morfrey surprised her by sighing, and Brynwen thought he might have rolled his eyes as well. "It's a hassle to snap him out of his own thoughts when he gets like this." He turned back to Aesculapius. "I appreciate your good work ethic; however, I need your attention. Please," he added dryly.

Nothing.

"We are out of fresh strawberries."

Somehow, that awoke the studious man from his musings. "How are we out of strawberries so soon? I only had some yesterday. Or was it the day before?" He whirled around. The man's brown beard reached his ribcage, with a few white wisps scattered throughout. He wore a black robe that hung to his sandals. "Ah, your majesty, it is so good to see you. I believe I have made some progress. Here, let me show you—"

"No need at the moment, Aesculapius. I wished to introduce you to your new apprentice. This is Brynwen Masson."

Brynwen's eyes grew round. "A-apprentice?"

The king eyed her to keep silent, and she clamped her mouth shut as her heart thrashed in her chest. Apprentice for what? And I thought this man's name was Arthur.

Aesculapius—who was not after all named Arthur—fixed his gaze on Brynwen and his eyebrows rose in confusion. Then they lowered into recognition, and he smiled. "Ah, yes, Brynwen! So good to see you again. Iaso was afraid you mightn't come, but I knew you would make it. With the three of us working together, we may have a cure soon."

Confused and speechless at the compliment from a near stranger, it was a couple of heartbeats before she could respond. "I will do my best, sir. That is all I can do."

Aesculapius smiled and patted her hand. "A splendid answer."

"She will be a valuable addition to your work," Morfrey confidently remarked, implying familiarity with her capabilities. He looked at the older healer. "As usual, I require the report at the normal time. Please tell your daughter it grieved me to have missed her presence."

"As you wish, your majesty." The healer bowed.

When the door closed behind King Morfrey, Aesculapius let out a breath.

"Who was it?" The voice came from the room next to Brynwen on her left. Some "natural" light seeped in through a crack in the door. *No, not natural lighting.*

"King Morfrey kindly brought us our guest." Aesculapius beckoned to her with a sly grin.

A maiden poked her head into the room, eyes sparking with excitement. Isabel—or, rather, the maiden she'd known as Isabel. She held a basket full of calendula and hyssop. A braid of ebony locks surrounded her head while the rest lay straight down her back to her waist. A white dress with flowing sleeves and dark green embroidery adorned her slim form. Something about her reminded Brynwen of the nymphs in Cataractonium.

"Brynwen! Thank goodness you have come. We worried when no word came of your arrival this morning."

Tears threatened to fall and flood the room, but she choked them back. "Isabel. Or should I say...Iaso? And Master Aesculapius. Why did both of you use different names the other day?"

The older man nodded. "We decided that giving pseudonyms would cause less disturbance for those not familiar with our world. Forgive me for any grievance this might have caused."

"Not grievance." Brynwen shook her head. "Just confusion on my part."

Iaso's eyes widened. "Forgive my manners. You must be exhausted. We have a room ready for you to rest in until you're ready."

Being alone with her thoughts was the last thing Brynwen wanted at the moment. "If you don't mind, I'd like to help now, if possible."

Iaso beamed. "In that case, you can hang your satchel on the hook in that corner."

As directed, Brynwen hung up her satchel. She returned to the healers and pulled out the folded piece of fine paper from her pocket. "I have the list you gave me. What more can you tell me about the illness?"

Aesculapius set down the beaker and mixing spoon, both made of glass. "It began about a week ago, just after the Poplifugia Festival to Jupiter. All of Rellea attended. That night, many complained of abdominal and chest pains, nausea, and vomiting. By morning, they were all weak and bedridden. Twice that number fell ill later that day, including several nobles, servants from the palace, and citizens alike.

"Early on, we knew it could not be food poisoning. We made several known remedies, but the symptoms are irregular, and nothing has helped."

"Everything, it seems, including magic," Iaso replied, arms wide in exasperation. "Tonics, ointments, turmeric baths, tinctures. The three sorcerers in Morfrey's employ are helping in their own way, but their skills don't lie in healing. Our ideas and time are dwindling. Everyone grows weaker and weaker by the day." *We are helpless,* her expression said.

"Many elderly patients have died, but soon the younger and more healthy patients will fall. We have tried everything. King Morfrey is beside himself. He is also worried about the princess's health, should she become ill. She is his only heir."

"Have more people become ill since then?"

Iaso shook her head. "Mayhap a handful, no more."

"Interesting." The list of symptoms didn't sit well in Brynwen's stomach. Not at all. A dark feeling crept up on her.

"Despite their efforts, the king and his guard have been unable to find the source. It appeared suddenly, as if from nowhere. Not two days later, a huntsman returned from his hunt aboveground, traveling so far as York, and brought the rumor of a gifted healer who had cured two people of manticore venom. It took but a short time to discover her—you—in Derbyshire."

Gifted healer? This is too much. "But I did little to help with that. Circe was there, and—"

"Oh, we know all about Circe. She is a talented healer in her own right. While we thought about summoning her, *your* skills are the ones we require."

"But—"

"How did you do it?" Iaso asked, taking a step forward. "What ingredients did you use, if I may ask?"

Brynwen shook her head, knowing full well what had helped her save Padric and Gregorio from a horrible death. The Anti-Venom recipe from *On Healing and Other Remedies,* and the white caladrius bird named Nessie. The small creature's healing tears had helped save them. When Talfryn had discovered Nessie under the mausoleum of an ancient Roman legionary, they'd never expected her wondrous healing power.

She missed Nessie and wondered what had happened to the bird after healing Padric and Gregorio. Nessie had flown away immediately after providing her healing tears and hadn't been seen since.

Brynwen's hand stretched for the book on the hook but stopped, hovering in mid-air. *Is it bad to hide a book from its original owner?*

No. It wouldn't work for two reasons; one of which being the lack of the rare, vital feathered ingredient. *I won't bring Nessie into this. Even if I knew where she was, she deserves to be free.*

About to deny her involvement a second time, Brynwen stopped short and regarded the two healers, especially the elder one. Tingling in her fingers urged her to hold the book. To open it. A sudden realization dawned on her regarding Gregorio's previous statement. "Wait, you are Aesculapius. Are you not the world's greatest healer? Who surpassed your father Apollo and could heal anyone from near death?" *Who wrote the book in my satchel?* "Why haven't you discovered the cure yet?"

Scarlet flushed the man's cheeks, and his fingers fidgeted before him.

"Ah. Well, that was a long time ago. My abilities are not as they once were."

Even Iaso averted her gaze. "It is a time-consuming story."

Brynwen pursed her lips together in thought. "If you are his daughter, do you have special abilities too?"

Iaso squirmed, her fingers twisting together. "Yes. People knew me as the goddess of cures, remedies, and other modes of healing. But enough about us. We ask that you examine the patients yourself in order to make your own diagnosis."

Brynwen sighed inwardly. So many excuses. It was too much to hope for them to explain willingly what that meant, so she didn't argue the point. Clearly, there was a reason they needed another set of hands. *And yet, if Aesculapius had written the book, might it aid their search for the cure? On the other hand, if this was an imposter calling himself Aesculapius, he may exploit its abilities. "Keep it hidden for now,"* a voice in the back of her head warned. She didn't argue with herself about it.

The quicker they found the cure, the quicker she could ask King Morfrey to return her to Talfryn and Padric and the others—if they survived the cave-in. Her body shook with despair.

Remember the task at hand.

She repeated this mantra to herself two more times.

Her fingers itched to retrieve and open *On Healing and Other Remedies*, but she restrained herself although the book practically begged her to open it immediately. She still couldn't believe a master was asking her, a mere apprentice, for help. "All right. If we are to find a cure for sickness, I will need you to tell me everything you've tried. I mean *everything*. I also mean to examine the patients." Her hand brushed along the hidden leather spine of the book. "Before anything else, though, I'd like to freshen up."

After Brynwen splashed her face in a side closet with a waterspout not unlike what she'd seen at Circe's home in Cataractonium, she returned to the herbarium.

A light knock came at the door, and Aesculapius bade the knocker enter. At first glance, Brynwen saw a very petite person. But on second glance, her heart froze.

She shot to her feet, toppling the stool. All semblance of weariness wore off as she looked around desperately for a weapon. It was one of those goblin creatures who had attacked her group!

A hand clapped her shoulder. Whirling around, Brynwen halted her balled fist from striking just in time. Iaso stood there, her expression the opposite of fear. "We must fight off the goblin!"

"The what? Oh." Iaso spun Brynwen around to view Aesculapius and the creature, both with eyes wide in astonishment. "Meet our maid, Frania. She is a cobalus." Iaso must have noticed Brynwen's blank look. "'Cobalus' is another term for 'goblin' in this city. Although, no one above ground has seen one in eons. Come now, she won't bite." She half-dragged Brynwen to the door.

"Frania is a most excellent maid," Aesculapius commented. "You will find her very efficient and professional."

The cobalus, Frania, had short graying hair. She wore a gray dress with a pristine white apron, and her hands were folded in servile fashion over her apron as Brynwen had seen some maids from the Wilmots' manor in Chaddesden behave. Some brown spots adorned her hands, resembling freckles or birthmarks. Brynwen couldn't fathom how different Frania acted from her brethren who had attacked them earlier. She had seen some of these creatures in the streets of Rellea, but it hadn't clicked until just now.

The heat of embarrassment flushed Brynwen's cheeks. "Forgive me, Frania, please. It has been a day."

"Not to worry, miss." The maid gave a respectable curtsy.

The act made Brynwen feel more uncomfortable after her inexcusable actions.

"With that done, it is time to meet the patients," Iaso said.

CHAPTER 19

"All the patients have been accommodated here." Aesculapius indicated the grand wooden doors carved with ornate scenes from what Brynwen thought might be mythology.

Two legionary guards wearing blue stood guard, pikes pointed heavenward. A lump formed in Brynwen's throat as she thought about Padric and the other knights who'd been left behind in the cavern with the Druid. Were they and Talfryn all right?

The old healer opened the doors, and Brynwen's heart nearly stopped. Visions of the aftermath of the manticore's onslaught, with wounded knights and citizens wallowing on cots in the infirmary, flashed before her.

After blinking, the room changed to a grand room filled with makeshift cots and mats on the floor occupied by nearly one hundred humans and mythical creatures. Patients of all sizes and ages. She gripped her satchel until her knuckles turned white. The chill of doom spread through her bones.

"This is the grand ballroom," Iaso explained. "The banquet room, or 'less grand ballroom', as *Pater* calls it, is next door. We hope to not need it if another wave hits."

If another wave hits. The thought froze the breath within Brynwen's lungs. "So many patients." A far greater number than those she'd attended in Cataractonium at one time. *And so many have already died.* She pushed her sleeves up to steel herself. "Well, let's begin."

The first patient, a young human lad not much older than herself, lay on a mat on the floor. His skin was as white as the sheet of his makeshift bed.

"Wallace, this is Brynwen," Iaso said. "She is here to help. How are you feeling today?"

"Hello, ma'am." He looked up at her with bleary eyes. "Just great. Think I could run 'round this whole room." He chuckled for a second before choking and coughing.

Brynwen froze. Although he had lighter hair, the youth reminded her so much of her twin brother that a sob threatened to escape her trembling lips. Without thinking, Brynwen plopped onto the floor beside him until his coughs ceased. It took great effort to give him an encouraging smile and inwardly despaired over her brother's unknown fate. "Mayhap wait a few minutes before taking that run, eh?"

He grinned. "Yes'm."

"May I examine you, Wallace?"

"Of course, Miss Brynwen."

She raised his hands. Strong, used to hard work. She wondered what hard labor he did underground. Mining came to mind. "Do you feel tingling or numbness in your fingertips? Chest pain? Dizziness?" She went through a list of symptoms, and to most, he confirmed. Mild, giving her hope he'd recover within a week or two at the most, with plenty of rest and medicinals.

Once done with her ministrations, Brynwen gave the lad another smile and squeezed his hand. She rubbed some of her Miracle Mix onto his chest to help with his breathing. All the while, he seemed agitated. "I will be back soon," she promised.

"Wait," he said, groggily. "I need to tell you something."

"What is it?"

"It's…" He pointed at something to the right when his voice failed him. Brynwen looked to where he pointed but saw nothing out of the ordinary besides ill patients, attendants, Aesculapius, and Frania, along with some other servants and visitors. The servants present were humans, fauns, nymphs, and other cobali.

"I see nothing." But he'd already fallen asleep.

As she stood up, she hid her frown. If he awoke again before she left, she'd have her answer. Moving from one patient to the next, she spent a few minutes with each. It consumed most of the remaining day. In the end, tears threatened to fall from her face as she exited through the tall doors of the grand ballroom-infirmary. Wallace continued his slumber.

"Well?" asked Aesculapius. "What do you think?" She'd caught his glances in her direction several times, likely seeing how she interacted with the patients. This seemed like a test of sorts. He looked down at her; not as a superior or a mentor, but as someone on the edge of a precipice. Someone needing hope.

A hope she couldn't give.

With a heavy heart, it took many moments for the words to form in her mouth. She was already imagining his reaction. "Based on the symptoms, it seems to me like monkshood." She envisioned the pretty purple flowers whose sepal resembled the hood of a monk. Its common name was wolfsbane. Rosa, the midwife, had pointed it out to her a few times whenever they found some in the forest near home. Unfortunately, academics had never found a cure for it. The next few days would claim the lives of many, if not all, Relleans. It depended on the amount they ingested, their age, and general health. Picturing Wallace or any of the others' cold, lifeless bodies nearly sent her into hysterics. Unless...

A dire sadness came upon the immortal healer, causing him to look an additional thousand years old. "Yes, yes, *Aconitum*. Monkshood. We have reached the same conclusion as well."

"Could it have been an accident?" Brynwen asked.

"Nay." Iaso's face appeared chiseled from stone. "This was no accident. Poisoning one person or a household on accident is plausible, but this..." Her hand swept in the door's direction. "This was malicious intent of the highest level. Someone planned it to do the greatest harm to our people. At a festival, of all places."

Brynwen had to agree at its dastardliness. "Why would someone do this?"

"That is the greatest mystery," Aesculapius said.

"There's little hope if it's monkshood. But what if—"

"There you are, Iaso and Master Aesculapius!" a girlish voice cried. A blur dashed into Iaso's arms, nearly knocking her over.

Iaso laughed as she clutched onto the child until she planted the maid's feet firmly on the ground. Her dark hair, similar to her father's, was elegantly arranged in a half-bun, half-down fashion. Brynwen guessed her to be about ten years old. Iaso patted out the wrinkles in the young maiden's green dress. "Tut, tut, my princess. What will your governess say? Besides, what are you doing here, anyway?"

The princess!

"Yes, my child, is this not the hour of your study?" Despite his tone, Aesculapius grinned and patted the maiden's cheek with affection.

The princess shoved her hands behind her back. "Oh, pshaw, Master Aesculapius. We are playing a game. When Nanny Merta catches up to me, then we will return to the books." Her ebony eyes radiated defiance and mirth.

"And what of your guards?" Iaso's black eyebrow raised in question.

"Oh, them. Well, their armor makes them clunky and slow, so I went on ahead." She leaned forward, one hand cupping around her mouth to whisper. "They aren't very good at hiding."

"I see."

"Anyway, I wanted to bring flowers for each of the patients. Regrettably, I could only get a hold of a couple." She brought forth her hidden hand to give two flowers, both in rough shape. A pink flower with a bent stem, and a yellow daisy missing some petals. "Oh no, they're ruined!"

Giving the child a hug, Iaso patted her shoulder. "They are lovely and quite thoughtful, my dear Mandalin. The entire room will love them, I assure you."

"Can I visit now? I wish to see my friend Maressa."

Iaso shook her head. "Not today, I am afraid. I will, however, tell her you stopped by."

The princess's shoulders sagged. "All right."

"Princess Mandalin Richal," Aesculapius said, "I would like to introduce to you Brynwen Masson, our new healer."

Brynwen started at the introduction but gave the younger maiden a bright smile. "It is a pleasure to meet you, my princess." She made a small curtsy and managed to not trip over her skirts.

"The pleasure is mine," Princess Mandalin replied with practiced diction. She gave a graceful curtsy, then bounded up and down. "Well, I best be off to avoid...I mean, to continue our game."

"Oh, no, not so fast." Iaso caught the maiden's sleeve with deft fingers. "You are to go straight up to your suite. In fact, I will escort you. Come along."

"It was nice to meet you, Mistress Brynwen. See you later, Master Aesculapius." The princess waved at them.

"She is a wonderful child, really." Aesculapius sighed. "Filled with mischief and energy, but she is also very bright, like her father. I only wish she did not have to witness this hard time. One of her professors perished from the poisoning, and despite her behavior, it has brought her great distress."

"I can imagine." But Brynwen couldn't comprehend the motive behind poisoning a large group of people. The fact that the princess was the sole heir of King Morfrey made her uneasy about the future.

BACK IN THE HERBARIUM, the healers led Brynwen to the crowded workbench. With thorough expertise, they explained what each beaker, jar, and bowl contained, and what they used them for. Among the new things she learned were rosemary for hiccups and owls' feet for knee arthritis. They discussed unsuccessful procedures, partially effective ones, and rejected ideas. None of the more successful ones contained any owls' feet, she was happy to note.

They brainstormed formulas for hours, long after exhaustion set in. Aesculapius wrote each idea down in neat handwriting on the chalkboard—handwriting Brynwen had seen on every page of *On Healing and*

Other Remedies. He had about filled up the board when Brynwen became bleary-eyed.

After a deep yawn, she peered out the window of the herbarium. The sky was black. No stars or clouds. Her tired brain registered much too late to remind her that they were below ground. She saw Aesculapius look at her over the rim of his glasses.

"Ah, it is late. Please, Brynwen, sit before you keel over."

"I am fine," Brynwen said defiantly, leaning heavily against the table. "We must find a cure, right?"

"Sit."

Without another word, she plopped down on the stool two feet from her. The moment she did, every bone screeched in pain.

Aesculapius went to a crowded bookshelf and pulled a long, braided rope hanging from a small hole in the ceiling. Brynwen had seen the rope before but was unsure of its purpose.

A few minutes later, the maid knocked and entered.

Iaso gave a conspiratorial smile. "Frania, is Brynwen's room ready?"

"Yes, m'lady. The wardrobe has arrived as requested." This time, Brynwen noticed her words were precise and clipped, as though English was not her first language.

"Wardrobe?"

Iaso nodded with enthusiasm. "Oh, yes, you shall adore it. Come along. *Pater?*"

"Run along, you two. I have a couple more ideas to try before turning in for the evening."

Frania led the way followed by Iaso, with Brynwen trailing behind, enthralled by the grandness of the palace. Before, she'd been too rushed and bewildered to take notice. But now, she let the wonders sink in. Gray stones packed neatly together, tapestries and family portraits adorning the walls.

Up three winding staircases they flew with a deep cherry wood banister, passing gilt-framed paintings of people and landscapes, each one grander than the last.

Iaso pointed to the right. "On this floor is the Gallery of Art. Yes, I know. It is a very clever name for a hallway."

As they moved upward, a vivid memory struck Brynwen, of sneaking into the Wilmots' manor to find clothing for Padric from the wardrobe of his friend John. She chuckled, recalling Talfryn's discovery of a strange-looking plaid cloth and trying to pawn it on Padric to wear. In an instant, the prophecy darted into her brain.

The adamant. The nexus. End the curse.

She sighed. If she didn't get the adamant, Janus would win. Inevitable danger loomed, though she lacked knowledge of how or when. But she couldn't leave these people to suffer. She could only hope they found a cure quickly so she could return to her quest.

Tired thoughts turned to Padric, the way his mossy green eyes sparked when he was excited, when his hand rested on her back. When he kissed her…

"…Don't you agree?" Iaso asked beside her.

Like an arrow shot from a bow, Brynwen's mind returned to the present.

Concentrate. Don't get distracted. Distraction leads to death.

"Umm, yes, I completely agree." *What am I agreeing to?*

It happened so fast, she would have tripped up the stairs if her hand hadn't caught the railing. Heart thudding, she paused a moment to catch her breath. *Padric. Talfryn.* Because of her tireless work for the cure, she'd forgotten about them and her other friends. Visions of their broken bodies lying under miles of rock made her tremble.

Snap out of it.

When her feet continued up the steps, Iaso and Frania were only a quarter landing ahead and hadn't noticed her missing. Dashing up the steps, she caught up with them, none the wiser.

Iaso was still speaking. "…and this is the lord chancellor's wing. He oversees the comings and goings of the populace. Well, he will when he makes a full recovery. Here we are."

Brynwen's feet clacked on the stone floor of the landing and stopped short. There, in the hallway three doors down, stood King Morfrey, *Dis Pater,* lord of the underground himself. Behind him stood two cobali guards holding pikes aimed upward. All the blood drained from Brynwen's cheeks.

The breath caught in Iaso's throat, and she jerked backward. "On second thought," she said, barely audible, "I'll leave you to it, Brynwen. There's not much to fuss about, honestly. See you in the morning." After a quick curtsy and greeting to the king, she dashed down the stairs before Brynwen could bid her good night.

She didn't have a chance to ruminate on Iaso's behavior, however, because Morfrey stepped forward and bowed. *To her.*

She bristled, beginning to wonder if this was a common occurrence with everyone underground.

"Good evening," he said. "Please forgive my unexpected appearance, but I feared I had given you a negative impression of me earlier. I have a surprise for you."

How much more negative could it have been? She wanted to ask, but instead, she pulled herself together to keep her posture neutral and curtsied considerably slower than Iaso had. "Your Majesty." She cocked an eyebrow. "What surprise could you have for me?"

From her pocket, Frania produced a large, flat iron key. Opening the door, both servant and king retreated a step, allowing Brynwen to enter first. A soft light glowed from inside. The bedroom was small, with a human-sized bed in one corner, topped with a light-yellow blanket. A small writing desk with one chair sat ready to use near the window. To its right, she spied a trunk for belongings, and another small wooden table by the door with a pitcher and a large matching bowl. An oil lamp lit the room from the writing desk.

Morfrey turned to her, all smiles. "I fear your room is not much, but it is the best we could manage on short notice."

Brynwen cringed. Short notice my foot...

"All I have is my satchel. The rest of my things are at my camp."

He waved a hand in the air as though it were nothing. "Do not worry about it. You require a wardrobe, and within this trunk is clothing all in your size. You shall want for nothing. Here, see for yourself."

So, he had been planning her arrival for some time. Slowly, she knelt and opened the chest. Her breath caught. Dresses. Each in bright colors and patterns, like the houses of Rellea, folded and arranged in careful piles within the trunk. Picking up the top one in light blue, she unfolded it and gazed at its perfection. The material alone must cost at least twice the amount of all the property her family owned. *Dis Pater*—'Rich Father,' indeed. "This is all for me?"

The maid, Brynwen noticed, didn't bat an eye.

"Of course," the king replied.

"Th-thank you, your Majesty," she stammered. "They are lovely. But I couldn't possibly accept them." They were gorgeous, but she didn't think she could bring herself to ever wear them.

The king frowned. "Brynwen, they are a gift. Or, if you wish, think of them as payment for your services and recompense for leaving your belongings behind. Please accept them and wear them as you will." He didn't once mention the others left behind in the cavern. She hoped Ulrich had found them.

A war raged within Brynwen. If she didn't accept, it could hurt the king's pride. But if she did, then did that mean he owned her? To be honest, though, what other choice did she have? "Very well. I accept your generous gift."

"Marvelous." Morfrey rubbed his hands together excitedly. "Now that this errand is complete, I will leave you to your slumber and curing my city."

CHAPTER 20

The next morning, Brynwen arose at her normal time, just before dawn. Her mission was to check on the patients first thing. Early on, she had learned that royalty in the palace didn't leave their rooms until at least midmorning. This included the two master healers. In retrospect, they had worked late into the night, while Brynwen nearly dropped in exhaustion hours earlier. It was not a sustainable routine. Aesculapius and Iaso were confident that, with three healers, they could quickly find a cure for the mysterious monkshood poisoning. All the while, Brynwen kept the prophecy and the stone of adamant in mind. Once she had the cure, she could look for the stone.

Not knowing if anyone had survived the Druid attack or the cave-in stressed her to no end. If only she knew they were all right. She wished she had crystal orbs like Gregorio and Circe used to communicate with them. It occurred to her that Payla might have had one as well.

As she made her way to the grand ballroom, she hoped to find Wallace feeling better. All night, she'd pondered what he'd been going to tell her before falling asleep. Upon reaching the makeshift infirmary, she searched the beds for the young man, but he was nowhere to be found.

"May I help you?"

Brynwen spun to find the attendant, Clara, a human woman of about forty with dark hair and freckles all over her nose. "I am here to visit with the patients. Is Wallace awake yet? I wanted to check on his cough." She cast another pass at the room.

Clara's smile wavered. "Ah. I am afraid Wallace passed in the night. He appeared slightly improved before I left for the night shift, but he never awoke. I am sorry."

Brynwen's chest constricted at the news. "Poor Wallace, I thought he might survive." *Was I wrong in my assessment? What if I was wrong about everyone else, too?*

With diminished excitement, she made her rounds for an hour and arrived at the same assessments as the day before.

Numb, she returned to the herbarium.

Having a couple of hours to herself, she entered the healers' sanctuary and took a deep breath to cast aside her remorse for the dead lad. He had reminded her so much of Talfryn, and now it was like she'd lost him too…she shook her head. Would she ever reunite with Talfryn, Padric, and the others?

To make matters worse, Ulrich had found nothing of their whereabouts. Heavy storms kept his search team from scouring several flooding caverns and above ground.

To calm her agitated nerves, she made a fresh batch of chamomile tea. Steaming tea in hand, she studied the chalkboard with Aesculapius's neat handwriting. A couple of ideas came to her, concoctions she wouldn't normally use, but under the circumstances could prove fruitful.

A light knock came at the door. "Enter." She gathered her things to take notes, but the ink pot was missing from the large, cluttered scribe's desk. It wasn't on the workbench, either.

"Good mornin' marm." Frania entered the room, apron as tidy as ever, hovering inside the door. "We come to bring yer morning meal and see if you needed anythin'. Come, Alta, Celta."

Two young maids entered behind her each in black frocks and aprons like Frania's, one gray faun and one human with light brown hair, each carrying a tray with breakfast items. They looked familiar, but she couldn't place them.

The tray-holding maids curtsied at Brynwen, the food they carried filling the room with the scent of cooked eggs, bangers, a load of buttered toast, and fresh fruit. *Heavenly.* They headed straight to the table by the couches.

Mouth watering, Brynwen's eyes roamed over the desk one more time for the ink pot. "Have you seen the ink pot? I thought it was on this table yesterday."

Frania headed straight for the tall bookcase. A knowing grin raised her lip. "When the master's got a bout of inspiration, he's like to put it anywhere." She stretched her arm up and plucked the pot from next to a large green tome on the third shelf. "Here 'tis, marm."

"How'd you know it would be there?"

"It's near one of his fav'rite books 'bout herbs an' the like." She proffered the pot to Brynwen.

"Thank you." Accepting the ink pot, Brynwen gasped. "Oh, Frania, your hands. They are getting worse. Do they hurt?" The brown splotches had grown larger, making it look like a rash of some sort. Unfortunately, her limited knowledge of cobalus physiology prevented her from identifying the cause.

The maid blushed and quickly hid her hands behind her apron. "'Tis nothing, marm. Tain't contagious, neither. Just an ol' rash from picking some herbs from the garden. Sensitive skin, you know."

"Well, I have a salve that may help." She found the Miracle Mix and, with careful fingers, lathered a healthy amount on them.

"Thank you." Frania's blush deepened. "I've got to be going," she murmured. "Alta, Celta, let's go." She dashed out of the door, the two remaining maids glancing at her in confusion, then followed.

"Huh, I guess she doesn't care to have a fuss made over her." She shrugged, then picked up the ink pot and sharpened quill.

Returning to the workbench, she pulled out *On Healing and Other Remedies* and opened the cover to the front page. "HA" appeared in its normal spot. Not for the first time, Brynwen reflected on the fact that only the book's title page, labeled "HA", never changed. She quickly imagined two ingredients she wanted the book to find—carrot and oleander—and then randomly flipped to a page. The title "For Relief of Digestion" appeared when she pressed the paper down. Some ingredients she'd expected, but others surprised her. "Perfect, that worked." Picking up a worn quill with a long brown feather, she dipped it in the jar of ink. She scribbled them down on the back of yesterday's parchment notes and made fast work to add some observations of her own.

"Now, how about a cure? Please?" She opened to the first page again. In her mind, she formed a detailed picture of an elixir the patients could drink to cure their illness. Bracing herself, she flipped to another random page near the center.

Anti-Venom Ingredients:
> *Rosemary*
>
> *Hyssop*
>
> *Calendula*
>
> *....*
>
> *Caladrius*

No. She slammed the book shut. "I can't use these ingredients, book," she hissed. "Why do you insist on showing this to me every time? Did I break you somehow?" The term "fed-up" was an understatement for how she felt. "I have limited time to find a cure, do you understand? People are *dying.* I need a little help here. I *beg* you."

The book did not answer. Instead, it sat there, as taciturn as ever, taunting her with its chosen ingredients blaring in her face. "Why would your master make such an unhelpful, ungrateful tool?" With a grunt of frustration, she closed her eyes and let her head fall upon the uncooperative book with a thunk.

> *Beneath the depths, a kingdom's plight*
> *Paths run with nary a light.*
>
> *...*
>
> *Find the adamant to end the curse*
> *Or end your days with this last verse.*

"Why does the prophecy keep coming up at the most inopportune time? Janus and his threats are the least of my worries right now." Absently, her fingers twirled around her auburn braid. What she wouldn't give to have Padric here. Besides his presence, which filled her heart with warmth, his encouragement could aid in solving this puzzle. Right now, even a quip from Talfryn, helpful or unhelpful, would be welcome.

"Mayhap I need to think more like Talfryn." She chuckled. "It would at least cheer me up. And look at me, I am speaking to a book. What have I come to?" Picking up the quill again, she wrote another idea for the cure. This triggered a chain of thoughts. Time flew by as she worked. She didn't hear the door to the hallway open until it had already closed and the singsong voice wishing her good morning filled the room.

"Well, someone has been busy. You must have been here for hours."

Startled, Brynwen's bottom slid off the stool; her arms flailed to keep herself from falling to the floor. "Oh!" Her hand fell on a leaden paperweight of a toga-wearing Apollo playing the lute. The statuette held firm, and her feet met the floor without incident.

Heart zipping every which way inside her ribcage, Brynwen held onto the table for another second to stabilize herself. Finally, her balance evened out.

Chuckling, Iaso held out her arms to keep Brynwen steady. "Forgive me, Brynwen. I did not mean to startle you. There, sit back down before your heart gives out. There's a good lass."

"You are here early," Brynwen said when the breath returned to her.

"On the contrary, I am quite late. There were a couple of errands I did not wish to burden the staff with, then there was...what is that?" Her eyes had wandered to the workbench and landed on the opened *Book of Healing and Other Remedies*. Her skin grew ashen, and her fingers fluttered an inch over the pages, then she yanked them back as though they'd been bitten. "Where did you get this?" Her voice had lowered to a whisper. *A frightened whisper.*

"An acquaintance let me borrow it for a while." It was true, Circe had let her borrow it. But deep down, Brynwen prayed the goddess might forget about it indefinitely. It was too good a resource to give up. Except, of course, when she needed it most. "It has worked wonders at home, but since coming here, it has yet to find a cure for our patients."

Iaso bit her lip in thought. Then, braving a chance at touching the tome, she flipped the pages backward until it landed on the title page, with "HA" in the top right corner. Two fingers glided over the initials.

She slammed it shut.

As soon as Iaso had touched it, a pit had formed in Brynwen's stomach, a soft susurrus of warning filling her brain. She longed to snatch *On Healing and Other Remedies* back into her possession.

"Who let you borrow it?" Iaso asked with slitted eyes. "No, don't tell me. But you must remove it from here, quickly." She hauled Brynwen to her feet. Her hands hovered with uncertainty over the book for a couple of seconds before she scooped it up and practically threw it into Brynwen's arms.

This was not the reaction Brynwen had imagined Iaso would have when she saw her father's book.

"But why? Iaso, this book can help us find the cure for the poison. We just need the proper ingredients. If we work together, we can find the right combination." *Without a caladrius*, Brynwen wanted to add. She missed the bird, and half wished Nessie were here without having to exploit her miraculous ability.

Seeing the questioning look in Brynwen's eyes, the dark-haired maiden sighed and rushed to the door. "There is no time to tell you now. You must take it away—burning it in the kitchen fireplace would be best, though I know it won't work. At least the other piece is gone." With a quick peek into the hallway in both directions, her head bobbing like a hen, she thrust Brynwen into the hall. "I will tell my father you went to fetch a…a snack." Without another word, she shut the door, leaving Brynwen in bewilderment out in the drafty hallway.

Oddly, Gregorio had had the same reaction when he'd seen the book. *"It was destroyed thousands of years ago. At least, it was supposed to have been. It is a dangerous book, Brynwen. You must be rid of it."*

Two people were frightened of the book. Talfryn was wary of it in another sense. And yet, its presence hadn't affected Circe in the least. *Why? And what did she mean by "the other piece"?*

Shaking her head, Brynwen packed the book into her satchel, its heaviness a welcome weight. Whatever the meaning behind Iaso's and Gregorio's behavior, they were upset by the book's presence. How could one book, albeit a magic one, cause so much turmoil? Was it the book itself, or something in the book? Something to have made Jupiter nearly kill Aesculapius for. Whatever the cause, she was determined to find out. *But first, for my friend's and master's benefit, I must take the book somewhere safe.*

But where?

CHAPTER 21

That afternoon, having all but forgotten the alarming incident from the morning, Iaso accompanied Brynwen to the market for supplies. Many shops and stalls had regular trade with above ground merchants, and she was happy to learn that they sold many items and seasonal foods she was used to finding at home. Of course, other exotic novelties caught her eye as she shopped. Iaso stopped at a stall toting an array of colorful mushrooms and encouraged Brynwen to continue shopping and she'd catch up.

Turning the corner around a ribbon shop with a sign above the door painted in pinks and reds called *Stripes and Curls*, Brynwen nearly collided with a maiden exiting the store. "I beg your pardon." She stepped to the side to let the maiden pass, when she noticed her height and the midnight blue of the cloak she wore.

"Payla?"

The maiden's eyes widened with delight. "Brynwen! Oh, thank Mithras you are all right. I imagined all sorts of terrible things happening to you when you went inside that portal." She looked like she might hug Brynwen, but restrained herself.

Happiness bubbled up inside Brynwen's chest, a feeling she hadn't felt in a while. "I am so relieved to see you. Are the others with you?" She didn't recognize anyone else in the vicinity.

The immortal's face fell and she shook her head. "I jumped into the portal right after you, so I don't know what happened to them. Afterward, when I tried to contact my cousin with my crystal orb, it didn't work right. I think it got frazzled from being inside the portal."

All of the happiness Brynwen had felt a minute before quickly faded and her chest constricted, nearly choking her. She wouldn't be seeing Padric, Talfryn, and the others anytime soon, if at all. She tried not to think of their bodies lying crushed beneath miles and miles of rock. "Wait—you *jumped* into it?" Brynwen asked in wonder. Except for the instant travel part, she couldn't understand the appeal. Each magical door or smoke-filled journey left her feeling sick and irritable. "If you were right behind me, why didn't you appear in the same place as me? Where have you been all this time?"

Scarlet blanketed the maiden's pale cheeks, accentuating her freckles. "I admit, it was a bit rash." She pointed to her left. "When I entered the portal, I didn't see you anywhere. Before I knew it, I exited into the middle of the city, with people gaping at me as though I'd grown a third horn on my head. I found a place to stay, and soon, I picked up rumors of a new healer who came to help with the terrible illness, whom I surmised was you. I'm glad to see I was right."

"Right, it's"—she lowered her voice—"poison. The two healers are having trouble keeping the patients stable, let alone finding the cure. You may have heard of them—Aesculapius and Iaso."

Payla's jaw dropped. "They are alive? I thought Aesculapius died thousands of years ago. Well, in that case, I'd love to ask them about this fungus I get sometimes on my—"

"Payla, focus." She scanned the area, expecting to see Iaso walking up at any moment. "What's in your basket?" She spied balls of blue and red thread and pieces of colorful string. Was she going to take up knitting? Did priestesses of Mithras knit?

"Oh, these. They are to practice my magic on. Which leads to something I must tell you, but not here."

"I can't right now," Brynwen replied. "I'm not alone."

Payla looked around and blinked. "Of course not, you're with me."

"Ha, ha."

The horned maiden grinned. "Tomorrow, then?"

Brynwen hesitated, then nodded. Unless an emergency happened, Brynwen could manage rearranging her morning. "I can meet first thing." She almost told her about the cave-in on Padric, Talfryn, and the others, but the thought caused her breakfast of eggs and fruit to turn sour in her stomach. *I'll tell her tomorrow.*

"Good, see you here at the ribbon shop."

Just then, Iaso came into sight. The maiden waved in the air with a basket filled with a rainbow array of mushrooms. When Brynwen looked back, Payla was gone.

"I have been waiting for these mushrooms to come into season for some time, and I wore down the seller until he gave me a good price. I love haggling."

"Of course." A wry smile lifted the side of Brynwen's lips. *Looks like we've both had positive encounters today.*

CHAPTER 22

The next morning, a child cobalus squealed as he ran through the streets, his too-long green tunic reaching down to his toes, as his older sister chased after him through skirts and boots of customers in the market. Brynwen smiled, thoughts of the market in Chaddesden flooding through her mind. Waiting for Payla by the ribbon shop at the agreed-upon time, she was picking through a merchant's basket of lavender, her mind whirling with all the treatments she could use with it. Her hands itched to open *On Healing and Other Remedies* to verify if she could guess the right ingredients for those remedies.

"Ah." Turning the three bundles of herbs over in her hand, she grinned in satisfaction. "This should be enough." She paid the seller, an older male faun with wrinkles, white hair, and an orange cap, with the coins Aesculapius had given her—after some haggling, of course. Next, she needed to find sage and rue.

She was in the middle of paying for some sage when she spied a cobalus exiting the *Stripes and Curls* ribbon shop. With a grimace, he looked from left to right as though trying to be inconspicuous. If it weren't for his clothes, she wouldn't have thought anything of it. They were worn and reminiscent of a uniform, like one of the Druid's rogue minions. *He* must *be an amateur if even* I *can spot him.*

He moved off.

Should I follow?

"Miss? I said two is a good price for the sage."

Not taking her eyes off the cobalus, Brynwen dropped it back into the stall. "I'll be back for it later." Anxious nerves propelled her to chase after the elusive cobalus. "What is he doing here?" she muttered. "If he's here, could the Druid be nearby?" All the hairs on the back of her neck stood up. If the cobalus led her to the Druid, she could have King Morfrey send his legionaries to capture him. Now, more than ever, she wished she knew what had happened to Talfryn, Padric, Aeron, Franco, and his family. Even Rawlins. She missed them so much and wished they would show up like Payla did.

Despite the cobalus's shorter legs, Brynwen struggled to keep up without drawing attention. Once, she ducked behind a vendor stall to escape notice, much to the odd stares of the sellers and patrons. When he resumed, she followed him for another few feet before being forced to look intently at a bolt of bright orange—a color much too bold for her tastes—and look small and inconspicuous.

"May I help you, miss?" The middle-aged seller's skin was the color of caramel, his head wrapped in white cloth. She thought it was called a turban but couldn't remember if that was right or not.

A flush crept up Brynwen's cheeks. "Thank you. I was just passing through." She froze as a carving on the stall's pole caught her eye. The image featured a crude circle with horizontal and vertical lines, and a bull's face in the foreground. Something about it seemed familiar.

Remembering her quarry, she curtsied and exited the stall before the wide-eyed clerk could ask more questions.

However, the cobalus was gone.

No, no, no, no.

Flustered, she continued down the way he'd been heading, peeking frantically into the shops, stalls, and at all the passersby.

"Where did he go?"

She felt like the biggest fool, trying to be clever. *It was a stupid, pointless endeavor, and Padric would be so ashamed of me.*

Suddenly, the creature popped out of a butcher's shop, a small bundle of paper tucked under his arm. Per his custom, his scowl deep, he glimpsed all around, then sauntered off a few feet before making an immediate right into an alley.

Brynwen's heart pounded in her ears when she spotted him and practically forgot about hiding in her rush to follow. *I'll not lose him this time.*

Rounding where the creature turned after a cobbler's shop, she squinted into the dark alley. The hair on the back of her neck stood on end. *This is a bad idea.* She straightened her shoulders. *A very bad idea.* Took a step inside. *This is such a bad idea, even Talfryn would agree.* With each step she took, the shadows deepened until they almost eclipsed the light. There was no way of knowing how far the alley went, if it let out on the other side, or ended at a wall.

She bent over and removed the small knife hidden in her boot. *Courtesy of Rawlins,* she thought with annoyance. *Whom I'm sure works for the Druid and Janus. Responsible for countless terrible actions. If only I'd told Padric and Talfryn about him instead of being a coward and staying silent.*

What if Payla and I are the only ones left? What if....? No, stop thinking about it. It won't help them or me.

Staring into the darkness, reason began to take over. Maybe a touch of fear. *I should go back and find Payla. But if I leave, the cobalus will be gone.* It took another moment to pluck up her courage, squeezing the blade until her knuckles turned white.

With resolve, she plunged into the depths. Just steps in, Brynwen heard the swishing of fabric. Her breath caught as a tall, dark figure loomed in front of her. A flash of light from the street sparked in the creature's yellowish eye as his firm hands clamped down on her arms and rammed her into the wall. Spikes of agony flashed through her shoulder blades and head. Seeing stars, she thought she imagined another set of eyes, at mid-height, blinking up at her. Two more sets of yellowed eyes joined them.

Warning bells went off in Brynwen's mind as she struggled to twist her arms free.

"I knew ye'd follow," her captor hissed in her face, his breath foul. "The master'll be happy this time. See fellas, a li'l extra work's all's needed."

"Good one, Glop," one newcomer said.

Glop, the cobalus. How can he be this tall now? And these others...

Brynwen tried in vain to come up with a plan of escape, trying to remember the strategies with the dagger Padric and Talfryn had shown her weeks ago. It was useless, though, as the knife dropped from her sweaty fingers and clanked onto the hard ground. *This really isn't good.* The surrounding cobali snorted and chortled as they pressed closer to her, their fowl breath stealing her air.

"There must be some mistake, good sirs. I'm looking for the...the bread shop."

"Bread shop, yeah?" Glop's yellow eye tried to see through her.

It's over, Brynwen thought with despair. *I knew I should have waited for Payla.*

"Just bring 'er, Glop," the cobalus directly below Glop said. "We gotta go 'fore someone sees us."

"We've got a minute er two, Dink." Glop licked his lips in such a way it made Brynwen's stomach curdle. The glint of metal flashed near his face—a dingy dagger. "Now, lass, don't make me use this."

"The master wants 'er in one piece."

"I said just a min—"

A commotion sounded from the street. Brynwen cast a quick glance over her shoulder to find a cart flipped over and a group of citizens arguing over it with raised voices.

Funny how a random incident can give one an idea, isn't it?

"Please let me go," she begged in her most pleading voice. "I will do anything."

"Anything?" The grip blissfully lessened a fraction. "Well, in that case..."

"...to get free of you!" With all her might, Brynwen jammed her foot into his tiny one.

"Owwww!" To her surprise, the shout of agony came from his middle.

"Dink! What're you doing!" Glop jiggled and crashed to the ground, his body breaking in half. No—he fell from Dink's shoulders!

Before the others could react, Brynwen shoved the closest cobalus on her left into his fellow. Four voices shouted and fell to the ground. A short cobalus with a crushed appendage had tears streaming down his face. Dink, she thought. He hobbled on one foot, looking about ready to crumple to the ground. Brynwen made to leave when Glop leapt to his feet, waving his rusty dagger at her. Recovered, the other four gathered next to him, weapons drawn, each in worse shape than the last. Fierce, yellowed eyes glared up at her.

"Nuh-uh, yer ladyship. Yer comin' with us."

Nothing Brynwen could say would sway them.

Suddenly, a flash of light struck Glop. Red bloomed from a wound in his chest where a dagger hilt stuck out. The creature gaped at it with a rounded mouth. The next instant, midnight blue fabric rippled beside Brynwen as the cobalus fell to the ground for a second and final time.

Dink looked at his fallen comrade in horror. "Glop?" he asked with a quaking body. His shabby clothes were covered in fresh blood splatter. His eyes traveled up the long cloak and settled on Payla's face. She gripped one dagger in her hand, its twin resting in the body of the expired cobalus. She plucked a third from somewhere within her cloak, pointing both of them at the remaining would-be captors.

"As a priestess of Mithras, I will allow you to live if you answer some questions for me."

Brynwen gaped. In the few weeks she'd known the maiden, she had never heard Payla speak like this to anyone.

"Well?"

"He—he'll kill us." Dink's knees knocked against one another.

"One question?" Brynwen asked. "Why does he want me?"

Eyes turning black with terror, he appeared about to shake apart. Then he said, "For the ritual."

"Shhh!" one other hissed.

"The ritual?" Payla asked.

As one, the cobali spun on their heels and disappeared into the darkness. Payla made to follow, but thought better of it. Feeling sudden fatigue, Brynwen sagged against the wall, all of her energy spent.

"I told you to wait for me." Payla's voice was back to normal as she leaned over to retrieve her dagger from Glop's body with a strange detached casualness. She wiped the blood off on the dead creature's dirty clothes. Brynwen wasn't sure she liked this side of Payla. The priestess.

"I did, but I saw this cobalus"—she pointed with her foot—"and thought he would lead me to the Druid, if he's here."

"And then you planned to do what, exactly?"

That's a good question. "How did you find me?" She changed the subject, feeling her cheeks flame. In fact, her whole body felt like it was in flames. She stepped out of the shadows.

"I followed your trail..." Payla trailed off and her eyes became saucers.

Following her friend's gaze down to her body, Brynwen could only stare. A worn, wooden knife hilt stuck out from the top of her satchel, a dark stain spreading on the fabric and onto her blouse. *Blood*—her blood.

The knife. It wasn't in Glop's lifeless hand.

"Well," Brynwen said with detachment, "that's probably not been cleaned...ever."

The alley tilted. Then the ground came up to meet her.

CHAPTER 23

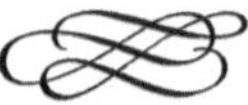

$\mathcal{P}$adric's first sensation was a splitting headache. Something tickled his face. Groaning, he found little solace for his pounding head.

"He's awake," came a voice.

"Finally," said another.

Slowly, Padric cracked his eyes open. Dark eyes gazed into his own. Padric started.

The eyes drew back. They connected to a fuzzy brown face and a black nose. Other blurry images hovered over him.

"Give him some air." This third voice he knew for certain…*Gregorio.* The immortal knelt next to Padric and touched his shoulder.

After a couple of blinks, Padric's vision cleared enough to discern Gregorio, Aeron, and Ulysses peering down at him with grim expressions; and, in Rawlins's case, his eyebrows were deeply furrowed. *Is that concern on his face?*

Scratches and dried blood covered the faces of Rawlins and Aeron. Like Padric, they had taken a battering from the Druid's cobali. They were no longer in the cavern, either, but outside under some trees.

Gregorio leaned forward and studied Padric's face for a few seconds before nodding and reclining back on his heels. "He will be fine. Padric,

I suggest you stay put for a little while. You have a large lump on the side of your head. A fraction of an inch another way and you would have died in an instant." He pointed unnecessarily to the right side of Padric's head.

Lucky me. Padric nodded without causing much more pain. "Fine," he said carefully. "Where is—" *Brynwen...* He felt his face screwing up as he remembered her being taken through some sort of oval light. Then Talfryn had panicked and fought against his captors with savage abandon. Payla disappeared. Padric's chest constricted as the memory abruptly stopped. *Something is wrong.* With aching muscles and a throbbing head, he glanced at each of his friends.

Gregorio set his jaw. "I told you not to move."

"Where is Talfryn? Lenore?"

Gaze lowering, Gregorio indicated to the right with his head. The others parted for Padric to see. He slowly turned his head to the left and gasped. Talfryn lay unconscious a few feet away, tunic removed, and bandages wrapped around his arm and ribs. Peeking out of the white bandages were fresh cuts and bruises all over his face, torso, and arms.

An eternity seemed to pass as he gaped at his unmoving friend. Mouth dry, the words finally came. "Will he...?"

Gregorio raised a pacifying hand. "He will live."

"No thanks to those little monsters." Rawlins's scowl returned as he squeezed his knuckles. "They nearly twisted his arms right off."

Padric winced. "Will he recover?" *Please.*

"With care and time, I think so—physically," Gregorio replied. "Yet, mentally, I cannot deem to guess. Nor for Lenore, after losing her family like that."

Lenore sat in a secluded spot not ten feet away, her face a blank as she stared off into the distance. Bandaged from wrist to elbow, her arm hung limp in her lap.

Aeron sighed. "But they are alive."

"Indeed. Yet our guide's wife seems to be in a state of great shock," Gregorio said sadly. "She will follow simple commands but does not seem to care about much else."

Guilt rent Padric's chest at his complete failure. Franco. Cecil. Simon. Payla.

And Brynwen.

"What got into him?" Aeron regarded Talfryn. "His eyes were savage, and he raved like a wild man."

"You might, too," Padric replied, "if you had lost your sister a second time. It was quite taxing on him on the first occasion and nearly broke him. I do not blame him for his actions this day in the least." His mind drifted to Brynwen. *Is she hurt? Where is she? What will happen to her? How can I rescue her?*

Aeron shrugged his shoulders. "I suppose you're right."

Gregorio swallowed, and his voice lowered. "They told me of Brynwen's fate. Why would they wish to take her?"

"One thing I am fairly certain about: the Druid had not expected Brynwen to be whisked away like that." It was all Padric could do not to scream, to shout at the top of his lungs, to declare the injustice of their separation to the world. His chest threatened to burst, but he shoved his pain down, down, down. *We must move on,* his father would say. So, for now, he would. His voice became hoarse as he asked, "Pray, did anything else happen in the cave? What of Payla? I thought...well, I thought I spied her cape near the bright light where Brynwen disappeared."

"I saw it, too," Aeron said. "She must have gone after her."

"That is something my cousin would do." Gregorio smiled. "Alas, no correspondence has come through to my orb, but I will try to contact her presently."

"Do that." At least it was some action that might bear fruit. A long-awaited breath escaped Padric's throat. While the others got up to go about their duties in camp, Padric made a mental list of all the things that must be done.

Rawlins lowered to one knee beside him. "We'll find them."

"But we have no tracker."

"Hasn't stopped us before."

"True." Padric paused in thought. "We should look at Gregorio's maps again."

"There ya go."

A flash of lightning fell to earth in the distance, accompanied seconds later by rolling thunder. A raindrop splashed on Padric's forehead. He had not noticed the darkening clouds until now. "Once we find shelter, that is."

❦

"WE NEED A PLAN."

In vain, Talfryn tried to concentrate on the conversation while Gregorio changed his bandages, but everything hurt. Everything. Even his pinkie toe. The cold and dampness of the tiny cave didn't help, either. Ulysses sat on his other side to help keep him warm. Well, warmer.

"We need a plan," Rawlins repeated. His gaze pierced Padric, but the blond knight refused to yield an inch. "The adamant, Brynwen, and Payla won't find themselves."

Padric poked the fire with a dry stick. "I agree, but we cannot do much until Talfryn has gained his strength."

"Once the rain calms, I can search ahead for any clues, if there are any left," Aeron suggested. "Pop into the next village and ask if they've seen anything. I can take Lenore as well."

Padric shook his head. "It would be unwise to divide the company just yet. Talfryn is too vulnerable."

"I'm right here, in case you lot've forgotten," Talfryn snapped. "I still have all my limbs"—although he couldn't exactly move his left arm at the moment—"and can go anywhere you can. I'm not an invalid." *Hopefully. Maybe.*

Grandfather always said tomorrow is another day.

Yeah, well...

Talfryn had awoken early the previous morning in the shallow cave, with Gregorio ministering to him. It was the worst wake-up he'd had in his entire life: pain shooting throughout his whole body and not knowing where he was. Even worse was when he'd remembered his sister being dragged into that bright oval thing. The gaping emotional hole in his chest, which had finally closed in Cataractonium, had reopened again as though with a bent pitchfork. Just when everything finally seemed almost back to normal, he'd lost Brynwen. Again. It was as though someone'd ripped an appendage from his body without warning.

Now, his arm lay useless in a sling, thanks to the sacrifice of one of their blankets; and no thanks to those ugly goblin-cobalus things. But just about any shift of his body hurt his shoulder. Gregorio'd said it was dislocated, but he didn't know how to fix it. "Books are my specialty, not the human body." *If only they'd put these things in books! Like the scary one Brynwen has.*

A tiny tap-tap-tap-tap sound came from behind Gregorio. Like tiny feet scurrying around. It grew silent, then Talfryn heard the tapping sound happen again, making him miss some of what was being said. He thought he saw something darting around where the fire didn't quite reach. That was when he felt Aeron's eyes scrutinizing him.

Avoiding his stare, Aeron's gaze flitted back at the other two knights. "The trail will grow colder the longer we wait. When Talfryn is ready, we'll need to move fast."

Arms still folded, Rawlins made his gruff reply, "I agree."

Talfryn shook his head. "Wait, what about Bryn? She's in danger." No one understood what this separation was doing to him. Or what it could do to her.

Ulysses nodded his head to get Gregorio's attention, his huge antlers taking up all the open space. Some sort of mental communication seemed to go between them. Gregorio smacked his own forehead as he would a disruptive pupil. "Of course, *Dis Pater*. I nearly forgot. If he is around here, he may have had something to do with the disappearance of Brynwen and Payla."

"I wonder." Padric tapped his chin. "If that is the case, Brynwen might be in no immediate danger. We have no notion that *Dis Pater* is or was a dangerous or vengeful king, do we? Did his people not ask for her help?"

Aeron nodded. "I concur. Being with the king of the underworld may be less than ideal, but Brynwen is likely safer with him now than with us."

Incredulous, Talfryn nearly choked. "Are you serious? Why'd he take her? We can't just leave her to this maniacal king, whoever he is. She may be safe now, but who knows when he'll snap like Helius did?" He looked daggers at Padric. "You, of all people, should understand."

"I do understand, Tal. But I would not lead us into perilous depths without reviewing all of our options. My deepest wish is to rescue Brynwen from this retched king, but we must think of the prophecy as well. And"—he sent a meaningful look to Lenore—"when we meet up with the Druid again, we shall rescue Franco and the children."

It was then that Talfryn dared a glance at Lenore. She sat in the corner, a blanket wrapped around her for warmth, staring into the fire as though lost.

Lost.

Like him. She looked so alone; it made his heart bleed. While he'd lost one sister, she'd lost her entire family. It made him feel like a louse.

"Be of good cheer, my friend." Gregorio placed a hand on Talfryn's good shoulder. He smiled, his youthful face so full of hope. It awed Talfryn how young Gregorio looked until he really examined the man's eyes and was reminded how old the immortal really was. "We shall rescue them all, have faith."

Faith in whom? His gods? My God? In Padric? This was something he'd never asked Gregorio, since he'd spent so much time with mortals.

From his satchel, Gregorio extracted not a book but the same spherical glass which they'd used to speak to Circe, Helius, and Pasiphae. He noticed Talfryn and Padric looking at the glass. "I tried contacting Payla earlier, but there was some sort of interference. I will try again, but I fear this rain is making it more difficult than it should be otherwise." Standing up, he moved toward the rainy cave entrance, raising it over his head and holding it this way and that, even standing on his tiptoes in a comical gesture as though straining to place it on a high invisible shelf.

Meanwhile, Aeron whispered something softly into Rawlins's ear.

The stoic knight clenched his jaw for a couple seconds before answering, then turned back to his lieutenant. "This is a bad idea, Padric. *Sir.* We think you are emotionally compromised. You, too." He glanced at Talfryn. "Can either of you make an objective decision about our predicament without throwing your hearts into it? Don't get me wrong, I like Brynwen and Payla, but we've got a mission to accomplish."

"It's all about the mission with you," Talfryn interjected. "She's my sister. If you only want the adamant, then I'll go for her myself."

"If you want to get yourself killed, go right ahead."

Ulysses and Gregorio stared at them helplessly.

"I probably will, no thanks to you, Invisibility Boy. Where's my hatchet?" His hands shook as he searched for his weapon, his shoulder on fire. *Looks like I'm on my own. How can they be so heartless?*

Padric stepped between the two, his eyebrows set in a straight line. "Rawlins, Talfryn, calm down this instant—"

Gregorio bristled, throwing his hands into the air. All speaking ceased. It was the most vexed Talfryn had ever seen the tutor. "I have remained silent long enough. Long have I observed you mortals, and yet even after history repeats itself many a time, you cannot see the world because you do not want to. Might I remind you young fellows, there might be more than meets the eye, here? Think. Do you not wonder how this may all be part of the prophecy? That Brynwen's being taken could have happened by design?"

Padric paused, his eyes glistening. "You are brilliant, my friend." He clapped Gregorio on the arm. "Indeed, it was she whom the Oracle bestowed the prophecy. It is *her* mission. Meaning, by being in *Dis Pater's* underground realm, she may be one step closer to the adamant we seek."

"Are you sayin' we let her do this on her own?" Rawlins's eyebrows furrowed.

"I am suggesting we give her all the aid we can—we merely need a way into *Dis Pater's* kingdom."

All eyes turned to Gregorio. He chuckled. "Do not look at me. My maps do not show entrances to underground kingdoms. Although, it would make a fascinating project for the future." He tapped a finger on his chin.

Shoulders relaxing, Talfryn breathed in relief and looked over his shoulder. *I'm coming, Bryn. Hold on.* "So, I'm going to need to break my fast before we start searching the next fifty caves for an entrance." He winced as pain lanced up his left arm. *Oh, right. Being able to move my arm might help, too.*

CHAPTER 24

The next morning, the rain continued to attempt entry into the cave. Talfryn felt chilled, wet, and hungry, but not in that order. Reaching into his pack for a snack, he noticed crumbs everywhere. The habit of keeping a few extra crackers for his dog, Finn, or his goats, Hay and Stack, stuck with him, even when away from home.

"All right, who ate my snacks? I had some crackers in here."

Everyone denied it. He doubted it was Padric this time, as the knights had tied him down all night on the opposite side of the fire.

"Do you eat in your sleep?" Aeron asked, munching on his own snack of dried venison.

"Nay." *Well, not recently, anyway.*

Later in the evening, Talfryn sat on guard duty. Shoulder throbbing, he tried everything to get comfortable, but it didn't work. Padric stayed up with him for a bit until he became exhausted. Within a minute of the knight falling asleep, his limbs shrank, gray fur covered his body, and white horns grew out of his hair. It might have fascinated Talfryn a few months ago as Circe's captive, but after having to endure the same changing every evening for a fortnight himself, he took it in stride. The major difference was that Circe's captives had become animals at sunset, whereas now Padric turned once he fell asleep.

His mind wandered, thinking about Ulysses and animal transformations, when he heard the scurrying of tiny animal feet again. Definitely not a bear, but something small. On instinct, Talfryn reached into the small drawstring sack of crumbs from his pack. "I'm guessing you've returned for the rest of my crumbs." With his mouth and good hand, he opened the drawstring and scattered a small mound of crumbs three feet away on the ground. Then pulled the strings taut with his teeth. "Eat up," he murmured.

Remaining still for a bit, he mused whether the creature would come out or if he'd scared it away with his movements. *What kinds of animals live in the marsh?* He'd seen a handful of squirrels, and they'd shot some grouses.

However, nothing happened by the time he and Rawlins switched roles. Disappointed, Talfryn settled into his blankets for an uneasy slumber.

When he woke up in the morning, the pile was gone to the last crumb.

He sighed. "The little miser. There's always tonight, I guess."

"Talfryn," Padric knelt next to the farmer's bedding. "How fares your arm?"

Talfryn hid his grimace as the discomfort came back to his shoulder at the reminder. *Thanks!* "Oh, it's great! Everyone should dislocate their shoulders once in a while. Gets you out of doing chores and a chance to think philosophically about life."

A chuckle fell from Padric's lips. "It appears Gregorio has been speaking with you. You must regale me with your philosophical discourse. After I build a fire, of course. Speaking of which, may I borrow your tinder box? Mine broke and everyone else has mysteriously misplaced theirs."

"That's odd." It took a couple of tries to get his limbs to work to sit up and rest his back against the cave wall. Unfortunately, he couldn't hide his grimace.

Padric's expression fell, but he tried to hide it with a quick smile. It was clear he felt responsible for Talfryn's current state. But really, Talfryn had no one to blame but himself for his childish outburst in the cavern. The cobali probably jumped him because they thought he was crazy. Admitting it didn't make him miss his sister any less, though.

"Sure. It's in my pack." Somehow, his pack had moved from his side to just out of reach. *Did I kick it over there in my sleep?*

Reaching his hand into the brown pack, Padric felt around for a couple of seconds before recoiling as though scalded by a fiery poker. "What the…something bit me." He held up his hand in consternation, revealing a small indentation on his pointer finger. *Like teeth.*

An angry string of squeaks came from the pack, the fabric moving around as though alive. Then a head popped out of it. Small and red and furry—a squirrel!

It flicked its tail back and forth like a forefinger berating their unacceptable behavior and invading his new home.

"Ha ha!" Talfryn laughed in relief. "I think we've found our crumb and tinderbox thief."

CHAPTER 25

Three days later

Padric parried, then thrust with his sword. His movements were stiff after four days of sitting in the cramped cave while storms raged outside. The sun had finally peeked out from behind the clouds as though to prove it still existed. Sidestepping out of harm's way, he feinted right and lunged, his faun hoof sliding on the wet ground. His opponent, Rawlins, dodged and brought down his sword. The following seconds were a blur as they got into the groove of fighting in earnest.

Gray clouds hovered overhead, threatening to burst. They matched his mood to a tee, goading him on. The weather had delayed their search for Brynwen, Payla, and the adamant, and the Druid had gotten away with Franco's family. Gregorio predicted that the rain would let up for less than a full day, so there was little time for sparring to shake out their muscles' disuse before they must return to the cave.

Meanwhile, their supplies ran thin, leaving Gregorio, Aeron, and Lenore to scrounge for food and a bit of kindling to dry out in the cave before the rain resumed. After a couple of days in the cave, Lenore's melancholy had lessened somewhat with Gregorio's ministrations. But they could not take her to the village until all the storm clouds passed—whenever that might be.

Time, time, time.

Bounding off a boulder, Padric struck hard and moved fast, only making Rawlins strike back all the harder.

"I'll win today, but *I* won't cheat," Rawlins ground out with the hint of a grin.

Padric narrowly missed losing his eye. "I do not think so. And being a faun is *not* cheating." It was their age-old tradition when sparring, to taunt one another. Somehow, it lightened his mood exponentially.

"Oh, come on, Padric. Don't let him *goat* you on!" Talfryn chided.

Padric rolled his eyes.

They battered each other, well past the point of sweating, leaving long ruts in the mud. For a bit, Padric thought to have the upper hand, and made to feint again, but his hoof slipped in the mud.

He landed with a slurping thud. Looking up, his heart froze as Rawlins stepped in to finish the fight, sword twirling high in the air. Brynwen's warning about Rawlins suddenly came to mind. *"I am afraid... it is about...Rawlins."* Followed by Roana's *"Beware the false one."*

The sun filtered through a break in the clouds, and a sudden bright light flashed in Rawlins's eye. He stumbled. "What the blazes?" Blinking several times, he swung in a wild arc.

With reflexes like a cat, Padric swiped upward, stopping less than an inch from Rawlins's chest. "Do you yield, friend?"

A second light dazzled Rawlins. Flinging his sword to the ground, he dug both palms into his eyes. "Blimey, it's brighter'n the sun. Aye, aye, I yield. Make it stop."

"Where did that light come from?" Padric asked, huffing.

Recovered somewhat, Rawlins reached out a hand. Both Brynwen's and Roana's words repeated in Padric's mind, gripping his chest with unease. *No,* he thought, putting all his conviction into it. *Not Rawlins. No...* He hoped his oldest friend made no notice of his hesitation as he clasped Padric's arm to haul him up.

Padric viewed the hills, then turned his attention to a whistling Talfryn sitting on a soggy fallen log, all his attention on polishing his hatchet with his one good arm. The red squirrel zipped across his shoulders, ran down to tag the hatchet's handle, then dashed to his shoulder again, as though playing a game. The hatchet sent a white lightning bolt zapping across Padric's eyes. "Talfryn!" he cried as he grabbed for his aching face.

"Do you think it's clean enough?" Talfryn asked brightly. The squirrel, which he'd named Miser, sniffed and inspected the weapon.

Still blind, Padric glowered in the farmer's direction.

The clouds swallowed the sun as Talfryn looked up. "Umm, what? Why's everyone staring at me?"

"You good for nothing," Rawlins snapped, making fists. "Are you trying to blind us all?" Nostrils flaring, he marched to within a foot of Talfryn and grabbed at him. Eyes growing wide, Talfryn tried to scoot backward with one arm but was too slow as Rawlins's deadly hands grabbed fistfuls of his tunic.

The squirrel lunged for Rawlins's hand and bit down hard.

"Owww!"

Ulysses came over, his antlers dangerously close to Rawlins's arm.

"Release him, Rawlins." Padric waited until the knight's fingers uncurled from Talfryn's tunic. Since entering the Dales, his friend's sour mood had become ever more erratic, and he did not like it. *But what can I do about it?* "What is it, Ulysses? Did you see something?"

With a slight movement, the peryton indicated over his shoulder at the hills of the marsh, over the sea of purple.

"The light came from over there?" Padric asked. "It could be a dropped coin or trinket, mayhap."

Rawlins frowned, scanning the hillside. "Or an eavesdropper." Like the one he had seen in the Gordale Scar.

In truth, since the attack in the cavern, Padric had sensed someone watching them, had thought to have seen the slightest movement in the distance at times. With small effort, he changed back into full human form. It was becoming easier to transform into a faun or centaur and back again the more he practiced it; yet each time, a sharp pang of doubt of accidentally turning into a goat and getting stuck again tugged at him. All this, despite Gregorio's encouragement that he was doing quite well.

"Whatever the case, the others should return with supplies presently. If the clouds hold up, we may scour the hills. Does that satisfy you, Rawlins?"

"A mite." The storm clouds began to roil and he gave Padric a wry smile. "Care for another go? Winner gets to spar with Aeron next." In a blink, Rawlins disappeared as though behind a door.

"Now who's cheating?" Padric asked with false ire. With a smirk, he changed into a centaur. A raindrop fell on his head as he transformed into a faun.

"Mmm! I love the smell of wet goat." Talfryn scrunched his nose in anticipation.

❧

"Where is it?"

"Where's what?"

Talfryn startled awake, the shouts from two vexed knights disturbing his pleasant dream about gamboling in the green fields at home with Brynwen and their goats. This time, Hay and Stack had left a patch of grass untouched for them to dance in. It was most thoughtful. Or…maybe their dancing preventing the goats from enjoying the best meal in the entire field. *Hmm.*

"My comb, you fool," Aeron snapped. "It was wrapped up with my shaving knife." In frustration, he patted his raven hair down, but it leapt back up in random spikes.

Yep, now the whole dream is gone, and I'll never know which way it'd end.

"Well, I didn't take it." Rawlins indicated his own disheveled hair.

"Did it fall out of your…" Talfryn's brain was still in a sleepy fog. "…your bag thing?"

"Nay, it isn't in my 'bag thing.'" Aeron looked about to punch something. Or someone.

Rawlins's chin jutted out in thought. "I'd bet it was—"

"You, tutor." Aeron pointed at Gregorio, his eyes in slits. "Weren't you on guard duty? Hand it over."

Gregorio frowned at the disgruntled knight. "I was, but why would I take your comb? It took me many centuries to discover that a comb like yours will only make my curls look frazzled and ill-tempered. So, nay, I did not take it."

"It wasn't him," Rawlins said.

Talfryn wiped his face with his hand and trudged to his feet, Miser's tail wrapped around his neck like a kerchief. "It's too early for this, fellas. Why're we arguing over a comb? And where's Padric? He can settle this."

"I agree, we should wait for Padric," Gregorio said.

"Mayhap *you* took it," Aeron accused Talfryn. "Poor farmer, too impoverished to pay for anything. Now you've resorted to stealing."

"Whoa, what?" Talfryn blinked, dumbfounded. "Seriously? In case you haven't noticed, miladdo, there're no pretty maidens to impress for miles and miles." Since he'd met Aeron, the knight never had a hair out of place, even in sleep. On the opposite spectrum, Talfryn could barely keep up appearances when getting up insanely early to feed the animals at home. "Anyway, don't you get paid enough to have like five of them in your pocket and stupid bag thing? Here, let me take a look in there." Talfryn took a step toward the brown bag.

"Don't touch it." Aeron grabbed Talfryn's wrist and twisted. Hard.

Miser screeched.

The others rushed forward in a flurry of raised voices and arms.

As if on cue, Padric and Ulysses crested the hill from the direction of the stream. Stripped to the waist, the knight sauntered toward them, a brown towel hanging over his shoulders. They sped up when the fighting ensued.

"What is the meaning of this?" Padric asked, his voice heightened. He dove into the fray. "Stop this. Stop it *now*."

Everyone stilled.

Breathing heavily, Aeron scowled first at Padric, then Talfryn, then threw the latter's arm aside like a dirty rag.

Well, this arm'll be bruised, too. Great, now I really am a cripple.

"What is this about?" Padric repeated. Despite not wearing his uniform tunic and rapidly-curling hair dripping all over his shoulders, he displayed all the authority of a superior.

"He took my comb. Lieutenant," Aeron added the title as an afterthought. Talfryn thought he was about to spit in Padric's face.

"I took nothing but sleep. Or lack thereof." Talfryn matched the knight's glare, refusing to rub his shoulder that now screamed in agony, nor the once-good wrist where a red welt was growing fast.

"This is unacceptable behavior." Padric eyed every man in the group, his eyes unwavering and scrutinizing. "Gregorio, prepare a quick morning meal with Lenore. Talfryn, help them."

The sheer annoyance in Padric's expression halted Talfryn from making any remarks. In silence, he followed the tutor-turned-cook to where the rations were kept near the fire. Rawlins kept his mouth shut.

Padric lowered his voice, his gaze directed at Aeron. "A comb, Aeron? A comb? Look, we are all weary from the time we have lost because of the storm."

Not to mention losing Brynwen and Payla to that scummy Dis Pater, Talfryn thought.

"This is not the time to worry about appearances. Shape up. We have more important things on our plate than your vanity." Aeron winced. "Besides, it could have been misplaced or left in the cave. Aye?"

Talfryn turned back to help Gregorio and Lenore, both frowning while rummaging through the food bag.

Talfryn squatted next to them. "What's the matter?"

Gregorio huffed. "I set out the journey cakes for our morning repast on top so I could prepare them first thing. But they are gone."

"Did you empty the whole bag?" Checking inside, he spied a bit of dried meat and berries, wrapped cheeses, a bag of nuts, and some other preserved scraps. No journey cakes. "Looks like someone was really hungry overnight. Or…"

Gregorio met his gaze.

"Someone stole it and the comb." A large shadow fell over them.

Startled, Talfryn jumped up.

Rawlins, arms folded across his chest, wore his usual scowl.

Gregorio cleared his throat and raised his voice. "Padric, if you are quite finished berating our associate, you'd better come here."

Padric approached with Aeron a step behind. It was as though a cloud had formed over Aeron's head, his cheeks and neck matching the crimson color of his tunic.

"Tell them," Rawlins said to Gregorio without waiting for Padric to speak.

"The journey cakes for our morning repast have gone. Talfryn, Lenore, and I double checked the bag and this area. They are simply gone."

Padric remained silent for a minute, thoughtful. "So. It appears our friend on the hill paid us a visit." He turned to Rawlins. "I thought you were keeping an eye on him."

"I've got to sleep sometimes," Rawlins replied drily. "Besides, he snuck past our guard."

"Who?" Talfryn, Gregorio, and Aeron asked in unison.

Padric lowered his voice. "Ulysses spotted him yesterday; a lone person over the next rise. It appears he is now brazen enough to steal our belongings."

Aeron clenched his fists as his personal cloud grew darker, ready to let out a storm. "When were you going to tell us?" *Perhaps Aeron's one of those types who get cranky when he doesn't eat enough in the morning.*

"When everyone was awake." Padric sat down on a stump, picked up a long stick from the ground and poked at the dying fire. "We do not know who he is, but before sunup, Rawlins got as close as he could and thinks he is a cobalus. He appears to be working alone, at least for now."

Aeron scowled. "The little gremlin. Then let's go get him." The lust for murder flashed in his eyes.

"Not that way—he might escape into the moor. We will lay a trap."

"A trap?" Talfryn asked.

"Indeed. We must make a plan."

"With pleasure." Rawlins's eyes gleamed, causing the hairs on the back of Talfryn's neck to stand on end.

Talfryn gulped. This wasn't the first time he'd seen the delight of the hunt in the knight's eyes.

"Now listen up, you lot. First…" Rawlins began.

Between Aeron and Rawlins, Talfryn was just glad he wasn't the one being hunted.

CHAPTER 26

*I*n the middle of the moonless night, a figure in a dark cloak and pointed hat halted behind the widest tree in the camp, where the goat slept peacefully, no doubt dreaming of chewing up everything in sight. He leered from one sleeping form to the next, the embers of fire in the center of the camp dying out. The scout, the same chap as the night before, would soon wake with a start to stoke it, so he had to act fast. The object he'd come for, the medallion and its chain, was clutched lightly in the hand of its owner—the skinny young man with dark curly hair. It caught the reflection from the fire. His gaze rested on it a good many seconds, mesmerized by its finery. It was much prettier up close.

Self-assured everyone lay fast asleep, the cobalus tiptoed into the camp on his worn leather shoes. Past the horns of the goat who was once a man. Past the dangerous-looking fellow, sleeping like a wee child with weapons in both hands. Past the strange deer with wings. He halted before the medallion and reached down for it, eyes shining and fingers wiggling in anticipation.

Talfryn, with one eye open, popped open the other. He grinned. The plan was working.

Earlier in the day, when the clouds had finally parted for a few minutes in the afternoon, Gregorio had planted himself to stand just so as he'd wiped his medallion clean to sparkling. He'd taken great pains to glint the sun off it toward the hills where Rawlins had seen the spy. It had been the right move.

Talfryn thought it was too simple a trap, but Padric and Aeron pointed out how easily one could lure in a thief, especially when he began to gloat after getting away with a couple of other crimes without difficulty.

Now, like everyone else in the camp, he threw off his blankets and leapt—well, he more like shimmied—to his feet. Beside him, Ulysses rose with his natural grace, Rawlins's net hanging from his antlers. Talfryn grabbed the other end of the net. His bad arm was strapped to his torso so it wouldn't get in the way. The blood pumped in his veins, ready to strike. "Antler-net time?" he asked with a grin.

Ulysses nodded, head down in readiness.

The shouting was loud enough to wake the dead.

Not to be left out, Miser squeaked out unintelligible instructions from the safety of a tree near where Lenore hid.

Aeron swiped at the cobalus with his dagger and missed. He yanked his hand back when the little guy snapped his teeth at him.

"Why, you little gremlin!" Aeron shouted.

Meanwhile, Padric transformed back into a human, and he and Gregorio chased after the thief. The medallion donned around its owner's neck where it belonged, swung every which way with his movements. Talfryn marveled at how fast the tutor could run for such a skinny fellow.

They maneuvered the cobalus toward Talfryn and Ulysses. The latter leapt over bedrolls and cooking supplies as though they weren't there.

"Just a little closer," Talfryn urged.

When the cobalus's eyes met Talfryn's, they were glowing yellow in the darkness, the shadows coming from the fire giving him a devilish air. A shiver ran up Talfryn's spine. It reminded him too much of his nightmares. Its uncanniness wasn't right. The creature dodged left.

So engrossed on the cobalus's eyes, Talfryn nearly missed Padric's signal. But Ulysses didn't. He plowed ahead, yanking Talfryn after him. They tore through the camp, Talfryn shouting whatever came to mind at the top of his lungs. Trying to keep up with a fast, leaping peryton was no light feat.

But Talfryn did it.

For all of five seconds.

Then his blanket, which had entwined itself around his ankle, got caught on a log. Down Talfryn went, dragging the net and Ulysses with him. Ulysses's antlers pitched, and he pivoted out of control.

Talfryn rolled and rolled, the blanket tearing to pieces. The net curled itself around and around him. Someone released a high-pitched scream. Suddenly, a set of glowing yellow eyes stared into his own.

Talfryn shrieked.

The little cobalus shrieked.

They were on a collision course with the blazing campfire!

CHAPTER 27

*P*adric saw the whole thing unfold before his eyes. He ground his feet into the earth to switch directions. In a second, he transformed into a faun and dashed after them. Dodging blankets and cookware, he reached for the net, but it recoiled out of his reach.

"*Pater,*" Gregorio cried in horror.

Net completely entangled in his antlers, Ulysses swerved in a panic. Screaming, Talfryn and the cobalus pitched toward the fire. Rawlins and Aeron halted in front of the burning logs, arms and legs braced. As one, they grabbed the net and yanked. They lost their footing for a step, but gained it again. At last, Padric got his hands on it. Together, they hauled Ulysses to a stop. The peryton staggered. His long, white wings fluttered at his sides, keeping him upright.

Padric returned to his human form, a wave of relief flooding his veins. "That could have gone better."

Rawlins materialized by his shoulder. "I'll say."

"*Pater,*" Gregorio repeated. This time his legs brought him to his furry parent, avoiding getting swatted by the large, white wings.

The net bulged as its inhabitants struggled.

"Lemme outa here!" came a scratchy voice from within.

"Arghh," Talfryn cried. "Did you just *bite* me?"

Feeling at his sides for a blade, Padric huffed. "A knife, please, before Talfryn gets eaten."

Crouching, Aeron flipped a dagger from his belt and sawed at the net.

By now, a thin, red ribbon streaked across the horizon. While his knights helped with the net, and Lenore picked up the disheveled camp, Padric danced over to Ulysses, his majestic antlers looking like the victims of a disastrous laundry line run-in. His expression was that of utter discomfiture. Padric would have asked the peryton what happened, but the poor creature was embarrassed enough as it was. Together with Gregorio, they made slow work of untangling his many-great grandfather's antlers while Aeron and Rawlins sawed at the netting below.

When at last the net fell apart, its reluctant inhabitants dashed their separate ways. Talfryn went right while the cobalus went left and toward freedom. If he had not been disoriented and run straight into Padric, he might have escaped.

Rawlins's nostrils flared as he reached out a hand to Talfryn. "That was a perfectly good net. Now it's ruined."

"It was. A little too good, I reckon." Talfryn glanced at Aeron. "Since I'm so *poor*, I'll have the cobalus buy you two new ones."

"Just one bite of stew?"

Pleading eyes regarded Padric through a filthy layer of grime. Arms folded across his chest, Padric kept his eyes on the cobalus and attempted to look bored. The last thing he wished the creature to know was how fast his heart raced, craving to retrieve information from him in quick fashion. "Not until you give us your name and the reason you have been spying on us and stealing our supplies. You give us something, we give you something. One for one. That is how it works."

The little fellow squirmed on the ground, surrounded by three armed knights, a farmer, a scholar, and a peryton with intimidating antlers. Despite this, he ogled the steaming stew pot as Gregorio stirred the contents, the delicious flavors wafting to the creature. Padric's stomach reminded him how hungry he was. This was another new quality of Gregorio's. He cooked nearly as well as Brynwen. Alas, food would have to wait until they received answers from the creature.

"Rawlins, did he have anything on him?"

The sergeant rummaged through the confiscated bag and paused, a smirk lighting up his face. "Well, well, look what we have here." He held up a comb made of bone.

Aeron gasped, took the three steps to Rawlins, and snatched the comb from his fingers. He scowled at the cobalus.

"Not much else," Rawlins said. "Just a dull knife, some hare pelts, this hole-ridden blanket, a few pieces of women's jewelry, some food crumbs, likely our journey cakes from yesterday. And this." He raised a small, plain metal ring.

"That is mine, good sir." Lenore's eyes lit up, the first Padric had ever seen them so. She held her hands out as though imploring the knight to relinquish a precious, holy relic.

Taken aback, the knight made a slight bow. "Of course, m'lady." He surrendered the ring to her with some reverence.

"We had no idea it was missing, m'lady." Aeron bowed as well. "Please forgive our oversight."

"Please," Padric replied as well.

Lenore studied the piece of metal with thoughtfulness, caressing its cool surface. "I thought it lost. It was given to me by my husband upon our nuptials, and I've never removed it. When I lost it, I feared the worst for him and our children." A tear trailed down her cheek. "But with its return, I have hope again. I thank you." Rawlins shifted his weight in discomfort under the intensity of her gaze. Without another word, she rose and paced away, kicking up mud as she sloshed to be by herself for a few minutes.

Rawlins was speechless.

The cobalus, on the other hand, looked somewhat green with the loss of his treasures.

Nevertheless, Padric spied the twinkle in his eye and gave pause. "Are you sure that is all? Check again."

And just like that, a few drops of sweat appeared on the captive's brow. After another few seconds, the tearing of fabric came from within the worn and crudely patched leather pack. Rawlins pulled out an item he had not expected to find on the creature's person.

"An old coin?" Aeron asked. "What are you planning on doing with that? You can't spend it here."

"That's mine!" The cobalus shouted. Teeth bared, he stretched his arms toward the coin. "Give it back!"

Keeping out of reach of the small arms, Padric accepted the coin from Rawlins and examined it, turning it about for study. Indeed, the metal was worn with the passage of hands and time. The profile of a man's face took up most of the space, with Latin words surrounding its margins. Unfortunately, they were worn as well. He related his findings to the others. Flipping it over, he studied it further. "A Roman Eagle. But it does not carry a laurel per usual. It is a…" Surprised, he flipped it over to the front once again. He could almost make out some of the letters. "D…I…"

"S," Gregorio said over his shoulder. He regarded the coin with greed —the greed of a scholar of history. "P-A-T-E…R."

"*Dis Pater*. So. The back is the Roman Eagle surrounded by some sort of treasure." A refreshed excitement flooded Padric's veins. *Please be the key*, he prayed. *Please.* "What can you tell us about this coin, cobalus?"

Silence.

"Well?"

A loud growl emitted from the cobalus's stomach.

"Suit yourself. My friend Gregorio has outdone himself in preparing a fine meal for us. But, alas, we only share with those who choose to cooperate." Padric nodded for Gregorio to dish out portions to the rest of the company. The tutor-turned-cook eagerly set about filling bowls, not wishing to miss a moment of the proceedings.

The wooden bowls passed by the cobalus's nose, his dark eyes following each bowl as it made its way to a different member of the company, drool slipping out of his mouth, until the very last dish passed him by and was set on the ground for Ulysses to enjoy. The goblin-faced creature's face crinkled in dismay. It was then Padric noted how young the creature looked. And thin. He could not help but wonder how long he had resided in the marsh by himself.

Padric bowed his head with the others to say grace over their meal. When taking his first bite of the savory rabbit stew, the herbs and spices complementing each other, Padric was increasingly thankful Brynwen had shared some of her cooking secrets with Gregorio. Otherwise, they might have starved to death by now. Nevertheless, he would be *more* thankful once she sat beside him again. He said an extra prayer to protect her from harm.

"Ombag."

"Beg par-on?" Talfryn asked, mouth full of food.

"Ombag. I'm Ombag," the cobalus said.

"Ombag," Padric repeated, testing the name on his lips between bites of well-seasoned stew. He finished swallowing. "What can you tell us about this coin?"

Glancing both ways, Ombag plunged into his explanation. "Found it in a deserted camp on th'other side of the marsh. Thought it was nice an' could use it for somethin'."

"But why'd you take my comb?" Aeron asked with little mirth.

"My back." Ombag lifted his hand over his head then moved it in an up and downward motion.

Padric sighed inwardly. "Aeron, focus." He returned his own focus to Ombag. "Deserted? Are you not affiliated with another group of cobali headed by a cloaked leader?"

The hungry cobalus shook his head. "I heard 'em, but didn't see no one take the family. I stayed out of sight and came in for prizes and vittles afterward."

Padric sized up the small creature once more. Yes, he was different than the other cobali they had met in the cavern. Of this he discerned no lie. Another look at Ombag's belongings gave Padric all the information he needed. He met Rawlins's gaze. His friend had come to the same conclusion. He returned his attention to their guest with renewed interest. "I see. The cobali we encountered before worked in a group. Your belongings are threadbare, and you are starving, yet the cave to the underground kingdom is not terribly far away. Thus, I must ask, why are you on your own?"

Ombag's eyes narrowed. "'Cos I'm a loner, that's why. No one ter tell me what to do or nothin'."

"It's more than that, though, isn't it?" Rawlins drawled. Suddenly, he stood next to Ombag. The raggedy creature cringed when the knight's shadow spilled over him.

"Wha—whaddaya mean?" Ombag's voice shook.

Aeron smiled. "He means you were ousted from your clan."

"You know," Talfryn said, "chucked out. Tossed to the wayside."

"Did you court the wrong maiden?"

"Or did you eat the wrong fellow's lunch one too many times? Because that happens sometimes." Talfryn nodded knowingly.

"Gentlemen, gentlemen," Padric interrupted. "We do not need to know why he was expelled from the caverns." Ombag's expression lifted in relief. "Nay, we merely wish him to lead us into the cavern and retrieve what was taken from us."

Ombag's breath hitched and all the color drained from his round face. "Nuh, uh. I ain't going back down there. Never again. No…" He trailed off as Rawlins placed his hands on his hips, the very stance Talfryn so endearingly termed: the stance of casual death.

Padric considered their guest. Threatening Ombag would only get them so far, so what else would he want? "Ombag, I will make a bargain with you."

The word "bargain" caught Ombag's attention. His head whipped around fast enough to cause whiplash. "Bargain? What sorta bargain?"

"Food for as long as you are with us. Relative safety in our numbers until you lead us to *Dis Pater*. Afterward, you are free to go where you will."

"That's all?" Ombag demanded. "If I'm ta risk my life going into the king's realm, it'll take more'n that to tempt me."

"What else is of worth to you?"

Despite the darkness, Ombag's gaze perused what he could see of the camp, surrounded as he was by men and a peryton. At last, his gaze landed on Padric's chest, and his eyes sparked. He nodded. "The trinket 'round your neck'll do."

Furrowing his brow, Padric put a hand to his chest and touched the cool metal against his fingertips. His Saint Christopher medal—a new one his mother had given him before leaving on this journey, with a fine chain as well. Astonished at learning of his losing the original one in the river on his previous adventure, his mother procured a new one for him and had it blessed by the priest at Saint Mary's church. Padric could not help but wonder with a smile if she had a stash of them hidden in her hope chest to give out at a moment's notice.

Hand clasping the gift, a desire to refuse flushed up Padric's neck. *What would he do with such a prize?* But, he realized, she would rather he gave it up than fail his mission. "This is all you desire?"

"Aye."

With heavy heart, he unclamped the chain and held it out to Ombag. "I charge you to keep this safe. It is a saint and will bless your journey with good travels."

"Yeah, yeah, I know all about Saint Christopher. My pa had a whole cache of 'em in a box, hoping to get a good deal for 'em someday. Heh, might've found one by now if it weren't for...Anyway, this is what I want."

"Very good, it is yours," Padric said. "Ulysses will take Lenore to Malham and return by nightfall. At first light, we will all go to the cave."

Ombag's Adam's apple trembled, but he kept Padric's gaze.

Talfryn beamed at Padric in heartfelt thanks.

Be strong, Bryn. We are coming!

CHAPTER 28

$\mathcal{P}$adric swallowed his irritation.

"It's right around here, I know it," Ombag said.

"You said that before. I am positive we passed this way earlier." They had walked nearly six miles around several cave systems and seven false openings. Everything looked familiar at this point.

"I stopped counting after the fourth time," Talfryn interjected.

Ombag bristled. "It's been a while since I was here, all right?

"We're lost, aren't we?" Aeron grumbled.

"No, no." The cobalus's eyes darted about the rocks in all directions. "It's here, I promise. The opening is a particular stone. We just need to… ah ha! There it is, over there. There's a gray stone jutting out by that fifteen-foot rock wall. Press that, and you're in." He scooted behind a large boulder next to a clump of tall, wily shrubs.

"You are *sure* this is the place? Ombag, why are you hiding?" An eerie feeling came over Padric. He pulled on his bow.

The cobalus nodded, his brows furrowed in deep rivulets. "Look, I showed you where to get in. Can I go now?" He spun around, ready to dash out of their circle.

"Not so fast." Aeron and Rawlins barred his way, their weapons drawn, dwarfing the cobalus with their great size. Ulysses sidled up next to them. Ombag cowered at his presence, holding his hand up in defense.

They all moved behind the rocks and shrubs.

Without removing his gaze from the cobalus, Padric spoke to the peryton. "Ulysses, watch the wall for us a moment."

The peryton complied, peeking his antlered head over the short rock wall.

"Our deal was for you to lead us to *Dis Pater*," Padric said, "not to the impassable wall where he may or may not be hiding. The longer we linger, the more danger Brynwen and Payla could be in. We have a mission, of which they are an essential part." The last thing he wanted to do was plead with the creature. Would that it never got to that point.

Ombag muttered under his breath.

"What was that?" Padric asked, unable to understand the garbled speech.

"If we go down there, we'll all be dead in no time."

"What do you mean?"

"Well, actually, we might die *before* we go down there."

"Ombag." Padric pinched his nose, feeling the headache coming on. "Speak plainly. I hope you are not trying to get us killed."

"Look, his Kingship has it out for me, and since he didn't help you out th'other day, he's likely got it out for you lot, too. Ya see, if the king took her, he's probably taken what he wants from her. She's a goner now. 'Side's, he's got the entrance watched."

"Why did you not mention all this sooner?" Gregorio asked.

"You know how the sayin' goes. 'Habits die like strangled hens.'"

Talfryn shook his head, the squirrel bobbing on his shoulder. "That's not a saying."

A shock of ice struck Padric's heart as he pictured *Dis Pater* piercing Brynwen's heart with a sword. It took every ounce of strength to take the next breath. "Why would he want to kill her? She has no possessions he could hope to gain. No dowry. Unless…"

Unless he wants the stone of adamant as well.

The agony must have surfaced on Padric's face, for Ombag's mouth screwed up. "Does she mean that much t'you?"

Talfryn nudged his way forward and rescued Padric from answering. "She's my sister. That stinker took her from me, and I want her back." The fingers on his good hand clenched into a fist.

Ombag fell silent for several excruciating seconds, seemingly thinking it over. At last, he looked up. "Fine, a deal's a deal. If the king needs her, she might have a chance for a while." *But I'm not very hopeful,* his expression said.

"Once we deal with the guards." Teeth clenched, Talfryn removed the hatchet from his belt.

"Well, yeah."

"How many?" Padric asked.

"Five or six?" Aeron said.

"Eight," Rawlins said. "There are two up top."

Padric nodded. "And we are outnumbered."

Talfryn squeezed himself between two rocks, hatchet at the ready. He waited for the signal at the top of the rock wall for Rawlins and Ombag to appear. It was Gregorio who had the genius idea of the knight taking Ombag up top, all invisible—it would be good practice of Rawlins's ability. It took everything in Talfryn not to chortle when the deadly fighter had to bend down to hold hands with the cobalus. Then they vanished from sight.

The cramped quarters were less than ideal while Talfryn counted the seconds with a little ditty he'd made up and studied the legionaries, as Padric and Gregorio called them. They wore leather and plate metal over black tunics that reached down to their knees. Their bronze helmets had what appeared to be a red broom at the top. He could imagine Brynwen sweeping the cottage floor with such a silly hat. One might call their outfits comical if they weren't standing completely still and serious and deadly.

"Hey, how did you get up here?" said a male voice from above.

"You!" shouted another. "You shouldn't be here."

Talfryn strained but couldn't catch the next part of the dialogue until it got really interesting. "Whoa, where'd *you* come from? I—ahh!" Scrambling, shouting, and the clank of metal on metal ensued. Three more legionaries had already begun their ascent up to their fellow soldiers' aid.

Now all that remained were the three on the ground. Padric, Aeron, and Talfryn rushed them. Talfryn was more of a distraction as the other two tussled with them a bit before knocking them out. In the meantime, Talfryn untangled the rope to tie up and gag them and set them to the side of the invisible entrance.

In no time, they were standing in front of the so-called entrance.

"Ombag," Padric said, "will you do the honors?"

For a moment, the cobalus hesitated. Finally, he nodded and stepped on a generic-looking rock near the wall.

The instant Ombag's foot touched the stone, a shimmering light emanated from it. The ground shook. Small rocks, pebbles, and dust fell from the rock face onto them, coating them all in a fine light brown dusting. Blinking particles out of his eyes, Padric tried not to sneeze. Talfryn sneezed in his stead.

Aeron snarled, brushing off his once-cream colored tunic, but a large brown smear was left behind. "This tunic was expensive."

Talfryn chuckled as he dusted off his own clothes. "And now it's a very expensive rag."

"Come now." Padric tossed unlit torches from the ground to Aeron and Rawlins. He lit his torch from a brazier on the rock wall. "There is no time to waste. You will be leading us, Master Ombag."

"Lucky me," Ombag replied wearily.

CHAPTER 29

"$\mathscr{H}$old still."

"I am holding still. Your hands are shaking."

"Well, *you* should be the one holding this tiny needle, not *me*. Why didn't you dodge the knife?"

"I didn't even see him stab me."

A little bit before, Brynwen had awoken on the cot in Payla's small two-room apartment which she had procured from a landlord. Side screaming in pain, Brynwen found the horned immortal rummaging through her satchel for ointments to stop the bleeding. Payla's face paled when Brynwen mentioned they would need a needle and thread.

She'd been very lucky. The glass jar of lavender balm in her satchel had deflected Glop's blow from going more than an inch into her side. Miraculously, none of the glass shards ended up in her wound, either. Unfortunately, the jar of lavender balm would never be the same, nor the bloodstains on her satchel and clothes, but they could be mended.

"All right, all right." Payla spoke between clenched teeth. "When this is over, I am teaching you defensive moves."

Brynwen nodded. Since their return from their adventure at Circe's and Helius's home, Padric had promised to teach her more defensive moves. He'd taught her a couple of simple things, but she'd yet to really practice them. Time always seemed to escape their grasp. "Yes, please."

"Brace yourself."

The needle punctured her skin, and the acute pain made Brynwen nauseated and light-headed. The strong smell from the Miracle Mix plus alcohol wafting up from the wound didn't help either.

If Payla didn't kill her with the stitches first.

When it was over, Brynwen's side smarting, she studied her friend's handiwork. The stitches weren't quite straight, but they weren't terrible, either. "It's different being on this side of the needle."

"More painful, too, isn't it?" Payla gave her a wink.

"Quite."

"I can imagine. I have only had to sew up a comrade a couple of times, but that was over a thousand years ago. You could say I'm a bit rusty."

Brynwen observed the tiny room, filled with a short cot against one wall, a stove against another, one door, and a small dirty window. The wooden table with four mismatched chairs where she and Payla sat was in the center of the room. Next to the bed she spied the basket filled with balls of thread from the day before. And she noticed a cloth covering a round object that might be the communication orb.

Several questions popped into her head, but with an inner sigh, she pushed them aside for a later time. For now, she had important matters to discuss, and then she needed to return to her work in the herbarium. They were probably missing her by now.

"Payla, how does the portal that brought us here work?" She had wanted to ask Magician Ulrich if he could make one for her to contact Gregorio and Ulysses but hadn't had the chance. Not knowing what happened to Talfryn and the knights was slowly killing her.

"I don't pretend to know exactly how portals work; but it is like a door made of magic. When he—I assume *Dis Pater* or one in his employ pulled you through the portal, he essentially pulled you from one room to another via a magical pathway. I wasn't thinking when I leapt in. But when I came through, I didn't have a hand to hold, so it dropped me directly into a fountain in the center of Rellea. I'm just glad it was not in the ocean or some terrible hole in the ground."

"I see." It made some sense, but it was still a lot for Brynwen to take in. "Like the smoke Circe and Helius use to go from one place to another."

"That is precisely right."

"Well, I'm glad you're here all the same."

"Me too. So," Payla said, "have you a cure for the poison yet?"

Brynwen released a huff, which pinched her stitches. "Not at all. It's monkshood poison. Every time we think we've got a breakthrough, it doesn't quite work out. At least, not for long. We are rapidly running out of ideas and time. King Morfrey is desperate to find the culprit to prevent a second attempt."

Payla nodded. "I had heard King Morfrey II was the ruler now."

"Do you know him?" Brynwen asked.

"I met him once, long ago, but he wasn't known as *Dis Pater* then." Payla rubbed her face with her hands and stood up to pace around the small room, lost in either thought or memory. Her horns glinted in the lamplight.

"He isn't quite what I had pictured a king to be." Especially when she'd thought King Morfrey would throw his master healer into the dungeon for a rather hasty remark, but didn't.

"The original *Dis Pater* was his father. My mother and I met him and Morfrey millennia ago. The king was shorter and very clever. The earth's treasures were his specialty, and he knew where all the richest deposits of jewels were. My mother heard a rumor once that *Dis Pater* made some sort of deal with the genius architect Daedalus to help keep his riches safe.

Daedalus? I've heard that name before, but where? "If *Dis Pater*, the first, is immortal, how did he die?"

Payla shrugged. "I have heard much since arriving here. The official word around Rellea is that he just…vanished, leaving Morfrey in charge. He isn't as ambitious as his father was. In fact, Morfrey was originally against moving underground. I don't think he liked what the search for riches did to his father. The *Stripes and Curls* shopkeeper has all sorts of theories as to what happened to *Dis Pater.*"

This perked Brynwen's interest. "Oh? Like what?"

"Well…you should really hear them for yourself. Some are quite interesting."

Maybe even something about the Druid and why he wants me. "May I speak with her?"

"I think that can be arranged."

"Perfect! But first, I need a small favor. Can you…" Taking a deep breath, her heart ached with grief as she removed *On Healing and Other Remedies* from her satchel, fingers clutching it for dear life. "…hide this for me?"

CHAPTER 30

So it happened that Payla, armed to the teeth under her cloak, guided Brynwen back through the streets to the market and the *Stripes and Curls* shop without incident. The satchel hanging around Brynwen's shoulder felt too light, every step a reminder of the book's absence. She wished she had something to dull the ache in her side too.

Outside the door, she spied the familiar metal engraving of a bull's head surrounded by lines next to the door frame. Before clutching the handle, Payla fingered the design with thoughtful strokes. Taking a deep breath, she pulled the door open.

Brynwen wanted to ask about the engraving, but something in Payla's face stilled her. She'd ask later.

When they entered the shop, the older matron brightened when she saw Payla, who had bought the balls of thread the day before. She opened her well of whispers willingly. She looked like a human with greenish-white hair, but there was something different about her eyes. The irises were too blue.

"Oh, aye, his Majesty is kind. His father a'fore him weren't bad, but he were very demanding. So, many of us worked in the mines or refined minerals and gems.

"That sounds rough," Brynwen said.

"Aye, but he protected us—him and his legion—from enemies. Gave us homes. Livelihoods. Well, the saying goes 'round two hundred year ago, he—er, the miners—found somethin'. Somethin' he'd been searching for too many years to count."

"What did they find?" Brynwen asked.

The shopkeeper shrugged. "'T'were immediately hidden and locked away. But some say a shiny gem or some'at."

Shiny gem? Brynwen's heart doubled its pacing as the prophecy raced through her brain. She turned to Payla. "Could it be a stone, by chance?"

Payla's expression brightened.

"Aye." The matron nodded. "It could. After that, *Dis Pater* became more reclusive. That's when his son took over, mind. Then, fifty years ago, the precious item were stolen, and the ol' king tore the palace and city up looking for the culprit. Found him and punished him, he did.

"'T'were peaceful for many a year. Not long ago, though, the ol' king disappeared. Some say he's locked in the tallest tower o' the palace, others that he went down to the Builder's Realm and ne'er came out again. Others say he tired of life underground and went up top. My mam thinks he was so old, he died in his sleep and turned to ash."

A shiver rode up Brynwen's spine, thinking about turning to ash and dust.

"What do you think happened to him and the gem?" Payla asked.

The shopkeeper shrugged. "Oh, well, no one ever asks what I think." Brynwen raised a brow in disbelief. "It's hard t'say. But I think he tired of all the responsibility for so long."

"I see. Who is the Builder?"

"Daedalus!" Payla said, triumphant. The shopkeeper nodded. "Forgive me, I met him once. His inventions were quite clever. But Brynwen, your, ah, verses. Daedalus built this fantastic maze called the Labyrinth."

Beneath the depths, a kingdom's plight
Paths run with nary a light.

Dawning fell on Brynwen. "Also called a 'nexus.' The old king found the stone of—" Payla gave her a warning look. "Or gem or whatever it was"—she said hurriedly to cover her tracks—"and placed it in the Labyrinth."

"Which is exactly what our *friend* is looking for."

'Friend' wasn't at all what Brynwen would call the Druid.

"The Labyrinth is below Rellea," the shopkeeper said. "That's where *Dis Pater* sentenced the thief."

Brynwen tried to imagine a huge maze somewhere below their feet. They were already so far underground—how could there be more open space below? It wasn't so long ago when her only concerns were growing herbs, making salves, and tending to patients. *How did my life come to this?*

Tugging on Payla's sleeve, she pulled the maiden to the side and lowered her voice. "Now I suppose I know why he wants me. But I don't know what exactly the verses mean, especially the curse."

"Mayhap," Payla said, "the stone of adamant is cursed. It would explain why *Dis Pater I* became miserly, and why he hid it away in the Labyrinth."

A new excitement bubbled up in Brynwen's chest. Finally, something constructive. *Find the adamant to end the curse.* "We must get into the Labyrinth."

However, instead of excitement, Payla's face lost its parlor. Retreating a step in the cramped store, her back pressed against a stack of boxes. They teetered, but when she stepped forward again, they righted themselves.

"That'll be hard," the shopkeeper said.

Brynwen and Payla whipped their heads around. The older woman gave a sad smile. "Forgive me, I didn't mean to pry. But the entrance has been hidden for over two hundred years—except for maybe the current king, no one seems to remember where it is, least of all me. But no one ever asks my opinion."

"Thank you for the information." Payla flipped the shopkeeper a coin and grabbed Brynwen's arm to steer her out of the door. "We must go."

CHAPTER 31

alfryn and the others waited with excruciating anxiety for Aeron and Ombag to return from their scouting mission of the opening into *Dis Pater's* underground city. They'd descended what seemed about twenty miles underground, although Gregorio surmised it was only about seven or eight. *Whatever.* His feet hurt from the hard packed rock and dirt of the winding cave tunnel; his forehead still smarted from smacking it on way too many low ceilings in the dark. He was hungry and had new respect for the scary-crazy Rawlins. The knight had delighted too much in sneaking up on a second set of unsuspecting guards and rendering them unconscious.

Note: Never become Rawlins's enemy. As long as he and Eliva never gang up on me, I'll be fine. Right?

On the positive side, it distracted him from his throbbing shoulder. Also, his worry that Miser might get lost in the dark.

Finally, Aeron and Ombag returned to Talfryn's great relief.

Aeron began speaking the moment he reached them. "Like Ombag said, Rellea is a big city. And it's remarkably bright, as though the sun were shining!" His eyes shone in awe. "The entrance has a ramp with many layers that go down and down to the base of the city. At the bottom, we spied a pair of legionary guards."

186

Ombag nodded soberly. "From what I remember, the guards change post twice a day. At sun-up and at sundown."

Raising his hand to his chin, Padric set his mouth in a straight line. "This is a problem, but not unforeseen. We knew it wouldn't be easy. How can you tell when the sun sets down here? We are miles underground."

"Gets as dark down here as the upper world," Ombag replied. "There's a sorta sun and moon, which make day and night look just like above ground, but that's about it. The king's magicians can't make stars very well, so they gave up on that centuries ago."

"That is something. I do not suppose there is any cover on the way down the ramp."

"None whatever," Aeron said.

"This will take some thinking. Ombag, when does the sun set?"

"Same time as upper world, so anyone goin' up won't get confused. My great gran'pop once told me of a time when it once got outta whack—"

"That's enough." Rawlins leaned over Ombag in his 'casual death' pose, with arms folded over his chest and several days' stubble adding to the intimidating effect. The cobalus clamped his mouth shut. "'At's better," Rawlins muttered and leaned back against the wall.

Gregorio held one of his maps under a torch, squinting at the open page. "It should not be too difficult to figure out. Let us see, we entered the cave at one hour after noon, and we descended roughly seven miles in the dark with torches..."

Padric sat in silence to listen while Rawlins and Aeron murmured about the weapons and such they missed at home. This interested Talfryn, but he didn't think they'd appreciate his thoughts on the subject.

As he waited, Talfryn became antsy, shaking his leg to have something to do. Having only one good arm didn't help his anxiety. This could be their only chance at rescuing Brynwen and Payla. Maybe they'd already escaped and found the prophesied adamant stone.

Absentmindedly, his hand reached into his saddle bag, rummaging for a snack to settle his nerves.

"Are you going to eat all that?" Ombag asked beside him.

Talfryn eyed the sliver of journey cake that had appeared as if by magic in his hand. "Umm, I guess not." He held it out to Ombag, who tore off a couple bites' worth. The cobalus munched noisily, but it didn't bother Talfryn one bit. Living in a house filled with mostly menfolk, he was used to it, and couldn't help but chuckle whenever his brother Samuel's betrothed, Edina, came over for a meal and scrunched her nose at them. Ah, those were the days!

"Why're you here?" Ombag said, spluttering crumbs all over his lap.

"I'm going to save my sister and friend. Why else would I be here?" Talfryn asked, indignation growing in his throat.

"No, no, I mean, why're you here with this." He pointed at Talfryn's arm in the sling. "You can't fight in that, if it comes to it."

"I can, and I will. Maybe I won't be as good, but I can still wield a hatchet with the rest of them." *I won't be left behind.*

"Huh, we'll see."

"You've got all the charm of a stoat, you know that?" Talfryn asked with a half grin. He took a bite of the cake, leftover from yesterday's meal, and savored it on his tongue. Not quite as good as Brynwen's, but Gregorio had a knack for cooking and baking. Changing the subject, he asked, "What can you tell me about the peoples of Rellea?"

Ombag gave him a quick census of the populace, of the types of humans and creatures who were found there, the economy, and a few more things he couldn't help speaking about. Everyone in the cave stopped what they were doing to listen.

"Will they recognize you when we get into the city?" Gregorio asked.

"It's been almost fifty years, but a cousin or two'd know me. But if we keep to the back streets and shadows we might sneak by."

Talfryn nearly choked on his journey cake. He beat his chest a couple times to clear his airway. "Fifty years? How old are you?" He didn't look much over twenty-five.

"Near sixty-five, but I'm pretty young for a cobalus. We can live close to three hundred years."

"Isn't that something?" Talfryn asked, feeling old for the first time in his life. "Fifty years is a long time to stay on the moors. You know, people think it's haunted."

"Haha," Ombag laughed. "Serve's 'em right. Makes it too easy to steal out there. It's not an easy place to live, that's for sure."

"How'd you end up in the moors anyhow?" Talfryn had been dying to ask this question ever since he'd met the creature.

The cobalus's face crumpled.

"Never mind," Talfryn said. "Forget it."

"Nah. I've held it in so long, it's just..." He cleared his throat. "Ya see, my pop was a master thief. 'Ombag the Pilferer' they called him. He'd steal from anyone, all challenges accepted. Taught me, he did. Well, one o' his more shady friends thought it'd be right hilarious to dare him to steal somethin' from the king, a large and shiny gem *Dis Pater*'d been hoarding for centuries. He and Pop shook hands, all cocky like, and the next night he took me with 'im to get it. Well, he didn't know security'd been updated. After snatching the goods, we got out. But it were a trap. Pop got caught. I ran for a bit, and then all this guilt and gumption came o'er me. I turned back, but by then they'd dragged him off. I got my mam and two lil' sisters outta Rellea and hid in the moors."

A pang of sadness for the little thief overcame Talfryn. "What happened to them?"

"I heard the king was so upset, he sent Pop into the Labyrinth. Mam died of a broken heart after a couple of years. My sisters ran off once they were old enough to make better lives. I thought maybe I could get Pop outta the Labyrinth someday but was too scared to go back." He hung his head in shame.

"Maybe *Dis Pater*'ll have forgotten by now," Talfryn said.

"Huh. You don't know *Dis Pater* a'tall, do you?"

AFTER WITNESSING the cobalus do some sleight of hand to annoy Miser, Talfryn begged him to reveal his secrets. Unsuccessful at trying to present indifference, it was clear Ombag relished showing Talfryn a few of the basics. The creature'd had little in the way of company for a very long time.

After a bit, Padric took a brief trip to the entrance into Rellea. Upon his return, he knelt in front of the cobalus. "Ombag, will you do one more favor for me?"

"Oh, no. I've already dared life and limb for you lot. I'm not doing it again."

"I understand." He bade them all follow him to the entrance. "Rawlins, can you make us all invisible and remain so long enough to get to the bottom?" Until now, the knight hadn't made anyone other than Ombag invisible, and that was only for a few minutes.

Remaining in the shadows, Rawlins studied the ramp and guards below. He nodded. "I can do it."

When twilight hit, Padric instructed Rawlins to turn invisible. The knight stood ready, face intent. But nothing happened.

"What is wrong?" Padric asked with a frown.

"Mayhap he can't do it while we watch?" Talfryn noted.

Rawlins's chilling frown fell on the farmer, his deadliness sweeping over his body. "That's not it. It's harder to work down here. Hold on." Closing his eyes and setting his jaw, after a few seconds he finally began to fade and blend in with the rock wall behind him, clothes and all. Talfryn had to blink a couple of times to make sure what he saw was real. He'd seen the knight practice disappearing a few times over the past several days but witnessing it in the dark was something else.

Before he disappeared completely, Padric gave a grim smile and lunged for Rawlins's arm. Immediately, he began to fade. "It is working. Quick, everyone—take each other's arms."

Talfryn, Gregorio, Aeron, and Ombag grabbed hold of each other and formed a chain. At the end, Ulysses grazed against Aeron. Talfryn expected some sort of tingling or other feeling, but nothing came, other than that he couldn't really see the others, just a halo outlining each of their bodies. "Woah. How did you know that'd work?"

"'Twas but a guess and a hope," Padric said.

"I have found that is a normal occurrence in magic," Gregorio said.

"Enough prattle. Let's go. I can't hold this all night, you know."

"By all means, lead the way," Padric said.

They tamped out their torches and laid them to the side of the tunnel. It got dark quickly, the only light coming from the entrance.

At first, they traveled slowly, concentrating on keeping a hold of each other's hands. Soon, the easy slope of the ramp loosened their trepidation, making their descent tick up to a foot race.

As they moved down, Talfryn got a few good glances of the city before them. Never had he seen buildings so close together and piled on top of one another. He bet they'd look more impressive during the daylight. At the far end, possibly one to two miles away, stood the palace with turrets and towers.

As silent as could be, they descended to the lowest level to within ten feet of the legionary guards without incident. Even though it was getting dark, Talfryn noticed the livery of the guards was black instead of the faded red ones in the Druid's group several days ago.

His thoughts were interrupted when Gregorio's foot accidentally nudged a small stone, and it skipped a couple of feet down the ramp. Suddenly, the guard on the left side of the road shot to attention and spun around. Everyone in the invisible group halted and held their breath. Talfryn's heart thundered in his chest as he reached for his hatchet.

"Did you hear that?" The guard squinted up at them, nose scrunched.

His partner likewise stood to attention and looked around with a shrug. "I didn't hear nuthin'. Prob'ly yer belly growling again."

"Hmm," the first one grumbled. He patted his stomach as if that'd make it quiet. "Could be, I s'pose. It's almost mealtime."

"I reckon you're right." Both cobali returned to face forward at their posts.

After a couple minutes, Talfryn felt the familiar tug on his arm to continue. He steadied his breathing as much as possible, but his heart would have none of it. It wasn't until they miraculously passed the guards, so close Talfryn could tickle either one's nose should he have chosen to, that he began to breathe easier.

Five steps away.

Fifteen steps away.

A tiny celebration went off in Talfryn's head. *We did it!*

Then, a loud, echoing noise emanated from the tunnel they'd just come through.

"Keep going," Padric instructed in a whisper.

"Intruders, intruders!" came a voice, echoing throughout the whole cavern. A small creature came into view—another cobalus. "Intruders in the cave!" he shouted again, hands cupped around his mouth.

Rawlins led them two more steps before the shouting began in earnest. Gregorio turned to him with wide eyes. That was when Talfryn realized they weren't invisible anymore.

Padric unsheathed his sword. "Into the city. Hurry!"

Aaron glared at Rawlins. "You didn't hit those guards hard enough."

Rawlins glared back as he drew his weapons. "We were in a hurry, all right?"

"Can we argue later?" Talfryn dared a glance backward. The guards gave chase at once.

"Please," Gregorio replied. He retrieved the glass orb from his pack. He muttered some Latin at it. It had just begun to glow with clouds spinning around inside when he spoke urgently. "Payla?"

Ombag wailed, scrambling on his shorter legs. "I'm going to die."

All semblance of order broke as Talfryn followed the others into the city, his shoulder jarring with each step, but the pain quickly became undermined by his will to survive.

"Halt in the name of the king!"

Yep, Talfryn thought, *we'll stop because you asked so nicely, and then we can have afternoon tea and become fast friends.*

Gregorio glanced over his shoulder. "Payla, I hope you can hear me…"

They plunged into the city with little effort, eliciting strange looks from citizens of all shapes, races, and sizes. Talfryn paid little attention as he ran for his life, keeping up with the others.

A few steps ahead, a terrified Ombag stumbled. He would've fallen had Talfryn not caught his tunic and shoved him along.

They turned down a side street, the legionaries a few paces behind. Talfryn thought they'd lost them when they turned a corner and a group of five more happened to be walking their way. They pivoted down one side street, then another. Market stalls flew past, and Talfryn had to dodge a screaming, goose-wielding matron. At one point, he thought he spotted Payla's dark cape. The shouting and patter of feet grew louder, and he quickly forgot about Payla.

After walking down dark tunnels for miles and miles, then running through the city streets, Talfryn was getting weary, when suddenly they came to a screeching halt. At least a dozen legionaries, consisting of cobali, nymphs, fauns, and many other creatures Talfryn hadn't ever seen before, barred the way, their shiny coats of the king's blue and cudgels gleaming in their hands. From behind, the uniformed soldiers halted.

They were surrounded.

CHAPTER 32

Stationing himself in front of Gregorio and Ombag, Padric considered their less-than-ideal odds. The other two knights imitated their lieutenant and formed a sort of circle to shield the others. Their last ill-fated encounter with a band of creatures soured Padric's stomach; their only saving grace now being more possible escape routes.

Talfryn, hatchet in hand, was the first to speak, with a wide grin on his face. "Well, fellas, I must say this is the biggest welcoming party we've ever received. I'm touched."

An impressive centaur with long, brown hair braided down his back stepped forward, a gold badge pinned to his tunic under his left clavicle. "Lay down your arms and you won't be harmed."

Padric cocked an eyebrow. "Is this how you treat guests of your fine city?"

"Invited guests don't sneak into cities unannounced," the leader reasoned.

Touché.

"We may have been invited in if someone had but asked. May I inquire to whom I am addressing?"

"I am Aanx, Tribune of the Fourth Cohort. We have you surrounded. You will put down your weapons and come with us, now."

Cohort? Padric held in his grimace. He knew if they surrendered to Aanx now, he would throw them all into prison or the dungeon for an interminable time. It would make their chances of rescuing Brynwen infinitely harder. Let alone finding the prophesied stone of adamant before Janus did.

"Ombag?" One cobalus soldier of lesser rank stepped forward, his expression one of indecision. "Ombag, is that you?"

"Ombag, the Pilferer of Rellea?" Aanx made no attempt to hide his disgust.

The weight of the soldier's admission seemed to have sunk in, and he shook his head. "This is his son, Sir: Ombag the Younger. I thought… well, I thought he was dead. And he's not at all like his—"

"So." The leader's head swiveled back to Ombag, who was trying to hide behind Rawlins, and studied him. "The Pilferer's exiled son has returned. The king will enjoy this happy reunion." He said *happy* with all the joy of a cat pouncing on a cornered mouse. "Hand him over, and the king might consider leniency toward you and the rest of your group."

"Ah, now I see why you didn't wanna come back," Talfryn said.

This was becoming disastrous. Padric refrained from grating his teeth in frustration. A slight movement from above caught his attention. Taking a quick glance in its direction, he espied a tall, hooded figure on the roof of a one-story home, the mysterious "daylight" reflecting off a familiar thin dagger. "Forgive me, Captain Aanx, but I do not care for these terms."

Aanx shrugged and a grin slid up his face. "Those are the only terms, take them or face the consequences."

"Well, then." Padric tightened the grip on his sword handle. "I choose neither. We simply cannot obey your terms. As much as it pains us to decline the invitation of staying in your fine cells, our friend must remain with us."

At that moment, Payla flipped into their midst to land in a crouch.

Padric reached behind to grab Gregorio's arm and launched toward the closest alley. Without a hitch, Payla's long legs pounded the pavement. Behind them, Rawlins caught up Ombag; Talfryn, Aeron, and Ulysses followed. The peryton spread his wings in an upward swoop, batting the forward legionnaires. They stumbled backward into their comrades with angry shouts.

Padric and his friends crashed through the surprised soldiers as though playing a game of Red Rover.

Following Payla, Padric kept his grip on Gregorio, praying they could keep up with the maiden's long legs. Behind them, Aanx bellowed orders at his soldiers. "Capture them! I want them alive!"

Padric wheeled left, then made a quick right. Aanx's men were relentless in their pursuit.

"Where are we going?" Padric asked Payla.

She pointed straight ahead, finger crooking to the right. She continued at a race, turning right, then another left down a side street. Fewer footsteps pounded after them. After a couple more course changes, Padric was completely turned around. But at least none of the soldiers had kept up.

"Padric," Gregorio huffed, a pace behind him. "I am spent."

Head drooping, Talfryn waned as well. Even Padric felt the muscles in his calf tighten.

"Payla, are we near somewhere safe?" Padric asked. "Not everyone can keep this marathon pace."

The cloaked maiden slowed to a jog and peered around her hood. "Two more blocks." Then she bounded off again.

"City blocks," Ombag whined.

Steeling himself, Padric lunged forward for—hopefully—the last dash.

Rounding another corner, Payla charged straight for a wall at the end of an alley.

Padric's breath hitched. "Payla!"

But she leapt through what appeared to be a curtain. Momentum too fast, Padric barreled through the opening and collided into Payla. They flew across the room, over a table, and rolled thrice on the floor before crashing into the wall.

Dazed, Padric blinked a couple of times before the world stopped spinning. At last, he glanced up into a pair of deep sapphire eyes. Eyes just like Circe's. He could not catch a breath.

"Are you all right?" she asked, swiping back her hood to reveal her curved horns.

He wheezed. "Your elbow…is on my chest."

"Oh, forgive me."

With ginger movements, she withdrew her elbow from his sternum, and Padric sucked in a welcoming deep breath. "Thanks." As he did so, he took quick study of the room he had crashed into. It was a sparse apartment, with a small bed in the corner and a window with a thick gray curtain pulled all the way across letting in the barest crack of light. A table knocked on its side lay beside two fallen wooden chairs. A cupboard and a small unlit hearth finished up the room's contents. Talfryn and Gregorio were sprawled on the floor gasping for air while veryone else had either sagged against a wall or chair.

Study complete, Padric drew his attention back to Payla. "You came at just the right time." He rubbed at the new sore spot on his chest.

She grinned and held up her orb. "Thanks to a direct request from my favorite cousin."

From the floor, Gregorio gave a weak wave of acknowledgement.

"Where are Franco and his family?" Payla asked.

Aeron clenched his fists and glared at the immortal. "We could have used your help in the cavern. Now our tracker is gone."

"Oh." The skin of Payla's face became drawn. Then she scowled, showing her teeth. "I trusted you to help them."

From the floor, Gregorio cleared his throat. "Calm down, little cousin. They rescued Lenore, but the Druid and his minions captured Franco and the children. We surmise the Druid wants his tracking skills if he cannot have Brynwen."

Jaw clenched, Payla regarded the group, her gaze resting last on Aeron. "I knew she needed aid, so I made a choice."

Talfryn sat up. "Have you been in touch with her? How is she?"

"She is fine, Talfryn. A bit preoccupied with her task of finding a cure for the townsfolk, but otherwise she is well."

"So, she is not a prisoner, then." Much of the weight of uncertainty surrounding Brynwen's fate released from his shoulders.

"That is correct." She explained Brynwen's part in researching the cure for monkshood poisoning as well as their encounter with the rogue cobali in the alley.

Padric frowned at the cobali's failed kidnapping attempt. "So, the Druid does still need her. But whatever for?" *It is the never-ending question!* He gave Payla a summary of what had happened since their separation and introduced Ombag.

Aeron cleared his throat. "I'm sure Ombag, Son of the Pilferer, knows a way to help rescue Brynwen."

The cobalus crossed his arms in a huff. "Nope, nope, nope, I'm done, I say. No more." With that, he turned around and faced the wall.

"Why not ask *Dis Pater* to release her?" Talfryn asked. He shifted and winced, trying to get comfortable.

"We are not exactly on friendly terms with the local constabulary," Padric reminded him. "Although...what of that cobalus legionary? He seemed to know Ombag."

"Sounds like a long shot," Rawlins muttered.

"We've got to try something." Talfryn tried to stand and failed. He plopped back down on his bottom.

Rawlins growled. "Not like that yer not."

"Rawlins." Padric gave him a dirty look.

Gregorio and Payla came to Talfryn's side. The horned maiden studied his arm. "What is wrong with it, Talfryn?"

Glad of the distraction from the tension in the room, Padric gave an inward breath of relief.

"Dislocated," Talfryn's face had paled and sweat covered his forehead. "I don't think the run did it any good."

"It wouldn't, no," Payla said. "May I?"

Talfryn nodded, and she unwound the bandage with careful movements. Brows furrowed in concentration, she felt a couple of spots with ginger fingers. "I think I can fix it."

Talfryn's face became pale to the point of green. "Ummm, have you done it before?"

Doubt rose in Padric's chest, remembering the clumsiness of the horned maiden when they had first met. He had seen a couple of successful and unsuccessful fixes of shoulder dislocation before and prayed this would be the former.

"Well, no, but I saw it done once or twice. Worst case, we would have to amputate."

"Right here." Gregorio pointed to his shoulder. Talfryn missed his wink.

"Nuh, uh. That gives me absolutely no confidence in—"

With one motion, Payla rotated his arm.

Crack!

"Owwwww! Oh my gosh, oh my gosh, oh my arm. I'll never plow another field again. I...wait..." Talfryn wiggled his arm a bit, his face radiating joyfulness. "Hey, that's better!"

"Looks like amputation is not needed after all, Tal." Padric smiled and clapped Payla on the shoulder. "Payla, I never doubted you."

THE SHADOW HAD HEARD the commotion of the knights entering the city. One could not miss it. Following the din, the Shadow located its protégé among de Clifton and his rabbles escaping a club-wielding group of legionaries. The Shadow made eye contact with the knight, who nodded without missing a step as he bolted from the legionaries.

Now, the Shadow waited in the dark recesses of the alley outside the lodging where they hid. When the "moon" moved directly overhead, the knight at last emerged. *"This way,"* the Shadow instructed, and the two traveled a safe distance down the alley.

"This will do."

The knight whispered his greeting. "Master, I don't have long. What news of the adamant?"

"It is as we suspected. The tracker is close to finding the second hidden entrance. Then we must deal with the adamant's guardian." Much to the

Shadow's delight, the tracker's children helped keep him especially motivated in finding the entrance.

The pupil's eyes glinted in eagerness. "Leave that part to me, Master." He rubbed his forearm absently—the one which the healer had sliced weeks ago. It still bothered him, whether physically or mentally, the Shadow knew nor cared not.

"As you wish, but do not dally."

"Yes, Master. I won't fail you."

"Now, before you go, there is one more thing you must do…"

CHAPTER 33

Brynwen paced her room. She knew such pacing might ruin the plush carpet, but she didn't care. Two problems stared her in the face. Their patients were dying one by one without a cure in sight, and she was no closer to finding the stone of adamant. The prophecy weighed on her like a sack of wheat, desperate to be solved. She was running out of time for both. *A happy prospect for such a day.* No amount of chamomile tea could untie all the knots in her stomach.

The last two nights, after leaving the herbarium feigning tiredness—which wasn't wholly untrue—she'd snuck out of the palace and made her way to Payla's accommodations to ask, nay, beg *On Healing* to cooperate and give her the antidote for monkshood. But each time, it had shown her the same exact answer, its most important ingredient, the caladrius.

Part of her wished Nessie the caladrius were here to help solve their plight. They'd only needed one of her tear drops. *One!* So much power wielded in such a tiny, winged body. The other half of her was glad the bird couldn't be used in that way. The poor creature was already doomed to live a solitary life because of her healing gifts and exploiting it would only doom her to a life of complete misery. Besides, Nessie's tears had a short time limit, and treating so many people would be nearly impossible. This way, Nessie was at least free—wasn't she?

Indeed, there was a good reason why the book should have been destroyed centuries ago.

"There must be something else I haven't tried. Some specific way I need to ask it. But what could it be?" she queried the room at large. She twirled her braid. "'I'm down to my last jar of oats,' as Mother would say."

Her conversation with the *Silks and Curls* shopkeeper came to mind, about *Dis Pater I* hoarding a gem. "Could it be the adamant the Druid is after?" she asked the book.

A knock came at the door. It had a specific rhythm. Stepping over to the painted door, Brynwen rapped a reply rhythm. She waited a couple of seconds for the third pattern. Once it completed, she turned the latch and grinned.

"Oh, good, I was afraid you'd forgotten the pattern." The princess strolled into her room like she owned the place—which, technically, she did.

"Well, I had a couple of times to practice, my princess."

"Indeed," she said, her voice proper like a queen. Then she broke out into hysterics and launched herself onto Brynwen's bed. She bounced on the soft mattress a handful of times.

The child's excitement was infectious, and all Brynwen's current worries melted away as she sat down beside the young maiden.

"Are you excited about my birthday celebration tonight?"

The short-lived happiness Brynwen had felt faded with the question. She wished it could be postponed until after the patients had been cured but couldn't bring herself to ruin the princess's day. *Perhaps we could all use a little celebration to cheer us up.* "I am thrilled to be invited, my princess. Cook says the most delicious dishes will be served."

Mandalin's eyes rolled with delight. "Oh, only the most scrumptious delicacies and cakes!"

The previous morning, on her visit to the market, she'd found a perfect pink ribbon for the princess's hair. It was short notice, but she hoped the spunky maiden liked it. As the princess sat on her bed,

Brynwen was glad the ribbon was hidden in the drawer by her bed. She just needed to wrap it in a bit of paper from the herbarium.

Bouncing some more, Mandalin asked, "What will you wear? Iaso is going to wear a new dress made specially for her, and she's very excited about it. Have you decided?"

"Oh," Brynwen said, taken aback. "I…hadn't thought to much about it. But there are a few pretty dresses in the trunk I might look at."

Before she had finished speaking, the princess leaped off the bed, scrambled to the brown chest in the corner, and flipped open the lid. It hit the wall with a thwack.

She lifted the top dress, a light green Brynwen had worn the day before, admiring its shape and embroidery. Then she tossed it onto the floor.

Brynwen balked and rushed toward the fallen dress. "My princess!" Before she could pick it up, a pink frock made its way to the ground. The third one, in brown, Brynwen managed to catch but the fourth landed in a wrinkled mess at her feet.

Steam just about exited from her ears. *Of all the childish things!* Brynwen bit back her grimace. These were the nicest clothes she'd ever had, and the princess was throwing them around like worthless rags. It would be a pain to refold and get them all to fit in the trunk nicely once again. "My princess, I appreciate your kind gesture and all, but I don't think—"

"Oooo. It's perfect. You will look *beautiful* in this one, I know it."

The princess held aloft a blue dress with lace up the wide flowing sleeves and edging the bodice. It was exquisite and must have cost the king a good sum of money. She didn't even remember seeing it in there before. "Where did this lovely dress come from?"

"It was at the very bottom. All you had to do was look."

"Well, yes, I suppose so…"

"You must try it on."

"I will, after I do some work."

"Nay, Brynwen. Now. Or I won't go to the party."

Brynwen regarded the princess with arched brow. "You would miss your own party because I didn't try this dress on right this minute? Isn't that a little dramatic, *my princess?*"

"Pleeeease." The princess squinted her eyes and scrunched her nose, trying to look as cute and innocent as possible.

She succeeded.

Chuckling, Brynwen finally gave in. "Fine, if you will—"

A knock came at the door.

"Now, who could that—"

"Enter," Mandalin sang out. A huge grin traveled from ear to ear.

In walked the faun and human maids Alta and Celta. They curtsied at Mandalin. Unfortunately, Brynwen still didn't know which maid was which.

Brynwen glanced from the maids to Mandalin. "Princess, what…"

"Alta and Celta, you know what to do. Go on, go on." Mandalin stuffed the blue outfit into the faun's hands and shoved Brynwen toward the changing screen in the corner.

As the human maid helped her into the chemise, the faun got the blue dress ready to slip over Brynwen's head.

"If it's not too forward, marm," the faun asked, "might I ask how the antidote is coming for the illnesses?" She raised the blue dress for Brynwen's arms to slide into. It sparkled as the light hit the shining threads and beads, dazzling Brynwen's eyes.

Once again, Brynwen lamented having to attend the party instead of working on the cure. "We learn a bit more every day," she replied as vaguely as possible. "Have you two had a chance to visit the patients?"

"We have indeed, marm," the human said. She tugged on the blue laces, making Brynwen gasp for breath. "Celta and I visit every day, when we get the chance."

Aha! That's where I'd seen them before. The first day, while Brynwen was meeting Wallace and the other patients, they were there along with Frania and some other servants and healers.

The faun maid fussed with buffing out any wrinkles in the dress. "My friend is a patient there. She's getting better, though. Perhaps you've met Vesta?"

Daggers of pain grated on Brynwen's ribs. Were these laces supposed to be so blasted tight?

"Oh, yes, she is so…sweet and…patient," Brynwen said between huffs of breath. "I am pleased with…her recovery." *Unlike some unfortunate souls who didn't make it.* Wallace's death still bothered her. She still couldn't believe she had been so wrong about his health. Perhaps there was another complication?

When Brynwen emerged from behind the changing screen minutes later, she paused. Surrounded by a rainbow of discarded dresses, Mandalin's eyes went round as saucers.

"Is it really that bad?"

"Not at all, Brynwen, it fits perfectly. You look beautiful." She continued to stare for another couple of moments. "All the lords and nobles will ask you to dance! Won't that be romantic?"

A flush of heat covered Brynwen's nose and neck. There was only one man she wanted to dance with, but alas, he wasn't here. "Well, my princess, now that's sorted, will you help me clean up this mess?"

"But that's what the maids are for. Besides, it's my birthday." Doe eyes met Brynwen's.

Ignoring the imploring orbs, Brynwen gave her the same pointed look she bestowed on difficult patients.

"Well, I suppose I could help a bit."

"Thank you."

Along with the maids, they picked up the dresses and figured out how to fold them. Meanwhile, Mandalin went on and on about her expectations of food and desserts for the party and how Alta and Celta would help with her hair and makeup.

Oh joy.

They were just about to lay the first dress in the bottom of the trunk when Brynwen noticed something on its inner wall. Leaning in closer, she made out a burnt picture, like a brand, no bigger than her forefinger. It was a crude circle with the familiar bull and horizontal and vertical lines. Just above the bull's head was a dot. Was it a mistake or a part of the design? She hadn't really paid attention to the other carvings she'd seen. "What is this symbol? I've seen it all over Rellea."

Mandalin gave it a cursory look. "Eh, it's nothing special. It's just the Minotaur in the Labyrinth."

"But why is it everywhere?"

"Father says my grandfather really liked him, and he is a great protector."

A great protector? "What is he protecting?"

"Not sure."

Another knock came at the door. "Princess, are you in there?" came a voice from the hallway. "It is time to dress for your birthday celebration. You don't wish to be late."

Before Brynwen could move, the human maid opened the door.

Mandalin's governess stood in the hallway, decked out in her black frock and lacy veil. Brynwen had seen her from afar, but this was the first time she had seen her in person. Kind, familiar eyes met hers.

Glancing down at the matron's hands, Brynwen gasped. She knew those hands. Hands wracked with arthritis. "Nettle, beeswax, rosemary, and peppermint oil."

"What?" the matron asked.

"The ointment I gave you for your hands a couple of weeks ago. You wore a veil like this and came with Aesculapius and Iaso. Merta?" *Was that her name?*

The matron smiled as though approving of a smart pupil. "Very good, Miss Brynwen. It is regretful we did not officially meet until now, but I had other concerns to care for." Merta patted Brynwen's hand, her smile blossoming and making her aged face look twenty years younger. "We all thank you for coming, and I know you shan't let us down." She turned toward her young charge. "Come on, my dear, so you'll be ready for your party."

Mandalin pouted but left with the Matron with little fuss.

"Mistress," the human maid said, sizing up Brynwen's long auburn tresses. She opened a small cabinet on the small table by the window. "Please sit. This may take a while."

❧

Borrowed hood shading his face, Talfryn turned the worn latch to Payla's apartment. The meager food from his sack wafted up to his nostrils, causing his stomach to groan. It being late in the day, the market had been picked over. All his disappointment was mirrored on Gregorio's face. *When was the last time we ate anything of substance?*

Entering, Ulysses paced the small apartment, his wings folded tight and antlers scratching against the walls. Payla and the three knights stood huddled in the corner of her apartment, out of Ulysses's way, deep in discussion. She'd gone on another errand at the same time as them but had returned first. In that time, the others had gotten cleaned up from their trek in through the cave.

The frown on Rawlins's and Aeron's faces summed up their conversation.

Near them on the floor sat Ombag, knees up against his chest.

The peryton noticed Talfryn and Gregorio enter and greeted them with relief on his face.

"It's good to see you, too, buddy." Talfryn patted the stag's thick neck, narrowly missing an antler to the eye. Twice.

After greeting his furry father, Gregorio set his half-filled bags on the table against the wall. "The market was pretty scarce, it being the end of the day, but we found some food."

Talfryn set his meager bags next to the others. "It's also the princess's birthday feast tonight. Who knew *Dis Pater* had a daughter?" It wasn't something he'd really thought about. Then again, most monarchs had families, didn't they?

"He would have had more," Payla said, "but his wife died in childbirth to their only surviving daughter. He has yet to find a new queen, if he so desires one."

Before heading to the market, Payla had told them about the reigning *Dis Pater,* King Morfrey II, being the son of the original, and that he guarded the labyrinth beneath the city. It didn't settle in Talfryn's stomach that they'd have a feast while lots of people were ill or dying from an incurable poison.

Gregorio began to unpack the fresh supplies and raised a shoulder to his chin. "Yes, well, when you live in a hidden underground city, your choices are limited."

Grunts of agreement sounded around the room.

"Well, miladdos." Talfryn sat down in a rickety chair. He still couldn't get over how much better his shoulder felt, despite the incessant ache and being tucked into the sling. *How can I ever repay Payla?* He turned to her. "Did you get us an audience with the king?"

A gray cloud shaded Payla's expression. "Nay. He is too busy to see anyone, even a priestess of the Temple of Mithras." She sounded indignant, as though priestesses of Mithras were some sort of higher nobility.

His heart sank. It was their best chance at seeing Brynwen. "That's too bad. Do you have another cunning plan yet?"

A silent look passed between the three knights and Payla. Padric answered. "It is the bones of an idea. Two of the three people we need are in the palace. *Dis Pater* to open the Labyrinth for us, and Brynwen, to find the stone of adamant in said Labyrinth. Ombag is here with us."

Rawlins leaned against the wall, hands close to his weapons. "Why d'you think he'll be any use to us? I say we let the little squirt go. He's nought but trouble."

"He is the son of the Pilferer. A pilferer would be useful on this occasion."

"Yes." Realization dawned on Payla's face. "Ombag is a pilferer like his father. Ombag the Elder would have taught his son everything he knew about stealing."

Rawlins shook his head. "He's not a very good thief. Got caught. Like father, like son."

"I heard that," Ombag objected.

"But it's true, ain't it?"

The cobalus crumpled. "Aye, it's true."

"But what did you and your pop pilfer?" Talfryn asked.

All eyes fell on Ombag. He bristled under their scrutiny, but he rolled his shoulders backward. "We stole a gem; the brightest an' best of the king's collection. Straight outta his vault. No one'd done that a'fore."

Gregorio shook his head. "I daresay not. The gem was never found?"

"Never." Payla's nostrils flared. "I think the Pilferer somehow took it with him when they threw him into the Labyrinth for punishment."

"Sneaky old man," Aeron said.

"We must go into the Labyrinth to retrieve the adamant. Ombag, will you help us reclaim what you and your father stole?"

Talfryn's eyes shone with respect for the situation. "Then you can pilfer from the Pilferer."

"Indeed." Padric chuckled. Then his smile dropped. "We must keep it from the Druid at all costs."

A frown marred Gregorio's studious face. "If we are not too late already."

Aeron's forehead scrunched in thought as he tapped his chin with his forefinger. "That's all well and good and all, but how do you know Ombag will be able to find it? Or that he'll want to help us?"

"I do not. But our options are finite, and the prophecy states an ally will guide us. Ombag, you could right the wrong of your family and make peace with the king. You could be free."

Rawlins frowned. Any mention of the prophecy, Talfryn noticed, seemed to make the knight uncomfortable. Not exactly like Talfryn loved being told to get a bunch of stuff done or else it's the end of the world, either. Rawlins regarded the cobalus in challenge. "Nah, I don't think he has it in him. He'd rather save his own hide than help the likes of us."

Ombag sat quietly on the floor, seemingly ignoring the conversation revolving around him. Talfryn couldn't help but wonder if the little fellow *was* the "ally" from the prophecy. Without him, though, they were kind of in a rough spot. However, that prospect wasn't looking too good right now.

"Anyway," Padric continued, "our best route—"

"Our only route," Rawlins muttered.

Padric gave him the side eye. "Right, our *only* route is to enter the palace during the feast."

To their great surprise, Ombag leapt to his feet, chest puffed out, his face all smiles. "And I'm the only one here who can break us in."

hy is this so heavy? Brynwen strained her muscles to scoot the heavy oaken chair closer to the long table of the banquet room until a male servant standing behind her in full livery took pity on her and pushed it in the rest of the way.

"Thank you." She was most grateful. It might have taken her the entire evening to pull the chair on her own and earned her several snickers.

He gave her a brief, silent nod before returning to his post.

Now, she was able to observe her surroundings. She had entered the room with Iaso and Aesculapius, but they had been escorted by a servant to the head table, while another guided her to the next table over. To her surprise, he placed her next to Ulrich, the magician who had made the portal to bring her there. Most of the seats were occupied, but the king and princess had yet to arrive.

The enormous chandelier at the center of the room was lit with hundreds of beeswax candles. Gilt plates, goblets, spoons, and knives rested in front of each diner, polished to reflect the light. Servants filled goblets before anyone asked for refreshment. She noticed Alta and Celta had been pulled into filling goblets, too. "This is quite elegant," she noted.

"Indeed." Magician Ulrich's grin reached from ear to ear. "The fête for Princess Mandalin is always a grand affair. Everyone looks forward to it all year."

"I can imagine."

They spoke for a few minutes while more guests entered. A lovely couple in complementing outfits sat across from them and joined in the conversation of bats amassing further into the caves when the trumpets blasted into the "less grand" ballroom.

A more regal sound Brynwen had never heard. Everyone stood. It was all Brynwen could do not to step on her new dress and fall flat on her face as she got to her feet. The kind servant helped with her chair again.

In strolled an imposing figure in livery, his face a full measure of decorum. In a loud voice he announced, "All hail, His Majesty, King Morfrey Richall the second, king of Rellea, and Her Royal Highness, Princess Mandalin Richall of Rellea."

King Morfrey entered with the princess's shorter arm curled through his. She was all smiles, practically bounding in. They were resplendent in complimenting colors of satin, he in royal blue and she in a dark pink gown. Pinned to her dress was a brooch of brilliant cerulean. Brynwen could tell signs of the king trying to look straight ahead and at the same time restrain his excited daughter. All the while, Brynwen noticed his gaze teetering in Iaso's direction. The pair made it to their seats without a hitch, with Aesculapius to her right and another noblewoman to his left. Everyone clapped their hands with great enthusiasm.

After a few seconds, the king regained his feet, and all fell silent. He peered around the room once before centering his gaze. "My dearest friends, thank you all for coming to this most anticipated event for our dear Princess Mandalin. While we are saddened that not all of our friends and brethren could be here with us this night, we shall keep them in our thoughts and prayers. Tonight, our princess's greatest wish is that we dine not in her honor, but in theirs."

A tear threatened to slide down Brynwen's cheek, likely ruining her face powder, but she didn't care. A pang of guilt pressed against her chest. *I should be helping our patients instead of sitting here.* Her gaze made its way to the head table where the other two healers sat. A pained expression pinched Iaso's face, but Aesculapius seemed nonplussed and took a long sip of wine.

King Morfrey raised his goblet. "To Princess Mandalin!"

"To the Princess!" all voices exclaimed. Goblets rose in the air, some sloshing their contents all over their arms and the table.

Almost immediately, the first course arrived: bowls of pottage. The kind Brynwen's family ate was made with vegetables such as cabbage, leeks, onions, garlic, and herbs from the garden. Sometimes they used carrots. This, however, Brynwen could only guess was frumenty. Her friend Isemay once explained to her that the richer stew included sugar, saffron, almonds, currants, meat, and eggs. As Brynwen brought the first bite of pottage to her mouth, her taste buds went wild with pleasure. It was rich, salty, and sweet, and she relished each flavor with delight. *Perhaps I can buy some of these ingredients from the Wilmots' cook. It would likely take a whole month's pay of midwifery and healing.*

They were just tucking into the second course of roasted wild boar when a commotion arose from outside the room. The tall oaken doors burst open with a crash.

Gasps and a few screams rent the air. King Morfrey shot to his feet, the tablecloth he'd been using as a napkin jerked up with him, dumping his roast boar onto the table and tipping over his goblet. Red wine spilled and stained the cloth near Mandalin's plate, then dribbled onto the floor. One pitcher in each hand, Alta, the human servant, was in the midst of filling the princess's small goblet. When the commotion began, she raised the pitcher.

The clattering of feet entered the room, though no one was there. From the hallway, palace guards ran to the hall, and two of the guards inside the ballroom moved toward the door. However, the doors began to close on their own and shut the guards out.

What's going on? Brynwen thought her heart would burst like the doors as dread flooded her veins.

"Papá!" Mandalin cried. She lunged for his arm in pure terror.

CHAPTER 35

"Now," Padric said.

When all the palace's kitchen staff had gone about their own tasks with attention drawn away from the enormous roast boar, Padric lifted the front of the platter. Talfryn, Gregorio, and Aeron took up the other ends. Donning borrowed servant wear from a cupboard and aprons hanging from hooks near the door—and without anyone so much as raising an eyebrow—they carried the boar from the chaotic kitchen and followed a handful of servants toting two more boars and heavy pitchers of what Padric expected was the king's near-best wine.

Somewhere behind, Ulysses, Payla, Ombag, and Rawlins stalked after them in the shadows. Surprisingly, the secret entrance Ombag had found paid off. No guards stood near it, and it took little to jiggle the lock. Depending on how things went, he would advise the king to make the entrance more secure in the future.

Delicious smells of the boar wafted up to Padric's nose. Mouth stuffed with an apple and surrounded by fruit baked with cinnamon and sugar, the meat made his mouth water. They could not arrive at the feast soon enough, especially for Gregorio, who labored under the meat's weight. Aeron muttered under his breath. Padric thought he discerned grumbling bits of either "It couldn't have been a pheasant," or "I'm dressed like a peasant."

No one batted an eye when they placed the boar on the table of honor and backed up like the others. Better yet, not one person seemed to notice when they did not return to the kitchen with the other boar-bearers.

As servers sliced into the meat for the first course, Padric studied King Morfrey. His appearance did not meet the expectations one would surmise of a "Rich King." On the contrary, while his clothes were well tailored and of the finest quality, they were not excessive in the least. Padric assumed the young maiden wearing a tiara beside the king was his daughter, Mandalin. She bore the same dark hair and complexion as her father. Eight guards and fifteen servants were stationed in strategic locations around the ballroom. Last, but certainly not least, he scanned the sizable room for Brynwen. Little hope did he have that she would be here, as she was vital in aiding the ailing Relleans. He planned on demanding the king take him to her. So, when Talfryn indicated his sister sat in a seat close to the head table, he would have disbanded his post had it not been for Gregorio's staying hand.

"You two shall reunite soon, my friend," Gregorio whispered.

Padric was about to protest when he spotted her head bobbing in conversation with her neighbor.

It was only for a moment's glance before she disappeared behind another, but it was enough. His heart leapt with joy and relief surged through his veins. Besides her hair style, he couldn't quite place what was different about her, but she was as beautiful as he had ever seen her. The temptation to shrug off Gregorio and leave his post on the wall grappled with his sense of duty.

Aeron seemed to sense Padric's emotions and cocked his head toward him. "Our friends will be here soon."

Ah, yes. And with that, he resolved to stay put—although he glared at Aeron first. In a few minutes, if all went well, they would approach *Dis Pater* and plead their case. *And take Brynwen with us.*

"I know a few of these nobles," Gregorio said. "It has been years since I saw any of them last. But I wonder how they came to be in Rellea."

"Would they recognize you?" Having Rawlins and Payla carry their weapons might have negative consequences if anyone recognized them now.

"I am not sure."

A sudden commotion emanated from the hallway. Shouts and the clash of steel.

"Get ready," Padric said. Nonchalantly, he withdrew the knife from his boot. Aeron and Talfryn mirrored him while Gregorio extricated a large tome from his satchel. "*Signore,* what do you plan to do with that? Read them into submission?"

"Sleeping spell?" Talfryn offered.

The tutor shrugged. "Bash some heads?"

Padric grinned. "Works for me."

From the hallway, the ruckus of palace guards grew louder. Two of the guards inside the ballroom moved toward the door.

Talfryn leaned forward with a smirk on his face. "Guess it's plan B, then."

Padric grimaced. "I would expect no less from Rawlins."

Before they could reach them, the thick doors began to close on their own.

A blur of brown and white soared through the door. Screams erupted in the room as it flew around the tables once before slowing down to descend.

"Now!" Padric cried. As one, the group dashed toward the closing doors.

The next instant, Rawlins, Payla, and Ombag materialized before the barrier, weapons in hand. Together, they made a formidable trio. They tossed gleaming weapons at their friends. Padric grinned wide as he once more gripped his sword, bow, and quiver.

White wings spread aloft, Ulysses landed with all the grace of a prince of stags.

The music stopped.

"Your highness," Padric began.

However, he was forced to pause his entreaty as the guards rushed at them with weapons high. Metal clashed against metal. Ulysses generated formidable gusts of wind against two foes with his great wings.

Despite their efforts, though, they were backed into the door and surrounded. At last, they surrendered their weapons to the stone floor. However, no one said anything about removing the other daggers from their boots.

"Who are you?" demanded the king. Power radiated off him.

Quip ready, Padric stepped forward to answer when Brynwen stood, her chair scraping against the smooth stone of the floor. Her expression was one of elation, relief, and astonishment.

All the air fled from his lungs as Padric beheld his maiden transformed into a goddess. The cobalt blue of her dress hugged her body in ways he had never before seen. Her hair was piled high atop her head and adorned with white beads. So struck, he could neither move nor speak.

"Your Majesty, we are travelers." Gregorio's voice changed from his normal studious tone to one of practiced courtesy and charm as he stepped next to Padric. "Come on a mission most urgent from Derbyshire. We apologize most humbly for this irregular intrusion, but we implore your help. I am Telegonus, son of Ulysses of Ithaca and Circe, at your service." Despite his lanky figure, he bowed low with great poise. When he righted himself, he bestowed the family seal from his blue bag and indicated toward the others. "These are my companions."

Dis Pater regarded them with stern severity. "Why would the son of Circe seek my aide when she is in the upper world? And why is there a peryton in my ballroom?"

A few snickers arose in the air.

"It is a matter we wish to confide in private, your Majesty. This peryton is an important member of our party."

"So, you thought it best to break into my palace, steal my servants' clothes, and pass yourselves off as staff. Who is to say you are not the perpetrators who came to thwart the people of my city?" A vein looked about to burst in the king's temple as he stared angrily at them.

He thinks we poisoned the townsfolk?

"Guards, take them away."

"Stop!" Brynwen dashed around her table, down the center aisle, and halted in front of the group, arms held out wide as though she could protect them with her body. "Your Majesty, please, these are my friends. They mean you no harm."

Padric reached for her arm so he could pull her behind him. "Brynwen, what are you—"

"Do not touch her," a guard said. "Miss, I suggest you remove to your seat at once."

Padric's hand froze.

"Papá, why are these men intruding on my party?" The princess's small hand grasped the king's sleeve. She looked near to tears. When she turned back to the intruders, a sudden smile brightened her cheeks. "Have they brought me a new pet, Papa?"

Mortification added to Padric's embarrassment. He had not meant it to go this way one bit, ruining a child's birthday celebration.

"They will go soon, my dear. I am afraid you cannot keep the peryton."

Brynwen fled to the king's table. "Your Majesty, please hear me. These are the friends who fought with me in the cavern the day you brought me here. They are brave and loyal, and would not dream of hurting you or the princess." She spun to look at them, her eyebrows furrowed in expectancy.

"Sire," Padric said with a bow. "Might we implore two minutes of your time to explain ourselves? Then if you do not believe us, you may do with us as you will." All hope rested on the king's being in a happy mood. Well, at least a temperate mood.

"Your Majesty." A beautiful young maiden with raven hair stood up from the head table. She seemed familiar somehow. "I believe Brynwen and these men. If they wished us harm, they might have done so already."

The king regarded the maiden, Brynwen, and the intruders, allowing three long beats of the heart to lapse before making his answer. "Very well. In light of my most trusted healers' requests, you may. But it had better be the most enlightening story I have ever heard, else you shall spend the rest of your days alternating between the stocks and the deepest part of the dungeon. Some of you, no doubt, will live a very, very long time in solitude and contemplation."

Padric nodded his thanks. *No pressure.* "You see, sire, we had no means of entry. For weeks have we searched for your beauteous underground city. My kinswoman, the Priestess Payla of the Temple of Mithras, petitioned for an interview with you but was denied. Our options and time were limited, sire."

"And you are?"

He bowed low. "Sir Padric de Clifton of Derbyshire. These are my fellow knights: Sir Aeron Drefan, Sir Ranulf Rawlins, Talfryn Masson, brother to Brynwen Masson, and Ombag the Younger." Lying about Ombag's name would help no one since he was known in Rellea.

The king flinched with a start at Ombag's name, but he did not interrupt.

"Telegonus and Payla, you know. And this," Padric said, regarding the peryton, "is Ulysses of Ithaca." Padric had almost forgotten his title.

Dis Pater raised an eyebrow in interest. "*The* Ulysses of Ithaca? I thought you would be taller." The hint of humor raised his lip a fraction. Some nervous laughter followed from the tables.

"Yes, well," Padric continued, "I am sure you have heard of the trouble in northern Yorkshire at the solstice."

"Reports have come to me, yes. But I thought it was all wrapped up. Were my reports wrong?"

"Things can change quickly, unfortunately."

Hard eyes fell on Padric and his companions, resting longest on Ombag. "Guards, secure Ombag the Younger. The rest of you will follow me to discuss this in my private chambers." He bade the music to commence and the revelers continue to feast, as he would soon return. Lowering his head, he spoke some parting words to his daughter, who nodded soberly.

Half the guard formed around Padric, Brynwen, and their companions, and they followed *Dis Pater* out the door.

CHAPTER 36

*P*adric and the others filed into the alcove near the throne room. The clinking of Ombag's chains still echoed through the halls, even though he had stopped moving since entering the room. Scanning the space, Padric discovered it to be a sitting room filled with two long couches, a table, and chairs carved with scenes from Roman mythology. Murals lined the walls depicting the Minotaur in various parts of the Iliad. Above the grand fireplace, hung an emblem with a Minotaur and some parallel and perpendicular lines. A circular dot filled the center.

Dis Pater closed the doors behind him. Only two of his most trusted guards stood by with raised pikes. "In truth, we had expected you to arrive long ago if you had survived the cave-in. However, the last few days have been hectic. I might have apologized for the inconvenience had you not broken into my palace. Impressive but unwise. Now, tell me everything."

Padric tore his gaze from Brynwen to regard the ruler. Gone was the angry facade of the king in the ballroom, replaced by a man suffering great stress. It made sense to Padric that there were two kings. *Dis Pater,* the hard-handed ruler of Rellea, and Morfrey, the man, almost human. A father.

Padric relinquished the first part of the story to Brynwen. She explained Janus's treachery, the prophecy, the curse in Rellea, the adamant, and their encounter with the Druid in the cavern.

Next, Padric explained how their guide, Franco, and his children had been abducted by the Druid and his band of cobali. "We believe the adamant is in the Labyrinth. We must go there to retrieve it before they do."

"How many entrances to the Labyrinth are there?" Gregorio asked.

"My father only divulged one entrance, although there is rumor of another nearby. There are more hidden around the world."

The tutor scratched his chin in thought. "Then they may already have a head start since they have Franco."

"Yes, *Dis Pater*." Padric folded his arms over his chest. "That is why we need Ombag to guide us."

The king winced and scoffed. "First, you may call me 'Your Highness, Sire, or King Morfrey. *Dis Pater* was my father's title. Second, the son of the Pilferer? Not happening. No one from that family was ever permitted to set foot in Rellea again. He has crossed the barrier, and for that he will pay the consequences."

Talfryn gulped. "Wha—what is that?"

"Execution first thing on the morrow."

Talfryn gasped in dismay.

Gregorio set a comforting hand on Talfryn's shoulder but spoke to the king. "Was that not more than fifty years ago, Your Majesty? Ombag was but a child. May we not bargain for his life?"

"I am sorry, but I cannot. My father made the decree, and I cannot break it."

"But why is what they stole so special?" Brynwen asked.

"And why is the punishment so harsh?" Padric added.

King Morfrey's hands fidgeted before him until he clasped them together. "In all honesty, I do not know. My father refused to tell me why it meant so much to him. We do not even know how it came to be in our mountains. But it did something to him. When we found it two hundred and fifty years ago, he disengaged from all but me. He became a recluse. Fifty years ago, when Ombag the Elder and Younger stole the priceless gem from our vault, he went mad with rage. My Legionary captured the Pilferer, but his son escaped. My father sent the little thief into the Labyrinth as punishment—and sealed him in with the Minotaur. The gem was never found."

Helius's bout of madness began over two hundred and years ago as well, Padric thought. *Could it be a coincidence?*

The king continued. "Afterward, he banished Ombag's family from Rellea, never to return below ground. The first person of his bloodline to do so would die. He signed the decree with his own blood; that is how sincere he was."

"Since your father's gone, though, can't you change the decree?" Payla asked.

The king shook his head. "I am afraid it is final. If you wish to pay your final respects to the prisoner, you should do so tonight."

Ombag's knees trembled. Somehow, the little fellow was keeping it together fairly well.

"But," Padric protested, "we need him to retrieve the adamant before the Druid reaches it."

"Ah. That is where you are wrong. They shall not reach it."

Payla wrung her hands, her hip bumping into a chair hard enough to tip it onto two legs before righting itself.

"With Franco's gift of tracking, the Druid may already have a head start."

King Morfrey crossed his arms. "I very much doubt it."

"What do you mean?"

"The labyrinth below the palace is guarded by the Minotaur. None shall get past him."

Hands frozen in front of her, Payla's breath caught. "Asterion?" Her hands resumed their agitation twofold. Forehead beaded with sweat, her hand accidentally knocked over a silver dish on a side table. Aeron rushed to her side before her knees could buckle.

"That is good news, isn't it?" Brynwen asked. "Your brother can help us protect it."

"Payla?" Padric's blood chilled by the immortal's reaction to her own brother's name. "What is wrong?"

A frantic knocking came at the door.

Morfrey scrunched his lips together in frustration. "Enter."

A legionary centaur popped his head into the room, his expression grim. "Sire, we have a problem. It is urgent."

"What is wrong?"

"Many of the guests have become ill, including the princess."

CHAPTER 37

They burst into the ballroom. The scene before them shocked Brynwen. Many people were doubled over in their seats, including Brynwen's table mate, Magician Ulrich. Others lay on the floor, moaning or unconscious. *Or dead*, Brynwen thought with a harsh breath. Everyone else screamed or ran around as though lost, begging anyone they found for help. All was chaos.

Brynwen stared at the scene, shattering her heart. "Not again." Suddenly, her dress's bindings felt too tight, the desire to swoon threatening to overtake her. She caught hold of the doorframe and took a deep breath.

"What's wrong with them?" Aeron asked.

"Monkshood, I'm sure of it." The poisoner had returned. Flashes of anger ripped through her, banishing her sadness. "It must stop."

"Bryn," Talfryn entreated her, "what can we do?" Padric and the others stood by, ready for orders.

Their confidence in her helped to mollify her clenched chest. "Help them into the infirmary in the ballroom next door as quickly as you can. In there." She nodded toward the exit across the way.

"On it."

She stopped at the sides of a few of the ailing people to ask for their complaints. To her utter dismay, they confirmed her fears of the poison. Unfortunately, she didn't have her satchel on her. It had taken great effort for Alta to persuade her keep it in her room before going to the celebration. "You won't need it tonight, Mistress," she'd said. "It's a party."

It was imperative to consult with Aesculapius and Iaso about their plan of action. They'd already used up most of their honey stores, and these patients seemed worse than their predecessors. A bit of luck struck when she spotted a familiar maid in a pristine apron.

"Frania!" She caught up to the frightened cobalus. The poor creature wrung her hands. "Frania, can you please run up to my room and bring my satchel?"

The maid nodded and smiled in thanks for having something to do. "Yes, mistress."

Brynwen got back to work.

"Brynwen!" The cry hailed above all others. The call came again before she located Iaso, waving at her in desperation.

"I'll return," she promised her current patient in a laced white dress with severe stomach pains.

When she saw King Morfrey holding his shaking daughter in his arms, the energy Brynwen had been using crashed into a stone wall. She fell to her knees beside the young maiden. Out of habit she studied Mandalin's pallidness and symptoms.

Complete despair crumpled the king. He looked thirty years older than he had a few minutes before. "Please, you must save her. I...I cannot lose her. She is all I have."

Her mind raced to discover how best to help intermixed with wondering what the book *On Healing and Other Remedies* would tell her now.

"We need to make more nektar," Iaso was saying. "It helped some last time."

Aesculapius wiped his head with a handkerchief. "Yes, but we are running low on honey."

"And it didn't work on everyone." Brynwen stood up. After a quick glance at the table, she found that the princess's goblet still had some liquid in it. The king's goblet, however, appeared untouched. She remembered seeing Alta, Celta, and the other servers refilling goblets right before Padric and company made their dramatic entrance. "When he'd launched to his feet, Morfrey had knocked the drink over toward Mandalin's plate." The goblet's contents would have been immediately replaced. Suspicion arose in Brynwen as she reached for the princess's goblet and brought it to her nose to sniff. Nothing. Next she regarded the plate. A couple of dried splotches of wine sat along the rim. Some of the wine had mixed with the juices from the boar meat. Scooping it up with a nearby spoon, she sniffed and wrinkled her nose. "Monkshood."

Iaso leaned in to waft the fragrance. "I concur, it is strong."

"Alta," Brynwen said in realization. "The servant Alta did this. She had two pitchers and poured drinks for the head table, one for Mandalin, and one for everyone else." Dread filled her stomach with bile as she realized Alta had been in the infirmary when Wallace wanted to tell her something important. Right before he died. "She may have killed a patient a few days ago, too." Alta had also persuaded Brynwen to keep her satchel in her bedroom.

"We must stop her," Iaso cried.

Just then, Alta came into the room from the infirmary.

"There she is." Iaso pointed at the maid. "Guards, stop her!"

Surprise registered on Alta's face as four guards surrounded her, their spears pointing at her middle.

Iaso came up to them. "She is responsible for the poisonings, captain," she told a guard with several pins on his left breast.

The captain nodded, never taking his eyes off the human maid. "You are wanted for questioning." He indicated the outer door with his spearhead. "This way."

"But...I..." All color drained from the maid's face, which had contorted in both confusion and terror. She bestowed Iaso with an imploring look, then her lost gaze fell on Brynwen.

The maid's woeful expression pierced Brynwen as the guards led her away. Guilt threatened to condemn Brynwen. *No,* she scolded herself. *Everything fits. This was right.*

"Thank goodness we found the culprit," Iaso said. "King Morfrey's guards will get a confession out of her. She shall not escape punishment."

Aesculapius sat down hard in his chair. Large drops of sweat adorned his forehead and cheeks.

"Master?" Brynwen said.

The old healer tried to chuckle and flinched instead. "It would appear they have poisoned me," he rasped.

"Not you, too." Brynwen closed her eyes, willing this day to end.

Iaso fussed over him until he raised a weak arm to block her. "Leave me be, child, and help the others. They…" His eyes rolled into the back of his head, and his face struck the table.

"*Pater!*" Iaso cried. She leaned over the slumped form of her father. His groans shook Brynwen to the core. "*Pater, Pater.*" Huge tears formed in her eyes as she raised them to Brynwen. "We must help him."

"We will." Brynwen placed a hand on her friend's shoulder. Her gaze fell on the remaining ill in the room, all hope hanging by a single thread. For a second, she thought of Gregorio's tale about Hercules and the Fates. Was this meant to be? Were they being punished for something?

No. We will help them all. God will help us. Somehow…

Think!

"I need the book," Brynwen muttered, wringing her finger in her hair until it hurt.

"What?" Iaso blinked back tears, snot pooling beneath her nose.

Talfryn and Payla came up and reached down to take Aesculapius to the next room.

Brynwen disliked repeating herself and said too loud, "I need *On Healing.*"

"You mean this one?" Payla hoisted a familiar tome from her small bag.

CHAPTER 38

$\mathcal{E}$yes growing wide, Brynwen's fingers moved toward it without thinking and caught it up, holding it with all the care a mother would her newborn. *I missed you so.* With a sigh she tore her gaze away from it. "How did you know to bring it?"

"I didn't. An impulse, as though Mithras were guiding my hand, made me get it for you."

Just then, Padric and Gregorio glided through the door. They saw the group and rushed over, their expressions revealing how bad the situation was in the other room.

She knew she must see the patients, but working out the antidote was imperative.

Iaso made to leave with her father, but her gaze landed on the book. Her body went rigid. Payla and Talfryn carried him without her. "What is *that* doing here? You said you would get rid of it."

"It doesn't matter now," Brynwen said. "Don't you see? The answer is in here—we just have to ask the right question."

"Nay—nay, I will not. This book is nothing but trouble."

"What is your quarrel with this book?" Padric asked. "Do you want to save your father and the princess?" Brynwen wanted to hug him for standing up for her.

"Because it was the downfall of my family." Brynwen, Gregorio, and Padric waited for more. "This book is filled with his earliest remedies. You can find anything you wish in here, yes?"

"Yes, well, almost." *Not the one I need the most right now.*

"You see, each remedy is teeming with all the power he received from his father Apollo. His very soul is in this book."

Gregorio's eyes widened in realization. "The book *is* his soul."

"At least part of his soul is, to my understanding. And then there is the adamant which enhanced his abilities."

Brynwen's ears perked. "Adamant? The diamond called adamant?"

"Yes. With it, he could cure anything, including manticore venom and the most vile of poisons."

"And Jupiter did not like it," Padric stated.

Iaso shook her head slowly. "Not one bit."

"Jupiter made you all forget, didn't he?" Gregorio nearly leapt in excitement. "That is why you have not been able to find the cure."

This time Iaso nodded. "He destroyed the book and the adamant—at least, he *said* he destroyed them. My entire family was forced to take a concentrated potion for forgetting. Most of our healing powers were lost except for the most basic remedies. We are shells of our former selves." A tear streamed down her cheek. "It was a very long time before I remembered any of the past myself, but I can still do very little to help anyone."

"That is awful." Brynwen shook her head. It was impossible to think of Jupiter removing everything she'd ever learned from her mother and the midwife, Rosa, in an instant. "You feared that if he saw the book, he might start using it again."

"Yes. *Pater* remembers very little from that time, and I wish to keep it that way. Not only that, but Jupiter warned us that if ever one of my family were to use the book again, he would find and kill us all. But now you have the book, Brynwen, and you can read it even though you do not know Latin. Do you know what that means?" She and Gregorio shared a look.

"You are Aesculapius's descendent." Gregorio nodded with a large smile. "Yes, yes. I see it now."

"Yes, and Jupiter could come after us here at any moment."

"We're related?" Brynwen couldn't hide her shock. She didn't know how to process that information.

Gregorio pulled a tome from his bag. "This is all very interesting. Years ago, I found an appended excerpt from *Naturalis Historia* by Pliny the Younger, hidden in a secret recess of the Library of Alexandria before it burned…"

"Signore, forgive me but we have little time," Padric reminded his tutor.

"Ah, forgive me." Gregorio opened the journal and thumbed to the page he wanted. "It spoke of one who had been called Hepius who possessed the stone of adamant, which augmented his healing to a godly level. With it, he wrote the codex *De Sanatione atque Aliorum Remediorum*, or *On Healing and Other Remedies.* His very soul poured out into the book. But when Jupiter put an end to Aesculapius's powers with the forgetting potion, he confiscated both the adamant and the book. Some sources say he destroyed them, but Pliny believed they were indestructible and merely hidden. My mother, Circe, received the book, but as far as I know, no one has ever found the adamant."

Iaso nodded grimly. "It is true, the adamant and *On Healing and other Remedies* are to be used together."

"A stone and a book." Brynwen's eyes skipped over the cramped script of the master tutor's journal and halted at the sketch in the corner. "Gregorio, what is this symbol?"

"The Labyrinth and the Minotaur? It is a symbol attributed to Daedalus. Because of him, the Minotaur had a place to reside and take sacrifices of the populace for decades. But I do not recall why I drew it."

"I've seen this symbol all around Rellea. But what is this dot above his head?"

Iaso stared at the dot in question. "Why, I always thought it was just a part of the design, and never really took notice of it before."

"I wonder." Gregorio tapped his chin in thought. "A stone?"

Padric raised his arms in frustration. "This has been very interesting, but what does it have to do with the book, the adamant, and the poison?"

> *...Beneath the depths, a kingdom's plight*
> *Paths run with nary a light.*
>
> *...*
>
> *Find the adamant to end the curse...*

Brynwen shook her head, trying to shake the meddlesome prophecy away from her thoughts. *Why does it always come at the most inopportune time? Unless...*

"Wait." An idea came to her. She picked up *On Healing and Other Remedies.* "'Find the adamant to end the curse.' What if...what if the prophecy doesn't refer to Janus at all, but to the Relleans' ailment? 'Curse' could mean poison, couldn't it?" Opening the book to the first page, she concentrated her thoughts on curing the princess and turned to the page the book had been guiding her to for days. If only she had been paying attention, the citizens might have been cured by now! *And poor Wallace mightn't have died.* "The book keeps leading me to this same anti-venom antidote. I disregarded it over and over because it called for an ingredient I don't have—a caladrius. But I think the book has been trying to tell me to use this recipe because it doesn't have an exact anti-dote for monkshood, nor all of its ingredients. I think the adamant could replace the caladrius in this instance. And that it is the same thing Janus and the Druid are after."

Padric nodded and smiled in encouragement. "I think you have something there, Bryn."

Warmth rushed through her at his smile. *How dearly I missed it.*

Eyebrows furrowed, Iaso nodded. "I concur."

"A curse..." Gregorio mused.

Padric began to pace. "But who would want to curse the people with poison?"

Gregorio scratched his youthful chin with thin fingers. "The curse and the adamant, the Minotaur and the Labyrinth."

"The Minotaur guards the Labyrinth." Everyone turned to see King Morfrey standing in the door, his crown disheveled and eyes bloodshot. "Whatever my father placed in there with him has been guarded for centuries."

"Is he still taking sacrifices?" Gregorio's face was ashen.

King Morfrey's nostrils flared in disgust. "There have been no sacrifices to the Minotaur since Minos's time. For now, the creature seems… *content* in his role as guardian."

"My brother, content?" Stunned, Payla sat down in a chair. "Even as a child, he was hotheaded and never idle."

"Wait, how is he still alive if Theseus killed him?" Gregorio asked.

Payla bit her lip, a habit one wouldn't expect from a priestess of the Roman gods. She opened her mouth to respond.

"We don't have time for a history lesson—Sorry, Payla." Brynwen closed *On Healing and Other Remedies* and turned to the king. "Sire, we must retrieve the adamant. First, to save Princess Mandalin and your subjects. And second, to keep it out of the hands of the Druid and Janus. We are certain it is in the Labyrinth."

Hope and despair both shone on King Morfrey's face. "You would risk encountering the Minotaur to rescue my people?"

Brynwen nodded. "We would."

Padric eased next to her. "We do have one demand, Your Majesty."

"And that would be?" Morfrey regarded Padric with unease.

"Ombag is to be our guide."

"Why him? He hasn't ever been in the Labyrinth. Besides, how do you know he will not merely try to escape once he is free?"

"Because, despite his family's actions, he might have some honor left. That, and he may wish to know what became of his father. He was very young when the incident happened."

"You have a valid point," the king said dryly. After a few tense seconds, he folded his arms. "You may have the Son of the Pilferer. If you all succeed, you are to bring him back to me to serve his punishment."

Gregorio lurched forward. "But, Your Majesty, he will not help us if he knows he is to still die."

"I do not care what you tell him—hold him at sword point if you must. But, should he betray us it will be on all your heads."

Brynwen's eyes locked with Padric's, her heart racing, before he looked away. Was this Ombag really worth the risk?

"Yes, Your Majesty," they all said.

"Forgive me, but I must stay to attend the patients and my father," Iaso said. She looked to Brynwen.

"I will stay." Gregorio bowed. "I will help you if I can."

&

WHILE KING MORFREY excused himself to get the key to the Labyrinth, release Ombag from the dungeon, and see about having the magicians perform a perpetual fire spell on the torches to take into the Labyrinth, Brynwen hugged her brother tightly.

"I missed you, too." Talfryn wheezed.

"Why do you keep nearly getting killed when I'm not around?" she scolded. In truth, she was so relieved to see her brother in one piece, and thankful Payla hadn't accidentally ripped his arm off, she didn't care what he'd answer.

"Well, it wasn't exactly in my plan for the day, ya know."

When she released him, a pair of mossy green eyes stared back at her. The scent of leather and sage filled her senses. All at once, she was overwhelmed with joy and warmth and love and...it was like the morning after Nessie's tears had cured him, and he was whole again. She knew she could withstand anything when they were together.

"Bryn, my love, my sweet." Padric's breath tickled her ear. "You look radiant this evening, as bright as a star in the summer sky." As a balm near a fire, her heart and all her cares melted into his embrace. She wished he would speak to her thus all night, but her cheeks reddened when she remembered there were others present.

She gave him a mock frown. "Took you long enough to find me."

"Not for lack of trying." He gave her a wide grin.

She took his gorgeous face in her hands, and pushed aside the blonde curl resting in the middle of his forehead. The way he looked at her, she was sure he would kiss her.

From behind Padric, Rawlins stepped into view. Dark memories—the hooded man, the knife, the fall, the scar on Rawlins's arm—came to her at once. Her body tensed, unable to stop her eyes from following him. He returned her gaze, and his face scrunched. Then he moved away.

Padric frowned. "Bryn? What is wrong?"

"I have them." Payla barged into the room, her horns etching a jagged line along the wood of the ballroom's doors at her hasty entrance. She puffed a couple of breaths. "Two balls of thread."

Rawlins eyed the material. "And those are for…"

The edges of Payla's lips raised into a grin. She held up a red ball. "This one will keep us from getting lost in the Labyrinth. And this one" —she raised the blue ball—"is to tie up my brother should he choose to be…um…unhelpful." A frown lowered her grin. "I worked all week on them to get the spells right."

Padric took a step closer to the thread for study and returned Payla's earlier smile. "Similar to the one Ariadne gave to Theseus. Well done, Payla."

"Won't they be an eyesore for anyone we don't want to find us?" Rawlins asked.

"He has a point," Aeron said.

Into Payla's bag went the red and blue thread. "When unwound, the red will be invisible to anyone but the holder of the thread. As long as it doesn't get severed, we ought to be able to retrace our steps without issue."

Rawlins sat on the banquet table in a slouch. "I guess that'll work."

"They will be most helpful. Thank you, Payla." Brynwen recalled Gregorio telling of the Minotaur in the Labyrinth, and her skin began to crawl. *I can't believe it. We're going into the Labyrinth. But will these two small balls of thread be enough to bring us out alive?*

PART III
LABYRINTH

"No one can hurry me down to Hades before my time, but if a man's hour is come, be he brave or be he coward, there is no escape for him when he has once been born."
— Homer, *The Iliad*

CHAPTER 39

"I hope we have enough of this," Padric heard Aeron mutter from behind. Aeron was in charge of unwinding the thread for the first stretch of their expedition into the Labyrinth. It reminded Padric of the thread his mother and sister used for embroidery.

Torches in hand, the group descended the crude stone steps, presumably carved by someone long before *Dis Pater* founded Rellea. Padric could not help but wonder if it was an original part of Daedalus's Labyrinth or a later addition. Judging by the strong scent of mildew and dust, it would not surprise him. Strong animal scents wafted up to him, turning his stomach.

"Payla, there is something I have wondered. If Theseus killed Asterion, how is he still alive? Were the stories wrong?" *Like the myth of Ulysses's demise.*

"Aye, they were wrong," she said darkly. "To make Theseus a true hero—*some hero he turned out to be*"—she said the last with a growl—"the stories portrayed the Minotaur as dying by Theseus's hand. But after Theseus left the Labyrinth, and as my poor brother lay dying, my mother prayed to Jupiter, and I to Mithras, to spare his life." She noted Padric's skeptical look and nodded. "He may have been a monster who devoured people as sacrifices, which I don't condone in the least, but he is still my brother. The circumstances of his horrible upbringing were made possible by my stepfather, Minos, who could not bare to love him."

She paused for a bit, and Padric thought she would say no more. Casting a look at her, he saw the glower that filled her eyes.

She huffed a breath. "Not long after we prayed, to our great surprise, both Jupiter and Mithras came to us. Together, they conferred over Asterion. A great cloud appeared over the gods and Asterion. When at last it dissipated, my brother gasped with breath—he had been brought back to life! Whole, but...different. There was a reddish glow about him. Without a word or acknowledgement, he strolled into the Labyrinth and did not return. The gods' work done, they returned to Olympus without explanation. I never saw my brother again, but I know he is alive." Her hand flew to her heart.

Padric wondered if it was a twin-sibling feeling or merely an ability immortals might acquire over time.

After about one hundred yards, the stairs ended into a narrow walkway with walls ascending straight up to some point above the torch light. Padric waved his torch a little higher, but the top never came into view. The ancient odors only grew stronger, and Padric scrunched his nose in disgust. *Sometimes*, he mused, *having enhanced senses is a curse.*

"I believe we are now in the Labyrinth," he announced.

Beside him, Rawlins grunted in assent. He gazed uneasily ahead. Every so often, Padric saw his friend's eyes move to Brynwen, a strange expression darkening his face. *What is that about?* Roana's warning came to mind, but he shook it off.

Padric caught sight of a small skeleton the size of a rodent against the stone wall.

Rawlins eyed the skeleton. "How long, d'you reckon, 'till the monster catches our scent?"

"For all we know, he might be on the other side of the Labyrinth." Aeron didn't sound convinced by his own comment.

Padric shook his head. "I hate to be the bearer of bad news, but he will likely find us much sooner than we think. He could already be onto us."

"Padric is right," Payla agreed. "Asterion is very resourceful and can sense when others are around and take advantage of their obliviousness."

Tugging on the red ball of thread, Aeron gulped and glanced behind them, then spun his head forward again.

"That's reassuring," Talfryn muttered.

After another fifty paces, they halted at a perpendicular fork in the path. As before, the walls traveled straight up without a visible top.

"Which way should we go?" Brynwen stood ahead of Padric, next to Payla and Ombag. Talfryn wandered up to her and checked down both dark pathways.

"I wish Franco were here," Payla said. "He would be a great asset right now."

The cobalus bristled as he decided the best course. "Left."

Padric spoke up, "Ombag is our guide now, but, ultimately, this is your quest, Bryn."

Shifting her gaze from one dark passage to the other, Brynwen twisted the end of her auburn braid around her forefinger. "Gregorio said to keep to the left, didn't he?"

"I'm pretty sure." Talfryn sounded much less than sure. "I mean, he said it like right before we plunged into the darkness, so...yeah." He shrugged.

Why is she having a hard time concentrating? Padric wondered. He spied a corner of *On Healing and Other Remedies* sticking out of her satchel. The realization of its magical properties both amazed and concerned him. It enhanced all of Brynwen's remedies; yet at the same time, it seemed to be siphoning all the confidence she'd had in healing prior to finding it. *Did Circe know of its power when she lent it to Brynwen?*

The others were growing restless. He had to do something.

Plucking up her free hand, Padric entwined his fingers with Brynwen's and leaned forward to whisper into her ear. "Bryn, take a breath. Do not doubt yourself so much. You are doing well."

"I just don't want to mess this up. We have one chance." She leaned her head against his and squeezed his hand. "Thank you," she whispered back, her breath tickling his cheek. Luckily, no one could see the scarlet rushing up his neck.

Brynwen cleared her throat and stood straight as a ramrod. "We will go left."

Padric's chest swelled as his beloved moved to the left.

"Yes, that's right. I mean, left. We'll, uh, go left." Talfryn scratched his head and took a step forward.

"Leeeft, Tarryn." Ombag steered Talfryn down the left tunnel.

"It's Talfryn. And I'm going, I'm going."

Padric couldn't help but chuckle. A low growl emanated from somewhere in the labyrinth, halting his mirth. "So, the walls do not go all the way up. Weapons check." Bows and arrows ready to draw, swords at their sides, and daggers in their boots.

"Didn't you say that hero fellow, Theseus or some such," Rawlins said, "had the string, but the Minotaur didn't see it? What if he finds it, regardless?"

"How did he get the thread past the monster?" Aeron asked.

Padric grimaced. "Payla already explained only the holder can see it."

"Wait, wait, wait." Aeron stopped short. "What if the Minotaur can smell us and sneak up on us? It won't matter that the thread is invisible then, will it?"

He nodded grimly. "We are well prepared for that."

Rawlins's neck grew taut, his veins protruding. "So we're inviting him to dine on us."

Aeron nodded. "He has a point, sir."

"Drop the thread," Rawlins instructed.

Aeron dropped it.

"Nay." Padric stooped to pick it up. Their plans were slowly unraveling. At this rate, the Minotaur really *might* find and kill them all. "What has gotten into you both? Do you wish us to be lost in here forever, as prey to the Minotaur?"

"*I'm* fine." Rawlins shook his head. "And no. But if the Minotaur comes after us, I won't promise he won't die, Payla's wishes or not."

Padric handed the ball of thread to Aeron. "Then we should catch up with the others and get what we came for and pray we avoid him." Their friends' footsteps sounded further away.

Rawlins gave Padric a black look and trudged down the left tunnel.

Captain Garrick de Clifton would never tolerate such insubordination. But he was not here, and who was to say Padric would never act in the same manner? *Something is very much wrong with Rawlins. I must speak with him alone.*

THE SHADOW GRINNED as the guide, Franco, led the way through the Labyrinth. *Dis Pater* had good reason to choose him to guide de Clifton to his cavern. He had no idea he was a descendent of Mercury, the Roman god of roads and protector of travelers. Now, Franco spent little effort finding a path through the maze of tunnels, although he had no idea why. All he need know was that if he failed, his sons would become a feast for the Minotaur.

They might become his feast regardless.

"Ow!" The youngest tripped and fell on his knees, his yellow hair flapping into his eyes. Arms bound behind his back with thick rope, he nearly yanked his connected brother down with him. The eldest lad teetered to retain his balance.

"Get up," the closest cobalus said. He took out his whip and snapped it at the lad's back.

"Stop it!" shouted the eldest.

Two lashes, laid with quick succession, struck his chest. He went down.

Franco shoved aside the evil creatures. "Leave them be! My sons are hungry and tired."

The cobalus ignored him. "Get up, I said." Worse for the wear, the lads got to their feet without complaint.

The other cobali poked their sharp-ended sticks at Franco.

"Papa!" the youngest cried.

"It's all right, Simon. We will get through this." Raising his hands, Franco retreated to the front of the group again.

"Will you, though?" the Shadow's raspy voice carried to the front of the queue. *"Continue. For your children's sake, tracker, you will complete your quest."*

The man's shoulders shook, whether in rage or fear, the Shadow couldn't care less. All was going to plan.

Until a low moo came from behind.

CHAPTER 40

After three hours, Padric and his friends had found many more animal skeletons, scattered bones, and cobwebs along the walkways, down side passageways, and at dead-ends. Here and there, they heard the scurrying of minuscule feet.

Something bade Padric call the party to a halt. He had heard something. His gaze fell on the opening to a side passage. There was nothing special about it, just the smooth stone like all the others. And yet…

"What is it?" Aeron asked, reaching for his sword.

A faint sound found Padric's ears. A report he had heard before. "Is it my imagination, or does anyone else hear a humming sound?"

Rawlins shook his head. "Not me."

"Me neither," Ombag said quickly. He tried to scurry straight ahead.

The hum began to tingle in Padric's chest, drawing his feet toward the passage. "I think we should go this way."

Ombag whined.

"Padric." Brynwen caught his arm and lowered her voice. "Is that a good idea? Remember Lilith?"

Closing his eyes, Padric concentrated on the hum. "It is hard to explain, but it resembles Circe's magic. Nothing like Lilith." His skin crawled as he recalled the once-beautiful succubus who had tried to kill him and Talfryn not too long ago. Back then, he had not known about his abilities.

"Look at you, Padric." Payla smiled. "Your power is progressing nicely. I say we have a look."

"Blimey, it's not another baby snake monster, is it?" Talfryn rolled his eyes. "I just got over my fear of 'em."

Padric barely refrained from laughing when he recalled the little creatures who loved light. They would have been adorable had their skin not been poisonous. "You mean the *cerastes*?"

"Yeah, those. Drat...does, uh, does someone else want to hold my torch for a bit? How about you, oh, brave Sir Aeron?"

"Nay."

"Sir Raw...never mind. I'll just keep it."

The magic felt stronger the further in they traveled. After three more turns to the left, they entered a small room. Padric scratched his chest and arms as the tingling became an awful itch all over his body. "Whatever it is, it is here."

The room they found was unremarkable, including the things within it: a small wooden table and a single chair, all smashed to pieces. The sad remains of a moldy mattress, its straw contents poking out of dozens of holes, lay in a haphazard heap in one corner. A roughly-built shelf and cupboard, an empty chest, and broken cups, dishes, and jars were scattered all over the floor. In a rusty sconce resided a burned-out torch, cold to the touch. Lastly, Padric spied a fire pit filled with black and white ash. Where did the smoke go when it was lit?

Talfryn scrunched his nose and put his hands on his hips. "It looks like a bear visited this place."

"Aye," Padric agreed. "This is—or was—someone's home."

"Asterion." Payla stood next to the shelf and pulled out a rolled up piece of vellum. With shaking hands, she unrolled it. A child's drawing. The rendering was of a woman and two small beings with what looked like horns on their heads.

"Is that you and your mother and brother?" Brynwen asked.

"It is. I drew this for him when I was six. To remember us." Slowly, she rolled up the scroll and replaced it on the shelf.

The Minotaur's room was cramped with seven people crammed into it, but in short order they searched everything. With an eager Miser wiggling in anticipation on her shoulder, Brynwen opened the cupboard and found it filled to the brim with cobwebs. Cross at their findings, Miser chittered noisily and bounded to the floor.

"Language." Talfryn raised a battered and partially-eaten shoe from under the broken table. "You can finish this shoe off if you'd like, you little beggar." Miser gave him a black look.

Rawlins raised the rotten mattress. A cloud of dust escaped the remains, and half a dozen insects scurried out from under it and scattered every which way. The knight was about to lower it again when Padric stopped him.

"Wait. I see a faint shimmer under there."

Without hesitation, Rawlins hoisted the rest of the mattress away as it began to disintegrate in his hands. Heart racing, Padric got on hands and knees and wiped away the straw and grime, ignoring the moldy stench. The object shone brightly. "Got it." He wrapped his hand around it. However, it did not feel at all as he had expected.

"So shiny," Ombag said.

Talfryn leaned closer. "Is it the adamant?"

Payla frowned when she saw it. "It is a spoon."

Brynwen looked over Padric's shoulder for a better view. "A spoon?"

Padric nodded, disappointed. "That it is." A very ordinary-looking pewter spoon with no ornamentation whatsoever, except that it shimmered like the dawn. "A magic spoon."

Ombag's eyes grew completely round. "May I hold it it?"

Everyone in the room responded in unison, "Nay."

"What do we do with a 'magical' spoon?" Rawlins asked dryly.

"Eat magical food with it?" Aeron mused.

"Could be part of a set." Brynwen peered around the room again.

Rawlins shrugged in agreement. "Maybe not a complete waste, then."

All eyes met, and another search of the premises commenced. They emerged from the Minotaur's decrepit room with the pewter spoon, a matching fork, knife, and the sliver of a pewter plate, all with some bewildering magical properties Padric could not detect. Payla, who knew a little magic, was at a loss as well.

Padric divided up the prizes.

"Not a bad haul. Doubt the monster'll even miss 'em," Ombag said, coveting his new pewter fork.

Talfryn tucked his spoon in his undershirt breast pocket. Unsurprisingly, Rawlins slid the knife into his boot, while Aeron kept the plate, placing it in his pack.

&

"BRYNWEN." She jumped in fright as Rawlins materialized beside her. "Might I have a word? It's important."

"Rawlins!" Her heart threatened to pound out of her chest. *Might you be trying to drag me off to a dark side passage and murder me?* A quick glance away saw Padric and the others conferring in low whispers around Ombag, who had just returned from a scouting trip. It had been hours since their group had started the trek into the Labyrinth, and some news regarding the adamant would be most welcome about now. She patted the knife in its holster which Payla had scrounged up in the city for her. Maybe this time she wouldn't lose someone else's weapon. *Maybe.*

The action drew Rawlins's gaze down to her hand on the knife's hilt.

Her lips drew into a line as she considered bringing it out, slicing the other arm…or worse. A shiver rose up her spine. A healer's job was to heal, not to harm. *But what about an enemy? What would Padric do, if his enemy were one of his best friends?* "Shouldn't you be helping with the decisions?"

"Shouldn't you, too?" He raised an eyebrow. "As it's *your* prophecy?"

"So everyone often reminds me."

"It is decided, then." Padric's voice drifted from among the group. His frown made him seem less pleased than before.

Talfryn's head popped into view, and he spotted Brynwen. "Oy, Bryn. Rawlins. Ombag's found something."

The tension flitted off Brynwen as she sidestepped around the dreadful knight and rushed to her brother's side. With great effort, she pushed down all the fear and trepidation which tried to freeze her to the spot. *Would he kill me in front of everyone? Would he then attack everyone else with his disappearing power? I should have insisted he stay above ground.* It seemed ridiculous, but after all, Ranulf Rawlins *was* trained in the art of killing.

They followed the cobalus down the path a short way until he stopped at a fork and focused on the packed earth at his feet. They had taken many left turns, always left. And this turn was no exception. Brynwen's feet grew sore, and she thought they should be nearly to the center by now.

Gathering around Ombag, they made room for Brynwen to see for herself. The ground looked trampled for a few paces but she didn't quite understand what it all meant.

"Foot marks," Ombag noted.

Padric took in the marks and nodded. "Many, by the look of it."

"Only a few hours old." Rawlins knelt on the ground. "These foot marks here are small, like Ombag's. At least a dozen sets, but it's hard to tell."

Talfryn pressed his lips together. "I don't suppose they're down here for a nice picnic in the pitch blackness."

"Look here, Rawlins." Padric lowered his torch near the ground a few feet away. "I believe these were made by the soft boots of humans. An adult and two children." Padric's face screwed up in concern.

A gasp escaped Brynwen's lips. "If it's Franco and his sons, we must rescue them."

"We will." Determination filled Padric's expression as he took in the rest of the scene. Brynwen knew without a doubt he'd do anything he could to save them. "Besides, we cannot allow the Druid to get the adamant first."

"Large human foot marks here. And here." Rawlins pointed at several much larger and heavier marks, appearing to leave deep impressions into the rock. Drops of dark, almost black, drying blood had splattered against the stone. The large marks led off in the opposite direction of the victims.

Payla's head shot up. "This is Asterion's work. Assuming it is the Druid's group, it appears he found them first." Her face crumpled in a pained expression.

Brynwen studied the dark substance, a sick feeling flooding her stomach. "Is it...human blood?"

Payla slid a finger along the blood on the wall and examined it. She shook her head. "Cobalus."

"So, does he hunt like a fox, so he'll leave us alone for a while, then?" Talfryn's face had gone ashen.

A chortle came from Payla. "Ha! It will only encourage him all the more to taste their blood. It is humans he likes best. He may be after the humans in this group. I daresay, it won't be long before he smells us."

"Oh." Talfryn spoke through clenched teeth. "That's uh...great to know. Thanks, I so love the threat of impending doom looming over me."

"What is this mark?" Padric had wandered to the side farthest from the blood splatter. "It appears to be some kind of dragging foot mark, but it does not match any other marks around here."

Everyone crowded around the place indicated.

"Never seen that before." Aeron unwound another yard of thread.

A haunting moo report echoed around the underground maze. The sound bounced off all the walls. Brynwen's heart lurched as she brandished her knife. Everyone else had the same idea.

Talfryn's head bobbed in both directions. "Time to go."

EVER KEEPING TO THE LEFT, they traversed the Labyrinth in the same direction as the group holding Franco and his sons. It wasn't long before the tracks veered off down a distant hallway. What was most interesting to Talfryn, though, was how Payla's magic ball of red thread never decreased in size despite the distance they traveled. He'd let out enough thread behind them to more than triple the amount of what the party's clothes were made of, combined.

Every strange noise made Talfryn jumpy. With each minute, he knew his life expectancy had somehow outwitted fate. He sent up another prayer through St. Christopher to keep him, Brynwen, and the others safe from the monster.

The intense distress of Franco's wife, Lenore, had haunted Talfryn ever since the day they'd rescued her from the Druid. Talfryn didn't know her family at all, but he understood her great worry for them more than she'd ever realize. His closest cousin and one of Padric's knights, Leowyn, had been kidnapped by Circe to work on her father Helius's temple. Worry had eaten a hole in Talfryn's chest for the months he was gone.

Unfortunately, Leowyn never had the chance to make it home. Because I wasn't quick enough. But maybe we'll be quick enough to save Lenore's family. And get the adamant, of course.

First, they'd have to pick their way through the Labyrinth.

"It is humans he likes best." The way Payla'd said that phrase sent all kinds of shivers up Talfryn's neck, not to mention bringing back nightmares of his recent past. *Nope. Not going there.*

They'd gone through another set of dead ends big enough to be a sitting room when they stumbled upon something odd. Well, really, Ombag saw it first.

"Shiny?"

"'Scuse me?" Talfryn asked and bent his knees toward the creature. "What's shiny?"

"Up there." He pointed into the sky.

Blinking as he looked up, Talfryn saw nothing but blackness. "There's nothing there..." Until there *was*. Talfryn stopped and stared. Soft, but unmistakable, a ray of pink sun stretched across the sky—or ceiling, or whatever was up there. "Ummm." He blinked again.

"Talfryn," Brynwen said wearily, "why are you two staring at the sky?"

"Just look."

After a few moments, she gasped and squeezed her eyes shut. Talfryn steadied her with his good arm. "Bryn, what's wrong?"

"It's the adamant...we're getting close, I can feel it. The prophecy is getting more urgent, like it's trying to exit my brain to travel the Labyrinth and find the diamond itself." She winced.

A sort of panic engulfed Talfryn as he stood by, helpless. He hated seeing his sister this way, but what could he do? Lying to her and saying, "This'll all be over soon" wouldn't be of any use. This prophecy stuff was beyond his comprehension, and it wouldn't stop until they'd secured the adamant-diamond-stone and gotten it far away from Janus.

Padric approached and took her hand. In an instant, her shoulders relaxed, and her eyes popped open.

Talfryn gaped at them. *How does he do that?*

"Why is it pink? Never mind, we are losing valuable time." A scowl spoiled Aeron's impeccable features, but he lowered his gaze to the ball of magic thread. "The other group will get there before us if we keep dawdling."

"You are right," Padric agreed. Talfryn could almost hear fabric rip as the knight tore his gaze from Brynwen. "We should resume. Ombag and Rawlins, find that pink glow."

"On it!" Ombag's eager determination was unlike anything Talfryn had seen reflected in the cobalus's face and stance before. It took no time for his short legs to outdistance them.

Talfryn grinned as he released another bit of red thread. "Guess all he needed was a shiny bauble to follow."

Aeron slowed his pace until his steps were even with Talfryn's.

"I can take the thread for a while."

He thinks I'm tired.

"I can handle it until the next shift change. Thanks, though."

"As you wish."

"D'you like being a knight?" Talfryn's question just popped out of his mouth. He didn't know much about Aeron despite having been traveling with him the last couple of weeks. In spite of a couple of incidental outbursts, the knight seemed a decent fellow. Sometimes, Talfryn had fancied about becoming a knight, but knew he was too old now, at nearly seventeen. If he'd really wanted to, he should have begun training as a page years ago with Leowyn.

"Aye. Never imagined I'd be on an adventure in a cave like this, though."

"Never imagined we'd be kidnapped by a real goddess, either." Talfryn chuckled.

Aeron laughed. "Nay, can't say I would have. Say, I'm famished. Do you still have some of those cakes the *Signore* made?"

"Yeah, sure." Transferring the thread to his slung hand, he reached into his bag. Soon his fingers grazed the wrapped snack, and he snatched it up. While he dug around in the pouch, Miser chittered and moved around his shoulders excitedly, knowing exactly where the treats were kept. "Here you go."

Miser made a high-pitched squeak of irritation at Talfryn's sharing with the wrong person.

"Calm down, Miser. I see your parents didn't teach you about sharing."

"Thanks." The knight unwrapped the food and broke off a piece before wrapping it up again and handing it back to Talfryn. He nibbled the cake and grinned. "I'll have to get his recipe. If you'll excuse me, I must speak with the lieutenant about our next steps."

"Sure, see ya." Once Aeron picked up his pace to reach Padric, Talfryn gave the squirrel a look. "Well, at least you didn't bite him. So, I guess you've learned *some* manners."

❧

Run. The animal part of Padric's brain kept screaming at him. All around, the scent of the Minotaur overpowered his senses—sweat, blood, and mustiness. The monster's *odor* had become apparent upon entering the Labyrinth. However, once they discovered the creature's altercation with the other group, it increased one hundred fold. *Run now. It is close. It will tear you up from head to toe.*

He scolded the remnant of his horse, Firminus, which remained in his head from his first encounter with the sorceress Circe. *Quit it. Now is not the time to be afraid.*

He had killed a succubus.

He had defeated the manticore.

He had thwarted Janus's deadly plan.

He could keep control now. He hoped.

His stomach clenched into a tight cramp. It was all Padric could do to concentrate on the next step. Then the next.

"Padric." A strong hand gripped his arm. "What is wrong? Is it your animal sense?" Payla.

He could only nod.

A spasm knocked him to his knees. "Not now." The horse wished to be free. *Free!* Clenching his teeth, he squeezed his eyes shut to abate the pain.

Another set of arms engulfed him. Gentle, with the scent of honey and lavender. "Padric, I thought you'd mastered this."

"So…did I."

"You must fight it, Padric."

"I am trying. Why is no one else as affected as me?"

Payla squatted beside him. "I was afraid this would happen. My brother is responsible for this, I fear. He is close, stalking us. His greatest ability is to strike numbing terror into the hearts of men. And livestock." She gave Padric a pointed look as he shuddered.

"Padric is not livestock," Brynwen said in a defensive tone.

"Glad we didn't bring Hay and Stack, then." Talfryn chuckled. "They'd cause mayhem."

"And be dead." Rawlins reached for his daggers as Talfryn frowned. "If he's coming, we'll be prepared."

"But the diamond," Ombag protested. "We're so close. Let's keep moving."

As they argued, Padric's mind wandered. Gregorio's lessons on Roman mythology, Theseus and Ariadne, and the Minotaur. The special thread Ariadne procured for Theseus. The fine details Gregorio knew about the Minotaur which the books never mentioned.

"Talfryn," he said. "You have done it again."

"Oh no, what'd I do this time?" Checking all around him and patting down his tunic, the farmer's face scrunched as though trying to figure out what he had messed up.

Taking a deep, shuddering breath, Padric related the plan. "We will need a distraction."

"A distraction, eh? Would a goat suffice?" Rawlins smiled wickedly, his voice growling with conspiracy.

Talfryn grinned and rubbed his chin as he looked pointedly at Padric. "Yesss. Now, if only we had a goat."

Padric did *not* appreciate the way his friends looked at him.

❧

PADRIC-GOAT CLOPPED out into the open. The four-way opening made the area seem spacious and lighter compared with the rest of the Labyrinth. A lit torch lay on the ground as though abandoned.

This is my worst idea yet. The Minotaur will never in a millennia fall for this trap.

He waited. And waited. And longed for snacks that never came. And waited some more.

It took every ounce of willpower to keep control. Every few minutes, he let out a "naaaah" sound to inform the Minotaur of his whereabouts. The only thing that kept him from changing back into human form was the constant build up of terror inside his chest, threatening to burst his esophagus. It kept him focused—well, as focused as a ravenous goat could be.

Rawlins waited with Aeron and Payla around the corner in a dead end tunnel. Behind them stood Brynwen, Ombag, and Talfryn.

The goat part of Padric's brain had just come up with the brilliant idea of lying down when a low sound came down the passageway to the right. It grew louder. The shuffling of feet on the passageway's stone made the hair on Padric-goat's neck raise.

"Naaaay," Padric-goat said. "Go awaaaaaay."

But the footsteps kept coming.

"Why are they here?" Payla asked.

"Padric, come back," Aeron called.

First, a cobalus turned the corner. Then another, followed by Franco. He had no weapon. Half a dozen more cobali, two human youths, and the Druid in the same heavy gray robes emerged. One by one, they were startled by the bored goat lounging in the center of the passageway.

"Fresh meat," said one of the cobali with a long, scarred gash stretching from his forehead down to the opposite jawline. He withdrew a long dagger from his belt sheath.

A shorter creature shoved his way forward. "See, I told you I smelled goat."

"Meat." The others agreed and stepped forward with hungry eyes and terrifying grins.

Instinct bade Padric duck as an arrow whizzed past his ear. The animal part of his brain squirmed.

That was close.

Padric thought to transform into a human when the hair on the back of his neck stood on end. After two agonizing seconds, the sound of a low, menacing moo emanated from somewhere nearby.

The grins on the cobali vanished.

His heart rate increasing, Padric tried in vain to hear which passageway the sound came from. The ground began to shake, jarring his jaw.

Out of the shadows in the tunnel to his left, a huge blur of brown sped toward Padric-goat. A deafening, deep bellow emanated from the charging beast.

"Naaaaah," Padric-goat called in challenge. At the last moment, he sidestepped. The Minotaur raced past, his red eye gleaming at his prey in both bewilderment and consternation.

So far so good.

It bounded off the opposite wall and leaped at Padric, sharpened nails glinting in the torchlight. Its horns narrowly missed the opposite wall.

Disregard that.

Padric scrambled forward. The swish of the Minotaur's hand tickled the gray hairs on his back as he dodged their deadly swing. The creature bellowed in outrage. The prick of agony struck Padric's abdomen as he flipped and rolled to the wall where his weapons lay. In a flash, he bounded up on two goat legs—a faun. Releasing the dagger and sword at his sides, he barreled into the wall, ran up two steps, and shoved off to flip into the air. Like the manticore, the Minotaur bellowed in rage as Padric's body twisted overhead.

Behind them, the cacophony of shouting, both familiar and new, covered the Minotaur's unintelligible threats. Led by Rawlins and Aeron, the fighters in their group faced off against the cobali and the Druid.

For now, Padric had his own worries with the Minotaur.

CHAPTER 41

Tucked into the recess out of sight from the fighting, Brynwen heard every blow between Padric and the Minotaur Asterion, as well as Aeron with Payla against the Druid and his cobali.

In a rush, the same pounding headache from Roana's most recent visit returned to Brynwen. She lost all bearing on the room, the floor, the ceiling. "What's wrong with me?" she whispered and fell to her knees. Her torch hit the floor in a clatter.

"You all right, Bryn?" Talfryn was by her side in an instant.

Ombag scoffed. "What's wrong with your eyes? They're moving around all strange."

No, this was all going so wrong. "It's this blasted prophecy." Brynwen kept her eyelids clamped shut. Nevertheless, it didn't stop the words trailing in never ending lines, in never ending text, swirling in figure eights and circles. Like Hay and Stack running in endless circles around her, but ten times faster. *This is Roana's fault. If it weren't for her, I wouldn't be in this mess.* There was no way and no one to read *On Healing and Other Remedies* to see if there were some sort of cure for the blindness caused by a prophecy—if such an incredible thing existed, she would kiss Aesculapius for it.

A new panic grew in her chest, that she'd fail to save Princess

Mandalin, Aesculapius, and the Relleans. Fail to finish the prophecy. That Janus would win and manage to destroy the world in a new way. Whatever he needed the adamant for, she couldn't let him have it. Not while she breathed.

Suddenly, the text stopped spinning. In another moment, so did her head.

Getting to her feet, she brushed off her skirts out of habit. She concentrated on Ombag instead of the irritating text lingering at the edge of her vision.

Ombag squinted at her, as though scrutinizing her sanity. "So, you're fine now?"

"For the moment." *Who knows when it might happen again?*

"Good. Then we should go get that adamant diamond o' yours."

Talfryn twisted the hatchet in his hand. "Coast's clear. Let's go."

TALFRYN WATCHED as Padric fought the Minotaur in the tunnel to his right. It always amazed Talfryn how well Padric fought as a faun, and even more so as a human or centaur. Maybe someday he could fight like that, too.

To the left, Rawlins, Payla, and Aeron rushed toward the rogue cobali. They wasted no time in picking off a couple of the weakest warriors. Talfryn sidled up to the edge of the wall, his hatchet at the ready. Brynwen and Ombag stayed close behind him as they watched in horrified fascination.

A group of four cobali guarded Franco while three others stood by his young, bound sons. The Druid stooped over the cobali nearest Franco's younger son, Simon. He couldn't have been more than eight years old.

"It's time," Talfryn said without turning around. "They won't notice us. I don't think."

"That's reassuring." Brynwen took a quick gander around his shoulder.

"I—I'll lead." Ombag's voice shook. He'd already crushed his hat between his hands, but his forehead was creased in determination "Great, let's go."

No one paid any attention as they slid out of the hiding spot and ducked into the empty tunnel. Toward the pink glow and hopefully the adamant.

A heart-wrenching shout came from behind. Brynwen stopped short and glanced back, giving a start.

"Bryn, come on—" He'd spun his head to find one of the rogue cobali dragging Simon away from the group toward the Minotaur. "What's he doing?"

"I don't know, but it can't be good. We should help him."

"There's no time, and I'm not leaving you. 'Sides, I promised to get you two to the adamant." *That, and the last time I let you go by yourself, you almost died.*

Brynwen nudged him. "Tal…"

Talfryn huffed. He had no idea what the cobalus had in mind for the lad, but he couldn't leave his sister. She reached for the knife in her belt.

"Stop, Bryn." With a quick movement, he halted her action. His heart ached as he made a split decision. "I'll get Simon. You two find the adamant. Get going, and be careful, will ya?"

"He's got a point," Ombag said. "We gotta go."

She hesitated and winced at the lad's scream. Then nodded with set jaw. "Be safe." She clutched Talfryn's arm for a second then withdrew down the passage with Ombag.

"You too," he called after them.

Returning to the fray, Talfryn ripped off his sling and followed Simon and the cobalus. Luckily for him, the lad dragged his feet, causing the smaller creature great anguish.

"Oy, you," Talfryn called from behind, spinning his hatchet around in his hand in what he hoped was an intimidating display. He was positive the squirrel on his shoulder made him more daunting. "Leave him alone."

"Help!" Simon called out.

The cobalus growled but continued to pull Simon along.

"I said *stop*." Talfryn flung himself at the cobalus. All three went sprawling to the ground. Simon lay dazed while the cobalus fought tooth and nail. He bit Talfryn's hand hard. "Ahh!" Talfryn's hatchet clanged on the ground. "Hey, if you keep that up, I'll bite you back." But the creature didn't seem to care about what he'd said. "Miser, go for it."

Miser launched at the cobalus and latched onto his cheek.

Embittered, the cobalus swiped the red squirrel off his face and grappled Talfryn to the ground, its yellow eyes glowering at him. It was as spry as Ombag, and more desperate.

Talfryn got a couple jabs in before it pelted him in the cheek and ribcage again. They rolled a couple more times. An elbow to the cheek, and the cobalus's head struck the rock wall. He went down.

Stopping to catch his breath for a couple of heartbeats, Talfryn checked on Simon. He stirred and sat up.

"Let's…get out of…here, Simon," Talfryn panted. With effort, he got Simon and himself to their feet. "I'm Talfryn."

They took two steps before a heavy weight came crashing down on Talfryn's back. Screams and fists pummeled his head, ears, and shoulders. The attacker smashed at his hands when he reached up, leaving smarting welts on them. The previous injury to his left shoulder did him no favors.

"Talfryn," Simon called as though far away.

The pounding continued, dropping Talfryn to his knees as the thrashing continued. "Run, Simon. Run."

Instead, he heard the lad's footsteps and shouts as he berated the creature attacking him.

Talfryn couldn't move. Couldn't think.

Suddenly, the weight lifted, and the pounding stopped. Thinking he'd gone deaf at last, Talfryn blinked. He touched his ears with ginger movements. They were still there.

"You can get up now."

Startled, Talfryn glanced up. Rawlins held the limp form of the cobalus in his hand. "Um, thanks. I'd've had him in another minute."

"Yeah. Sure." With a bored expression, the knight dropped the creature like a sack of flour.

Simon stared at the two of them with wide eyes. A few yards off,

Aeron and Payla stood over a group of fallen cobali, the latter cutting through Cecil's and Franco's bonds.

"Are you all right?" Talfryn asked Simon. In shock, the lad just stared at him. "We'll get you out of here soon."

The moo-howl which came from beyond the torchlight reminded Talfryn that their task wasn't yet over. Padric must've led the monster away from them.

Rawlins scowled. "Give me the binding thread."

"I should do it," Payla said. She took a step forward, breathing heavily. "He's my brother, he will listen to me."

"Not in his condition, he won't. If you go, he'll never forgive you," Rawlins pointed out.

Payla hesitated a moment, then nodded miserably and tossed the shining blue ball to him. He caught it and dashed down the corridor.

"Simon, will you take care of Miser for me?" Talfryn held the squirming squirrel out.

The lad gave a solemn nod and accepted the squirrel.

"Thanks," he said, then sped after Rawlins. "Wait for me!"

"You've done enough already." Rawlins's tone held all the warmth of a frost in December.

"Yeah, well, I'm coming anyway."

The stoic knight made no answer to that.

ROUNDING THE NEXT CORNER, Talfryn and Rawlins stopped short. Padric the faun fought with the monster. It was everything Talfryn never wished to see with its bull's head, long, pointed horns like Payla's, and biceps each as thick as an anvil. However, compared with the *aeternae's* mottled fur, bone horns, and inch-long claws, the Minotaur was a handsome creature.

Both partial-man-partial-beasts had multiple cuts and lacerations all over their bodies.

Landing in a crouch, Padric was too slow to dodge the thick arm that struck his back. He went flying and landed ten feet away with a thud, then rolled a few more feet after that. His sword skittered along the packed earth.

"No!" Talfryn cried without thinking.

The half-bull swung his huge head around, its horn scraping against the wall in a fit of sparks. Thick smoke puffed out of his nose, a golden ring dangling from said nose, just asking for someone to pull on it.

Rawlins glowered at Talfryn before turning back to the bull.

"Sorry," Talfryn said to his back.

They met the Minotaur halfway. The monster regarded Rawlins as the bigger threat, could see all the deadliness in the knight's silent presence without speaking a single word. Rawlins handed Talfryn the thread.

"Glad you've got confidence in me."

Rawlins snorted. "Don't mess this up."

"Oh. Yeah." Talfryn watched for a fascinated minute as muscles, claws, and blades clashed before remembering Padric sprawled on the floor a few feet away. Guilt didn't really equate to what he felt as he knelt next to his friend.

Padric groaned. "Are you not supposed to be with Brynwen and Ombag?"

"An insane cobalus attacked Simon." The bruises on his upper body probably wouldn't heal for weeks, even with a heaping lathering of Brynwen's Miracle Mix. "They went to find the adamant. Can you get up?"

"I believe so." First, Padric's body shuddered, then his goat legs dissolved into his human legs, complete with trousers and boots. With halting movements, he got to his feet and retrieved his sword.

"It's getting easier, then."

"Aye," Padric agreed. "Come on. The Minotaur is as clever as he was in the stories."

They turned, and Rawlins seemed to be doing well. Until the Minotaur feinted, catching the knight by the shoulder and slamming him into the wall. Hard. He slammed him again. Then his long nails glinted before slicing Rawlins's left arm from shoulder to elbow. Dark blood flowed and trailed down his appendage.

Ignoring the gaping wound, Rawlins continued to slice at the Minotaur, his body fading out of sight and then reforming another foot away. But the power took its toll. Finally, Rawlins's body stopped flickering. Enraged at the tricks, the Minotaur rammed the knight into the wall a final time with a sickening crunch.

"Rawlins!" Padric cried through clenched teeth.

Talfryn thought Rawlins's chest must have been crushed as he crumpled to the ground.

Nails outstretched, the Minotaur reached down for Rawlins.

"I've got this. Get Rawlins."

"Tal…"

Gripping the tail of the thread, Talfryn lobbed the ball over the Minotaur's head. He'd then dash in and wrap the thread around to bind him. Easy, right?

Instead, it bounced off the bullish head and landed harmlessly on the ground a few feet away.

Perfect.

Steam blew out of Asterion's nose as his hands halted an inch from Rawlins's face.

"Uhh, great." Talfryn rolled his eyes at his own stupidity. "Hey. You. Asterion. Didn't your mother tell you that if you break all your toys, there'll be nothing left to play with later?"

A loud moo-ish howl emitted from the Minotaur. He spun to swipe at his new toy, a long gash on his chest and across his nose. A quick jump backward saved Talfryn. Instead of his chest, the monstrous fingernails sliced through his sleeve and scraped against his arm. Before he could get in another swing, Talfryn leaped in for a strike, aiming to draw the fight away from Rawlins. Heart thundering in his chest, he reminded himself, *Just make a tiny distraction.*

"By the way, I spoke to your mother the other day. You know, Pasiphae? Nice lady. When we told her we were coming here for a visit, she asked us to say 'hello' to you."

The Minotaur's muscles tensed.

Behind the monster, Padric moved with silent caution toward the fallen thread.

Talfryn kept his attention on his quarry. Also, prayed he didn't *become* the quarry. "She also wants to know why you never write."

The Minotaur's large rounded ear twitched, and he cocked his head to the side, regarding Talfryn with something akin to an inquisitive dog.

"Just once in a harvest moon, she'd like a reply letter from her son. You know: 'How're you doing, Mother? What've you been up to? Met a pretty heifer the other day.' Is that too much to ask of a long-lost son?"

Then something strange happened to the Minotaur. Some sort of emotion passed through his ebony eyes. He hung his head as though ashamed of his actions, that he'd been a bad Minotaur-for-a-son, and should find a scroll and quill somewhere in this huge maze to write his witchy immortal mother a letter of apology.

Huh. All those years of scolding the farm animals must've paid off, after all.

The Minotaur uttered a moan of lament. For a split second, Talfryn's triumph melted into remorse about his deception. The creature was Payla's brother, after all, and he didn't wish her any harm. But then he spotted Padric checking on the battered Rawlins, and his resolve returned. The Minotaur was a monster. It had killed loads of people. He didn't even know if the monster had a soul or any sort of real conscience.

Padric continued toward the ball of blue thread.

That's it, Padric. Easy, slowly...

As Padric stooped to pick up the thread, his boot scraped against the stone, making the slightest sound. The knight halted immediately and flinched at his blunder. But it was too late.

Talfryn weighed the hatchet in his hand, preparing for the worst.

The Minotaur's head shot up, and he spun around. Talfryn leapt again, aiming for the monster's hairy back. Without a glance backward, Asterion swung out and struck Talfryn clear in the chest.

All the air wheezed out of his lungs as he struck the wall. His vision winked in and out as he slid to the ground. A warning snapped in his brain—*don't go dark.* Shaking his head, he shot to his feet and gulped in a breath. Sharp pain shot through his rib. Then he was off to attack the Minotaur again.

Padric's sword flashed as he swiped at the monster, but the Minotaur was beyond angry now. The thread danced its way between the monster's feet. This time, Talfryn succeeded in hitting the Minotaur's backside with the flat of his hatchet. The monster let out a wail and turned on Talfryn. He winced, choking on his wail. Glaring first at Talfryn, then Padric, he darted away.

And tripped on the thin, shiny thread.

The Minotaur's bulk crashed to the ground. A howl of pure rage came from him, shaking the hidden rafters.

"Go!" Padric yelled.

"I sure hope this thread's really enchanted." Talfryn scooped up the ball and sprinted to the Minotaur.

By then the monster was bellowing and attempting to get up. Padric tackled its back and Talfryn tossed him the ball. He wound it around a sharp horn as the Minotaur tried to buck him off. Many more cuts and bruises later, the muscly monster was secured. He lay on the ground, bound from head to foot in thin, shining thread, glaring at them with red eyes.

"Huh," Talfryn said, "I guess it works after all."

Then, before his eyes, the gashes on the Minotaur's nose and chest began to fade.

Talfryn reeled back. "Did you see that?"

"I was about to ask you the same thing," Padric replied. "We should go."

Talfryn and Padric lifted the unconscious Rawlins between them. They limped along toward where they'd left Payla, Aeron, and the others. Scuffling sounds came around the corner. "Not again." He wished he hadn't hooked his hatchet onto his belt so soon.

Aeron appeared, sword in hand, a wild look on his face. His usually neat, dark hair was disheveled and covered in dust. He took one look at Rawlins and his eyes furrowed. "Is he...?"

"Alive, for now," Padric replied.

Relief spread on Aeron's face. "Praise be. And the Minotaur?"

"Captured." Padric hiked Rawlins's weight better onto his shoulder. He indicated the bound creature.

"Don't get on his bad side." Talfryn was past ready to set the heavy, unconscious knight down. He'd seen wild animals, and the Minotaur was as wild as they came. If Brynwen and Ombag had found the adamant by now, maybe they'd all be out of the labyrinth before it released itself. The voice in the back of his head laughed at that.

When they reached Payla, Talfryn couldn't have been more glad to set down his burden. The knight's dead weight made him feel heavier than he should be. Rawlins groaned. Somehow, it made Talfryn feel slightly better.

"Will he make it?" Talfryn asked. There was so much blood.

Padric had already knelt next to the bloody knight to examine his wounds. "He is strong, but I pray so." He raised his gaze to Aeron and Payla. "What happened here?"

Talfryn took a moment to really take in his surroundings. Franco leaned against a wall with Simon beside him, curled up into a shaking ball of legs and arms, but his brother was nowhere in sight.

Payla shifted her weight to the other leg. "The creepy little Druid in the cloak returned with a smoking potion that sent everyone to the ground. He took the remaining standing cobali and Cecil with him." She scowled. "It was poor timing, both their group *and* the Minotaur arriving at the same time."

"Indeed, but it could not be helped." Padric tore off a strip of his tunic and wrapped it tightly around Rawlins's bleeding arm. "Rawlins needs care from Brynwen. We must find her, and quick."

CHAPTER 42

Keeping the pink glow in her sight, Brynwen and Ombag followed the Labyrinth's walls.

"This is a terrible idea," Ombag muttered. "It could be a trap."

"I know, but we don't have much of a choice." Brynwen rubbed her neck. It became more sore the longer they walked after keeping an eye on the strange light source for so long. For some reason, she didn't trust the glow to stay visible forever like the sun at dusk, when it tucked into the hills on the horizon.

She sent up another prayer that their trek to the adamant was nearly at an end. And that Padric's fight with the Minotaur ended in the knight's favor. And that Franco and his sons escaped the horrible little hooded Druid with the wrinkled, almost translucent hands, and his rogue cobali. Whoever he was, Brynwen couldn't allow him to find the adamant before her. The problem was, he had the best tracker in York-shire with him.

The gold and red letters of the prophecy flew by her vision again, but not as intensely as it had been a little while ago. She blinked to assuage the dizziness that came on, her shoulder brushing against the passageway.

"Hold on there." Ombag steadied her with his surprisingly strong grip.

Rubbing a tiny amount of lavender oil on her brow and neck earlier had done little good. A nagging feeling tightened her chest. "We're almost there?"

"Aye." Ombag craned his neck. "It's getting brighter."

"I've been wondering…why is the adamant a pink diamond? Shouldn't it be white or the like?" *Not that I know much about jewelry.*

"Diamonds've been known ta be pink, yellow, or light blue. Being a thief, I'd know."

"That's fair."

After only about twenty more paces, the tunnel veered to the left and opened up to a glow so intense it blinded them. For a few moments, they had to shield their eyes.

When she looked up after several blinks, her breath caught as the diamond gleamed, suspended in air, its light pink rays like a single-colored rainbow. "It's magnificent." Her feet took two steps of their own accord. Never taking her gaze from it, a hunger grew in Brynwen's stomach. With the adamant and the book, she could heal every ill, every disease. Perhaps Aesculapius had abused the power, but she would see that their usefulness never outgrew their purpose. *Yes,* she told herself. *I can do it. And at the same time keep it out of Janus's hands.*

As her eyes adjusted to the light, she noticed that several passages converged into one large round area with the pink diamond suspended in the middle. "Ombag. We're at the center of the Labyrinth."

But Ombag's eyes weren't on the passageways. His gaze was drawn to the large pink gemstone. It was then Brynwen noticed the small skeleton holding it. And the giant spider web filling the entire center of the Labyrinth, suspending the diamond and skeleton well out of reach. Below the web they could see naught but darkness. *How far down does it go?*

Brynwen's muscles went rigid with fear. *How didn't I notice all of this before?*

Several minutes passed before Brynwen plucked up enough courage to withdraw a step. "Umm, Ombag? How…" She gulped. "How large do you think the spider who spun this web is?"

The cobalus sat on his knees, a large tear sliding down his cheek.

"Ombag? What's wrong?"

The creature sniffled. "That's…that's my pop up there."

Shocked, Brynwen regarded the skeleton again. "How do you know?" It was small, the size of Ombag. A bit of hair stuck to its skull and most of its tunic and trousers had disintegrated long ago, all except the belt around its waist.

"The belt. It were his lucky one, an' he wore it the night he was…"

Ah. Well, it doesn't seem to have been very lucky for Ombag's father at all in the end.

"I am so sorry, Ombag." She didn't know what else to say. "Forgive me, but we must hurry and get the adamant. I wonder how he found where the monster was hiding it."

"Yeah, well." He wiped his nose with his sleeve and rose to his feet. "That was pop. Too clever for his own good."

"Can you climb this web?"

"Slight problem, there. I'm afraid'a heights."

"Well, they aren't my favorite either."

"Yeah, but…"

His hands wrung his hat, and he squirmed, unable to look at the remains of his father.

Ah, I see. Placing a hand on his shoulder, she squeezed it gently. "I will get it, don't you worry. You just keep watch." *And pray I don't fall into the giant hole.* She studied the web and frowned at the unsavory prospect of climbing it. Never had she liked cleaning the tiny cobwebs that littered the corners of her cottage, but this…well, this topped them all a thousandfold. If only Talfryn were here, he'd be all for climbing the sticky nest.

Brynwen grabbed the edges of her dress and cringed, wishing she'd thought to change into her old clothes at the palace instead of wearing the most beautiful outfit she was ever to wear. "I hope the king doesn't want this back after tonight," she muttered. Quickly, she gathered the ends together and tore off a disgusting piece of web to wrap around it so she could move her legs more easily, very aware of the small creature studying her. "Don't you dare look up my dress." She gave him a withering look.

He shrank away. "Wouldn't think of it."

Unease spread through her as she removed her satchel and placed it on the floor by the wall. Taking a deep breath, she gripped a handful of sticky grey-white web. A sudden gasp of dread filled her. Her heart pulsed, making the prophecy's gold and red letters pulse with it, creating an ache in her temples.

She took a shaky breath. *I can do this. I've* got *to do this. The princess and her people are depending on me.*

But, seriously, why does it have to be spiders?

"Here goes." Right foot first. Then left. After jerking loose her right foot, it made a strange suction noise upon release. *Ugh.* The same trouble happened with her hands, and some of the sticky web stuck to her fingers. "Eww, I don't think that'll ever come off."

"Yer doing great," Ombag encouraged.

"I've only gone three steps."

"See? Progress!"

Brynwen rolled her eyes and detached her other hand and left foot. It was a painstakingly slow process. It was only an eight- or nine-foot climb, but it was the most difficult distance she had ever managed. Perspiration from the effort built up on her brow, her neck, hairline, and just about everywhere else on her body. "This must be what it's like to give birth," she mumbled.

The bright light of the diamond only increased her headache as she ascended. It also obscured her vision, so, much of the time, she closed her eyes and climbed blindly. Often, she'd open her eyes to the carcasses of long dead critters. Meanwhile, each time she raised her hand, more of the sticky web came with it, to the point it looked like she had on mittens with bits of dead things in it. Some hadn't been dead very long, which didn't help her nerves or nausea one bit.

A faint hissing sound came from close by. Straining her neck, she looked in all directions but saw no movement. "Did you hear anything, Ombag?"

"Nope."

Every so often, Ombag sent her a phrase of encouragement. She clenched her teeth against several angry retorts.

Finally, her hand fell upon the small foot of the skeleton. The smooth bones made her skin crawl. Disturbing visions of how Ombag's father had ended up here ran through her brain unbidden. Her gaze fell first on his preserved belt with the wide buckle. Some sort of runes were etched into its metal surface. His skull looked up toward the invisible ceiling.

"I am sorry your life ended this way, Master Pilferer," she said. "And I am doubly sorry about taking your prized possession. But please understand that I must use it to save the king's people up above. I'll give your belt to your son, so you're never forgotten." Somehow, saying this made her feel slightly better about the situation.

When she touched the belt buckle to try to unlatch it, the leather strap freed itself from the bones with surprising ease. The movement caused the bones to shift and its head tilted so the empty eye sockets looked directly at her with his skeletal smile. A silent scream escaped her parched mouth.

"You made it!" Ombag cheered. "Now, get the gem and toss it to me."

Heart pounding loud enough to wake the dead creature, she lobbed the belt onto the floor.

"Hey, you almost hit me!"

Ignoring him, she reached a cocooned hand up toward the shining pink diamond. For the first time, she took a good look at it, ridges and all. The hunger of power grew inside her soul.

A prick to her finger brought her back to herself. Guilt rushed through her. "Nay, as much as I'd like to, it wouldn't be right." She bit her lip. "I'll give the king the adamant to hide away in his vault but keep the book. That won't be too much, will it?"

"Are you talking to yourself up there?" Ombag asked, hands on hips.

Brynwen's face reddened, but it wasn't from the trek up the web. "Of course not," she retorted.

With a huff, she gripped her web-mittened hand over the pink diamond. It didn't budge. "It's stuck." She shook it, the action vibrating the entire web. The Pilferer's hollow bones bumped against one another, giving the morbid impression of dancing.

"I will dance over your grave," came his voiceless promise. The hissing sound happened again.

With a final mighty tug, Brynwen wrenched the adamant free. "Got it!" *Strange. It doesn't stick to my hands like everything else has.*

"Great! Toss it here."

It took a minute to wriggle her body enough so she could lob it at him. If she missed it would go into the abyss, and all would be lost. "Ready?"

"Yes," he said with a raised voice.

She tried not to think about the greedy tug that seemed to play on his lips and in his eyes. *It's just the light messing with my mind. Right?*

Swinging her wrist, she let the gemstone fly. It caught the torchlight, its colors illuminating the place with dazzling light.

Ombag caught it with deft hands. The hands of a thief.

His eyes widened as he beheld the diamond. "It's gorgeous. Just like when pop and I pilfered it from the king's vault."

"Wait," Brynwen called, still partially dazed by the light. "You what?"

"Yeah, didn't I mention?" He opened his sack, stuffed the stone into it, and flipped the flap over; the hint of a glow the only evidence of the diamond's existence. "This isn't yer savior stone. Nah, it's the one from the king's vault. And it's not a diamond or adamant or whatever you need, it's a sapphire. I know, I know, they're usually blue, but hey, money's money, am I right? Well, it was nice knowing ya, Brynwen Masson. You're nice people, but I gotta go. Tell Talridge no hard feelings. G'bye now."

With that, he raised the torch and spun on his heel.

Her chest tightened as he scurried away with the only torch. "Ombag? Where are you going? Come back. How am I supposed to get out?"

"Keep to the left, remember?" The little runt cackled as he left the room in pitch darkness.

CHAPTER 43

*D*esperately, Brynwen tried to get her arms to cooperate, but the webs had tangled in her dress and hair and arms and legs and...

The hissing came again. But this time louder, close by.

Very close by.

"Ombag?" she whispered. "Is that you?"

The web vibrated a bit, like someone walking on a mattress while she lay on it. She could feel every step, the hissing increasing. And with it, Brynwen's limbs began to shake.

"*Welcome.*" The hiss sounded like speech. It was practically on top of her. "*It will be a nice, short visit, won't it?*"

Hairs raised on the back of her neck and her body shook uncontrollably. She tried to think. *What would Padric do in this situation? He'd fight... but with what?*

Something slimy dripped onto her head.

She tried to pivot away, but the slime followed her. When she moved her foot, it was stiff. Her eyes grew wide.

The knife!

Raising her foot was the hardest action ever. Something fuzzy brushed against her shoulders.

Hurry, hurry, hurry.

"Stay still, squirmy creature. Don't you wish to play?"

"I'm not really in the playing mood right now." She tried not to imagine how the monster creature wished to "play."

Quaking fingers finally reached her boot. *Success!*

The "fingers" brushed her again, caressing at first. But then they gripped at her, the fuzzy ends sticky like the webbing.

No! No, no, no, no, no.

Her web-covered hand scooted into the boot. She grinned as she touched the knife hilt. Before she could grip it, the maybe-spider raised her up as though she weighed nothing. Suddenly, she began to spin fast. Thin strands of something wrapped around her ankles. Brynwen couldn't think as she spun round and round, unable to move. Bile burned in her throat as she grew dizzy. Briefly, she thought of praying, but no words came. She'd never see Talfryn or Padric again. Grandfather and Samuel. Her new friends somewhere in the Labyrinth fighting the Minotaur.

Pressure like rope wrapped around her thighs and hips. In a defensive measure, she raised her arms to her chest as Padric had taught her. Something thin and hard was stuck on her hand.

"Fine," a voice said. "I've come back to—"

Blessed torchlight shone again.

And yet *not* blessed, as Brynwen glimpsed the hundreds of eyes and sharp pincers of the largest spider in the world. It's bulky body outweighed her ten-to-one.

Surprised at the sudden brightness, the spider hissed and reared back in pain.

"What in the name of *Dis Pater*?" Ombag swore.

"Ombag…" She couldn't believe he'd come back! "Do…something."

"Uhh. Right!"

A few moments later, objects came hurtling at the monster. Glass jars and pouches. A roll of bandages bounced off several of its black eyes. Things from her own satchel!

"Ombag! What about your own stuff?"

"Sorry."

The whirling halted, although Brynwen's head kept spinning.

The monster reeled in pain as the uncorked jar of Brynwen's Miracle Mix slammed into its eye. Ointment splattered into its crevices. It couldn't blink, but it could *wail*. Shaking her in rage, something nicked her arm. She breathed in sharply and spied the object in her hand. The knife! It must have stuck to her sticky hand when she'd touched it in her boot.

It took a bit of work to coincide sawing and jostling by the giant spider.

Something heavy struck the spider's face. *On Healing and Other Remedies*!

Now the spider was angry—as was Brynwen. It scurried down the web toward Ombag, murder in its many eyes.

"Nice spider." He backed up two steps as sweat poured down his face.

With renewed vigor, Brynwen sawed at the web. At last, the sticky substance tore away. Her arm was free.

It got bright again like a pink sun. In his excitement, the diamond must have fallen out of Ombag's pack. The distraction was enough.

"Thanks." She stabbed at the dark, hairy appendage wrapped around her waist.

It shrieked and threw Brynwen into the web. Her knife hand stuck to the web like glue. Tugging was no use.

"Enough of this! Dinner is served." It bore down on her, pincers wide, striving for her head.

This time, Brynwen knew it was the end. At least she'd die trying. This time, she did send the Lord a quick prayer of thanks for her short life and all the wonderful people she loved and the experiences she'd had. *'The Lord giveth and the Lord taketh away. Blessed be the name of the Lord.'*

CHAPTER 44

"*S*top this!" screeched a raspy voice in her head. "*Stop at once, Aranea.*"

Startled, the giant spider paused, its dripping fangs inches from Brynwen's face. It raised its head in curiosity.

Hair stuck in the web, Brynwen couldn't move her head much, but saw him out of the corner of her eye. The Druid.

"Druid," Aranea said with disdain. "*I see you are still hanging on by a thread.*"

The Druid ignored her. "*I shall not request it again, Aranea. I know where your children hide in the shadows of this Labyrinth. Where they wait for you in the darkest recesses for their food. Release the maiden and your children shall be safe from my wrath.*"

Children? This nightmare creature had *children*?

Aranea's roar of outrage sounded like her hisses. "*But they are hungry. They must eat or they will perish. This one is skinny but will sustain them for some time.*"

A lump filled Brynwen's throat. She wouldn't be just one monster's meal, but many.

The Druid pulled out a vial from his robe. "*Not with this potion. One drop will rip their insides apart until there is nothing left for you to find. You will be* alone."

"*Bah! What is this child to you? She is a weak human, a meat sack.*"

Meat sack? Brynwen's brows knit together in indignation.

"*She serves a purpose. Go, whilst your children still live. I spied other creatures who wandered into the southern end of the Labyrinth for your children to feast upon.*"

The spider was quiet for a minute, contemplating the Druid's words.

"*I will leave. But if you find yourself in my dwelling ever again, my children and I shall relish in your demise, Druid.*" She spit out the cloaked figure's name as though it tasted bitter on her tongue, then ascended the web backward in silence.

Relief flooded through Brynwen when the web stopped trembling. However, her relief was short-lived as she beheld the Druid.

Ombag crossed his arms. "Who are you?"

"Why did you save me?" Brynwen asked at the same time.

"'*Thank you' will suffice.*" The Druid ignored Ombag. As before, his hood covered his entire face. Or was it a woman? It was hard to tell by the old voice and hidden face. The only skin to be seen was the blue-veined hands, which appeared transparent, folds of the gray cloak visible behind them. For some reason they reminded her of shadows.

Brynwen glanced down the endless blackness beneath her. Unless she wanted to guess at the chasm's height, she and Ombag wouldn't be escaping that way. They were trapped.

"*There is nothing left for you to fight for, I am afraid, child. Nowhere to run,*" the Druid said. "*You and your friends—those left—will wish for death in the end. Your brother and handsome knight, both torn to tatters by the Minotaur.*" The unnerving voice seemed to smile as it spoke of Padric's and Talfryn's demises. "*Please tell your friends of my sincere thanks for leaving the present for me.*"

She started.

The Druid laughed, a cruel, ancient sound. "*That is right. In their attempt to tame the beast, they have dropped it into my hands.*" He raised his transparent appendages for effect.

"What do you want with the Minotaur?" Brynwen asked. Nothing made sense. First the pink sapphire, now the Minotaur. *And what do I have to do with it?*

"*Soon, my dear. Soon, you and I will be face to face again, and all shall be revealed. Patience.*"

Another cryptic message. Unless...

"If you have the Minotaur, why do you need me?"

"*At last, we come to it. You have other uses to me and my master. The abilities you inherited from your family, for one. You, my dear Brynwen, are the key.*"

Brynwen cringed at how he said, 'my dear.' "My family?"

"*The family of Aesculapius.*"

With everything happening, she had forgotten that information.

"*Think on it,*" the Druid mused. "*With everything to lose, you have a choice to make. Regardless, I shall see you again very soon.*"

Before Brynwen could respond, the shadowy figure disappeared, taking with him all her hope.

As the Druid vanished, a volley of arrows and steel struck the place where he had stood a moment before.

"He got away!" Aeron cried.

"Brynwen! Ombag! Praise Mithras you are all right." Payla's singsong voice rang through the center of the Labyrinth and echoed down below. She hadn't realized how much she'd missed it after her ordeal. "We despaired when the pink light winked out, but when it relit the sky, we made haste to get here."

Strong hands gripped Brynwen's arms and legs and detached her from the web.

"Really, Bryn. I leave you alone for a minute and you get yourself into another mess. Tsk, tsk!" Talfryn's scratched face grinned down at her.

"It appears we came just in time." Padric knelt beside her, her heart fluttering at the sight of him, thankful he was unharmed except for a few scrapes she could fix with salve—once she made more, no thanks to that little imp.

The others of their party stood around them, including Franco and Simon. She didn't see Cecil or Rawlins, though.

Ombag approached with a sharp knife and made to saw at the web-rope around her legs. Unwilling to have him near her, she swatted his hand away. He retreated a couple yards, every bit as shamefaced as he should be.

"See," he said, "you shouldn't ever trust a thief."

"Clearly." Emotions still rampant and close to tears, her voice and fingers shook with abandon. "This blasted web…Why did you do it, Ombag?" It was the first time she'd really looked at him since he'd left her to die.

"I—"

"And don't give me any excuses."

"Well, I—"

"I want the truth."

Mouth agape, the creature blinked. As though what she asked wasn't something he normally did upon request. He looked around him, all eyes wary. Talfryn stiffened. Payla brandished her shining daggers.

Ombag's shoulders sagged in defeat. "You deserve it after wha' I did to ya." He took a resigned breath. "Fifty years ago, when my pop and I stole from the king, we didn't just steal somethin' shiny. We stole his sapphire, his prized possession. Locked in the deepest vault. I didn't lie 'bout that. He wrapped it up tight. Well, that being my first big outing, I got excited and cocky. Thought we were in the clear. We were nearly ta home when I got the hankerin' ta look at it. Careful-like, I unwrapped it layer by layer. It blinking blinded me! I dropped it, and pop picked it up and quickly wrapped it up again. But 't'were too late; the legion saw the light and came a'runnin."

"That's when they caught your pop," Talfryn said.

His gaze met Talfryn's for a brief moment before launching them down at his feet. "Aye. An', well, I ran. I didn'a think ta stop and help him. Nope, I ran and hid like a frightened ninny all night long. When we came down here and saw the bright pink light, I knew what it were. Somehow, Pop kept it hidden on his person when they threw him in the Labyrinth."

Brynwen felt the fool. Again. "So, if this isn't Aesculapius's stone of adamant, where is it?"

The creature shook his head miserably. "Heck if I know."

In other circumstances, she might have taken pity on him. "You tricked me into finding it so you could steal it all over again. You knew it was a trap, too, and left me to die at that monster's hands."

Ombag's whole body winced. "Seemed like a good idea…fer a minute."

"Don't think I'll let you off the hook for rescuing me after leaving me to die."

"Nah, Miss Brynwen. I promise ta do better."

A resigned sigh flitted from Brynwen's lips. She figured that was the best she could hope for. "Now we must begin our search for the adamant all over again." What she wanted to know was how *Dis Pater* had kept the identity of this shining stone hidden from his son for so long.

"I don't think so. I think…"

As much as she distrusted him, she thought he'd learned his lesson—at least a little—and urged him on.

"Your eyes went all crazy when the Minotaur came by."

Talfryn started. "You're right, Ombag, they did. What of it?"

"What if he has it?"

"The Minotaur?" Brynwen thought back. He was right. When they'd left the Minotaur behind, the prophecy calmed down in her brain. "He's the adamant's guardian."

Padric followed the logic with a nod, squeezing her sticky entombed hand. "What better way to guard it than to keep it on his person?"

Payla's eyes grew large. "Mithras and Jupiter." She slapped her palm on her head, hard. "That was how they revived Asterion. They interred the stone of adamant into his body to heal him, making him immortal. Yes, that must be it. It was not long after Jupiter stripped Aesculapius of his powers. It never occurred to me before, since both Aesculapius and his tools were rumored to have been destroyed."

"Oh, no." Brynwen felt lightheaded. "What happened with the Minotaur? Where is he?"

Talfryn spoke up. "We tied him up with Payla's special thread and left him like we planned."

Now she felt that she *would* faint. "We're too late."

"Why?" Padric asked. "We could not carry him even if we wanted to, what with Rawlins's injuries."

Ombag rolled his eyes heavenward. "Because of you clever lot, the Minotaur's been handed over to the Druid like a little calf to the sacrifice."

"What do you mean?"

"It means, miladdo, he has what he wants."

CHAPTER 45

*B*rynwen allowed Talfryn to cut the web away with his small knife, cursing spiders and all their creepy ilk. By the end, they had twin amounts of web stuck to their persons. Despite everything, she found herself giggling at her brother.

"We must get Asterion back," Padric said.

"How?" Payla asked. "We do not know where Asterion is, right?"

Aeron shook his head. "Nay, but we know where he was."

"I could try to track them from there," Franco offered. "They still have Cecil, I won't leave without him."

Padric drew his hands through his hair in frustration. Some of the webbing from his hands got stuck in his hair, giving it extra volume. "Rawlins will not make it without aide right now."

Rawlins! Brynwen had forgotten about him. Just hearing his name plummeted her mood more. Wounded badly, he lay on the ground on the other side of their group. *How could they possibly want to help that traitor?* She still hadn't had a chance to tell Padric or Talfryn. She'd do it before they all left.

"Brynwen," Payla spoke gently. "Rawlins needs attention."

Brynwen realized she'd been staring at Rawlins. She wondered what expression Payla had seen. She thought of telling the immortal her suspicions, but her words wouldn't work. "I will stay with him." *For now.*

She met Padric's gaze of concern. With reluctance, he tore his eyes away to give orders.

"I will stay and keep guard," Aeron offered, "and help Brynwen if she needs it." He cast a worried glance at the wounded knight.

Padric nodded. "Payla, Franco, with me. Talfryn and Ombag, stand guard here with Aeron. We will return presently."

"What about me?" asked Simon. Miser sat on his shoulder, his tail wrapped around the lad's neck.

Padric knelt on the ground and put a hand on the lad's other shoulder. "Will you and Miser help guard Brynwen and Rawlins from any bad creatures that come by?"

"Including sp-spiders?"

"Including spiders."

Simon nodded in determination.

"Excellent." Standing up, Padric squeezed Brynwen's hand and kissed her forehead. "See you soon."

"Stay safe." She squeezed his hand in returned desperation. A bad feeling crept over her.

At their departure, a void filled Brynwen's chest. She took a moment to pray that Padric and the others would remain safe and avoid the Druid, then rummaged in her bag, but *On Healing and Other Remedies* wasn't in it. Alarm spread through her until she remembered what Ombag had done.

Leaping up, she sought the book in the mess of webbing. There, near the center, was the book, *her book.* It lay open, most of its pages torn up from the monstrous spider stomping all over it, and her medicines had smeared all over the pages.

Usually, it drew her to it, speaking to her, asking what she needed. But it was silent.

"Book."

It was dead.

Aesculapius's soul was dead.

Her soul was dead. The spider might as well have finished her off.

The heart within her chest wanted to burst in agony.

"Bryn." Talfryn put his arm around her shaking shoulders. Blood covered both of them. "I'm so sorry about your book. I know it meant a lot to you. But Rawlins needs help." He didn't know she'd stalled aiding Rawlins, half hoping he'd bleed out before retrieving her extra bottle of Miracle Mix.

"The book is gone, Tal."

"I know."

"You don't understand. I need it." He gave her a skeptical look. "Everyone will die without it, I know it."

Grabbing her arms, he made her look up at him. "Stop it, Bryn. I'm sorry it's gone, but Rawlins will *die* without you."

"Or mayhap he'll die *despite* me." She spit the words out.

Her brother rolled his eyes. A witty retort usually followed, but this time, he just looked at her in pity. "Not this time, Bryn. Let it go." His voice was tired, quiet. He stretched, and from the spiderweb withdrew the bottles, pouches, and bandages within reach that hadn't been damaged. Without another word, he released her arms and trudged to the wall to slide down beside Simon.

Sitting by himself in the far corner, Ombag fiddled with something in his hands.

If she hadn't known any better, she'd have said that Ombag and Talfryn had planned her book's demise. She spun around so she wouldn't have to look at them anymore. It seemed the only people left she could trust were Aeron and Simon.

She steeled herself for what was to come. Kneeling next to Rawlins, Brynwen's skin crawled. She set down the tattered satchel and its remaining contents, none of which had miraculously been broken or destroyed. The knight was unconscious, his normally deadly demeanor neutral. Someone had tied a tourniquet on his upper arm to staunch blood flow from the three deep claw wounds. To their credit, it had worked. This would be the third time the knight ended up in her care. But this time around, she knew the truth about him. Padric's oldest friend. *A liar and a would-be murderer.*

There would never be a day when she'd forget what he had done to her, Padric, and Talfryn. Under the stolen cloak he'd donned, pretending to be someone she cared about, someone she trusted. What irked her was that she had trusted him. Padric worked with him every day, yet he'd been deceived. She was about to voice her objections about Rawlins to Talfryn, who looked as dejected as one could be, but decided against it.

"I could sit here and pretend to heal you, you know," she muttered to the unconscious knight. "And if you died, no one would know." *I would know,* her conscience said, cracking her heart.

The vision of her mentor, Rosa, came before her. She startled Brynwen with harsh words she'd never heard her utter. *"He is your patient; your responsibility. It matters not what he has done, so long as you did your best to aid him. Always remember, Brynwen. We are not maimers of people, but healers of people."*

Brynwen sucked in a breath. A war raged within her. Short, but with feeling and great debate. In the end, Rosa was right, as always.

With some satisfaction, she tore away what remained of Rawlins's tattered left sleeve. There it was, the scar on the forearm. As she relived the moments when he'd tried to take the amulet from her, she had dealt him a long, jagged cut with his own dagger. Yet, as she studied the scar, it didn't seem right. It was straight and clean, and not as long as she'd remembered. After over six weeks, it should have fully healed unless he hadn't taken care of it, but this looked newer. Her brows knit together, trying to pick up all the details. *I must have misremembered. It was dark, and I hit my head. That must be it.*

With reluctance the flavor of bitter herbs, Brynwen located the flat, unharmed container of Miracle Mix and a cloth, which she dampened with water from Talfryn's water skin. If he awoke while she was tending him, she didn't know what she'd do.

She had just begun wiping the blood away with a damp cloth when Rawlins stirred. His eyes popped open and his muscles tensed, causing a face-altering grimace. *So, he does feel. Good.* When again he looked up and saw Brynwen, his muscles relaxed. "It's only you," he growled.

This spurred Brynwen's resolve to scrape more harshly. A satisfied smirk raised her lips when he groaned. She checked that Aeron guarded the entrance to their sanctuary and the other three huddled a little ways off. *Good.* "You didn't kill the Minotaur, if that's what you're wondering." He opened his mouth, but she interrupted. "And by the way, it's been captured by the Druid, no thanks to you."

"You didn't fight it."

Finished scrubbing the blood off, Brynwen threw down the bloody rag on the ground with a sloshy plop and opened the jar of rosemary and hyssop salve. She leaned in closer and hissed, "Padric and Payla are out there right now and could be attacked by the Druid and his minions again. I bet you warned him, and he'll soon be after the rest of us. By the way, this might sting."

The knight's nostrils flared as the stinging agent touched his open flesh but said nothing. His silence turned Brynwen's stomach. He wouldn't even try to deny it. Was he gloating behind those cold eyes? Lastly, she uncorked the shallow jar of Miracle Mix. "I know what you are. I've seen the scar you try so hard to hide from everyone." She slathered on a generous amount into the grooves of each of the three claw marks and some of the other scratches on his face, arms, and bruised torso. "What I don't understand is why you would betray Padric, your closest friend since you were children. You're just lucky he loves you like a brother or else I would let this wound fester like the plague." She unrolled a bandage and wound it around his arm. "And if you so much as disappear to stab us all in the back, I will not hesitate to use a tainted potion on you directly from Aesculapius's laboratory. Think on that as you lie there." She tied off the bandage with a satisfying squeeze. It was a bluff which she didn't know if he'd fall for. If he believed her to be a witch, then all the better.

Expression impassive, Rawlins raised his uninjured arm toward her. A shadow fell over them, and he dropped it to his stomach.

"Brynwen, may I be of assistance?"

"Aeron," Brynwen said, breathless. "Thank you, but I'm done here." Without another look at her patient, she corked the jar with a little more force than necessary and stuffed it into her poor satchel. "Let me check your cuts over here." She led him away—if only it could be miles —to where Talfryn sat with Simon.

·ཊ·

Padric muttered under his breath as he inspected the empty spot where the Minotaur had been bound with Payla's magical thread only a few minutes before.

"If I hadn't made the thread, he would still be free." Payla held her arms as though cold. "If they do anything to my brother…"

"If I had not left him in a vulnerable state, the Druid would not have taken advantage of the situation."

Franco sniffed. "We were all fooled. The only thing he wasn't counting on was the king snatching Brynwen in the cavern. He was really mad after that."

"Hardly surprising," Padric mused. Mad enough to bring the cavern down on top of them. "As you lead, tell us about the Druid."

The tracker studied the floor and trembled. "He speaks in your head." A moment later he began following the invisible trail of the Druid and Minotaur.

Padric nodded, remembering the feeling of a jagged knife slicing through his head as the Druid spoke to them. He thought the tracker was taking everything well considering his harrowing experience thus far. Being a former soldier, he likely kept his emotions in check and at the same time raged on the inside.

"He demanded we not be 'damaged' in any way, although he let those nasty creatures poke and threaten my sons well enough." His eyes clouded over as he remembered.

"Did he say what he needed the adamant for?" Payla asked.

Franco shook his head sadly. "He didn't speak very much. But he seemed able to direct his mind-speech to his minions."

Payla gave Padric a look, but he did not know what it meant. Only that it made his stomach curdle. Franco saw it, too.

Before he could ask, the sound of running feet came from the direction they were headed.

"Turn back," Padric directed.

"Aye," Franco agreed. His jaw twitched and changed course.

Despite picking up the pace, their followers kept up. After a bit, a grunt grabbed Padric's attention. He had just enough time to shove Payla out of the way before the wide fishnet fell atop them.

Tangled in the net, Padric and Franco squirmed for an exit as the rogue cobali danced around and hooted in triumph at capturing their quarry. Completely surrounded, Padric's struggle halted when the points of spears protruded through the holes at him and Franco.

CHAPTER 46

*B*rynwen paced the area, staying well away from the entrance into the rest of the Labyrinth. Everything was going horribly wrong. If only she'd known the adamant was *in* the Minotaur sooner, they might have found a way to defend him from the Druid. But she still didn't know how to extract the adamant from the Minotaur or what the shadowy figure planned with it. There was something vital she was missing, and between Rawlins's treachery, the book's destruction, and the prophecy's text constantly trying to blind her, she couldn't think properly. She, Talfryn, Aeron, and Ombag had discussed the Druid's reasoning a bit, but never came to any good conclusions.

With a cursory look at the helpless Rawlins, Brynwen finally decided it was time. Her stomach clenched as she cleared her throat. "There's something I must tell you all."

From the entrance, Aeron turned to her. "What is it, Brynwen?"

Talfryn mustn't have liked her expression, as he stood up and came over with furrowed eyebrows. He shared a quick look with Ombag, who approached with caution.

She felt trapped with these men regarding her. Taking a deep breath, she finally released the information she had kept to herself for so long. "Rawlins has a scar on his arm."

None of those present made any inclination of understanding.

"Right here." With her finger, Brynwen drew a long line from wrist to forearm on her own appendage.

Talfryn blinked a couple of times, then his eyes widened in recognition. "Are you saying Rawlins is the man in the cloak who tried to kill us?" He raised a hand to rub his neck in disbelief. "But—but he's our friend."

Aeron's eyes bulged. "Are you sure? I've known him for years, and never would have believed it."

"I'm positive. I cut him myself." Brynwen wrung her hands in her skirts. "He's been lying to us this entire time, and is in communication with the Druid."

"All this time, eh?" Aeron regarded his comrade, now his enemy, lying on the floor and shook his head ruefully. He unsheathed his sword. "I suppose it does make sense that the Druid would have someone on the inside, although Rawlins is the last person I'd ever suspect. Well, we should tie him up and keep guard over him at the least."

"I still can't believe it." Talfryn shook his head. He frowned at Rawlins who dozed fitfully. "I mean, I guess I can, with how much he smiles."

Aeron cocked an eyebrow. "He's never smiled."

"Exactly."

Brynwen hugged herself, glad to have finally gotten this burden off her chest. "I still can't believe it either, but that doesn't mean it's not true."

A few minutes later, Brynwen was twiddling the magic knife from Rawlins's boot, the one from the Minotaur's room. Talfryn had thought to search the boot and remove the rest of the weapons hidden on his person: three sets of daggers in varying sizes—two in his boot, his broadsword, and a hidden bandolier of mini throwing daggers under his tunic. And finally, the magical pewter knife.

Without thinking, she practiced some of the moves Padric and Talfryn had shown her. No time like the present.

"Brynwen." Aeron approached with his winning smile. "I see you practicing knife defense. Which ones have Padric taught you?"

"Oh. Well, he's taught me three of them so far. There's the back-handed one." She gave a half-hearted demonstration. "And these other two whose names I can't remember." She demonstrated those, with slashing and stabbing, although she knew the pewter knife wasn't great for stabbing.

"Those are good techniques. But there are a couple I think you should learn as well. If you will permit me. May I?" He indicated the magical knife.

"Of course." She handed it to him.

"Talfryn, would you care to help me with this demonstration?" Aeron asked.

Interest piqued, Talfryn leaped to his feet. "Sure. What d'you want me to do?"

"Come stand over here. Good. Now, raise your arms like you are going to attack." They went through the motions of learning the technique. Brynwen watched in fascination as Aeron moved in and feinted one way then the next, pretending to stab Talfryn in the stomach. Then Talfryn proceeded to pretend to die very tragically.

Talfryn sat up with a wide grin. "I've seen this one. Can't remember where, though."

"Very good. Then there is this one which I think will thrill you." Aeron gave Brynwen a mischievous grin.

Brynwen nodded, eager to learn more. "All right. What is this one called?"

"*Ultima gambit*," he said in Latin.

Intrigued, Simon sidled over, Miser perched on his shoulder. "Can I try it?"

"Not this one, lad. Talfryn, stand over there. I will come at you. Be ready."

A large smile plastered all over Talfryn's face as he readied his fighting stance: arms loose, knees bent. "Ready."

"Talf...ryn," Rawlins drawled. "Don't..."

Eyes blazing, Aeron cut him off. "Ignore him, Brynwen. He just wants attention. Now, as I was saying, you step forward and—" Taking one step forward, in one swift movement he plucked the dagger from his side holster and flicked the knife like lightning. Talfryn flew backwards and skittered on the ground.

It happened so fast, Brynwen didn't react right away. "Talfryn?"

He didn't move.

"Talfryn!" She bolted half a step before a hand clamped on her arm.

Untethered, Simon dashed to the fallen farmer. Miser leaped off and landed on Talfryn's head, chittering in frantic excitement.

Rawlins attempted to get up against the wall, but slid to the floor with a groan.

Struggle as she might, Aeron's grip tightened. "Stay, Brynwen. There's naught you can do for him now."

"Aeron, release me!" Brynwen cried. The face that stared back at her was cruel, his dark eyes pools of malice. "You killed him." Frantic, she tugged at a string tie on his left sleeve. The strings pulled loose easily. Too late, Aeron jerked his arm away. The fabric opened six inches, big enough to show the long, jagged, scabbed-over gash. It took every ounce of strength to keep her body from quaking down to her boots.

"You wretched vixen!" He snatched her wrist and twisted it painfully behind her back. His breath was harsh against her neck. "Lucky for you, my master wants you unharmed. Otherwise, I would have no qualms about slitting your dainty throat this instant."

From the side, a blur appeared, along with a cry of "Relleeaaaa!" But before Ombag could stab Aeron's leg with his magic fork, Aeron kicked him into the wall. The cobalus slumped to the ground.

Brynwen twisted in his grasp, desperate for escape to help her brother, but he clamped down all the tighter. "Why?" she sobbed. "Why would you do this?"

A wicked smile revealed perfect teeth. "You wouldn't begin to understand." From somewhere on his person, he withdrew a dagger. "I've daydreamed of piercing de Clifton's heart with my sword, and you're going to help."

Her eyes flew to her unmoving brother and then to Rawlins, who looked at her in helplessness. *Forgive me. I was wrong. I was so wrong!*

The dagger hilt struck her head and everything went dark.

CHAPTER 47

rynwen sat up with a start, but the throbbing in her head
made her groan and lie back down again. It was another
couple of minutes before she opened her eyes.

A dim room greeted her, the only light source was a torch outside
the open door. *Or wall*, she realized. *I'm still in the Labyrinth.* A rogue
cobalus in tatters stood just outside the room. With a pang, she recalled
what had happened at the center of the Labyrinth. Talfryn, lying so
still...

Blinking back tears and anguish, her throat was beginning to tighten
when someone stirred beside her. As her eyes adjusted to the dark, she
recognized Cecil.

The lad sat against the wall with head and shoulders drooped toward
his knees. He let out a shuddering sigh. Brown hair at all angles and
tunic rumpled, he did not appear hurt except for a small cut on his neck.

"Cecil? Are you all right?"

With effort, Cecil unrolled his shoulders and looked up with puffy
eyes. He only nodded.

She placed a hand on his shoulder and let him sit in peace for a time.
Heaven knew she had enough to think about for half a lifetime. All of
her failures, all her dreams came tearing down around her. It had been

Aeron in the cloak all those months ago. Technically, he'd still worn it afterward, as he'd led her and the others along on a leash, feeding them lie after lie. And now he and his master had the adamant. *Cecil is leverage for later, but for what purpose do they need me?*

They had to escape.

"Cecil," she said after collecting her thoughts. "Have they hurt you at all?"

His shoulders raised and he shook his head.

"Do you know why they took us?"

Another shake.

She regarded him thoughtfully. It was clear the lad was scared to death.

He gazed at her in earnest, as though she should have the answers. On her life, she wished she did. "Your father, Sir Padric, and Payla are on their way to find us." He gave her a blink that more resembled a bird than a lad, then hung his head again. "It is true. They will find us soon, I'm sure of it." *If the Druid hasn't found them first...*

It was not long before Aeron and a rogue cobalus came for Brynwen and Cecil. The traitorous knight led them with a silent scowl, so unlike the facade he had borne on their journey. They traveled a short distance down another passage where part of the wall had broken and crumbled rock lay in heaps on the floor. Her heart pounded in her chest with each step. *How can Cecil and I escape?*

In one of the passages they passed, Brynwen whiffed something rank. She could have sworn she heard grunting from the Minotaur, but Aeron's thick body stepped in her line of sight. Before she had the chance to think much of it, though, they entered a "room" where a half-dozen torches lit the Druid and his followers.

When they approached the Druid, he stood at the foot of a ragged blanket which had once been black. On it, she recognized the tools of a healer's trade: mortar and pestle, three empty shallow bowls, two wooden spoons, two jars, a miniature brazier with an unlit candle underneath, a scale, a sieve, and a pewter goblet. There were bowls filled with herbs, spices, and petals she recognized except for the last two with vibrant colors. One of the unknown herbs was a reddish-orange color, and the other was bright yellow. Last, a jar filled with liquid, possibly water or wine. The display was the last thing she'd thought to see when Aeron brought her here.

"All is nearly ready," the Druid said with eagerness.

"Ready for what?" Brynwen asked. "What do you expect me to do?"

She could almost discern a smile on the cloaked figure's covered face. *What is it about villains and cloaks?*

"First, you shall make a potion of healing. Then you shall extract the stone of adamant from Asterion's body. It is in the center of his chest, where his heart used to be."

"Used to be?"

The Druid's hood shifted. *"Yes. The stone of adamant replaced Asterion's heart so he could live forever to protect the Labyrinth and the adamant."*

Payla mustn't have known this, or else she would have brought it up earlier. "Why do this now, though?"

"My master wills it, so it shall be done."

As vague an answer as any she'd heard of late. She shook her head. "I am a lowly healer's apprentice with mediocre skill. Would you not wish for someone more qualified?" Someone like Aesculapius or Iaso. Not that she wanted the Druid to capture and force them to do this very thing.

"Only the descendent of Aesculapius may take the stone from the beast once placed. Sadly, their skills have dulled over time. Aesculapius would not be able to tell the difference between a potion and a glass of wine.

"Yet, young Brynwen, your power is only beginning to bloom. Your skill with the manticore venom caught Lord Janus's attention. To think, after this, with the proper training, you might be the leader in medicine within a few years and become more powerful than your forebears. Your name will become renowned in all the world. Sonnets will be sung of your great deeds. My master Janus has seen it."

Brynwen held in a laugh at the joke. Janus, the god of time, who could see into both the future and the past. The god who had, just last month, tried to destroy the world. Now he wanted to heal it? And why did everyone think she had healed the manticore venom on her own?

Yet…something about the Druid's offer picked at the back of her brain. Training, *real* training. She could heal anyone at all, without a caladrius or a book. A sort of excitement filled her being.

"Do we have an agreement?"

The awful truth of the offer slammed in her face, and all joy fled. *What am I thinking?* "Nay." Her voice didn't falter. "Even if I said yes, there is no guarantee Janus would keep his word. He lied to Helius to get him to nearly commit mass murder. I won't do it, not for all the healing power in the world."

"Not even if your cooperation might save the life of another?"

Brynwen shifted her weight, wondering where this was going. The Druid beckoned someone forth.

"The traps we originally set for the Minotaur have caught something almost as valuable." He gestured, and Brynwen spun around. There, with a half dozen spearheads pointed at their chests, stood Padric and Franco.

CHAPTER 48

*N*o!

All the blood drained from Brynwen's face as she beheld him.

Hands tied behind his back, Padric stopped short when he saw Brynwen with Aeron and the Druid. Franco ran into Padric's arm. Their abrupt halt incited the wrath of the rogues, who shouted in rough voices, jabbing mercilessly at them with their spears.

Taking a desperate step toward them, Brynwen's foot never connected with the ground as Aeron snatched her arm and yanked. Her squirming and scowling made him squeeze all the more. Nonplussed at her poor attempts to escape, he seemed to enjoy the pain he caused her.

Rage blaring through her, she stomped on his foot. She took small satisfaction in the wince and low growl of frustration he produced.

Until he clenched her wrist and grinned at Padric like a hungry wolf. "Good to see you, Lieutenant." He said "Lieutenant" with all the love the sole of a boot shows to a roach.

"Aeron. I should have known it was you." Padric's eyes turned to slits.

"Mayhap I am a very good actor."

"Mayhap," Padric replied dryly. "Or mayhap you are desperate for attention and begged Janus to take you in."

Aeron's eyes darted as sharp as daggers in Padric's direction, and his hand shot to his sword hilt. His earlier admission, *I've daydreamed of piercing de Clifton's heart with my sword,* might come to fruition after all.

"Enough. Bring the prisoners here," the Druid hissed. He turned to Brynwen. *"Now, child, you have a choice. You can make the potion to extract the adamant from Asterion's body for me or you can watch your friends die and extract it regardless."*

"Whatever it is he is asking, Bryn, do not do it," Padric said. The heel of a spear smacked into his cheek, and he stumbled. When he regained his balance, blood trailed from a cut on his cheek.

Brynwen clenched her fists. The bite of her nails cutting into her palm kept her focused and held the trembling at bay. If she did as the Druid asked, it would mean Janus would win and change the world forever—and not for the good. Padric and these innocent people would die. Aesculapius, Princess Mandalin, and the Relleans would die from monkshood poisoning. She'd only begun to love Padric. Cecil had barely seen the world yet. And what about his brother, Simon, and their mother Lenore, who waited for them in Malham? Brynwen's poor brother lay dead or dying in the Labyrinth, and she couldn't save him.

Stalling for time was all she could do now. "What will Janus do with the adamant?"

"That is between him and me. Now, get to it."

The rogues shoved Padric and Franco next to Cecil against the wall.

Without the book, Brynwen might botch up the attempt at making the potion. Thus, her ineptitude might somehow save Padric and the others. Choosing not to think of the alternative, she drew in a deep breath.

Resolved, she gave the Druid a solemn nod. "I'm ready."

Heart reeling, she lowered herself to her knees and prayed to God for guidance. For strength. *Lord, can You hear me this far below ground?*

For a fleeting moment she thought she could do this.

However, after inspecting all the items before her on the blanket, fingers itching to hold the ruined *Book of Healing*, she knew she couldn't. *Right, I'm going to get us all killed.*

Aeron held out a small, brown, leather-bound book that looked as old as the Druid's wrinkled skin. "The ingredients for the potion are on the third page."

Hesitating a second, Brynwen took the book and opened to the first page. The ink had faded, but it appeared to be a journal or something similar. Aeron's offending black boots remained near her as she turned to the third page with neat, cramped script. Not one word of English ran the length of the page of what looked like a list of some sort, but whether it was ingredients or a shopping list, she couldn't be certain.

"I can't read this," she said. "I think it's Latin?"

Aeron regarded her with raised eyebrow. "But you read Latin in your *Book of Healing*."

"Yes, but that was a magic book. This"—she tapped the cover—"is just a regular book." *I think.*

He snatched the journal and flipped through some of the pages. "It's too ancient for me to read." His eyes slid over the top of the book to Padric. "I bet you would know this, Lieutenant. You will read the ingredients aloud while she puts them together."

A rogue shoved Padric forward. Jaw clenched, he said nothing.

Aeron pressed the book into Padric's chest. Since his hands were tied behind him, it fell to the ground.

"What is your reward for this betrayal, Aeron?"

"Just read it or I will start hurting Cecil over there. One finger at a time. And don't change the wording around to be sneaky. The Shadow and I will know."

The Shadow? Does he refer to the Druid?

Padric deadpanned. "If I am to do this thing, then I will need space."

"How is this for space?" He punched Padric in the stomach. As Padric doubled over, Aeron shoved him to his knees. "Looks like enough room to me. There, you two look cozy now."

"If you make the wrong potion, he dies." Aeron motioned for the guards to hold their spears at Padric's throat.

Despite the terrible situation before them, Padric's presence helped to alleviate a smidgen of the tension between Brynwen's shoulder blades, but not enough to rid her of the distaste for the deed before her.

Once Padric's wind had returned, the Druid clapped his hands together. *"Perfect. You will begin now."*

TALFRYN GROANED. Chittering filled his ears and sharp, little nails dug into his face.

"Am I dead?" He wanted to be dead with the way his heart ached.

"Not dead," Simon confirmed.

Talfryn popped an eye open, then closed it as Miser pounced on his face. The red squirrel chattered at him angrily, berating him for trying to die when they'd just become friends and all.

It felt like rocks crushed in his chest as he sat up. Nearby, a dagger lay on the ground, and Ombag lay on his side in what looked like an uncomfortable position. "What happened?"

"Thought you were dead. Aeron threw his...dagger at you." Rawlins sat against the wall, face ashen, clutching his injured arm.

"Did I make him mad somehow?" Talfryn poked his finger through the new hole in his tunic and touched the tender spot on his chest but found no blood. "That's going to bruise...what's this?" Torchlight glinted off of something in his tunic. Reaching inside his collar, he removed the metal utensil from his undershirt pocket. The pewter spoon, bent and misshapen. "Huh, forgot that was in there. Thanks for your sacrifice, spoon." *And thank you for protecting me, Lord,* he remembered to raise up the prayer.

"Wow!" Simon's eyes went round.

Rawlins grunted. "Took your sister, too."

"He what?" Dropping the spoon, Talfryn shot to his feet. "So you're not...but he is...*Why didn't you lead with that?* Where'd he take her?" Pausing to take a breath, he seethed at how they'd been tricked, and he hadn't seen it. "I'm going to get her back."

With considerable effort, Rawlins pushed himself up the wall with his good arm. "I'm coming, too."

"Rawlins, you're in no shape to—" The deadly look the knight bestowed made Talfryn's face pale. "Yep, you look hearty enough to me. Ombag, you all right over there?"

"Yeah, just a bit…dizzy."

"Great, let's go, then! Simon, bring Miser. We're getting your brother back too."

❧

FOR THE SECOND time that day, Talfryn held Rawlins's arm over his shoulder. This time, though, the heavy knight was awake and taking the lead at a brisk pace, especially for one who'd lost so much blood. *Probably stores extra blood in his muscles. And yet, he seems just as grumpy asleep as awake. Figures.*

Next to Talfryn, Simon hurried in silence as though in a trance. Talfryn's heart went out to the lad who'd been through loads of trauma in such a short amount of time. Too much trauma, period. Miser sat on Simon's shoulder, content to be near Talfryn's food pouch.

"But why would Aeron take Brynwen? I thought he was on our side." *Why is this happening again?* His heart couldn't take it if something befell her. If Aeron really had betrayed them, then no one'd be able to stop Talfryn from tearing him apart. Given enough incentive, maybe he'd end up as ruthless as Rawlins.

Remaining silent, Rawlins's face reddened. His bandaged arm had been tied to his chest so it wouldn't bounce around.

Ombag worked double time to keep ahead of them, the torch bouncing with his short-legged steps. "Been wondering, what'd you do ta make Brynwen think you were going to betray us?"

The wounded knight grimaced. Or was it a growl? Sounded about the same coming from him. "Stop wasting time with stupid questions. Keep movin'."

A dark shadow leapt out at them.

Startled, Talfryn reached for his hatchet.

"Thank goodness you're here," came the pretty voice, so close to Circe's.

Ombag raised the torch so it lit Payla's face, her eyes shining in worry and tears. Her horns almost glowed in the darkness.

"Payla! Where'd you come from? Where's—"

"They were captured. A huge net fell from the sky. Padric shoved me out of the way, and I landed in a side passage. Then a handful of rogues took him and Franco away and didn't even notice me."

Rawlins emitted a scowling curse. Payla flinched and made some sign with two fingers over her sternum.

Talfryn's heart sank down past his boots and into the floor. What else could go wrong?

"That isn't all. I followed from a distance and know where they were taken. I stayed and listened in for a bit. The Druid wants Brynwen to remove the stone of adamant from Asterion's body." Creases formed on her forehead.

And there it is!

"Well, at least it's not *all* bad news," Talfryn surmised wryly.

Rawlins's eyelids narrowed to slits. "How do we know you're not in league with the Druid?"

Payla blinked. "I suppose you will just have to take me at my word."

To Talfryn's surprise, Simon approached Payla and tugged on her tunic. "Payla, are my brother and papa there? Are we going to save them?"

She knelt, his head coming up to her collar bone, and placed her hands on his shoulders. Her eyes shone with a determination Talfryn hadn't seen before. "We will do everything we can to rescue your father and brother, Simon. Won't we?" she asked, peering up.

"Of course," Talfryn responded with feeling. His own sister and friend were in danger, and he'd do anything for them.

"But how?" Ombag asked. "There's only the four of us."

"Six." Talfryn ruffled Simon's hair for five. He pointed a thumb at Rawlins. "He counts as two."

Miser squeaked as loud as ever.

"All right, all right, seven. Sheesh."

Simon smiled for the first time, a crooked affair with a dimple.

Rawlins stepped forward, dragging Talfryn with him. "It'll be my pleasure to break some cobalus and Druid heads."

Ombag paused and glanced up at them with fear.

"He doesn't mean you, Ombag," Talfryn said. For good measure, he glanced at Rawlins's face but didn't like the expression he saw there. "At least, I don't think he means you."

"*otio Evulsionis,*" Padric read aloud. "It translates to 'Potion of Extraction.'"

"Charming." Brynwen jabbed the pestle into the mortar on the ground in front of her.

Rope chafing his wrists behind his back, Padric made a quick scan through the ancient recipe list. It contained the herbs but not their amounts. It had been written from at least the time of Christ, if not before. Gregorio would know the precise time period. He thanked the Lord the immortal was not stuck in this mess with them.

Out of the corner of his eye, Padric noticed the Druid standing nearby but keeping in part to the shadows. In all honesty, he seemed to belong there. Strange how the hand in shadow looked whole while the one in the torchlight looked transparent or translucent, depending on the angle. Who—or what—was he, and how had he enticed Aeron into working for him? The bigger question, though, was how a Druid had ever become enmeshed in Olympus's politics? Historically, they were enemies.

Brynwen had laid everything out the way she liked it yet with much less enthusiasm than usual.

Padric translated the ingredient list. "Rosemary, hyssop, turmeric..."

Brynwen took her time with each ingredient. Each movement and grinding with the mortar and pestle comprised of thoughtful attention to detail, which opposed the furrowing of her brows, making her look older. Too old for her nearly seventeen years. Would they live to see her birthday next week?

There had to be a way out of this. A way around more than a dozen armed cobali, a trained murderous knight, and a magic-wielding Druid.

"Could you repeat that last one?" Brynwen asked.

Remembering himself, he cleared his throat. "Ah, that is *geranium*, which translates to…geranium." He continued to read the list.

Aeron leaned in closer for a perusal, causing Padric's skin to crawl.

His former friend puzzled him. How had Aeron become involved with Janus and this Druid? It was hard to believe this was the man in the cloak who had tried to kill him and Talfryn. Who had essentially pushed Brynwen off a cliff. Now, Padric recognized the familiar way he had fought at the river outside the ruins of Mamucium. Padric had thought the fighting style similar to many of those in his unit, but he had not been able to place it at the time. Aeron's every stroke of the sword had meant not just to disarm but to kill. The dagger thrust into Padric's side weeks ago proved that.

What have I done to earn his hatred?

To his knowledge, Padric had always tried to be fair to each knight in his unit, giving them all the same opportunities and accolades according to their strengths and abilities. There may have been a time or two when he gave preferential treatment to someone, but nothing to warrant wishing him dead. Nothing came to mind as to why Aeron's disdain for Padric was enough to stab him, to try to drown Talfryn, and to harm Brynwen. It could have been only orders from the Druid or Janus—but Aeron seemed to enjoy his role of authority over him.

Padric reached the bottom of the page. "That is all of the ingredients. There is nothing more."

"What?" Brynwen's eyebrows furrowed. "But what do I do with all these herbs?" She reached out to flip the page over, but Padric shook his head. Two spear points bumped into his neck, nearly breaking skin. He winced. "This speaks of the final step to remove the object from the body."

"But how am I supposed to make this? It doesn't give instruction on how much of each type."

"Bryn, I need you to focus. Every skill you require, you have."

"But, Padric—"

"Trust me." A war arose within his mind. They needed to fail to remove the adamant, but at the same time, it was needed to heal King Morfrey's daughter and people. It was up to Brynwen, now. He would try to buy her some time if he could.

"Druid, how did you know the stone of adamant was in the Labyrinth?" He braced himself as Aeron made to strike him.

"*Enough, Aeron!*" The Druid raised his hands for emphasis. "*I shall answer the youth, for it is a fair question. Dis Pater made a visit above ground a few years ago and has been graced as a houseguest of Janus ere since. It took some convincing on our part to help him see our view. Soon, you shall all see the true greatness of Janus.*"

"With the help of the stone of adamant." More like *Dis Pater* had been captured and forced to reveal the stone's whereabouts. The idea made him sick.

"*Indeed.*"

Padric wanted to gag. "Janus's only greatness is for telling time and making other people do his dirty work." He sent a pointed glare at Aeron. Ignoring the spear scratches, Padric leaped to his feet to get in Aeron's face. The startled knight retreated a step. "You have a choice to walk away, Aeron. Walk away and never look back. Janus and this Druid are not to be trusted. Who is to say neither of them will ever betray you, too, as you have done to me? To our fellow knights? Have you no friends among them?"

Deliberation seemed to pass through Aeron's eyes for a moment. Then he blinked, and a grin Padric had never before seen on the young man took shape. Wrong...he *had* seen it on someone else. The eyes. The ebony hair. It sent chills through Padric's body as it dawned on him. *How did I not see it before?* "But nay, you are in too deep, and not just as a mere lackey. You are Janus's descendent."

"His son, in fact," Aeron replied with a smirk which Padric dearly wished to strike. It explained why he looked little like his father, Arthur Drefund, with light brown hair and very different facial features. Padric had always assumed he took after his mother.

"Yes, yes, very good, children." The Druid's voice grated in Padric's head. *"Now you know. Get back to work, or my cobali friends here shall begin taking gouges out of the tracker and his son. You four."* He pointed at the group of cobali closest to him. *"Bring Asterion. The Minotaur will have his greatest performance yet."*

An event to rival Theseus's epic conquest centuries ago?

The unlucky cobali exchanged glances and one of them gulped. Without asking questions, they moved into the next passageway.

Brynwen looked at Padric, the expression of doubt on her face mirroring his own.

TALFRYN SWALLOWED DOWN HIS TREPIDATION. The Labyrinth was really getting to him now. Somehow, evading Eliva in Cataractonium had been more enjoyable than running around the Labyrinth. Especially if they had to *save* a monster like the Minotaur in the process.

"It is just up ahead," Payla said.

"I agree." Ombag scrunched his nose in distaste. Simon and Miser had similar expressions.

For the eightieth time, Talfryn checked for his hatchet on his belt. *Good. Rawlins hasn't keeled over from his wounds yet. Good. Payla hasn't gotten us lost yet. Good. We've met no more villains or traps. Great!*

They made it in no time, although to Talfryn it seemed like a lifetime. Payla pointed down the hall toward some firelight. They extinguished their ever-torches and hid them in a side passage, then proceeded.

The first rogue guard stood near the entrance with a lit torch. The slouch to his stance suggested how invigorated he was about this assignment.

Rawlins did his disappearance trick—which Talfryn wouldn't *ever* get used to—and took the guard out. Talfryn then dragged him into the closest side passage. So far, so good.

Talfryn picked up the fallen torch. Excitement over, the smell of unwashed fur and human body hit him like a wall. He scrunched his nose. "Yep, I think we found him." Also, the near deafening sound of snoring.

The cobalus thief spun in a circle. "Why do all you humans smell so bad?"

"Hey." Talfryn pounded his chest. "We work hard for our stench, thanks very much. Besides, I'd wager our Minotaur friend hasn't bathed in a couple thousand years. I bathe at least once a season." On the other hand, in the short time he was at Cataractonium, he'd bathed almost every day in the public bathhouse, which had become one of his favorite pastimes. Having missed it so much, he'd considered petitioning the mayor of Derbyshire to build a bathhouse but hadn't gotten up the nerve yet. Maybe when he got home.

Talfryn felt rather than saw Rawlins's eyes burning a hole in his head. "Anyway, Payla, did you find him?"

"He should be right...aha." She passed into a dead-end tunnel on the left, shaped like a small room. There, on the floor tied up in the same magical blue thread, sat the Minotaur, who looked every bit as deadly bound arm to toe as without.

Ombag took one look at the Minotaur and spun on his heel. "Umm, I'll keep a lookout outside."

Rawlins leaned against the wall and handed Ombag the fallen torch. "Stand outside and look like a rogue. Shouldn't be too hard," he muttered. Talfryn heard him, but Ombag was already in the main passage.

Talfryn gulped. He lowered his voice so the monster wouldn't hear. "Do we have to free him?"

Payla twisted her hands. "Yes," she replied. She knelt on the floor beside her monstrous brother, their only resemblance in character and physical attributes being the horns atop their heads.

Pulling Simon and Miser behind him for safety, Talfryn did his best to steady his shaking knees. He really didn't want to have to contend with the Minotaur a second time.

Asterion's eyes burst open and flashed red at Talfryn and Rawlins in hatred, as he struggled against the strong thread. However, when his gaze fell on Payla, his features contorted into confusion. A deep sound emanated from his throat. Not quite a moo but not quite a groan. *Recognition?* Talfryn had a strong urge to reach for his hatchet, just in case.

"Don't untie him," Rawlins warned. "Just 'cos you're family don't mean he won't rip your head off."

"Asterion, my brother." Payla reached up to touch his cheek, then lowered her hand. The creature raised a skeptical eyebrow. "Do you remember me? We once played in Mother's orchard when we were children. Only a few times, though, before…" She faltered, her eyes glistening. "Well, I am here now. To help you escape, if you'll let me. These are my friends. Please do not look at them that way, they only meant well."

A puff of smoke escaped the Minotaur's nostrils, steaming up the large gold ring dangling from his nose.

"I don't mean to barge in on family time," Talfryn said, "but it doesn't look like he wants to cooperate. We could leave and come back later?" Small hands gripped Talfryn's tunic in a vice. Simon huddled behind him in terror.

Payla pulled out her small, sharp dagger. "Asterion, if I free you, will you help us save our other friends? Our mutual enemy has captured them. We—"

"They're coming!" Ombag hissed into the room from outside. "No time to escape. Hide." He whipped his head back outside and spoke to whoever approached with an over-the-top raised voice. "It's *about time* you fellas got here. I've been standin' here for*ever*."

Talfryn looked around but there was nowhere to hide. Not even behind the bulking muscles of the Minotaur. They'd have to fight, then. He went for his hatchet.

"We're to take 'im to the Shadow," came a rogue's voice.

Who's the Shadow?

Rawlins gathered everyone in his wide arm span and smashed them into the corner. "Be quiet," he whispered harshly when Talfryn gave him a look.

Talfryn's heart trampled his chest as four cobali entered the room.

The rogues ignored the group huddled in the corner and made a direct path to the Minotaur. The one in charge went right up to him, hands on his hips. Even sitting on the ground, the Minotaur was over two heads taller than the cobalus. "Get up."

Not moving, the Minotaur slit his eyes and huffed a puff of smoke.

"I said get up. Lads." He stepped aside. The rogues raised their spears at the Minotaur's chest.

The monster puffed again in what sounded to Talfryn like a chuckle. He glanced over at the corner where Payla hid with everyone, then got to his feet abruptly despite the taut thread. So abruptly, the rogues fell to the floor in surprise. They rushed to their feet and pointed their spears at him.

"That's better," the leader said with puffed chest.

The group marched out of the room, the Minotaur hopping like a hare. The room shook at each connection with the ground.

Once they were gone, Rawlins released them.

"Good job, Rawlins. That was a good trick."

As a reply, the knight's eyes rolled up into his head and his knees buckled. Talfryn and Payla each caught an arm and gently dragged him over to the space the Minotaur had vacated. The very stinky space.

Ombag rushed in with the torch, illuminating the room. "They're gone." His mouth formed an "o" at the sight. "What happened?"

Payla sat with Rawlins's head in her lap, patting his cheek. "He overtaxed himself, the poor human."

Talfryn fidgeted with his hatchet. "We still need to save Brynwen, Padric, Franco, and his family, and now the Minotaur. *Am I missing anyone?* We need a plan. Or part of a plan." He fidgeted some more. "Why does this Shadow guy want the Minotaur?"

"The Shadow." Payla scratched her cheek in thought. "That name sounds very familiar. That Druid fellow has some shadowy aspects about him, doesn't he?"

"He seems pretty shady to me," Talfryn agreed.

Ombag rolled his eyes.

"Did you see his hands?" Simon asked with rounded eyes. "You could see right through them! Ugh."

"Ugh is right." Talfryn nodded, thinking. "But how does that help us? The Druid is the Shadow, Aeron is the traitor. They have the Minotaur and know he's got the stone of adamant, and Bryn needs to do something. Everyone else is a captive."

Rawlins stirred and his eyelids fluttered open. He groaned.

"Oh, good." Talfryn grinned. "Now that you're done with your nap, we can go about saving everybody."

CHAPTER 50

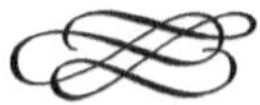

Brynwen tried stalling by taking her time with checking and rechecking the ingredients, chopping with excruciating slowness, and pestling them into the finest powder. Thinking and thinking of how to completely mess it up. But her hands seemed to be doing everything right of their own accord. To them, "removing a stone from a body" was the same as "removing pain from a patient." Except her patient wasn't sick but immortal.

All the while, she could feel Aeron breathing down her neck and the Druid—or Shadow or whatever he was called—scrutinizing her every move from his shadowy corner. Padric had new cuts on his handsome face and neck. Now she stared down at the ingredients ready to be assembled to retrieve the stone of adamant. The stone Aesculapius had used to heal people with any ailment, even those on the brink of death. Its power must match that of Nessie the caladrius, who could heal the greatest poison or venom in the world with a single tear. The adamant could replace the book in a heartbeat. If she could keep it, she'd become an even greater healer. And yet…

The nagging in the back of her mind scolded her, reminding her it was a bad idea. In the end, its power had cost the immortal healer and his family everything. Their memories, most of their skills, and nearly their lives. *No,* she thought with a pang, *it must be hidden or destroyed after this quest...if we live long enough.*

A loud grunt came from the other end of the passage. Startled, Brynwen whirled to see what had entered. The four rogue cobali led the Minotaur, bound with the blue thread. Brynwen blinked, admiring the frail-looking thread which kept the Minotaur secure. It seemed Payla's spell was strong enough after all.

He produced a bellowing moo when he entered, shaking the brazier and sloshing the water around in the bowl. He was more threatening up close than when he'd fought Padric in the half-darkness. With their spears, the rogues directed the Minotaur to kneel not one yard from Brynwen and Padric, and—oh, the stench! They both screwed up their noses at the offending smell.

"Now, Brynwen, it is time to make the potion."

It was no use; she had to do it. The water bubbled to a frenzy in the lit brazier, and Brynwen prepared the herbs for it. How this was to dispel the adamant from the creature, she hadn't a clue.

The moment she touched the first ingredient, rosemary, she knew what to do with it and how much to use.

A touch of Rosemary. Plink.

Three pinches of Hyssop. Plink.

A helping of Turmeric. Plink.

Garlic, chopped…

One at a time, she dropped the ingredients into the brazier as she stirred the contents together. The orange-brown turmeric gave the bowl a red tint and an earthy scent which nearly masked that of the Minotaur. Garlic mixed with sweat, though….not so good.

"Is it almost complete?" Aeron exhibited little patience.

Brynwen gave a half-smile of satisfaction. "It is if you wish for a half-complete potion."

Aeron closed his mouth.

Too soon, the potion was complete, and she stirred until everything was mixed perfectly. Finally, she carefully poured the boiling contents through a sieve into the pewter goblet. In her bones, she knew it wouldn't do anything other than help flush the Minotaur's system of impurities.

When at last she pried her gaze from the cup, the Druid nodded in satisfaction.

"Now, from the book, you will read the incantation." Brynwen made to protest, but the Druid continued. *"Brynwen, you will repeat each word precisely as Sir Padric recites it. Precisely, or else he, Cedric, and Franco will all die. Do you understand?"*

No! Brynwen raged. *This isn't how this should go.* "But I am no magician."

"Do you understand?"

Tears threatened to fill her eyes, but she blinked them away and lowered her head with a slight nod.

"Very well. And Sir Padric?"

"Yes?" He gritted his teeth.

"You will read it precisely, for I know each word."

Padric held back whatever retort he would have said as all the spear points came to rest on his throat. Sweat dripped down from his forehead as he seethed in helplessness. He cast Brynwen a solemn expression of remorse.

Bending over to read the incantation, he took a sharp intake of breath and raised his head as though struck. "This will kill him, Druid."

"Read it."

Padric scowled and glanced at the Minotaur before beginning.

> *Sicut verus magnusque morbus*
> *Qui manat in foramen omne*
> *Alienum relinque corpus*
> *Creaturae huic vitam redde.*

> As an illness true and great
> Seeps into every pour,
> Relinquish the foreign body
> And to this creature life restore.

Brynwen recited the ancient Latin syllable for syllable. As she uttered the final line, the goblet glowed. Her chest ached and head grew heavy. She strained to watch the Minotaur, and a single tear ran down her cheek. The creature, fabled as a despicable monster throughout mythology, had died like Lazarus once—but dying a second time would be unbearable for any creature.

And what about Payla, his twin? She would be devastated.

After a few moments, she noticed Padric gaping at her. He realized his error, and brought his head down to finish reading aloud. "'Bid the host drink the potion.'"

One look at the Druid, and she knew he would never relent in his plan. She rose without spilling a drop.

The Minotaur eyed the goblet with disdain and decried his unwillingness to participate. Every one of his muscles bulged as he tried to break his bonds, to no avail.

"I understand, Asterion," Brynwen said. "Believe me, we are as one in this."

Brynwen made to move when the barest gruff whisper reached her ear. "Be ready."

The next instant, the room burst into action. Rawlins appeared beside her from nowhere and dodged a spear. Hands freed, Padric rose to grasp and twist the spear from one of his captors. Payla threw a dagger at a rogue's weapon while Talfryn dashed into the room with raised hatchet.

"Talfryn!"

Renewed energy flowed through Brynwen's veins at the sight of her twin.

The Minotaur fought with his bonds and released a bellow, the ring in his nose flapping with the cry.

In all the blur of excitement, Brynwen barely spied the Druid dashing at her faster than his frail-looking body seemed capable. Ducking at the last moment, his ghostly fingers grasped the air.

"I don't think so." Sloshing cup in the one hand, she searched the ground for a weapon. The first thing her hand found was the lit brazier.

Blistering heat burned her fingers as she flung the fiery contraption at him. It hit the hem of his cloak and burst into flames. Screeching, the Druid stamped it out with a spell, leaving behind a sooty mess of scorched cloth.

Brynwen wove around the chaos of flinging bodies and weapons. The Druid followed, clawing at her. From somewhere on his person, he produced a corked vial. The green liquid contents sloshed as he uncorked the cylinder and tossed it in her direction.

CHAPTER 51

The first thing Talfryn noticed as he entered the room swinging his hatchet was the number of cobali. It rivaled the number he'd seen earlier by a score or more. *Have they been here the whole time?*

He spotted Asterion right away, being unhappily ignored and still bound in shiny blue thread.

The Druid was holding a glaring match with Brynwen. Talfryn had the urge to go help his sister, but the ones who needed him the most immediately were Franco and Cedric, on the other side of the room, with several cobali in the way. He grimaced as Aeron's knife inched its way toward Cedric's throat.

Thankfully, he'd left Simon behind in the Minotaur's stinky room, so he wouldn't get hurt.

However, Talfryn wasn't so sure they could save Cedric in time. He turned to Payla and said the first thing that came to his mind, "Throw your daggers."

"What?" She glanced down at her gleaming weapons. "I—I've never thrown these *at* anyone."

"Never?" It was Talfryn's turn to be incredulous. "But you practice on trees."

"Trees, yes. People, no. Besides, if I miss, I'll hit Cedric or Franco."

"Just great." *What else can we do?*

They dashed around the smaller cobali, glancing their weapons off oncoming spears and short swords.

Ombag stepped up beside them. "Why the long faces?"

"Ombag!" Talfryn made no attempt to hide his relief. "Need your help. Can you fly?"

"Only on Tuesdays. Why?"

"Umm, it's Tuesday. Sorry about this."

"About whaaaa?" His eyes grew round as Talfryn picked up the poor cobalus by the scruff of the neck and pants. He grunted under the weight. "You're heavier than you look."

"That's a compliment?"

"Oy, Aeron!" Talfryn yelled as he launched Ombag into the air. "Catch."

Turning at his name, the dagger swung away from Cedric's stricken face. Aeron's mouth formed a perfect "o" as Ombag barreled into him. The two went down.

Talfryn winced at their ungraceful landing. "Great job, Ombag! And I forgot, it's actually Friday."

Ombag got up first and brandished his knife at the surprised knight's neck. "I was having a lovely flight 'til your big rear got in th'way."

Before Talfryn could join in, the rogues were upon him. He slashed with knife and hatchet. Payla swept through the group with great dexterity, like a dance. It reminded him of Circe and the dryads Nalini and Eliva. He couldn't help but wonder if they'd had the same teacher.

Two cobali rushed Talfryn, and he sidestepped, but not in time to miss the spear heading for his weak arm. A set of shining daggers deflected the spear with ease.

"Thanks," Talfryn breathed.

Payla huffed, eyes shining and a huge smile on her face. "On your right."

Talfryn spun in time to parry the next blow and the next. "Go untie your brother."

The horned maid nodded, and dove into a somersault, smacking a rogue cobalus's chin on her way up, then bounded to her fuming brother.

Despite his growing stride, Talfryn wasn't fast enough for the third blow that came out of nowhere. The spear heel struck his head with a loud crack. He knew no more.

❧

FEINTING LEFT, Padric pivoted around the rogue. The blasted creature recovered fast and followed him in an arc, his eyes never leaving Padric's. *Clever. A fast learner, this one.*

Padric broke the short spear over his knee and brandished both weapons. A double blow to chest and head, and the cobalus landed, unconscious, on the blanket Padric had occupied moments before.

Another rogue came upon him the next instant. *How many are there?* They sparred and locked weapons, the polished wood splintering under the strain. Padric shoved to spin his opponent's weapon away, but the little fellow's brows furled, refusing to budge. "Yours is a determined lot."

"Some say brave," the rogue replied in a haughty tone.

"Or foolhardy."

A scowl bared the creature's remaining yellowed teeth.

To the side, the Druid flung a corked vial with green liquid at Brynwen. Padric's heart stopped as the shimmering vial passed through the air behind him.

Bryn!

The rogue blocked his path to her. Releasing his hold on the spears, Padric sidestepped to the right. Unbalanced, the cobalus stumbled forward with a confused cry.

The unaware creature stepped onto the smashed, smoking vial a split second after Brynwen stepped out of the way. He screamed as the vapors touched his skin. In writhing pain, he collapsed onto the floor, sores sprouting all over his skin.

While the vial had created a distraction, the Druid had practically floated over to Brynwen.

"Bryn, look out," Padric shouted over the din right before Aeron's steel blazed toward his face.

CHAPTER 52

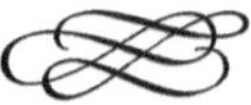

"*P*adric!" Brynwen cried as Aeron leapt at Padric.

"*I will take this,*" the Druid hissed in her head. Before she could react, ice cold fingers grasped her forearm. The potion almost fell from her grasp. All hope drained away as the freezing touch chilled her to the core. "*Now, I will finish what we started. When my master gets what he wants, he will make me whole again.*"

Brynwen's teeth chattered. None of her limbs seemed able to cooperate. "Wh-which is wha-what?"

A pause as the Druid seemed to regard her question. Then he said, "*My body will be returned as it once was, my power fully restored. My master and I will be without equal.*" From beneath the hood, his eyes sparked in long-awaited anticipation. "*Now, come with me.*"

Something must have happened to him long ago to make him this way. "Is that what he promised you? How can you be so sure he will keep that promise?"

Instead of answering, the uncommonly strong creature dragged her to where the Minotaur stood, his eyes red with rage. When they got to within a yard of him, the Druid stopped.

"*Give Asterion the potion. Asterion, you would be wise to take it without complaint, otherwise, the consequences will be great for your sister.*"

The Druid was having a day of doling out threats like cough syrup to a sick village.

It seemed the Minotaur didn't care for the demand. Smoke flared from his nostrils, his ears flicking in irritation as he refused to budge.

Glimpsing over her shoulder, she saw Padric still fighting with Aeron.

The flash of a midnight-blue cape behind the bulk of the monster caught Brynwen's eye before it disappeared altogether. "Perhaps he didn't hear you."

"He heard me very well. Asterion, you will receive your medicine with grace. Or would you care to see Payla suffer?"

Her heart nearly stopped. "Don't, Asterion. It's a trick."

"Silence!" The Druid's free hand jabbed her in the ribs. The potion swished around the inside of the goblet as Brynwen gasped for breath, and her knees buckled.

Two daggers fell at the feet of the Minotaur with metallic reverberations. Payla emerged from behind her brother, followed by two cobali holding spears at her chest. Disappointment filled her face as her hands pointed toward the ceiling in defeat.

Through blurry eyes, Brynwen thought the monster's bullish ears flicked again. After a second's hesitation, he complied and stilled.

With a tug on her freezing wrist, the Druid brought the cup to the Minotaur's lips.

"Stop!" Brynwen cried. "It doesn't belong to you." She imagined the princess dying on her bed, her father weeping over her as she breathed her last. Lost forever, the child's smile and enthusiasm would become the ghost of a memory. Next, she pictured Iaso holding Aesculapius's hand as his spirit left him. *I'm so sorry I failed you!*

With all her might, she tugged at the goblet with both hands. Irked, the Druid strained to keep a firm grip, his icy touch turning her arm blue. Her teeth chattered and chest tightened. Locked in a battle of wills, for every inch she succeeded, she lost ground.

She spared a glance at Payla, frantically sawing at the thread binding her brother. Her captors lay crumpled on the ground.

"You cannot win," the Druid breathed. The skin of his hands became invisible. *"Janus knows your past. Your present."*

Every breath was labored. Brynwen wanted to give in so badly. "And my future, too, right?"

"Would you like to know what he has seen?"

Do I? Will I die like this? Her body felt like a block of ice from the spring by her cottage in the dead of winter. She took a shuddering breath. Steam rose from her mouth. "Not really." She caught movement to her left and smirked. "Nor does he."

The taut thread securing the prisoner snapped and burst as the Minotaur flexed his muscles. With a startling cry that filled the entire passageway, he smacked the potion from Brynwen's hand. Her fingers stung as the cup flew into the air and crashed against the wall. The cup broke in half, its dark contents splattered against the wall and dripped down to the floor.

At the same time, Rawlins appeared holding Payla's forsaken dagger. He sent it flying into the chest of the closest cobalus enemy.

Stunned, the Druid released Brynwen's arm. In an instant, most of the chill fled from Brynwen. She shoved the Druid off of her.

Asterion grabbed the cloaked figure by the throat and raised him off the ground. Strangled, screeching gulps resounded in Brynwen's ears. It felt as though five hundred cats warbled in her head. She covered her ears to no effect. The Minotaur flung the Druid across the room where he hit the wall with a crack and landed in a dusty heap.

Immediately, the screaming in her head ceased.

As did her strength. Payla caught her and helped her sit down.

After catching her breath, Brynwen gasped. The Druid's gray hood fell back to reveal a bald-headed creature. Its grotesque features were so pale, so taut, as though it had lived without having touched sunlight or a good meal in the last thousand years. Green veins popped out of its head like carvings. Strange tattoos in faded ink covered the rest of its face and neck. Brynwen cringed in revulsion.

The Minotaur stalked after the three remaining rogue cobali. Incensed, he charged at them, his massive feet stomping on the ground.

He chased them down the corridor, their squeals and shrieks fading into the distance.

"Brynwen, your arm." Payla gasped in horror.

It was mostly blue, but the spot where the Druid had touched had turned black. "I have some salve…somewhere." But she couldn't recall where it had gone.

"I doubt salve will help that."

&.

PADRIC DUCKED and rolled as the sword swiped where his head had been.

Aeron grunted in frustration. "Hold still, won't you?"

Heart pounding in his ears, Padric scampered to his feet and dashed toward the corner where, earlier, a rogue had pitched his weapons behind a crate like picked chicken bones. He discarded the spear halves and lifted the empty, knee-high crate and flung it behind him. The satisfying smash and a second grunt of anger from Aeron made Padric grin.

There, glinting in the torchlight lay his discarded sword, bow, and quiver of arrows. Hand on the familiar hilt, his confidence swelled. "You know what the captain would say about displaying unnecessary anger on the battlefield."

Aeron growled.

Bringing the blade up as he pivoted, Padric's arms jarred with the force of steel striking steel. Aeron leaned in, his sword biting into Padric's like the teeth of one of Circe's lions into a piece of fresh meat. He clenched his teeth.

How could I have missed all the signs? Dressing well seemed to have been a quirk of Aeron's, but now Padric could see it was all vanity and obsession. His lost comb in the marshes had proven it.

Putting power into his shoulders, Padric finally budged his sword enough to slide Aeron's blade down its side. "Why?" asked Padric. "Why did you betray us?"

The knight pivoted and swung down hard while Padric parried, with little chance of making his own attack.

"Oh," Aeron replied with a sneer, "there are so many reasons, I cannot name just one."

"One being Janus's pawn?"

Aeron pulled back for the first time, causing Padric to misstep, but he quickly righted himself. "I'm no one's pawn. Anyway, that story is long and dull, and I'd much prefer killing you than boring you with details."

His search for an opening proved useful. As Aeron spoke, Padric lunged. They clashed and parried, strike for strike. It humored Padric that sparring with Aeron on the training field had never been as intense as when the former had tried to kill him.

As they fought, Ombag and a rogue faced off nearby.

Another opening came when Aeron overestimated his swing. Moving in, a rogue leapt backward between them, forcing Padric to change tactics. A dangerous glint bounced off Aeron's eye as his sword flashed in front of Padric's face. Then the dagger appeared.

A piercing agony flared up his ribs. Padric staggered, retreating a step. Touching his side, his fingers came away bloody. "Same old tricks, I see." It was only an artificial wound across his ribs, but it stung all the same.

"But they work." Aeron grinned and lunged again.

Back and forth they fought, parrying, and skirting around those fighting and fallen. For every cut Padric inflicted, Aeron did likewise. This dance of theirs would not last much longer. Brynwen and Payla were in trouble. He was tiring, but happily Aeron fared the same.

"Releasing the manticore and *aeternae* was my idea."

Padric's chest constricted as he realized the impact of Aeron's admission. "So, that was why no one could find you for a time. Your actions led to the deaths of Leowyn and countless others."

Aeron frowned. "Aye, it was a pity. He was a good soldier despite his modest background."

"What is that supposed to mean?"

They drew too close to Talfryn and a rogue locked in combat. Talfryn called a warning as another stab of pain bit through Padric's back. Everything became sluggish after that. Somehow, he dodged Aeron's next cutting blow. But Padric went wide on the upswing.

This time, when their swords clashed, they put in everything they had.

Suddenly, the Druid flew across the room and crashed into the wall.

With the barest glance, Padric noted most of the rogues were down. The Minotaur, Franco, and Cedric were free.

Aeron cursed. His eyes grew wild with fury and desperation.

A roar echoed through the chamber, and the Minotaur pounded down the opposite passage after the remaining squealing cobali.

"It's over, Aeron," Padric said. "Your master has lost."

"Never!" He shoved Padric in his battered ribs and bolted down the passageway.

Padric stared after him in confusion. "Why flee, Aeron?" The decision to follow and conclude what they had started or to return up top with the others dangled in front of him.

"Padric." Rawlins limped up with bloodied broadsword in hand. "Simon's down there."

Franco overheard and began running.

Padric sucked in a breath. "Stay with them, Rawlins." Down the corridor he darted on Franco's heels.

CHAPTER 53

Talfryn was shaken awake by an irate Ombag. "You *threw me?*"

It took a couple of seconds for Talfryn to comprehend the little fellow. A groan escaped his lips as he tried to move. His head throbbed. Then his memories of the last few minutes returned. "Seemed like a good idea at the time."

"Yeah, well, I could'a died."

"But you didn't."

"Well." The cobalus scratched his chin. "Guess I'm still in one-ish piece." He helped Talfryn up.

Everything was in disarray, and several cobali lay dead or injured. He spotted Rawlins hunched but standing guard over the unconscious Druid. Cecil looked around, lost. Brynwen and Payla knelt on the old blanket. His sister's arm was wrapped in a cloth.

"Bryn."

Hearing her name, Brynwen spun around. A wide grin spread across her face. "Tal!"

He picked her up and hugged her tight. "I'm so, so sorry I didn't protect you from Aeron."

"Nay, I'm sorry I was wrong about him. I thought he…" Voice failing her, her gaze dropped to the hole in his tunic. She touched it with two ginger fingers. They tapped against something hard.

Talfryn smirked and reached into this inner tunic pocket. "Magic pewter spoon. Don't leave home without it."

A chuckle escaped Brynwen's lips, and she play-shoved him. "Only *you* could be so lucky."

"Well, someone's gotta have all the luck, I guess."

Ombag huffed. "What about me?"

Brynwen smiled, seemingly having forgotten her earlier anger over him. "Thank you for saving me too." She bent down and kissed the top of his sweaty head. He blushed as bright as a cherry.

"Brynwen," Payla called from the blanket. "This is all I could gather. I am sorry." A few scraps of herbs lay in a small heap in her hands.

The healer's smile faded. "We have another problem, Tal. The book and herbs we need to make the potion of extraction are ruined." The small tome in question was the unfortunate victim of the lit brazier candle, which had been knocked over during the melee. Worse, all the spices in the bowls had been trampled to death. And Padric was nowhere to be found.

❧

AERON EMERGED FROM AN OPENING, propelling Simon in front of him. Tiny scratches marred his cheek and chin. Spotting Padric, he kept a hand on the trembling lad's shoulder and raised his sword edge against his neck.

Out of the room limped Miser, his red tail hanging limp. When he spotted Aeron with Simon, he chittered angrily at the vile knight, his little body shaking in rage. Padric could only imagine what curses he was throwing at their enemy.

Franco came limping up. "Simon. Stay calm, son." The tracker looked anything but calm. Padric refrained from ordering Franco to return to Rawlins. It would be futile.

"Release him, Aeron." Padric drew back his notched arrow on the bowstring. "It will do you no good to keep Simon as a hostage."

"And then you will allow me to go free, is that it?" Aeron snapped.

Simon whimpered as the knife nicked his skin, a trail of scarlet trickling down his neck.

"I didn't think so. This one will remain with me for a time. Just keep the Minotaur away from us, and he might live."

"Please, I beg you to let him go." Franco raised his hands. "Take me instead."

"Stay away, now." Aeron stepped back. The terrified Simon moved with him like a helpless baby rabbit.

Padric's face clouded with rage, and he dared a step nearer.

Aeron pulled on the blade another fraction. "Uh, uh, Padric. One more step, and you'll have to bring little Simon here back to his mum in pieces. If you shoot me, my sword will slip and kill him first. I dare say you wouldn't want that." He *tsked* and continued pulling Simon backward down the passage.

Padric's chest tightened, but there was nothing he could do that would not endanger Simon. "You will not get away with this betrayal, Aeron."

"I think I already have." He flashed another wicked grin. Padric wished nothing more than to break that perfect nose.

After five retreating paces where no one dared to move, let alone breathe, a loud disturbance fell upon their ears.

Boom, boom, boom. The heavy paces of the Minotaur.

Padric froze, unsure what the creature would do.

Worry crept over Aeron's face as the monster rounded the corner where they were headed. He pivoted to be perpendicular with the new and current threats.

The Minotaur halted when he saw the scene before him, gaze zoned in on Aeron. His chest heaved after his cobali chase. Fresh blood coated his arms and chest.

While Aeron took in the biggest threat in the corridor, Padric released tension on the bow. "When he releases Simon..." he whispered to Franco. He hooked the bow over his shoulder.

Franco nodded, determination in his face. "Got it."

Dashing the last three yards, Padric bared his steel. Franco followed close behind.

Hearing Padric's sword leave its sheath, Aeron knocked Simon to the ground as he drew his sword up.

Steel clashed as though their reprieve had never happened. But now, instead of his confident smirk, Aeron fought with a dour scowl. Whatever his connection to the Druid, everything had been bent on him achieving their deadly goal with the Minotaur. Padric directed Aeron away from Simon. In a flash, Franco grabbed the lad's hands and hauled him away.

"Why does Janus want the adamant?" Padric pressed as he parried.

Aeron rolled his eyes as he stepped left. "All your blasted questions. Your curiosity is tedious, you know that?" He blocked Padric's strike at his knee. "You and the Signore are always rattling on about inconsequential topics."

As Aeron spoke, Padric found an opening at his enemy's side. *He should know better.* Regardless, Padric thrust for it. Then the steel of the dagger hilt flashed toward his face.

Next thing Padric knew, he was sprawled on his stomach, an aching knot on his forehead. The mother of all headaches was so intense, he thought he might be sick. Only the ringing in his ears stopped him from passing out.

All at once, his vision cleared. His sword lay on the ground, forlorn and forsaken. He reached for it. Every sinew in his body screamed as he stretched his arm out. Then a black boot smashed into his hand.

Bright stars flashed through his vision.

"After you're dead," Aeron was saying, "I won't miss your drills." The boot twisted, and Padric truly thought he would pass out. Aeron's other boot kicked him in the kidney, hard. "Nor the lectures on weaponry. Gods, how I hate your voice." Another twist. Something in Padric's hand popped.

Holding in the gasp, it took all of his will not to make a sound. Padric refused to give Aeron the satisfaction. An inner voice cried out: *Do not give up yet.* Easier thought than done. Images of Brynwen and his friends blared through his thoughts. His family. They still needed him.

"I think it's my turn now."

Franco's shadow moved along the floor, his foot falls pacing behind Padric.

"Tracker." Aeron spat with disdain. "I've seen you fight; you can't best me."

"I don't have to best you, betrayer. I just have to keep you busy for a minute." In a blink, Aeron ducked, Franco's dagger flying past where the knight's head had been.

Clenching his teeth again, Padric swung his leg out and hooked it around Aeron's unencumbered knee. His leg buckled. Hand released, Padric lunged for his sword and twisted it up. It slid into Aeron's side beneath his ribs like cream on a pastry. Shock sprouted on the traitor's face as he sunk to his knees. He looked at the wound like someone watching a snail race.

A trickle of blood covered his lips.

The sword slid out of his foe as Padric dragged himself to his feet. He stared down at the fallen knight, the adrenaline leaving him, hand smarting. He shook his head at the loss of someone who he, until a few minutes ago, had deemed a friend. A brother in arms. *When did his heart darken? When did Janus come into his life?* It was clear Aeron held no squabbles over killing others. This in itself could not lightly be forgiven. "I still do not understand your choice in taking this path, Aeron."

"Don't you dare pity me." Aeron sneered and spat blood at Padric's feet.

"Despite my revulsion with your actions, I do. We were comrades once. Whatever led you to take Janus's hand and do all of this, I cannot fathom." He knew Aeron did not have the happiest home life, but this was an extreme he never would have guessed in a hundred lifetimes.

"We should go." Franco put a hand on Padric's shoulder to turn him. He had already retrieved his dagger.

"You should finish me, de Clifton. Don't leave me to that maniac Minotaur." Aeron indicated behind him to where the Minotaur still stood as a guardian over them.

The last of Padric's patience broke apart like stale bread. "As you left me to the river with a hole in my side? I think I will." He made a quick nod to the Minotaur. "Mayhap, in your final moments, you will reflect on your monstrous choices and pray to God for forgiveness."

"This isn't over." Aeron spat again, more droplets of blood spluttering on his lips.

Lips the maidens at home adored. Padric shuddered at the thought.

"I will haunt you until the end of your days. You shall never be rid of me."

Padric spun on his heel, not looking back. "Until we meet again, then." *Which I pray will never be.*

CHAPTER 54

"I've failed," Brynwen lamented, staring at the burned book and trampled herbs as though she could will them back into one piece.

"Can we get out of here now? I already plundered the ugly Druid geezer's robes." A huge grin spread across Ombag's face. He patted his bag like a cat who'd caught a mouse. Sure enough, his drawstring bag was filled to bursting, and the sound of glass clinked as he shifted his weight.

"Were all those potions in his robes?" Talfryn asked.

"Be careful with those, they can be dangerous." Brynwen remembered the green liquid which had maimed the cobalus earlier.

Looking around, Brynwen noticed that Cedric was following Ombag's example and poking at the dead rogue cobali. "Where are Padric, Franco, and Simon?"

Rawlins pointed. "They went down this tunnel."

As they dashed past the lifeless Druid, Brynwen didn't deem it worth the effort to look at the horrid creature one last time.

A cuff of ice caught Brynwen's ankle. With a cry, she crashed onto the floor.

332

"Nay!" shouted the Druid. His shrill voice hissed with desperation. *"You shan't escape me. Cobali, to me."* But they were dead or gone.

The cloaked being cringed, not letting go of Brynwen's freezing leg. Payla and Talfryn grabbed Brynwen's hands and tugged, but the determined creature had inhuman strength.

In his fretting, Ombag's sack shifted, and a bottle of red liquid poked its stoppered neck outside the bag's opening. Brynwen reached for it and slammed it down on the Druid's ugly white head. Everywhere the liquid touched began to boil, causing the creature to screech and writhe in agony.

As Rawlins brought down his sword toward the Druid's neck, the creature stretched its free hand into Ombag's shadow. His cold eyes sparked. With a creepy cackle they would never forget, the Druid's body dissolved into a mist of gray. The shadow absorbed the mist until it was nothing but a memory.

They all gaped at the spot in horror. Brynwen's skin prickled with goosebumps as though a hundred insects slithered all over her body.

"Shadow Druid," Payla said with shaky voice. "Time to go. We must find Asterion and the others."

Rawlins extended a hand to Brynwen. Raw guilt built up in her chest. Despite her cruel treatment of him earlier, he still wanted to help her. She took his hand. On her feet, she burst out, "I'm so sorry, Rawlins. I can't believe I thought you betrayed us and worked for Janus. Can you ever forgive me?"

He nodded. "I…" His mouth clamped shut, although his expression revealed he wished to say more.

"Oh," Payla said. "Very curious. You can't speak of it, can you? Aeron or the Druid must have put some sort of spell on you. When we return to the surface, mayhap my mother and aunt can find an antidote."

"That explains so much," Brynwen said.

An incensed moo carried down the corridor where Brynwen and Cedric had been held captive earlier.

All eyes met in fear, then they raced down the corridor.

They soon found the Minotaur, Padric, Franco, and Simon staring at a puddle of blood. Brynwen's heart burst as she saw them all together, cut and bloodied; even little Simon.

She embraced Padric with all her might. His strong arms caught her, and all the terror of the last few hours fled. When he released her with reluctance, all the warmth she'd felt went with it. The forlorn look in his eyes broke her heart. She cupped his chin and willed her love and hope to him, for God to give him strength in his suffering, although she didn't know for what.

Then he removed her satchel from his shoulder. "It is mostly intact." His mouth set into a grim line. "Aeron shall not bother us again."

She nodded and hugged the bag to her chest, her mind and heart conflicting, not understanding how Padric could feel any remorse for the double-crosser.

"So, what happened to Aeron?" Talfryn asked.

"I am not sure. He was dying. We left the Minotaur to deal with him whilst we searched for your things, and returned to find this." He gestured to the puddle.

The Minotaur mooed in Payla's direction. She frowned and turned to them. "Asterion says an arm came out of Aeron's shadow and pulled the dying youth into it.

"The Shadow Druid took him?" Brynwen asked.

Payla stooped over the blood with a dour face. "It seems so. At least now we know how Aeron planned to get out—through the Shadow gateway." She explained to Padric and Franco what happened with the Druid and Ombag's shadow.

"But why take Aeron's dead body?" Rawlins asked.

"He may not be dead yet." Vexation and guilt passed through Padric's green eyes.

"We don't have time for this." Brynwen cast a guilty glance at the Minotaur, then lowered her voice. "To cure the monkshood poisoning, we must extract the stone of adamant from Asterion. I think we have the ingredients for the potion in the palace's herbarium, but he must come with us. Will he come?" she asked Payla. "I will do everything I can to keep him alive." She prayed she could keep that promise.

Payla bit her lip and regarded her brother. "Allow me to speak with him."

"Asterion?" Payla stepped around the blood. She took her brother by the arm and led him a short distance, then spoke to him in Latin. Their heads were animated in discussion. After a couple of minutes, they returned to the group, a smile on Payla's face that didn't quite reach her eyes.

"He agrees. I think we can just make it." She removed the enchanted ball of red thread from her bag and her breath caught. "Oh, Mithras." Turning the ball, Brynwen gaped at the spliced end of the thread.

"Aeron," Padric and Rawlins said with ire.

"We can find the way out." Franco patted his older son's shoulder. The tracker sounded more confident now that his sons were returned to him. He nodded at Cecil. "Son."

Closing his eyes, it took a few seconds for Cecil to get his bearings. He pointed to the left. "This way."

CHAPTER 55

Taking a rest was out of the question, Brynwen knew, but she wished for it, nonetheless. After a few false turns, Cecil, with the aid of Franco, found his groove, and they made their way to the steep stairs, tired but eager for the long ascent up. Everyone breathed more easily once they reached the top. They were met by the relieved faces of Gregorio, Ulysses, Iaso, and King Morfrey. Several curious city folk gathered around the group as well.

King Morfrey pushed his way to the front, shoulders hunched and anxiety creasing his handsome features. He fidgeted and shifted from polished boot to polished boot as an antsy child would. "Did you get it?" All eloquence seemed to have left the ruler.

"In a sense," Brynwen answered. She stepped aside to reveal the Minotaur still lurking in the shadows of the Labyrinth. Next to him stood his horned sister.

The king's resolve hardened while several people gasped and scampered back a few paces.

Brynwen raised her arms. "Do not be afraid. He will not harm you. In fact, he has promised to help us. Come on, Asterion." She waved for him to follow.

Payla rubbed her hands together. "I am afraid he cannot leave the

Labyrinth. When he received the adamant, he made an oath never to leave. I will remain with him." She sunk into the shadows.

"Then I'll bring what I need back here."

"We will be swift," Padric promised with a bow. "Your Majesty, how fare the princess, Master Aesculapius, and the others?"

"Not good, I am afraid. They may have another couple of hours left in them or mayhap last until morning. It is hard to say."

"Where is Aeron?" Gregorio's face had turned ashen as they followed the king and healers to the palace.

Padric's body stiffened beside the tutor. "He was false, Gregorio. He worked with the Shadow Druid."

"Aeron?" Closing his eyes, Gregorio bowed his head. "I should have seen it."

"We all should have." Padric sighed. "But we saw what we wanted or were made to see."

This was true enough, Brynwen realized. She had wanted to see the good in all of the knights of Chaddesden and saw only what Aeron wished her to see. It occurred to her that the ordeal was more traumatic for Padric and Rawlins since they'd known Aeron for years, whereas she'd only known him for a month. It didn't make it any less painful for her, though.

While moving, she explained to Iaso what herbs were required for the potion. She nodded eagerly, quickening her steps enough so Brynwen had to work to keep up.

Each step up the staircase tied Brynwen's stomach in tighter and tighter knots. *How can I hope to cure the illness with only the stone of adamant and no book or journal?* The adamant itself was not enough, like Nessie's tears were not enough to heal Padric, Gregorio, and the other dying patients in Cataractonium, but needed a salve to go with it. She had one shot at it. *One.*

"Bryn." Padric put a warm hand on hers. Peering down at their hands, she noticed how her braid had wrapped itself at least three times around her finger. At the third landing, he guided her to stand aside. "We will meet you up there in a minute," Padric explained to the others. "Bryn, my sweet," he repeated once they'd gone, his whisper soft and brimming with concern. He placed her hand in his and rubbed the backs of her fingers with his thumb. The other hand had been given salve and bound in a bandage. She would inspect it more later. "Tell me what is wrong."

"I'm fine, just tired from the Labyrinth. You could use more salve on your—"

He shook his head with a wry grin. "Nice try, avoiding my question. Please, Bryn, you can trust me."

She grimaced, not wishing to admit to being the fool. "I know, Padric. It's hard to explain..."

He caressed her cheek and a trill of tickles pranced up her spine. "Try me."

It felt as though an apple had lodged in her throat. Three times she had to swallow to make it go away. With a tug, she pulled out of Padric's grasp and spun around, ashamed of what she had to say. "Well, I...don't know what to do without the journal or *On Healing and Other Remedies*. The book has been an impeccable aid over the last month. I couldn't have saved you and Gregorio without it. My patients at home have improved sevenfold since opening its pages. But now...I am lost. I am about to kill Asterion, and I will likely kill the princess and everyone else in the palace, too. They are dying, and I only have one chance to make the perfect antidote to a poison without an antidote, or else..."

"Stop." Sure, strong hands grasped her by the arms. Padric spun her and pulled her back into his chest. She breathed in his rich scent of sage and leather. Even after all the fighting and the adventure in the Labyrinth, he still retained the same wholesome smell. "Why do you believe the book will help you? You were already an amazing healer before coming across it—I can attest to that. The Lord gave you your gifts, Brynwen, not the book. While it may have helped you save me and Gregorio, it was you and Circe, your gift and prayer, that provided the antidote."

"It is kind of you to say so, but..."

He cupped her face in his hands. "But nothing. Trust your instincts, Bryn. Months ago, as I was convalescing in your cottage, I recall listening to you hum as you made the poultices and chamomile tea. The smile of contentment and love went into each chop and stir of the process. You pour your heart into your work, your soul." He pointed at her heart. "The book is a tool only, and Aesculapius and Iaso would agree. Being a descendant of the greatest physician to have ever lived, your powers are only at their beginning stage. Think on it."

"Bryn," Talfryn called down from the next flight of stairs. "Iaso is about to start without you. She's threatening to chop them up to make tea scones."

"I'll be right there!" Brynwen called, cracking a smile.

"You can do this." Padric slid his hands up and down her arms. "I have faith in you, as do Talfryn and our friends."

"No pressure," Brynwen said drily.

Padric took her hand and led her up the stairs. The little voices in the back of her head warred with each other. *Can he be right? Can I do this without any books?*

You have been doing this for years.

Yes, but not as well without the book.

A part of her wished she could turn the loud part of her brain off for a moment of silence so she could think instead of worry, which only ate at her insides.

"Is there anything else I can do?" Padric asked at the door to the herbarium.

She squeezed his hand, trying to remember every word of his beautiful speech. "Besides being wonderful?" Her stomach growled, remembering how little food she'd eaten that day.

He laughed and pecked her on the lips, making her heart go all a'flutter. "I will ask the cook to fix you something. We cannot have you fainting over the burners."

"Thank you," she said with a little laugh.

After kissing her forehead and making her blush some more, he, Talfryn, Payla, Rawlins, Ombag, and Ulysses went to see about food. Gregorio stayed to help out as much as he could, if only to be a grunt and hold a bowl or do some such task.

"Call us if you need help," Talfryn offered.

§.

"Where is *On Healing and Other Remedies?*"

Reaching for the jar of rosemary on the shelf, Brynwen's heart cried over its loss. "It's gone, Iaso. Lost to the Labyrinth."

At that, the tension from Iaso's shoulders uncoiled. She placed a hand on Brynwen's upper arm. Brynwen had expected a smug expression, but instead the healer regarded her with understanding. "I am sorry it had to be this way. And that I did not tell you about your relation to us sooner. I feared the knowledge might draw you to *On Healing and Other Remedies* even more."

"Man was not meant to have such a tool," Gregorio said. "Too much power corrupts the balance of the world. Mayhap it was the will of the gods. And your God," he added with a nod of respect.

Or maybe my God wanted to tell me something—He had to shout. A lot.

"Yes." Some of the anxiety squeezing Brynwen's stomach receded. "I see that now. But I miss it, all the same. It was a part of me, even if only for a short time."

Iaso nodded. "I, too, understand, and for a long time it was beyond frustrating."

"Me most of all," Aesculapius said weakly from the couch, face drawn.

"Papá, you promised not a peep."

"I said no such thing."

Iaso raised her hands in defeat.

Brynwen took a deep breath and Gregorio nodded to her with encouragement. *It is time. No more dallying.* The ingredients she had told Iaso about were set up before her. "Looks like everything is here. Let the ritual begin," she said wryly.

It took Brynwen little work to repeat Padric's every word as recited from the journal. Crushed and sprinkled into the warm brazier, she stirred until the correct consistency bubbled before her.

Satisfied, she poured the contents into a pewter cup.

CHAPTER 56

*P*ewter cup in hand, Brynwen hurried through the streets of Rellea with Iaso, Talfryn with Miser, Padric, Gregorio, Ombag, Ulysses, and Rawlins behind her. She dared not spill a drop. If she were a bystander, they'd have made an odd sight. Despite the late hour, a few curious citizens followed behind. But all her efforts were focused on retracing her steps to the Minotaur.

When the opening to the Labyrinth at the edge of the city came into view, Payla and Asterion emerged from its shadowed recesses.

Dried tears stained Payla's cheeks.

"I'm sorry we took so long..." Brynwen began. She was about to potentially kill her friend's twin brother. They'd needed all the time they could for a final meeting.

"It is well." Payla forced a smile that quickly faded. With a final squeeze of Asterion's hand, she stepped away.

In that moment, knowing what she had to do, Brynwen couldn't breathe.

Padric came up to her and cupped her elbow. "Bryn." His breath caressed her cheek. "I shan't ask how you fare, but know I am here. We are all here for you." When he released her, she thought she'd liquify into a puddle.

"It is time," Iaso said. Brynwen couldn't help but notice how the healer's hands twisted into the fabric of her green skirt. In vain, Brynwen tried to remember the words Iaso had made her memorize. Unfortunately, they had to be in Latin.

Taking slow steps, Brynwen approached the Minotaur. She felt so small and inconsequential compared to the mammoth creature whose horns were nearly as long as her arm and very sharp.

Instead of the rage she had seen in his demeanor earlier in the day, he now seemed calm. Resigned to his fate.

"Asterion." She tried not to let her voice shake. "This potion will remove the stone of adamant from your body. In so doing, it may revert your life to that which it was before. By your leave, the stone will help save the people of this city from certain death." Her mouth was dry. "Do you accept the fate of your gods?"

The Minotaur gave a slow nod of understanding. "I...do. I am... ready." The gruff, unused voice of the Minotaur surprised Brynwen.

Next, Brynwen was to recite the incantation. But her mind went blank. Heart racing, she tried to recall the words. Oh dear, how had Padric pronounced them?

You are a daughter of Aesculapius. Of Apollo, the whisper of a voice reminded her. It sounded nothing like the grating utterance of the Druid, but something more natural, wispy. Like her mother. The thankful trees from the forest outside the ruined Mamucium came to mind. *You are not alone.*

The presence of those she cared about entered her consciousness. Their love and support filled her. Most of all, they believed in her. When she hadn't believed in herself, they were there. Even Rawlins, whom she'd threatened in anger earlier, stood by her side.

That's it!

It's so simple. I am a daughter of Aesculapius and Apollo. But I am also a daughter of God, who gives me love and strength. Concentration narrowed on the task at hand, her breathing slowed. The Latin incantation came to her lips unbidden.

After she uttered the final word, the potion glowed a faint, whitish-blue like before.

"Is it working?" Talfryn asked in awe. Padric nudged him in the arm.

The Minotaur took the goblet from Brynwen's hand and drank with care until the last drop was gone. He extended his arm to return the cup to her, when his body shook with tremors. The cup fell from his hand and crashed to the hard ground.

Choking, he crumpled to his knees, clutching his chest.

Falling to her knees in front of him, Brynwen regarded the creature with helplessness. "What did I do?"

"The potion is working," Gregorio said. "The adamant is working its way out."

Sweat covered the Minotaur's face while a whitish-blue glow emerged over his heart. On instinct, Brynwen touched the spot on his thick chest. Pressure thrummed against her fingertips. She gasped when her fingers brushed against the smooth surface of the object. In seconds, the white stone rested in her hand.

Asterion slid to the ground. Blood streamed down his neck from the re-opened laceration of Theseus's two-thousand-year-old death stroke. Payla dove after him and caught up his head, tears streaming down her face. "Oh, Asterion! I will miss you. Rest well, my brother."

Asterion raised a massive hand to her cheek to wipe away a tear. "Pay-la. Don't...c-cry." Then his eyes dimmed, and his hand dropped to the floor.

"I love you too."

CHAPTER 57

*R*eturning to the herbarium, Brynwen and Iaso whipped up from memory the biggest batch of anti-venom they could for the princess and nearly fifty guests who had been poisoned by monkshood. A handful had unfortunately died while she'd been in the Labyrinth. The adamant emanated a healthy glow as it rested on the table next to the large bowl of ingredients, as though happy to be of use again. They used up every bit of the herbs the recipe called for, including the stores in the palace garden. Instead of making an oint-ment, though, they concocted a liquid to match its potency for the patients to drink.

Barely lucid, Aesculapius rambled on and on about kittens and salves made specially for ants and "those spiders with the long spindly legs."

"How do I use the adamant?" Brynwen asked.

Iaso drew her lips together and scowled. "The exact procedure is hazy, but it had to do with intent. As I recall, *Pater* would essentially ask the medicine to heighten its potential for the recipient. Sometimes he touched the adamant to the ingredients to increase their healing prop-erties as well."

"Taking the antidote won't make him remember all of his past, will it?"

"I...do not know."

Gregorio leaned over the glowing stone in fascinated study. "Did you know..."

Despite their rush, Brynwen smirked, ready for the tutor's ever-ready knowledge quips.

"...that the caladrius's power originally came from the stone of adamant?"

"It did?" Brynwen asked. "How old is Nessie? Has she been around for thousands of years?" She had to wonder about her little white-winged friend. It would make sense that she could be immortal, based on where the bird was found, caged under a dusty old tomb for who knew how long.

"Who is Nessie?" Iaso asked.

Not hearing her question, Gregorio scrunched his forehead in thought. "I'm not certain of her age. Yet, since there have only been a score ever seen, it may be so."

In less than a half hour, Brynwen swiped the sweat from her forehead. Some of the giant spiderweb still stuck on her forehead. She and Iaso had done it. An overwhelming wave of relief and exhaustion swept over her as she hovered the stone of adamant above their creation. *This must work. Please, Lord,* she prayed. *Please heal everyone of this terrible affliction.*

Sinking half of the adamant into the antidote, warmth spread throughout Brynwen's body, a caress of comfort and confidence. After a couple of seconds, the warmth dissolved but the feelings it had bestowed remained.

She picked up an empty vial and scooped up the creamy white liquid into it. Brynwen bit her lip. "We need a tester."

"Papá," Iaso said with determination. She rushed to her father and shook his shoulder, but he was weak and nearly gone.

"Are you sure?"

"Yes."

Uncertain, Brynwen handed her the vial. Without any hesitation, Iaso ripped the cork from the glass container and downed the contents into her father's mouth. He coughed and spluttered, and Brynwen was sure they'd killed him. In another minute, his breathing evened out and his muscles relaxed.

Brynwen didn't let out her held breath until he opened his eyes. *Praise be!* Encouraged, she got to work. Into two large baskets lined with fluffy white towels, they tucked the fifty-one other vials filled with the antidote.

Gregorio gripped her arm. "What if it only worked on Aesculapius because he is immortal?"

"We must risk it," she said. "There's no time to try again."

She opened the door to the susurrus of conversation emanating from her brother and friends, still gathered in the hallway. They were saying something about Circe and the Minotaur but stopped abruptly when she came out and watched her expectantly.

In her exhausted state, Brynwen almost giggled. "Yes," she replied to their unspoken query. "I think I have it. The king must know first." They hurried down the stairs and dashed into the princess's chamber.

The king launched to his feet. His eyes begged for happy news, but his mouth wouldn't form the question for the answer he didn't wish to hear. He looked so old and tired, nothing like the proud monarch who had demanded her help a few days before. The heir of the god of wealth and treasure was naught but a statue of his former self.

"She has it," Iaso said. "It worked on my father."

She was so sure, Brynwen didn't have the heart to say, "Mayhap."

The king made way for Brynwen to sit next to the princess. The lass's lips were blue, her face white as a sheet. Her dark hair hung limply around her tiny face. Brynwen unstopped the cork and raised the child's head. "Here goes," she muttered. With another prayer to heaven, she slowly poured the liquid into the little maid's mouth. Every drop.

They waited. And waited. If it worked on the princess and Aesculapius, it could work on the rest. Vacated by the king, the cushioned chair in the corner beckoned to Brynwen, but she remained standing with the others in silent hope. She turned to speak to them in whispers.

After a few minutes, the king gasped. "Mandalin!"

With a start, Brynwen spun around. Taking a breath, she dared to look at the child in the canopied bed, bracing herself for the worst.

The princess yawned. *She yawned!* Once finished with the action, she blinked up at her father.

"Pa-pá?" she asked in a hoarse whisper. "You've got those frown lines on your forehead again. Did I miss the party?"

A laugh emanated from the king, and he scooped up his daughter into his arms. Her mouth opened in an "o" of surprise. "Not at all my darling. You awoke right on time." He turned his gaze on Brynwen and Iaso and mouthed *thank you.* Then he proceeded to hug his daughter, presumably until dawn or he fell asleep, whichever came first.

Smiling, Brynwen turned to her friends with raised basket. "Follow me. I need all your help to dispense the antidote to the patients."

CHAPTER 58

The next morning, the artificial sun shone as bright as Easter morning. Brynwen breathed in the fresh air of the herbarium as she, Iaso, Gregorio, and Aesculapius—despite his daughter's urging him to rest—returned herbs and tools to the shelves. She was relieved that the book's destruction hadn't seemed to have any ill effects on him. Ulysses wandered around, keeping his antlers away from anything fragile. Everyone who had received the antidote would make a full recovery. Most of the tension she'd harbored the past few weeks had dissipated, but the king's guard hadn't gotten a confession out of Alta. She remained unwavering in her denial of having anything to do with the poisonings, nor was she aware of who might have been responsible. All the staff were questioned as well.

The whole thing didn't sit well with Brynwen, though. *Something is off, but what am I missing? How can I prove Alta did or didn't do it?*

Around lunchtime, the cobalus maid, Frania, came into the herbarium and deposited a tray of food on the low table by the couches. She unloaded fresh bread, its scent wafting over to the healers, a platter piled high with sliced cold cuts of meat and cheeses in shades of yellow and white. Next to it she placed a small dish of a creamy white substance. A cup filled with a dark liquid and a plate of small crackers remained on the tray.

"There you are, Miss Brynwen. Here's that savory cream you liked so much th'other day. Cook made it special as thanks for your help."

Seeing the maid brought up a question. "Oh, Frania, wait a moment."

The maid straightened. Something differed in the way she stood. Her face seemed more strained than it had in the last few days. Gray gloves covered her fidgeting hands, but a brown stain stubbornly poked out by her forearm as she straightened her apron. She gave a brief curtsy. "Yes, miss?" The practiced inflection in her voice gave no other indication of distress.

Despite her fatigue, Brynwen gave the maid a warm smile. "I feel like I haven't seen you in ages." The trip into the Labyrinth felt like a lifetime ago. "How is your daughter? Is she any better?"

Frania perked at that, and her eyes glossed over. For the first time, Brynwen noticed bags under her eyes. "Better every day, miss. I think she'll get to visitin' the princess again real soon." She curtsied again, and with deft movements, lifted the tray with the cup and crackers to leave the room.

"This food looks delicious."

Ulysses nodded in agreement.

Brynwen's stomach growled. "It is quite good. Cook outdoes herself every day." Both she and Gregorio picked up a slice each of meat, cheese, and bread and piled them on top of each other. Aesculapius and Iaso placed their food in neat portions on their plates.

Gregorio took a bite and then set a bit of cheese on the ground for his antlered father. "By the way, Brynwen. I never thanked you for your cooking tips on the trail. We ate so much better than on stale biscuits and hard tack."

"Glad to be of help. You are a good student." She grinned.

Picking up a spoon, she scooped a generous portion of the delicious, cheesy cream with chives and dill to place on top. But in her excitement, she'd scooped out too much, and a blob of it toppled onto her hand. She stuck out her tongue to lick it up when a frightening thought occurred to her.

Pursing her lips, she shook her head, but the meddling hunch wouldn't go away. Setting down the stacked food and cream with regret, she wiped off the cream with her napkin.

"I am going to see the princess again. Master and Iaso, will you both bring her some tea?" She said it before the thought completely formed in her mind. There was something she needed to check. The healers regarded her with curiosity but didn't ask questions.

"But you were just there an hour ago."

"Gregorio and Ulysses, you haven't met her yet," Brynwen said. "Come with me."

The tutor and peryton exchanged brief looks.

But Brynwen was already rushing toward the door.

TALFRYN STRODE up the staircase behind Padric. Rounding the next landing toward the herbarium above, they nearly collided into Brynwen, Gregorio, and Ulysses. "Oh good," his sister said before anyone could say anything. "Come with us to meet the princess."

"All right?" Talfryn shrugged, unsure what was happening. He was still exhausted from the previous day's events, but after a good sleep and mid-morning meal of roasted venison and spiced root vegetables, his energy had returned enough to see if Brynwen needed any help.

Padric and Gregorio followed, Ulysses's massive antlers towering over them. They descended the flight of steps and marched down the hallway to the princess's suite.

Instead of knocking, Brynwen opened the door into the princess's sitting room.

The cobalus maid stood there, startled, her hand reaching out for the latch. "Mistress," Frania blurted. She gave a rushed curtsy, clumsily trying to keep a hold of her now empty tray. "Be-beg pardon, I've got to get to the kitchen." She took two hurried steps before Brynwen barred her path.

"Wait, Frania. I have something for you."

Talfryn hadn't met too many cobali before that week, so he didn't know how warm they got in general, but he thought he noticed sweat beading on her forehead.

"For, uh, me?" Now her face blanched. *What is going on, and why is my sister so intent on giving the maid something?*

"For your daughter." Releasing Frania's arm, Brynwen held up a small jar with a cork stopper in it. "I know you said she is getting better, but I thought this ointment might help her. It is a special recipe I made."

"For Cinda?" Now the maid's eyes began to pucker. "How...how thoughtful, Miss. I..." She reached for the jar. A dark stain on her skin poked out of her glove.

Brynwen gasped. "Oh, Frania, your hand."

"It is nothing, Miss Brynwen, just scrubbing my hands too hard with lye. You know how rough it can be."

"Here, may I tend to it since I'm here? I may have another ointment to help with this."

"But I've got to go."

"Please, Frania." Padric took the maid's tray and gently turned her around into the sitting room. "Brynwen only wishes to help."

Talfryn looked from his friend to his sister and back again. *Something's going on, but what?*

As Talfryn stepped into the room, his jaw dropped. "Wow. This is so much brighter compared to the corridors of the Labyrinth." The room was furnished with two plush couches facing each other and two cushioned chairs facing inward to make a "u" shape. A large fireplace took up much of the wall to the left. A little table sat in the corner with two matching chairs, and on the right was a closed door.

Brynwen removed the gloves and brought Frania's hands to the window for better light. "Oh dear, this is bad. You see, it's spreading. It could be contagious."

"What?" Fright filled Frania's eyes.

"In fact, we should tell the king. He will wish to know about this. Iaso may wish to see it, too. In case I'm wrong, of course. But I don't think so." She spoke in the dramatic voice she used with difficult patients. The ones who tended to disbelieve how serious their conditions really were. "Talfryn, you've seen this before, haven't you?"

What? How'd I get dragged into this?

Over Frania's head, Brynwen gave him an expectant look.

Seriously? He bent to take a better look at the stains, which upon closer inspection, looked like minor burns. Not that he was a healer or anything to really know that. "Um, ooo, that looks really bad." He put on his most dramatic voice. "Sorry, Frania. I hope you won't have to lose your whole hand. Rosa—the head healer at home—had to cut Goody Brown's hand off. Right here." He stiffened his hand and brought it down like a cleaver onto the other, making a chopping sound for good effect.

Maybe I laid it on a bit thick...

Frania winced and looked about to faint. Her big, brown eyes pleaded with Brynwen. "Please, please, mum. I don't want ta die. It's been smarting something fierce."

Brynwen barged through the closed door without knocking and without waiting for an answer, dragged the poor, bonneted cobalus into the next room despite her protests. They barged in on King Morfrey sitting in a chair next to the princess's bed. On the bed, Mandalin was tucked under blankets of pinks and reds, scowling with her arms crossed. Talfryn had heard she'd have to stay in bed for a few days. However, her expression brightened the moment she saw Brynwen.

The king shot to his feet. "What is the meaning of this?" He gaped at the intruders.

Out from the corner, the elderly nurse, Merta, shuffled to the bed, confusion spilling across her features. In her hands she held a tea cup and saucer.

"Sire." Brynwen was nearly breathless. "We may have another epidemic on our hands."

"What?"

"Look." She held up Frania's hand. The cobalus tried hard to hide her face in her apron. "Her fingers have the first signs of *anatatumus disclosus.*"

"That sounds dreadful. Is it very serious?" The king retreated a step in horror, the back of his knee hitting his upholstered chair.

She nodded. "Your skin gets a rash that soon covers your entire body and your hair falls out. Your throat tightens, and you can't eat ever again. After two weeks—boils. So many boils, you aren't recognizable anymore. Then, death." She spun back to the cobalus maid. "How long have you had this pain in your hands?"

That sounds like hay fever, Talfryn thought. *Except the boils part. And death. Death is bad.*

"A fortnight."

"And how long has your daughter been sick with it?"

"She's not sick—that is, she's not sick from this."

"I see." Brynwen released Frania's hand and paced. "No, don't lower your hand, it may be fatal." Frania raised her hand up again with a squeak. "If she isn't sick from the same thing, she may be safe. But you should bring her to me for preventive treatment."

"Ah, no, miss. She's, uh, too sick to leave her bed. Bedridden, she is. Coughs and moans. She moans so mournfully, miss." She nodded with so much enthusiasm, Talfryn thought her head would pop right off.

"Might I intrude?" King Morfrey asked. "If it is a plague, should she not be put in isolation, and not be brought here for examination?" *Or burned,* King Morfrey's horrified expression asked.

"I agree, Your Majesty," Padric chimed in with a bow. "If her daughter is ill, she must be contained along with the maid."

"Your words have merit, Sir Padric." The king nodded. "We must keep this hidden. There is little choice in the matter. Put the maid in the attic until it dies down."

Now Frania began to tremble. "Sire?"

Talfryn placed his hands behind his back to try to appear like he knew what he was doing. He thought he saw the direction Brynwen was trying to go with the child. "Before that, Frania, we could bring some medicine to help your daughter. Where's her room?"

The panic intensified on Frania's face. She waved her arms, forgetting for a moment about her hand. "No, no, no, she can't see anybody. Give it to me, an' I'll give it to 'er."

"But we cannot allow you to leave." Padric raised a brow. "The plague, remember?"

A vein popped in the king's forehead, and he pumped his hands against his hips. "You all had better leave before I have my guards lock you in the tower. I will not have my daughter accosted by another illness."

At that moment, Aesculapius and Iaso entered the suite bearing a steaming cup of chamomile tea. Talfryn's nerves instantly relaxed when the fragrance wafted past his nose. *Brynwen must have taught them how to make it, because it smells just right.*

"See, papá, Master Aesculapius is up and about. Why not me?"

Brynwen continued her questioning. "How long *has* your daughter been sick, Frania? Was it the same time as when the first people became ill with monkshood?"

Frania nodded.

"And the same time you received this stain?"

Another nod.

"Ah, Master Aesculapius and Iaso. What do you make of this stain on Frania's hand? It has been bothering her for two weeks."

Handing the tea to the closest person—that being Talfryn—they took the cobalus's arm and studied it. They conferred in whispers and after less than a minute, they were in agreement. "It is minor monks-hood poisoning," Iaso declared. "It is absorbing slowly through your skin. See how the scars and bumps line up and the hand is turning brown?"

Brynwen nodded. "It is as I thought."

"Will I get boils?" Frania nearly fainted again.

"Your daughter is not ill, Frania, is she? She was either abducted by the Shadow Druid or you have her in hiding from them."

"That's absurd. Why would they—whoever they are—do that?"

"It isn't absurd. They needed you to poison the people of Rellea for an excuse to get someone to enter the Labyrinth and get the stone of adamant."

"The maid is responsible for the poisoning?" King Morfrey was incredulous.

"Yes." Padric nodded. "I understand the reasoning. Our being called here was the perfect opportunity for the Shadow Druid to set his plan in motion. He devised a plan to kidnap a high-ranking palace maid's child and force her to give an incurable poison to several people. Immediately, she was to spread the rumor that a hunter had heard of a renowned healer who could aid them. The king was then to send emissaries to invite the healer to his home. But before she could reach Rellea, the Druid planned to abduct her to perform the ritual of extraction to remove the stone of adamant from the Minotaur in the Labyrinth. The Shadow Druid had attempted to abduct Brynwen at least two times that we know about."

Gregorio nodded vigorously. "Yes, yes! And when that failed, the maid was coerced into poisoning the people again to force the healer into the Labyrinth to find the adamant. Is this not correct, Maid Frania?"

Brynwen's eyes glistened as she beheld the maid. "In your preparations of the monkshood distribution, some of the poison dropped onto your hand, producing the brown splotches and sores. One of the patients, Wallace, wanted to tell me something. I didn't know what at the time, but now I am certain it was that he'd seen you with the monkshood before the first occurrence. So, you killed him during the night when it was dark, and there was only one person on guard. Alta and Celta happened to be at the infirmary at the same time as you and me, and their presence there and at Mandalin's birthday celebration threw me off your trail."

Frania broke into instant tears and sobs, crumpling to the floor. "The Druid threatened to kill my daughter if I didn't do it. And I didn't want to kill the human lad, but I had no choice. I am so very sorry, Your Majesty. The p-princess wasn' supposed to get sick. Please forgive me." She rushed to the king and plopped on the floor at his feet, begging for mercy. The king, cornered, looked less than thrilled at the sniveling cobalus maid spilling tears and snot all over his regal blue silk slippers.

"Take her away," King Morfrey ordered in disgust. "And find her daughter before she floods the entire palace with her tears."

CHAPTER 59

*P*adric and the others found Frania's daughter alive but tired, tied up in a small, rundown house in the city, under guard by a couple of the Shadow Druid's rogue cobali.

"Rawlins wasn't about to miss the chance to break some more heads. Figuratively speaking, of course," Talfryn explained to Brynwen at the evening meal. They sat around the palace's medium sized dining table. Padric allowed Talfryn to tell the story of what had happened, how the rogues had fought like true goblins and gave the fights of their lives. They admitted the Shadow Druid had paid them to keep the cobalus maid alive and unharmed, but bound to a chair the entire time. The maiden had been ever so thankful, she'd given all of her rescuers kisses, and to Ombag, she'd given two. His blush had lit the entire room. And he still blushed.

Padric buttered his toast and grinned at Talfryn's story, shaking his head at some of the farmer's embellishments. *Dis Pater II*, or King Morfrey as he was called in Rellea, had set a grand spread for them in his infinite thanks for rescuing his daughter and people and ridding the tunnels of their mutual enemies. Four kinds of breads and rolls, roasted venison and pork, vegetables grown from their greenhouse, enticing fruits and berries with a sweet creamy dipping sauce, and sweet pastries to make one's mouth water. Padric might have indulged in a couple of those.

The sons of Franco fought over a cherry scone; Cecil in his quiet way and Simon with loud shouts. Miser cheered on whoever was winning, sneaking mouthfuls of the good food when no one was watching. Their father attempted to hush them but to no avail. When not shouting, Simon loudly spoke to Payla across the way about his adventures in the cavern, having forgotten all of his nightmares from the experience after a good night's sleep.

A bittersweet smile lit Payla's lips at the children's antics. Ombag, still free for the moment, sat beside her, devouring everything in sight while Ulysses nibbled from his own bowl of berries on the edge of the table.

Talfryn continued his tale. "On our way back to the palace, the rogues tried to escape, but Rawlins put the fear of his face in them."

Padric chuckled. "I confirm this is true."

Brynwen grinned. "I can imagine."

Padric could not help but notice how radiant Brynwen looked this morning. Gone were the worry lines creasing her forehead, and her hands were no longer always drawn to her satchel. Her expression brightened the whole room despite the artificial sunlight streaming through the windows. The bright, light-green dress with daisies and a white panel—a gift from the king—made her look resplendent. Each time she smiled, Padric had a strong desire to wrap her in his arms.

Rawlins nudged him. "You look like a sap."

"Ever the eloquent one, eh, my friend?" Padric's eyebrow shot up.

"'Course. I want to know why our enemies keep slipping out of our hands."

A headache formed above Padric's eye. Leave it to Rawlins to ruin a nice moment. "I do not know. But next time, we must be thorough and stop them for good." He lowered his voice. "And now that we know Aeron is helping them, I feel there are fewer people we can trust. Who else is our enemy?" His gaze fell on each person at the table. He could not fathom any of them ever siding with Janus, but he had been wrong before.

"Outside this table, we can't." Rawlins expression remained as wary as ever.

Payla slid her head over to them, her horn nearly stabbing Padric in the neck. "Sorry to overhear. But you have an opening for a new recruit, don't you?"

Padric regarded her with a grin. "Are you wishing to join the ranks?" He imagined his father meeting Payla as a green recruit. The image of Garrick's first impression did not go over very well.

The immortal's eyes grew round. "Oh, ha, ha, not me. I have enough of my own training at the temple. But you have got a decent fighter over there." Padric ducked as she indicated Talfryn with her head. The farmer was laughing at his own joke. "I think he would be a lovely choice."

"In fact," Padric said, "I had the same idea myself. Sergeant, what say you?"

Rawlins seemed about to reject the idea, but instead raised his shoulders. "A bit old, isn't he?"

"We could start him as a squire."

"Could do worse, I s'pose."

High praise, coming from him.

"We will discuss it more later." At present, he wanted Brynwen to have this moment worry free. The future might be uncertain, but they had a reprieve from the concerns of the outside world, and he wanted to enjoy it.

THEY SPENT a few more days in Rellea to help Princess Mandalin recoup and administer more antidote to the sickest patients. Afterward, King Morfrey and Magician Ulrich would lock the stone of adamant in the vault with enhanced magical security so it couldn't be stolen ever again. Alta had been released from prison with a royal apology. As for Frania, she remained in the dungeon until the king could make a decision regarding her actions, as they were coerced.

In the meantime, Brynwen imparted all she knew to the two healers, writing it down for them in a new journal that she made them promise not to enchant. "We don't want another altercation with your gods, do we?" They shook their heads in agreement. *How have I gone from pupil to teacher in a matter of days?*

It was two days after saving the people that Brynwen awoke to realize the prophecy's blazing red and gold lettering had disappeared from her vision. It was the first and last thing she had seen every day. She felt a fresh start in the air, like a new spirit, and she intended to use it. No more book. She would stick with what she knew and learn along the way. Rosa would be proud of her.

The black and blue marks left by the Shadow Druid had all but faded and pained her no more.

As they made preparations to return home, a pang came over her. She would miss the friends she had made here. It was hard making new friends, just to leave them again. She made a promise to several people to keep in touch.

"Will you write to me, Brynwen?" Princess Mandalin jumped up when Brynwen came to say farewell and brought her final cup of chamomile tea. At least Iaso had been able to duplicate it with ease, so the princess could have her fill of it for the rest of her now long life.

"Of course. Every month." She'd agreed to send letters for the princess and Iaso to the inn at Malham, and a messenger would pick them up.

Mandalin shook her head and folded her arms across her chest, imitating her father. "Mm, mm. Every day."

Brynwen laughed and set down the tea. "How about once a week? I need time to help others get better, you know." She poked the little maiden's nose.

The princess rolled her eyes and let out a puff of air which shot her bangs into the air before falling down again. "Fine, once a week. And when are you and Sir Padric getting married?"

Iaso hid her snorting chuckle behind her hand while Aesculapius sent his gaze to the ceiling.

Brynwen's face, neck, and ears turned impossibly hot. "I, uh…that remains to be seen."

"What's that mean?"

"It means…I must go."

"I love you, Brynwen." Mandalin gave Brynwen a hug. She noticed how quickly the child's strength had returned.

"I'll see you downstairs before we go."

Later in the afternoon, when the servants were preparing their bags for the trip home, Brynwen pulled Padric to the side.

"Padric, I've something to tell you."

"Yes?" He returned her smile.

"I am going to tell Grandfather whom I wish to court."

Padric's eyebrows furrowed as he cupped her chin. "Anyone I know?"

Scrunching her lips together, Brynwen gave his arm a fake punch. "Ha, ha."

Her knight laughed and kissed her hand as though for the first time, his gaze never leaving hers. "Mayhap this time will go better."

"I won't leave the cottage until he's heard me out and agrees."

A commotion came from the entrance into the palace. Ombag came out and dashed to Brynwen and the others, a long parchment trailing from his hand, billowing in the breeze of his strides.

"I'm free, I'm free!" He pounded the parchment into Talfryn's hands. Then he jumped from one foot to the other in jubilation.

"That's great." Talfryn smiled at the cobalus's enthusiasm. "But what is this?" He regarded the paper. Words in a fancy script lined the document, and there was a seal at the bottom. "Sorry, I can't read it. What's it say?"

"The king gave me a pardon." He pointed to a line of text in another language. "'In light of your efforts in aiding in the discovery of the antidote for the Princess Mandalin and the people of Rellea, you are hereby pardoned from indefinite exile.' Immediately. Forever and ever."

"Amen," Talfryn responded.

"What?" Ombag's face contorted in confusion.

"It means congratulations." Brynwen laughed and patted her new friend on the shoulder.

"Well done," Talfryn agreed.

Everyone else chimed in their congratulations and gave him hearty pats of approval.

"Thanks, everyone. Without you lugging my sorry self down here, I'd still be stuck up top." He scrunched his nose in distaste. Clearly, he wouldn't miss pilfering food and goods from people crossing the marshes.

"What will you do now?" Padric asked.

"Not exactly sure yet, but I report to the barracks tomorrow for a special project."

"As long as it's not stealing," Brynwen admonished.

"Ah, yeah, about that…" Ombag rummaged around in his sack and extricated a small jar.

Brynwen's eyes grew round. "That's my comfrey! I've been looking everywhere for that."

"Sorry…habits. Here's this."

"My Roman coin. Did it bring you any luck?" Payla winked.

"Well, I didn't die, despite *someone's* trying, so, I'd say so." He gave Talfryn the eye.

"You helped save lives. And—hey, I needed that yesterday." Talfryn snatched up his crucifix. "Do you even know how to use this?"

"I dabble." Last, he raised a St. Christopher medal on a chain.

Padric shook his head. "You did not steal this; I gave it to you."

"Yeah, an' like I said, I've got a bunch of 'em. You can use it more'n me." He stuffed the medal into Padric's hand and backed away.

Brynwen rolled her eyes. "Is there anyone you *haven't* stolen from, Ombag?"

Ombag glanced at Rawlins. "Him. Well, it's been fun not dying and all. Bye now!"

Once the company bid farewell to King Morfrey, Princess Mandalin, Aesculapius, and Iaso, they took the easiest path out of the cave. At the exit, the midmorning sun welcomed them. Brynwen breathed in the fresh air, the swaying heather in the marsh visible over the next rise. Next stop: home.

EPILOGUE

a week after returning from *Dis Pater's* realm and reporting to Circe and Pasiphae, reuniting with her family, and celebrating her seventeenth birthday along with Talfryn, Brynwen begged Payla to come on a picnic with them before she had to return home. Padric offered his family's orchard since his parents and sister had an engagement that afternoon.

The shade from the de Clifton orchard apple trees gave perfect cover for their meal. Padric set down the overflowing picnic basket while Talfryn and Rawlins spread out the blankets on the soft ground. "Bryn?" He rubbed his aching arm muscles. "Did you pack the whole market in this one basket?" He wiped sweat from his forehead with his sleeve. His mother would be horrified at his lack of manners.

"I may have overpacked a tad." She bit her lip. Taking Brynwen's hand, he slowly lowered her to the ground, and she curled her legs under her skirts. He knelt next to her. "I didn't want to forget anything."

"'Tis better than not having enough." Gregorio plopped down on the ground on the other side of the basket.

Brynwen laughed. "Very true. I'm just glad you, Ulysses, and Payla could make it to this picnic before she heads home tomorrow."

Next to Gregorio, Payla sat down and pushed back her hood. She shook her dark hair until it spilled over her shoulders, showing off her long horns. "Me too. And I, for one, am famished. I hope you packed the strawberry scones. I've heard nothing but praise about them."

"I did, although you are too kind." A blush crept up Brynwen's cheeks.

"I was hungry at the time," Talfryn admitted. "You know I'll praise anyone's food when I'm hungry."

Padric laughed. "That is quite true."

Brynwen snorted. She opened the basket, and the fragrance of all the food wafted over to Padric. Once the meal had been arranged on the blanket, everyone tucked in. Roast turkey legs, breads and cheeses, a medley of boiled vegetables with savory spices, an apple pie, a custard pie, strawberry scones, and chamomile tea, of course.

After the meal, Padric felt fit to burst.

They sat for a time and talked until well into the afternoon. At length, Payla got up and asked for an apple. "Never have I eaten a Derby apple before."

"I am sure it is similar to the ones near your home."

Payla shrugged. "Mayhap, but I would still like to try one." Examining the red fruit, she sought the best one.

Padric reached up for one nearby.

"Not that one, Padric." She pointed up another couple of feet. "That one." It was the biggest and reddest apple on the whole tree, without noticeable blemish. *Of course she wants that one.* Her eyes sparkled in a challenge.

Padric grinned. *Challenge accepted.* The trees were too fragile and tight for him to climb, but he had something else in mind. Centering his thoughts, the pain gripped his belly button for a second before it abated. When he opened his eyes, he had four chestnut horse legs and was a head taller. "That should do it, I think."

"Cheater." Talfryn faked a pout.

"All is fair in love and food," Gregorio said. "That is how the quote goes, is it not?"

Padric rolled his eyes at his friend. Raising up on his hind legs, he reached for the apple. His fingers had just encircled the red fruit when he heard three gasps. Plucking it from its stem, Padric swiveled his head to the direction of the gasps. His heart sunk to his hoofs.

His mother, father, and sister stood still as statues, shock on their faces. Mother looked ready to faint.

"Father. Mamá, Chelsea." His forelegs came down to earth harder than he'd meant, jarring his back. Glimpsing those on the blankets, he noticed Payla's horns sticking out on either side of her head and Gregorio looked like a seventeen-year-old youth. He spun around to face his parents, blood rushing to his head as he sought a plausible rationalization. "Allow me to explain."

THE END

A WORD FROM THE AUTHOR

Thank you for taking the time to pick up *Perilous*!

If you have a moment, I would really appreciate it if you would take a couple of minutes to leave a review on your favorite booksellers and social media sites.

- Amazon
- Goodreads
- Barnes & Noble

Reviews help authors find new readers and receive feedback about their works.

To receive alerts about the Rise of the Charioteer series, sign up for my monthly newsletter at: https://susanlaspe.com

AUTHOR'S NOTE

Did the Minotaur really have a twin sister? Only Pasiphae knows! In reality, none of the texts state that Asterion the Minotaur had any full-blood siblings at all (only half-siblings). This idea of adding a twin sister named Payla, whose disposition is the opposite of her monstrous brother, is loosely based on *The Man in the Iron Mask* by Alexandre Dumas. In Dumas's story, Louis the XIII's wife gives birth to twins, Louis XIV and Philippe. Instead of dying in childbirth, the younger brother, Philippe, is secretly taken away to live a quiet, incognito life in the French countryside and later, imprisoned in a mask of iron—until the Musketeers decide to rescue him in order to replace his terrible brother and claim the French throne.

WELL, FANCY THAT!

I was in the middle of writing *Perilous* when, one evening, I went to a Chinese restaurant for dinner. Upon opening my fortune cookie, it contained this fortune! How *fortuitous*, right? It's like they knew me!

"You will soon emerge victorious from the maze you've been traveling in."

ACKNOWLEDGMENTS

An author wouldn't be much more than a person with a pen without help from amazing people.

My husband Mark, who appreciates my hobbies and is always willing to read my work and discuss his feedback.

Fellow author Kelsey Gietl, who always encourages me to better my writing craft and bounce story ideas off with!

My awesome beta, ARC, and proofreaders: Rachael Johnston, Kelsey Gietl, Kirsten Wright, Carla Varner, Christine Emnett, and Kelsey Gietl. Your input is always most helpful!

Patric Tebeau for his amazing translations of all the Latin text in my books—including providing recordings of how to accurately pronounce them!

My dedicated editor, Sarah Everest, who spent much of the Christmas season editing my book and checking for accuracy.

To the Lord, who, like with Brynwen, gives me love and strength.

ABOUT THE AUTHOR

Susan has loved watching television and movies, reading, writing, and art since her earliest memories. The push to create her own stories was influenced by Grimm's Fairy Tales and the Percy Jackson book series, as well as a love of history (one of her favorite subjects in school). Author of *Sorcerous* and *Treacherous* from the Rise of the Charioteer series, *Perilous* is her third published novel. When not working or writing, she can be found doing one of too many craft projects, scrounging the pantry for chocolate, or playing board games with her husband in St. Louis, Missouri.

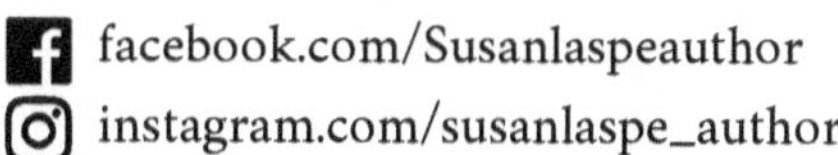
facebook.com/Susanlaspeauthor
instagram.com/susanlaspe_author

www.ingramcontent.com/pod-product-compliance
Lightning Source LLC
Chambersburg PA
CBHW051434190726
48289CB00001B/178